WHAT ARE YOU AFRAID OF?

"If you read my book, then you know that I thoroughly researched the victims," Carmen said. "There was no obvious connection. As far as I could tell they'd never met one another."

"So if there is a copycat killer out there who is following Scott's pattern, then his victims should look like this." He tapped the tip of his finger on each picture of a dead woman. "Young, old, black, brown, and white."

He tossed the book on the rumpled bed and returned to his backpack. Reaching in, he pulled out the photocopies of Polaroids she'd left on his desk.

"Look at the newest victims," he said, moving back to stand at her side.

Reluctantly accepting the papers he shoved in her hand, she glanced down at the pictures. "I'm not sure what I'm looking for."

He once again pointed to each picture. "They're all young, they're all white, and they're all blond."

She stilled, her gaze locked on the pictures. Even in the dim light Griff could see her face lose a shade of color.

"Carmen." Before he could halt the impulsive gesture, he reached to cup her chin in his palm, tilting back her head to meet his worried gaze. "They all look like you . . ."

Alexandra Ivy is a *New York Times* bestselling author of romantic suspense, paranormal and erotic romance. She has also written Regency historicals under the name Deborah Raleigh. A five-time *Romantic Times* Book Award Finalist, Ivy has received much acclaim for her Guardians of Eternity, ARES Security, Immortal Rogues and Sentinels series. She lives with her family in Missouri.

Find Alexandra online at **www.AlexandraIvy.com**, and connect with her on Facebook at **www.facebook.com/ alexandraivyfanpage** and on Twitter **@AlexandraIvy**.

By Alexandra Ivy

Pretend You're Safe
What Are You Afraid Of?

WHAT ARE YOU AFRAID OF?

ALEXANDRA IVY

HEADLINE
ETERNAL

Published by arrangement with Zebra Books,
an imprint of Kensington Publishing Corp.

First published in Great Britain in 2018
by HEADLINE ETERNAL
An imprint of HEADLINE PUBLISHING GROUP

1

Cataloguing in Publication Data is available from the British Library

ISBN 978 1 4722 5293 7

Offset in 12.04/14 pt Times New Roman by Jouve (UK), Milton Keynes

Printed and bound in Great Britain by CPI Group (UK) Ltd, Croydon, CR0 4YY

MIX
Paper from
responsible sources
FSC® C104740

Headline's policy is to use papers that are natural, renewable and recyclable
products and made from wood grown in well-managed forests and other
controlled sources. The logging and manufacturing processes are expected
to conform to the environmental regulations of the country of origin.

HEADLINE PUBLISHING GROUP
An Hachette UK Company
Carmelite House
50 Victoria Embankment
London EC4Y 0DZ

www.headlineeternal.com
www.headline.co.uk
www.hachette.co.uk

WHAT ARE YOU AFRAID OF?

Prologue

A voice in the back of Jeannie Smith's mind whispered that she should be resigned to her ugly fate.

She'd always known that she was going to come to a bad end. Everyone had said so. Her mother said it just before the older woman had run off with her latest lover. Her grandparents said it when they'd kicked her out of their house when she was just sixteen. And even her pimp said it when he'd caught sight of the infected track marks on her inner arms.

A bad end was what happened to girls like her.

And it wasn't like she hadn't had any warning. Since she'd started working as a whore she'd been beaten, robbed, and dumped in the gutter. It'd only gotten worse when she'd left the streets of Kansas City to become a lot lizard.

Trolling the truck stops and rest areas along the interstate was considered the lowest of the lowest, even for whores. Which meant that it was only for the most desperate women.

But even after all the beatings and rough sex she'd been forced to endure, nothing had taught her the true meaning of horror until the john who'd picked her tonight.

Which was weird, really.

He was so handsome.

Dark skin, glossy black hair, and rich brown eyes.

The sort of dude who could have any woman he wanted.

Of course, that might explain why she hadn't instantly been wary when he'd urged her into the long trailer attached to his semitruck. Not even when she realized it was equipped with a freezer. It was better than doing the john against the wall of the diner. Or on the hard gravel of the lot.

But as she climbed into the back of the trailer, she caught sight of the other men already waiting for her. Shit, she was in trouble.

She jerked her arm, struggling to free herself from her companion's grip.

"Hey, there was nothing said about this being a party," she protested.

One of the men stepped forward, his face wrapped in shadows.

"It took you long enough," he snapped. "There's a half dozen whores out there. What were you doing?"

The john holding her arm flinched. Clearly, the other dude was in charge.

"You said she had to be a blond. This was the first one I could find."

The man in charge snorted. "Well, while you were dilly-dallying the rest of us nearly froze off our balls."

There was a grumble of agreement from the shadows at the back of the trailer. Jeannie hissed in fear. How many were there? Four? Five? Maybe even more?

"You cleaned up from the last one?" the man holding her rasped, clearly attempting to hide his nerves behind an air of bluster.

"Of course," the other stranger drawled. "Our previous guest is hidden with the others. Now it's time for some more fun."

The numbing sense of resignation was abruptly replaced with a savage need to fight back.

Maybe her destiny had been decided on the dismal day she'd been born. Maybe her fate was to die in a bad way.

But by God, she'd spent twenty years fighting to survive. She wasn't going down easily.

She struggled against the bastards as they strapped her down and ripped off her clothes. And even when they took turns raping her.

She struggled until her original john was standing over her bruised and bloody body, a crowbar in his hand.

There was a brief hesitation as he gazed down at her. Almost as if the man wasn't certain he was prepared to commit the ultimate sin. Then, with the shadowed man whispering in his ear, he at last lifted the crowbar, swinging it with desperate power. There was an odd whistling sound as the metal cut through the icy air. Jeannie was strangely mesmerized by the sheer horror of what was happening. At least until she felt a blast of pain as it connected with the side of her face.

Then she felt nothing.

A bad end . . .

Chapter One

December 20, Rocky Mountains

The large overnight envelope was waiting for Carmen Jacobs on the porch.

She grimaced as she glanced through the frosty window of the front door. Her first instinct was to ignore the unwelcome reminder of the outside world.

She'd rented the isolated cabin in the Rocky Mountains precisely to forget the demands of her high-profile career. Or at least, that's what she'd told her literary agent. And in part, it was true. She'd spent the past twelve months flying from city to city to sign copies of her blockbuster book, *The Heart of a Predator*. Her hectic schedule had also included TV and radio interviews as well as speaking engagements. She'd even spent a month in California, teaching a creative writing class.

Soon it would all start again when the paperback version of the book was released.

She deserved a break.

But the deeper need to retreat to this cabin in the dead of winter was to avoid the yearly madness that was a mandatory part of the Christmas season. She wasn't a grinch. Okay, maybe she was a little bit of a grinch. But it wasn't her fault. She was a woman without a family. And, if she was honest, without any close friends.

Usually it didn't bother her to be alone. In fact, she preferred to concentrate on her career without being encumbered by people who would be a constant distraction.

At this time of year, however, she couldn't help but feel the lack of intimate companionships. Maybe it was the sappy commercials. Or the sight of giggling children who darted through the stores. Or the distant memories of when she hadn't been alone.

Whatever the reason, she always felt the urge to retreat from the world during this time of year. And despite the fact she'd just celebrated her twenty-sixth birthday, she had the necessary funds to grant her wish.

Sipping her morning cup of hot chocolate, she watched as the snow lazily drifted from the clouds, coating the porch in a pristine layer of white.

In a few more minutes the envelope would be hidden.

Problem solved.

She took another sip. And then another. The snow continued to float in the air. Silent. Hypnotic.

A swirling cloud of peace.

She tried to force herself to turn away. Her plans for the day included a long, hot bath. A leisurely lunch. Some prime-time romance in the form of a paperback novel. And later, a bottle of wine in front of the fire.

Nowhere in her schedule was a mysterious envelope.

Unfortunately, Carmen had one deeply imbedded character flaw.

Curiosity.

It was the reason she'd snooped on her eighth-grade teacher after catching sight of the woman disappearing into a storage shed with the principal. That little adventure had gotten her kicked out of school. Probably because she'd posted the pictures she'd taken on the classroom bulletin board.

Three years later that same curiosity had urged her to sneak into her grandparents' attic to try to peek inside the small safe that had once belonged to her parents. She hadn't managed to open it, but she'd been caught in the act. Her grandfather had grounded her for a month and her grandmother had cried. The tears had hurt more than being forced to miss the spring formal.

On the brighter side, her curiosity had inspired her to become a journalist. And later to interview five of the most prolific serial killers to ever terrorize North America. The book she'd written after the nerve-wrenching meetings had become a number-one best seller and launched her into the world of fleeting fame.

Like disco balls and Crocs.

With a grimace she set her half-empty mug on a nearby table. She wasn't going to be able to relax until she knew what was in the envelope.

She might as well get it over with.

Wrapping the belt of her heavy robe tighter, she reluctantly pulled open the door. An instant blast of frigid air slammed into her with shocking force. Crap. The cabin had looked so picturesque in the brochure. The pine trees. The snow. The majestic mountains.

She hadn't really considered just how freaking cold it would be.

Now she scurried forward, her fuzzy slippers sliding over the icy surface. She bent down, snatching the envelope off the edge of the porch. Next year she was going to a sandy beach with lots of sun and fun.

Straightening, she paused to glance around, ensuring there was no one lurking in the small clearing. Then, with a small shiver, she darted back through the door and closed it behind her.

She brushed off the few flakes that clung to her robe before she grabbed her mug of hot chocolate and returned to the kitchen. Since she'd arrived ten days ago, the cozy room had become her favorite spot in the cabin. The wood-planked floors. The open-beamed ceiling. The worn table that was set near a window that overlooked the frozen back garden. There was even an open fireplace where she'd toasted marshmallows last night.

Now she moved to pour out the old cocoa in the sink and rinsed out her mug. She wasn't an obsessive neat freak, but she preferred to keep her surroundings organized. A psychiatrist would no doubt tell her it had something to do with her need to control some small aspect of her life. She preferred to think that she was just tidy.

Taking a seat at the table, she wavered one last time. She should toss the envelope into the fire she'd stoked to life while she was brewing her morning cup of cocoa. Snap, crackle, pop, and all her troubles would be gone. Instead, she gave a rueful shake of her head and turned it over to stare at the front.

Her name was neatly typed, along with the address of the cabin. Then her gaze shifted to the return address, not surprised to find the name of her PR firm. There were fewer than ten people who knew where she was staying.

She ripped open the envelope, only to discover another envelope inside. It was a plain manila one, with her name scrawled across the front.

She scowled.

Usually this would be a desperate plea for help from some unknown person.

Since the release of her book, she'd been besieged with requests for her to investigate the murder of some relative. Or pleading with her to use her contacts to get their beloved son out of prison, despite the fact he'd bludgeoned his girlfriend to death or shot a neighbor in the head. On occasion some enterprising soul managed to discover where she was staying and shoved the information under the door of her hotel, but usually the requests ended up on the desk of her agent, or even her editor, who sent them on to the PR firm.

The same firm she'd given strict orders to hold all correspondence until after the first of the year.

Which meant that they knew better than to pester her with unwanted mail unless they were hoping to be fired. Something she doubted so long as her book remained on the bestseller lists.

So why were they sending her an overnight package?

A Christmas present? An appearance on the *Today Show* they'd been desperate to book for her?

There was only one way to find out.

Running her finger beneath the sealed flap, she pulled out the sheet of paper. Her gaze impatiently skimmed over the handwritten note.

Holiday Greetings, dearest Carmen. The new year approaches and I offer a challenge. You can be the predator or the prey.

She scrunched her nose. Well, that was cryptic. Her gaze lowered to the signature at the bottom.

The Trucker.

From one beat of her heart to the next, her annoyance was replaced by a bone-deep shock. With a gasp she was on her feet, knocking over the chair as she took a sharp step backward.

Crap.

The Trucker.

Details from her investigation fired randomly through her stunned brain.

Neal Scott. A forty-two-year-old truck driver from Kansas City who'd hunted whores and runaways along I-70 from Denver to Topeka. He'd killed at least twenty-seven women with a crowbar and dumped them along the highway. After his arrest in 1991 he'd admitted that he'd kept the bodies in the freezer of his semi until he found a new victim.

She pressed a hand to her racing heart, forcing herself to inch back toward the table. The envelope had been too heavy to contain only one thin sheet of paper.

Reaching out her hand, she grabbed the corner of the envelope and slowly tipped it upside down. There was a strange rustling sound and Carmen tensed. She didn't know what she was expecting, but it wasn't the stack of Polaroids that fell out of the envelope and splayed across the table.

Her breath rasped loudly in the silence as she reluctantly leaned forward. She'd seen the pictures before. They'd been found on Neal Scott when he'd been pulled over by a highway patrol. They had helped to prove Scott was the mysterious serial killer the press had dubbed the Trucker. As if the dead hooker in his trailer hadn't been enough.

Carmen pressed her lips together and reached for the pictures. She'd used copies of them in her book, which meant she was intimately familiar with the gruesome images.

On the point of shoving them back into the envelope, she stilled, her gaze locked on the shattered face of the young blond woman.

The picture was grainy, and there was blood covering the woman's brow from the brutal wound on her temple, but the rest of the features were visible.

Her face was thin, almost gaunt, with faint scars. There were newer sores on her chin. Probably from meth. And her long hair was tangled, as if she hadn't combed it in a long time.

She looked forty, but she was probably closer to twenty.

A woman who'd lived hard, and died even harder.

Carmen's hands shook as she shuffled to the next picture. Another blond. Her face was a little squarer and had been tanned to the texture of leather. But she shared the same painful thinness. And the same bloody wound on the side of her head.

There were three more pictures. All of them of young women who'd been brutally murdered.

They looked exactly like the Polaroids that'd been found on Neal Scott when he was captured. But not one of these had been used as evidence in the trial.

What the hell did that mean?

Had Scott been hiding the pictures? But where? And why send them to her?

Carmen dropped the Polaroids, wiping her fingers on her robe as if she'd been contaminated.

She had to do something. That much she knew. Unfortunately, her brain was churning without spitting out any answers. Like it was stuck in neutral.

Her gaze darted from side to side, at last landing on the large envelope that was still wet from the snow. Yes. This had started it all. The destruction of her fairy-tale vacation.

And she knew precisely who to blame for that destruction.

Cautiously backing away, she kept her gaze locked on the table. As if the pile of pictures were a rattlesnake that might decide to strike. At the same time, she stuck out her arm, blindly searching for the cell phone she'd left on the kitchen counter.

She knocked off an empty plate and tipped over a vase of flowers. Minor casualties. Then her fingers at last clenched around her phone.

Lifting it to a position where she could glance at the screen while still maintaining a close watch on the Polaroids, she hit the third button in her speed dial.

There was the sound of a buzzing as the connection was

made, then a prerecorded voice floated through the air, warning Carmen that the offices were closed until after the New Year and that she was to leave a message so they could get back to her as soon as possible.

Oh, and then a bubbly wish for her to have a happy holiday season.

Perfect.

She ended the connection and scrolled through her contacts to find the personal number of her PR person. Lucy Cordova was ten years older than Carmen, with the sleek beauty of a supermodel and the soul of a great white shark.

It was no accident she was the top in her field. She ate her competitors and spit them out.

"Pick up, pick up, pick up," Carmen muttered as the phone buzzed and then went straight to voice mail. "Dammit."

She hit redial. Same result. She hit it again.

On the point of trying a fourth time, her phone buzzed with an incoming call.

Lucy.

Thank God.

"Okay, Carmen," a voice croaked. Obviously, Lucy had decided to sleep in this morning. "What's the emergency?"

Carmen was forced to clear the lump from her voice before she could speak.

"The package that landed on my doorstep this morning."

"What package?" Lucy demanded, and then there was the rustle of covers as if the woman was crawling out of bed. "Oh, wait. I remember sending an envelope to you."

Carmen licked her lips. Why were they so dry?

"Where did you get it from?" she demanded.

"It came by messenger three days ago," Lucy told her.

"From where?"

"It was from the office of the public defenders who'd handled the Scott case," Lucy explained, her voice echoing as if she'd put the phone on speaker.

No doubt the woman was pouring her morning coffee. She was a caffeine fiend who was never without her insulated cup in her hand.

"Was there a letter with it?" Carmen asked.

There was a slurping sound, then a soft breath of relief. Lucy had just had her fix.

A second later she spoke, her voice stronger as the caffeine kicked in.

"No, there was no letter. Just a handwritten note that said they'd been forwarded all of Neal Scott's possessions after his execution and that they were just now sorting through the box."

Scott had been executed three months ago. "Why would they send it to your office?" Carmen demanded.

"The note said that they'd found the envelope and tried to deliver it to your condo. When there was no one home, they sent it to our office."

Carmen's gaze moved toward the nearby window. The snow continued to fall at a leisurely pace. As if it couldn't decide if it intended to pick up speed or just call it quits for the day.

I should be drinking my coffee and enjoying the winter wonderland, she thought. Instead, her peace had been shattered by visions of death.

Not the sort of Christmas anyone wanted.

"And you decided to send it here?" she demanded.

"I thought it might contain some new information from the killer," Lucy told her. "You know, something you could add to the paperback version that would spice up sales."

Carmen made a choked sound of distress. Having the Polaroids in her home—actually touching them—somehow made them far more disturbing than the black-and-white-copies she'd used in her books.

These were more personal. Almost intimate.

"The deaths of those young women are a tragedy, not a spice," she snapped.

There was an awkward silence before Lucy cleared her throat. "You know what I mean."

Carmen forced a strained laugh. She didn't know why she was angry with Lucy. The older woman had merely forwarded the envelope. She hadn't known what was inside.

"Yeah, I guess I do," she said.

"What's going on, Carmen?" Lucy abruptly asked.

Carmen's gaze returned to the table, her stomach clenching.

"There were pictures inside the envelope."

"What kind of pictures?"

"Polaroids of dead women. Five of them."

"Christ, I'm sorry, Carmen," Lucy breathed. "I assume they were from the trial?"

Carmen shook her head even though Lucy couldn't see her.

"No. I've never seen these before."

"Wait." The word sounded like it was wrenched from Lucy. She wasn't a lady who was often shocked. "Are you saying there are pictures of dead women that haven't been released to the public?"

Carmen shuddered. She was three feet away from the table, but she felt as if the unknown women were staring at her. Pleading for something she couldn't give them.

Justice.

"I'm saying I've never seen them. And you know the research I did," Carmen said. "I think it's possible that I'm the only one besides Scott to know they exist."

There was a sudden clatter through the phone, as if Lucy had dropped her coffee cup.

"God Almighty, this is fantastic!" the woman said, not bothering to hide her burst of glee. "Do you know what will happen to your book sales if you can add in pictures from new victims?" There was a pause, and Carmen imagined she could hear the calculator in Lucy's mind clicking away, adding up each new sale. "Hell, you could write a whole new book."

Carmen grimaced. She would be a hypocrite to act shocked by Lucy's response. The reason Carmen had hired her was because the woman was a ruthless master at taking advantage of any situation.

Even a situation that included dead women.

"These need to go to the authorities," she said in firm tones.

"Fine, but first we need to make copies," Lucy insisted. "It could be months or years before the cops will give back the originals."

"Let's worry about figuring out who these poor women are before we start cashing in, okay?" she said dryly.

As if sensing that Carmen wasn't in the mood to discuss business, Lucy did her best to squash her excitement.

"What do you want from me?"

Carmen took a minute. She was still rattled and it was unnervingly difficult to think. Like her brain cells were wading through syrup.

"I want you to call the lawyers and find out everything you can about the envelope," she eventually demanded.

Might as well start at the beginning.

"You got it," Lucy said, the crisp determination easing a portion of Carmen's unease. "I'll get back to you."

Carmen hung up the phone and forced herself to turn and head to the back of the cabin. She felt in dire need of a hot shower. It couldn't erase the images from her mind, but it might wash away the feeling that she'd been contaminated.

Entering the small bathroom, she dropped her robe and stepped beneath the spray of water. She shivered as she waited for the hot water to kick in, not for the first time wondering if she'd made a mistake in writing *The Heart of a Predator*.

It wasn't like she'd started off her journalism career with

the dream of spending her days in dank prisons interviewing monsters. And they were monsters—each of the five men she'd profiled had killed at least ten women, and most of them much more than that. But when her college professor had warned her that the articles she was writing for the school paper were too mundane to earn her any notice by any reputable newspaper or magazine, she'd forced herself to examine what she could offer that was different from every other wannabe journalist.

What truly made her unique?

The answer was simple.

Murder.

She was intimately acquainted with death. And the sort of man who could kill an innocent woman without mercy.

She'd reached out to Neal Scott, not believing for a minute that he'd respond to her request for an interview. He'd been on death-row for seventeen years and had never once spoken about his crimes. But her letter had been answered by Scott's lawyers within the week.

"Yes, Mr. Scott would be pleased to meet with Ms. Jacobs at a time of your convenience."

And that had been the start of her twisted journey through the minds of serial killers. A trail she thought would be over once the paperback book was released.

With a grimace she stepped out of the shower and dried off. Then, heading into the bedroom across the hall, she slipped on a pair of jeans and a heavy cable-knit sweater. Her blond hair was already curling around her face, making her look about twelve. She clicked her tongue as she pulled her hair into a tight ponytail.

Her grandmother might have thought that it was cute that Carmen looked like a perpetual child, but it was a pain in the patootie.

She'd just tugged on a pair of warm socks and returned to the kitchen when her phone rang.

Carmen hit the speaker button. "What did you find out?"

Lucy's voice floated through the air. "Nothing."

Her tension returned. Dammit. Had the older woman just pretended she was going to help in an effort to get Carmen to use the pictures in her book?

"Lucy, I'm not in the mood for games," Carmen snapped.

"I wasn't trying to annoy you, Carmen," Lucy said. "I meant the word literally."

There was no missing the edge in Lucy's voice.

This wasn't about making money. The woman was truly worried.

"Explain," Carmen said, dropping into a kitchen chair and rubbing her aching head.

Lucy cleared her throat. "I called the law office that represented Neal Scott, only to be told that they didn't have a clue what I was talking about."

Carmen frowned. "They don't remember sending the package?"

"They don't remember, because they never sent it," Lucy clarified. "In fact, they had direct orders from Neal Scott that all his possessions were to be destroyed after he was executed. He didn't want some prison guard selling his toothbrush on eBay after he died."

Carmen's gaze moved to the pictures that were still spread across the kitchen table.

There was no reason for the law firm to lie. At least none that made sense.

"You're sure the package wasn't from a different law firm?" Carmen asked.

"I'm sure. I even double-checked with the receptionist who keeps a log of packages we receive. Each one is labeled with who the package is for, and what company it's from."

Carmen felt an odd sense of dread lodge in the pit of her stomach.

"What was the name of the messenger company?"

"Dullus Express," Lucy said without hesitation. No doubt she'd anticipated Carmen's question.

"Do you have their number?"

"I already tried to contact them."

"Tried?"

Lucy released an aggravated sigh. "The telephone number that was left on the sign-in sheet actually belongs to a Chinese restaurant," she admitted. "And when I googled the name of the company I couldn't find it listed anywhere."

"So who sent the envelope?"

"I don't have any idea."

Carmen shivered. "Shit."

"Yeah," Lucy agreed. "Shit."

Carmen disconnected the phone. Right now she needed to think. Something that would be impossible when she had Lucy chattering in her ear.

Wrapping her arms around her waist, she glanced at the envelope before shifting her gaze toward the note.

Was it possible that the Polaroids had been taken by Neal Scott and never found by the cops? But who could have uncovered them? And why go to the trouble to make her believe that they were from the serial killer, including a note signed *The Trucker*?

Was this some sick joke? Her book had made her the target of all kinds of whackos. Could one of them have staged the pictures to attract her attention?

It was a plausible theory. There were all sorts of crackpots in the world.

But as much as she wanted to dismiss the Polaroids as a prank, there was something deep inside her that warned this was no joke.

She paced the floor, a terrible fear beginning to form.

If they hadn't been taken by Scott, and they weren't a prank, there was only one explanation for them.

A copycat killer.

She paced the floor, the horrifying suspicion churning through her mind. Was it possible? Was there some maniac out there who'd decided to follow in the footsteps of Neal Scott?

Was he even now bashing in some innocent girl's head?

Halting near the table, she reached to touch the picture that was lying on top, her dread hardening to determination.

There was nothing she could do to save them. Not if they were already dead.

But maybe, just maybe, she could give them justice.

Chapter Two

December 20, Rocky Mountains

Not exactly sure which authorities should be contacted, Carmen hopped into the Jeep she'd rented for her stay in the mountains and drove to the small town that was tucked next to the ski lodge. There had to be someone there who could hand the photos over to the proper authorities.

Unfortunately, she hadn't factored in the holiday season, or the flu bug that was making the rounds through the office. Or even the fact that the sheriff's wife had just given birth to a set of twins.

Arriving at the squat brick building, she was grudgingly allowed into the eerily empty station by a bored receptionist and left in a cluttered office to await the deputy who was on duty.

She clenched her jaw as the minutes ticked past. What could be taking so long? There might be a new killer on the loose and here she was, twiddling her thumbs as she waited for someone to remember she was there.

Unless the receptionist had forgotten to tell the officer?

She gave an impatient shake of her head. Even if the

woman had forgotten, this had to be the deputy's office. There were scribbled notes on the whiteboard attached to the wall. And a framed picture on the battered desk. There was even a filing cabinet stuffed so full of beige folders that a couple were sticking out, apparently trying to escape the clutter.

Sooner or later he would have to return.

Another ten minutes passed before the deputy at last strolled into the room. He was a short man with a thickness to his frame that had more to do with extra helpings of pecan pie than muscles. He had a square face with blunt features, like a bulldog.

Currently he was dressed in a brown uniform with a ball cap pulled low on his head. He brought with him the smell of coffee and a recently smoked cigarette.

"Ms. Jacobs," he drawled, casually dropping into his swivel chair.

With an effort, Carmen pasted a smile to her lips. "Hello, Deputy."

"You want to tell me why you're here?"

Carmen frowned. It was difficult to imagine how he could sound less enthusiastic. Clearly, she wasn't the only one having a bad day.

Leaning forward, she ignored his attitude and tossed the envelope on his desk, quickly revealing what she knew about how they came to be on the porch of her rented cabin.

He tipped the pictures onto his desk, flicking through them with seeming disinterest.

"They arrived this morning?"

"Yes."

More flicking, then without warning, he lifted his head to stab Carmen with a look of intense dislike.

"And you brought them to me?" He made the words sound like an accusation.

She frowned. "I didn't know where else to take them."

"Maybe to someone who . . . what did you say?" He pretended to consider his words. "Who isn't so busy sitting on their ass and eating doughnuts that they can't be bothered to investigate missing whores."

Carmen swallowed a sigh and sat back in her seat. Ah. So that was the reason for the big chill.

It hadn't even occurred to her that he might have read *The Heart of a Predator.* Stupid, really. The real estate agent who'd rented her the cabin had probably told the entire community that they had a famous writer coming to stay.

Which might have been fine if she'd written a top-selling cookbook.

Instead, she'd written about serial killers and had defiantly shared her opinion—although the local authorities hadn't shown much interest—about finding the missing women. And that the killers would have been caught much sooner if the victims had been from prominent families instead of whores and runaways.

She tried to keep her smile in place. "I'm sure this sheriff's office is quite competent."

"Why would you assume that?" His gaze made an insolent survey of her tense body. "You made the police departments look like a bunch of fools."

"That wasn't my intention," she said, even knowing that he wasn't going to believe her.

He didn't. If anything, his expression darkened. "No. You were all about making stone-cold killers into some sort of cult heroes."

Carmen shook her head. She wasn't going to argue the merits, or lack of merits, of her book.

"Look, I'm sorry if you were offended by my book, but I need your help to find out who sent those pictures." She attempted to bring the man's attention back to the reason she'd braved the icy roads to drive to town.

The deputy took a long, insulting minute before glancing down at the Polaroids.

"Did you touch them?" he demanded.

Carmen clenched her hands in her lap. "Of course."

"Then there's not much use in searching for fingerprints," he said, as if her touching the Polaroids magically rid them of any other prints. He grabbed the envelope and turned it over. "No postmark?"

"The original envelope was thrown away."

The deputy loudly cleared his sinuses. He sounded like a drunk goose.

"Convenient."

Carmen studied him in confusion. "What do you mean?"

"It might have cleared up some things," the deputy said.

"Things?"

He made a production of tucking the photos back into the envelope.

"Right now all we have is some pictures that might or might not be that of dead women," he said, his tone dismissive. "We don't have a date or place where the pictures were taken. Or even any indication where the supposed bodies might be now. I'm not sure what you want me to do about it."

Was he being serious?

"Obviously, I want you to investigate," she said, unable to hide her irritation. "Don't you want to know who sent them? And whether those women are really dead?"

His lips pursed. "Tell me, Ms. Jacobs, this wouldn't have anything to do with your book, would it?"

Carmen counted to ten. Then twenty.

At last she spoke. "Obviously, Neal Scott was one of the killers that I profiled," she admitted.

"I meant . . ." He tapped a blunt finger on the envelope. "Don't you have a new book coming out?"

She frowned. Why was he so fixated on her book?

"Not a new one," she said with a small shrug. "Just the paperback edition."

"Yeah, but having Scott back in the headlines would pump up the sales, right?" he drawled. "A few mysterious pictures that just happen to show up on your porch and all of a sudden the public is eager to snatch up your book."

Wham. The accusation slapped her in the face, making her flinch.

So that's where he was going.

She leaned forward, slamming her hands on the edge of his desk.

"Are you implying that I brought you these pictures as some sort of publicity stunt?"

"It wouldn't be the first time, would it?"

Angered by the man's stubborn refusal to listen, Carmen scowled.

"What are you talking about?"

"Didn't a woman show up at your signing claiming to be the mother of one of the victims in your book?" the deputy accused. "I read that she later admitted that she was an actress and that she was paid to create that scene."

Carmen flinched. It was an incident she'd tried to forget.

"No one ever could prove that the woman was actually paid to show up at my book signing, but it's possible one of the interns at the PR firm that represents me might have thought it was a good idea," she grudgingly admitted.

The deputy's lips curled into a sneer as he tapped his finger on top of the pictures.

"Maybe you should check with your PR people and ask them about these."

"I've already talked to them. They don't have anything to do with this."

"Easy to say." The man leaned back in his chair, looking as smug as a cat who'd just cornered a wounded rat.

Muttering beneath her breath, Carmen reached for the purse she'd set on the floor next to her feet.

"If you don't believe me, you can talk to the head of the PR firm yourself," she said, pulling out her phone. "They'll assure you that they didn't have anything to do with this."

He shrugged, ignoring the phone she held toward him. "That doesn't prove anything. It could be your own idea this time."

"If I wanted to use the pictures as a publicity stunt, I would have sent them to *The New York Times* or the *Today Show*, not to myself."

He shrugged. "But then you wouldn't have been the center of the story." He sucked some air through the gap in his front teeth. "This isn't my first rodeo, Ms. Jacobs. Women like you are always desperate for attention."

"Women like me? You mean journalists?"

"Women who've been featured in the scandal rags their whole life," he corrected. "You just can't stand for the spotlight to go away."

Her whole life?

Carmen forgot to breathe as her gut twisted with horror.

The deputy wasn't just referring to her book. He clearly knew about her parents. And the shocking details of their deaths that had rocked and dominated the headlines for months.

Her fingers curled tightly around the phone. Briefly she had an image of whacking the man across the face. He wouldn't look so smug with a bloody nose.

Then sanity made a timely return and she shoved the phone back into her purse.

Spending Christmas in a jail cell wasn't on her agenda. Not if she wanted to actually do something to try to discover the creep responsible for sending her the pictures.

"Can I assume that your only response to the photos is to call me a liar?" she bluntly asked.

The deputy suddenly appeared vaguely uncomfortable. As if he hadn't expected her to demand he come out and bluntly spell out what he preferred to imply.

"I'm saying the timing of these unknown pictures suddenly appearing when you're about to pimp another book is more than a little coincidental," he hedged.

"Fine." Carmen reached to pluck the envelope from his chubby fingers as she surged to her feet.

"Hey." He blinked, making a belated grab for the envelope. "Where are you going with those?"

Carmen was already headed toward the nearby door. "You don't believe me. I'll find someone who will."

She half expected him to rush and block her path. What respectable law officer wouldn't be anxious to ensure there wasn't a new killer out there?

But the deputy merely muttered a curse, his chair creaking as he settled himself into a more comfortable position.

"Merry Christmas, Ms. Jacobs," he called out.

"Jerk," she muttered, marching across the outer reception area and back into the frigid cold.

She shivered, slipping and sliding across the small parking lot to climb into her Jeep. Then, starting the engine, she flipped on the heater and stared out the frosty window.

She wasn't looking at the nearby slopes that were packed with brightly attired skiers clustered in small groups. Or even the dramatic, snow-covered mountains that loomed just beyond the ski lodge.

Instead, she tossed the envelope into the passenger seat and dug through her purse to pull out her phone. It was obvious she couldn't depend on law enforcement to help her. She'd burned too many bridges when she'd written her book. Not only by implying the police should have been more concerned about the missing women, but she'd been more than a little aggressive in demanding details that they hadn't wanted to share with the public.

Plus, as the deputy had so painfully exposed, there would always be those people who assumed she was somehow deranged because of her past.

She had to have proof. Absolute, inarguable proof.

So who could help her?

She scrolled quickly through the names. Most of them were from the publishing world. Or the media. But she did have a few connections who worked on the fringes of law enforcement.

She froze, her thumb hovering over the one name that could offer genuine assistance.

If only he didn't consider her a life form barely above a mold spore.

Chapter Three

December 21, California

The cottage was far enough from the beach to avoid the hordes of tourists who flocked to California every year, and hidden from the neighbors behind tall fences to offer a sense of privacy. The actual home had once been a traditional farmhouse with a screened-in porch and massive stone fireplaces. It also had a second floor where Griffin Archer had converted the cramped rooms into a spacious master suite when he'd moved in three years ago.

At the moment, Griff was seated at the shaded patio table that was perched near the drought-tolerant garden he'd chosen instead of the predictable pool. The landscaper he'd hired to design the yard had regarded him with a horror that Griff thought was excessive when he'd refused to contemplate even a shallow koi pond.

Rich people were supposed to be addicted to excess.

Griff liked things simple.

Polishing off his usual breakfast of a warm bagel with cream cheese and a glass of freshly squeezed orange juice, he studied his companion.

Rylan Cooper was a lean man with angular features and

Alexandra Ivy

golden brown eyes. His hair had been bleached light blond by the California sun and his skin was richly tanned despite the fact the younger man had recently returned to Missouri to live with his new wife, Jaci.

Since the day the two men had moved to the West Coast to set up their tech firm, which specialized in cutting-edge software for law enforcement, Rylan had looked perfectly at home.

Rylan had bought the elegant condo on the beach. He wore designer clothes that were perfectly tailored. And dated scantily clad models.

The clichéd California dude. At least until he'd returned home to marry the girl next door.

Griff, on the other hand, had never truly fit in. His brown hair was always a few weeks past needing a trim. This morning it was worse than usual, flopping onto his wide brow and curling over his ears. His skin was pale despite the fact he never missed his early morning run on the beach. He assumed it had something to do with being born in Chicago. Chi-Town skin was made for icy winters and dreary summer days, not sun-drenched beaches.

His face was average, with the usual nose and mouth. He'd always considered his eyes his best feature. Like his mother's, they were a dark brown and framed by thick lashes. Still, more than one woman had complained that they always looked distracted. As if he was thinking about something besides them.

They were right.

Oh, he liked women. A lot. But when he was working on a project, he found it difficult to think about anything else.

This morning he was wearing his running shorts and a loose sweatshirt. But even when he tried to dress up, he never could pull off Rylan's sleek sophistication.

And the truth of the matter was that he didn't care.

There was a reason Rylan was in charge of sales, while Griff concentrated on creating the actual product.

Thankfully unaware of Griff's inane thoughts, Rylan glanced at his wrist.

"I think that's all," he said. "I want to get to the airport early. This time a year it's always a pain in the ass to travel."

Griff set aside his orange juice. The two men had spent the past few weeks working on a new program that might very well revolutionize how countries around the world could track money that ended up in the hands of terrorists. Which meant Rylan had racked up enough frequent flyer miles to buy an airline.

"I want to schedule another round of tests before we start to install it."

Rylan rolled his eyes. Griff knew his friend and partner thought he was being obsessive. They'd run hundreds of simulations and the program had performed flawlessly.

"Homeland Security wants to have the program installed and ready to go by the first of March," Rylan said, as if Griff might have forgotten the looming deadline.

"They'll have to wait until I'm satisfied every bug is worked out," Griff said, his tone stubborn. "You know my philosophy."

"Yeah, yeah. Perfection is always possible." With a sigh, Rylan rose to his feet. He knew when Griff wasn't going to budge. "I'll give my contact a call." Planting his hands on his hips, Rylan glanced down at Griff. "At least tell me you aren't planning to work during the holidays?"

A lie hovered on his lips.

Rylan was his best friend. Hell, he was Griff's *only* truly close friend. But there were times when he nagged like he was Griff's grandmother, not his partner.

He wasn't really in the mood for a lecture.

But meeting his friend's steady gaze, he heaved a resigned sigh. Rylan could smell bullshit a mile away.

"I plan to catch up on some side projects that I put on the back burner over the past few months," Griff admitted.

Rylan narrowed his gaze. He was gearing up for a sermon. Probably one he'd already rehearsed in his head. Then, catching a glimpse of Griff's long-suffering expression, he threw his hands up in resignation.

"Jaci is never going to forgive you if you miss Christmas dinner," he instead warned.

"I'm not an expert on women," Griff said, ignoring Rylan's choked laugh. "But I suspect that your beautiful new bride would prefer to spend her first Christmas alone with her husband. Especially after she's had to share you for the past six weeks."

"That's what you would think, right?" Rylan demanded. "What woman in her right mind wouldn't want to serve me a romantic dinner in bed and then unwrap me like a Christmas present?"

Griff blasted his friend with an appalled glare. "Christ, Rylan, that's not a visual I want stuck in my head."

The younger man sniffed, conjuring up a wounded expression. "Instead, my wife has spent the past week cooking enough food to feed an army and complaining that I haven't tried hard enough to strong-arm you into traveling to Missouri." He paused, clearly hoping to instill maximum guilt. "She insists the holidays won't be the same without our family together."

"Family?"

Rylan smiled. The two men had met in college, and later moved to California.

"That's how she sees you," he assured his companion. "You got a problem with that?"

Griff's heart swelled with warmth. He hadn't been acquainted with Jaci until his friend had married her. But in the months since the wedding, he'd had the chance to get to know the sweet, levelheaded woman who'd instantly claimed him as an honorary brother.

He'd never openly admit that deep inside he'd been worried that once Rylan was married he'd turn his back on the business and his old friend. That's what usually happened when men fell in love.

Instead, he'd gained a little sister.

"No," he said. "No problem."

"Then you'll be there for dinner?" Rylan smoothly pounced.

Griff released a short laugh. There was a reason his friend was such a successful businessman.

"You just don't give up."

Rylan shrugged. "It's part of my charm."

About to inform Rylan that his charm was a figment of his imagination, Griff was distracted by the buzz of his phone.

His lips tightened, his fingers twitching as he resisted the urge to knock it off the table.

The calls had started yesterday. One glance at the name flashing on his screen and he'd sent them straight to voice mail. He'd hoped that after a dozen tries the woman would get the hint.

Futile, of course.

Carmen Jacobs was nothing if not determined.

Rylan glanced at him in puzzlement, easily reading the annoyance that was etched on Griff's face.

"A dissatisfied client?"

"Carmen Jacobs," he answered in clipped tones.

Rylan frowned. "Do I know her?"

"She wrote the book *The Heart of a Predator*," he reminded his companion.

"Ah. I remember." Rylan paused, studying Griff's clenched features. "She wanted to interview you, didn't she?"

Griff abruptly rose to his feet. As if going from sitting to standing could halt the image of Carmen Jacobs from searing through his mind.

No such luck.

With annoying clarity, he envisioned Carmen's curly blond hair that formed a halo around the perfect oval of her face. Her big eyes that were the precise color of bluebells, and the disarming flash of dimples.

It was the sort of face that inspired men to act like idiots.

Something he'd learned the same way he usually learned things about pretty women.

The hard way.

"Yeah," he muttered.

The phone stopped buzzing, only to start up again ten seconds later.

"What does she want now?" Rylan asked.

Griff was uncomfortably aware of a heat crawling beneath his skin. It had to be anger, right? Maybe embarrassment that he'd been so easily fooled by blue eyes and dimples.

"I don't know and I don't care," he said.

Rylan narrowed his gaze. "You look—"

"What?"

"Flushed."

Crap. Griff scowled, pointedly glancing toward Rylan's wristwatch. "Don't you have a plane to catch?"

"Fine." Rylan held up his hands in defeat. "But don't blame me if Jaci cuts off your supply of blueberry muffins."

Griff was genuinely horrified. Jaci's blueberry muffins were works of art. Moist and sweet with tart bursts of flavor from the berries.

"She wouldn't be that cruel," Griff protested.

Rylan's lips parted, but before he could speak, Griff's phone went on another buzzing rampage.

Griff muttered a low curse, in no mood to appreciate Rylan's sudden chuckle.

"You might give Ms. Jacobs a call back," Rylan told him. "Any woman that persistent is worth the trouble."

Griff folded his arms over his chest. "Ms. Jacobs and trouble are two things I don't need."

Rylan shrugged, turning to head toward the side gate. "Take care," he called over his shoulder. "I'll see you for Christmas dinner."

"Annoying ass," Griff breathed, snatching the phone off the table before he headed into his house.

Twenty minutes later he was on his favorite stretch of beach, jogging away his frustrations.

Breathing deeply of the salty air, he cleared his mind as his feet pounded against the hard-packed sand and a layer of sweat covered his skin. This was the best part of living on the coast. The early morning solitude when it was just him and the ocean and the beat of his heart.

Hitting the five-mile mark, he turned to stroll back at a leisurely pace. The slower speed not only allowed him time to cool down, but he could actually appreciate the view.

He climbed the steps to the parking lot, his mind already starting to turn to the work that was waiting for him at home. A mistake, since his distraction meant that he didn't notice the woman who was leaning against the hood of his red Tesla.

Not until he was less than a few feet away.

Crap.

His ex-girlfriends were right. He was too wrapped up in his inner thoughts. Otherwise he would have spotted the woman while he was still on the beach and taken evasive maneuvers.

Certainly, no other man in the area was so oblivious to the sight of Carmen Jacobs.

The swelling crowd hustled toward the ocean, many of the men coming to a halt to gawk at Carmen's slender body, which was curved in all the right places beneath her jeans and tight cashmere sweater. A few of them even managed to tear their gazes from the sweet swell of her breasts long enough to admire the silver-gold curls that brushed her shoulders and framed the delicate features of her face.

He knew what they were thinking. It was every man's fantasy to lure the sweet, innocent girl into his bed and thoroughly corrupt her.

It'd been his fantasy six months ago. For an entire week he'd shared his morning run with Carmen, stupidly assuming it was fate that had crossed their paths. He hadn't suspected the truth even when she started to question him about his work. Or when she acted as if she was fascinated by every word that left his lips.

It wasn't until he'd been reading the morning paper and ran across an article that featured Carmen Jacobs's lecture series at a local college that he realized there might be something dodgy about her sudden interest in him.

Digging into the pocket of his shorts, he pulled out his keys.

"Don't say a word," he warned, refusing to meet her gaze. He'd been sucked into those glorious blue eyes once before. Wasn't happening again. "Just get off my car and walk away."

"Hello, Griffin."

Her voice was as light and feminine as the rest of her, brushing over him like a caress. Griff clenched his teeth.

"What part of *don't say a word* wasn't clear?"

Out of the corner of his eye he saw her flinch. Had she expected him to do backflips at the sight of her? Probably.

"I need your help."

"Tough." He moved to open his car door.

She quickly hurried to stand in his path. "You have to listen to me."

He instinctively lifted his eyes at her fierce plea, a jolt of awareness blazing through him as he met the clear blue gaze. It was as swift and potent as the first time he'd seen her on the beach.

Annoyance sizzled through him.

"I don't have to do a damned thing," he growled.

"Please," she whispered, lifting a hand as if she intended to touch him.

Griff stepped back. "I'm sure you've been able to flash your dimples and get what you want your entire life, but they don't work on me," he informed her, giving a sharp motion with his hand. "Now get out of my way."

She folded her arms around her waist. Not surprisingly she didn't move.

Obstinate female.

"Look, I know we didn't get off to the best start," she said.

"Really?" He released a sharp laugh. "Which part? When you stalked me?" he demanded, referring to the mornings he'd found her waiting on the beach for him. "Or when you lied to me?" he asked, reminding her that she'd teasingly told him her name was Jane Doe. "Or when you tried to use me?" he concluded his indictment.

"I didn't . . ." Carmen's words trailed away as she took in his grim expression. Apparently, not even she could look him in the eyes and deny her sins. Not after she'd hounded him for weeks with endless calls trying to interview him for a new book. Then, when he'd bluntly refused, she'd decided to use the old "incognito" ruse. Pretty woman. Teeny, tiny bikini. Casual meetings on the beach. No doubt she hoped she could seduce him into blind lust before he could realize who she was. "I need your help," she repeated.

He snorted in disbelief. "Searching for some new victims you can exploit to create a blockbuster book for yourself?"

She paled, as if he'd hit a raw nerve, but her expression remained determined.

"This has nothing to do with my career," she said.

"Right."

With jerky movements she reached into her large purse, which was sitting on the hood of his car, and pulled out a manila envelope.

"I think a copycat is killing women and sending me the evidence," she said, shoving the envelope into his hand.

Griff froze. Had he heard her right? Did she say she was getting mail from a serial killer?

He studied her pale face, absorbing the brittle tension that vibrated around her before he opened the envelope and reached in to grab a stack of pictures.

Polaroids? Unusual.

Then he turned them over and his breath was jerked from his lungs.

Holy . . . crap.

"If this is some sort of joke, then it isn't funny," he breathed, shuffling through the rest of the pictures before shoving them back into the envelope.

He felt tainted.

As if just touching the disturbing photos was enough to infect him with evil.

"Of course it isn't a joke." Her voice was hoarse, her hands clenched into tight fists.

It was hard not to believe her. She projected a fierce sincerity that would be difficult to fake.

Still, he wasn't a total idiot. He'd been fooled by this woman before.

"Then you should take them to the cops, not me," he told her, shoving the envelope back into her hand.

She grimaced. "I tried."

He felt a small surge of relief. If the cops knew about the pictures, then surely they were investigating.

"And?"

"And they're no more fond of me than you are," she said.

"Imagine that," he said, then instantly regretted the words when she abruptly turned her head, as if trying to hide her hurt expression.

Okay, he was still pissed, probably more pissed than was reasonable, but he wasn't a cruel person.

"Which means that I need proof to convince them to take this seriously," she told him.

Griff sucked in a deep breath, his gaze lowering to the envelope. The images of dead women remained branded in his brain, making him wonder how any cop could need more proof.

"What did they say to you?"

She scowled. "They think the pictures are a promo stunt because the paperback edition of my book is coming out in a few days."

Ah. Well, that made sense. They lived in a world where people would set themselves on fire to gain attention.

"And is it?" he bluntly demanded.

"What?"

"A publicity stunt?"

Her eyes flashed blue fire. "I know it's hard to believe, but my book sales did just fine," she snapped. "I don't need stunts to be a successful author."

He held up his hands. "This has nothing to do with me."

He didn't know what he expected, but it certainly wasn't for Carmen to abruptly drop to her knees in front of him.

Tilting back her head, she sent him a defiant glare. "Do you want me to beg?" she demanded. She pressed her hands together, as if she was saying a prayer. "To grovel at your feet?"

Griff's brows snapped together. He didn't need to look around to know they were becoming the center of attention. The tourists were no doubt craning their necks to see if she was a prostitute about to do her business in a public parking lot, while the locals had their phones pressed to their ears as they called 911. The neighborhood was upscale enough to resent having people making spectacles of themselves in broad daylight.

That's what reality TV was for.

"Ms. Jacobs—"

"My name is Carmen," she interrupted, her eyes suddenly damp as her lips trembled.

Griff swore beneath his breath. He'd just told her that he was immune to her dimples. And he was. At least in theory. But he was no match for tears.

Crap, crap, crap.

Bending down, he hooked his fingers around her upper arm and urged her to her feet.

"Get up," he commanded.

She stumbled upright, swaying toward him before she regained her balance. Griff's hand slid up her arm, careful not to grip too tightly.

She was so fierce, it was easy to forget just how small and delicate she was. He had no intention of accidentally bruising her.

"Will you help me?" she demanded, standing close enough he could catch the crisp, citrus scent that clung to her skin. Her soap? Lotion? He sucked in a deep breath before he even realized what he was doing.

He shook his head in frustration. "Do I have a choice?"

"No," she assured him.

"Great." He glanced around the parking lot, which had filled to the limit over the past few minutes. "Where's your car?"

"I took a cab from the airport."

"You were that certain I would be here?"

She hesitated before giving a small shrug. "You're a creature of habit."

Creature of habit? Griff grimaced. Just great. She made him sound as exciting as a house slipper. An old, ratty house slipper.

With brisk steps he rounded the hood of his car and unlocked the passenger door.

"Get in."

She scurried to slide into the low-slung car, keeping her lips shut as he took his seat behind the wheel and switched on the engine. There was a low purr of power as he pulled out of the lot and headed across the highway toward the narrow road that zigzagged through the local neighborhood.

She at last broke the thick silence. "Thanks."

He sent her an annoyed glance. "Don't thank me. You were starting to attract attention," he informed her. "Just say what you came here to say."

She wiped the palms of her hands on her jeans. It was the only visible indication that she was anything but cool, calm, and collected. Then, with a concise attention to detail, she started to speak.

She told him about staying at the remote cabin and finding the envelope on the porch. She skimmed over her horror at pulling out the Polaroids, but he didn't miss the way her fingers curled into tight fists.

He didn't interrupt and she quickly moved on to the fact that the law firm that'd supposedly sent the envelope claimed they weren't responsible. Something that might have been a clerical error, until she revealed that the messenger company that delivered the package didn't exist.

She finished up with her trip to the sheriff's office, where she met with a deputy who'd immediately decided she was playing some sort of sick game.

From that, she'd decided the authorities weren't going to believe her without some real proof.

Whatever that meant.

He pulled the car into his long driveway, halting at the side of the house. Remaining silent, he climbed out of the vehicle and watched as Carmen hurried to join him. She had her purse slung over her shoulder and the envelope clutched tight in her fingers.

As soon as she reached his side, he led her to the back of the house to enter through the kitchen door.

He crossed the tiled floor to the sink to splash cold water

on his face. Later he would hop in the shower, but for now he needed to clear his brain.

Plus, it gave him a perfect excuse to put distance between him and the woman who he'd never expected to see again.

He reached for a dish towel to wipe off the droplets that clung to his heated skin, and then, turning around, he braced himself to tell Carmen he couldn't help her, only to discover he was alone in the kitchen.

His heart missed a painful beat.

She was gone.

Chapter Four

December 21, California

Carmen drifted around the spacious living room that was filled with overstuffed couches and chairs clearly designed for comfort, and the driftwood shelves that held rows of leather-bound books that were scuffed from use.

There were tall windows that allowed the morning sunlight to pour into the room, and bright hand-woven rugs on the planked floor. Across from her was a stone fireplace for the rare nights that it was cold enough to need heat. And in the corner was a large Christmas tree covered with a mishmash of decorations that looked as if they'd been handed down over the years.

On the walls were two oil paintings. She crossed to study them, a genuine envy tugging at her heart. They were original Turners. One of her favorite artists.

Both canvases had ships battling the elements as they struggled to cross a stormy sea.

Hmm.

Beauty amid chaos.

She didn't know if it was a glimpse into Griffin Archer's complicated brain or not.

The man was quite simply impossible to read.

From the minute she'd uncovered the fact that Dr. Franklin Hammel, the second serial killer profiled in her book, had been caught because of software invented by Griffin and his partner, she'd been fascinated.

Her first book had centered on killers. How cool would it be to write a book about the people who caught those killers?

But not the usual cops and sheriffs and detectives. They had hundreds of stories that spoke about their heroism. No. She wanted to delve deeper into the way technology was altering the way police tracked down criminals.

Unfortunately, Griffin Archer refused to even take her calls. That was the only reason she'd decided to use a different approach. If he wouldn't talk to her over the phone, then maybe she could convince him face-to-face. And the perfect opportunity had offered itself when the local college had requested she do a series of lectures.

When she'd traveled to California, she hadn't intended to try to fool him. Not consciously. But from a young age she'd trained herself to become a woman who never accepted the word *no*. How else could she succeed? So she'd used her journalistic skills to discover Griff's routine, and decided to approach him during his morning run.

The last thing she'd expected was to be knocked so off-balance by Griff that she forgot her own game.

He was nothing like she'd expected.

Okay, he was brilliant. That was a given. And clearly obsessed with his work.

But he was also gorgeous. The dark curly hair that made her fingers itch to run through it. The finely chiseled lines of his face. A slender nose. A wide brow. A strong jaw that added a stern masculinity to his features.

His eyes were velvet brown and he had a boyish, crooked grin that melted her heart.

Then there was the lean, sculpted body that made women stumble when he jogged past them.

She wasn't a nun; there had been men in her life. But none of them had made her brain shut down when they glanced in her direction.

In all honesty, it was supposed to be the other way around.

She smiled, sometimes she fluttered her lashes, and they did what she asked.

Was it any wonder she'd so badly blundered her attempt to lure him into giving her an interview?

"Making yourself at home?" a dark voice drawled from behind her.

She abruptly turned to discover Griff standing in the doorway, his expression stern.

"I'm sorry, I'm just naturally curious," she said, trying not to notice the awareness that sizzled through her. The last time she'd approached this man she screwed up everything by allowing her raw attraction to cloud her thinking. She couldn't afford to let it happen again. "You have a lovely home."

He folded his arms over his chest. "You sound surprised."

"I suppose I am," she admitted, her gaze skimming over the cushy furniture. The place reminded her of her grandparents' home in Indiana. Warm. Inviting. Lived in. "I saw your partner's condo featured in a magazine. This is nothing like it."

He wrinkled his nose. "I don't like feeling I'm living in a fishbowl. This is much more . . ."

"Comfortable," she said when his words trailed away. "The condo is a showroom. This is a home."

Something flared through the dark eyes before his lips flattened. Had he reminded himself that she was the enemy?

"Tell me why you came here."

She studied him. Was this a trick question?

"I told you. I need to convince the police these are real," she reminded him.

A sharp shake of his head. Apparently, she'd given the wrong answer.

"One last time," he warned. "Why me?"

She glanced down at the envelope in her hand.

A part of her understood his confusion. She had pictures of dead women. The cops should be all over the case, even if they didn't personally like her, or the book she'd written.

And deep inside she knew if she tried hard enough, she might find a police department that was willing to at least check into the possibility there was a killer out there.

So why was she here?

The answer was simple. She wanted him to find proof that the pictures were real so she knew beyond a doubt that this wasn't a hoax.

There.

She'd admitted it to herself.

She didn't want to press the issue if there was a chance she was making a fool of herself.

Acutely aware of his gaze that was watching the emotions flit over her face, she squared her shoulders.

"I need to know the truth," she told him. "You're the only one who has the skill to give me that."

He frowned, but he didn't throw her out the window. She considered that a win.

"Flattery, Carmen?" he instead drawled.

"It's not flattery," she retorted. "You're the best, and you know it."

"If I find out this is some sort of stunt, I'll make you regret trying to screw with me."

She spread her arms. "You can do your worst," she assured him.

Or his best, a wicked voice whispered in the back of her mind.

Carmen was quick to squash the voice. Griff wasn't doing anything to her or with her that didn't involve photos of dead women.

She grimaced. And as a means of dampening her lust, that was a doozy.

Releasing an exasperated breath, Griff pointed toward a doorway near the fireplace.

"Let's go into my office."

With long strides he was across the room and entering the attached office. Carmen scurried to keep up, her eyes widening as she stepped over the threshold.

Once again Griff managed to catch her off guard.

He was a computer genius. The golden boy of every government agency, including Interpol, who she'd discovered had offered him a very large fortune to head up their cyber-crime division.

His office should be the latest in high tech, right?

Instead, the room looked like it belonged to an English country squire.

There were no metal shelves filled with servers and blinking modems. No rolled-up cords that connected twenty computers into one seamless machine. No sleek chrome-and-glass furnishings. In fact, the only computer was a laptop that was set on a heavy walnut desk situated near the French doors.

"Give me the pictures," Griff commanded, waiting for her to hand him the envelope before taking a seat in the leather swivel chair.

She was vaguely aware of him opening a drawer of the desk to pull out a small scanner, but her gaze was traveling over the built-in bookshelves and collection of baseball cards that were framed and displayed in a glass case. The floors were covered by vintage rugs that looked like they'd come from a Turkish market, and the walls were paneled with glossy wood.

It was a manly sort of office, but with the same shabby comfort as the living room.

Her feet were carrying her toward the framed plaque on the wall. It had two small medals hung on ribbons mounted next to it and a folded American flag. Was it some sort of military award? Before she could get close enough to read what was stamped on the silver medal, Griff made a small sound of satisfaction.

Pivoting on her heel, she hurried to stand beside his chair. "Did you find something?"

He turned the laptop so she could see the screen. She flinched. He'd scanned the Polaroids into his computer, enlarging them so that they could make out every detail.

It only made it all the more gruesome.

The white faces frozen in horror. The weird hint of blue around the lips. The blond hair splayed outward like a tarnished halo. And the bloody wound that provided the only splash of color.

Griff used the mouse to click on one of the images, allowing it to fill the screen. Then he zoomed in on the stacked boxes visible in the background.

"A label," he murmured, continuing to zoom in.

Carmen felt a stirring of hope as she leaned forward. If the women were killed in the back of a freezer trailer as she suspected, the contents of the boxes might give them a real clue.

The image went fuzzy, then cleared as he did something else with the mouse. Carmen grimaced, releasing a disappointed sigh.

"There's nothing that says what's inside or where they came from."

"Actually, there is."

He used the tip of his finger to touch the screen. She leaned even closer, tiny shocks of pleasure racing through her as the side of her breast brushed against his shoulder.

She shifted an inch away, hoping he didn't notice the sudden heat that stained her cheeks.

"A bar code," she said, her eyes at last focused on the black smudge he was pointing at. "You can use that?"

"We'll soon find out," he told her, his slender fingers flying over the keyboard.

She blinked as the screen was suddenly filled with files that flickered by so fast she could barely see them before they were gone. Like a strobe light going full speed.

Did he always work like this? It was a wonder he didn't have a seizure.

At last he slowed and then stopped the files, enlarging what looked to be an order form.

"Did you get a hit?" she asked.

He sent her an amused gaze. "A hit?"

She rolled her eyes. Okay. She wasn't a tech guru. She could turn her phone off and on. What more did she need?

"Whatever you call it," she said.

He returned his attention to the file on the computer screen.

"The box is packed with containers of frozen pasta," he told her. "It left a warehouse in Denver, Colorado, on December sixth and arrived in St. Louis on the eighth."

"Of this year?"

"Yep."

Around two weeks ago, she silently calculated. "So these aren't from Neal Scott," she said out loud.

"Not unless he's returned from the grave," he agreed.

"Can you tell anything else?"

He clicked through more files. "I can give you the name of the truck line. Kirkwood Freight Carriers."

She reached into her purse to pull out an old-fashioned pen and small notebook. She scribbled down *Kirkwood*.

"What about the driver?"

"Lee Williams," he said, clicking onto another file.

Putting the name in her notebook, Carmen heard Griff make a small sound. As if he was startled by something he'd just discovered.

"What is it?"

"There was a police report filed," he said.

"On the driver?"

He shook his head. "No. Williams reported the truck missing."

Her gut tightened with dread. Abruptly she realized just how much she wanted to believe she was overreacting. It would solve everything if Griff told her this was all some sort of bad joke. She could fly back to her cabin and crawl beneath the covers until the holidays were over.

Maybe until the snow melted.

"It was stolen?" she asked.

He paused, reading through the file before he answered.

"The report says that the driver stayed the night at the Fairview Hotel in Kansas," he told her. "After he ate breakfast he went to the parking lot and discovered his truck was gone."

"Did they catch the thief?"

"No. The truck was found abandoned a few miles away. On the shoulder of I-70."

I-70. The hunting ground for the Trucker. Plus, a missing freezer trailer . . .

The dread intensified.

"There had to be video footage from the hotel," she said.

He used the mouse to skim to the bottom of the report. "There was a camera mounted in the parking lot, but according to the manager it was just for show." He shrugged. "It looks like the cops talked to a few customers staying at the hotel, but no one wanted to get involved."

Of course not. An eyewitness would have made this too easy.

"Predictable," she muttered.

He reached the bottom of the screen. "And since the truck was found with nothing missing, the report was closed and the driver finished his delivery."

She abruptly straightened. "If the case was closed, then I assume that means there wasn't a body found in the trailer," she said, speaking more to herself than her companion.

"Doubtful," he agreed with a grimace.

"A difference."

He turned his chair to study her with a searching gaze. "A difference from what?"

She hesitated before sharing the thoughts racing through her mind.

"Scott always left his latest victim frozen in his trailer until he could choose a new one," she explained.

He studied her for a long minute. "Why do you assume this has anything to do with Scott?"

"The M.O. is very close. Scott held his victims in the back of a freezer trailer before he smashed in the sides of their heads with a crowbar," she said. "And all of the victims had been prostitutes known to work in the parking lots of truck stops along I-70." She reached past him to pluck the envelope off the desk. Then, pushing her hand inside, she pulled out the sheet of notepaper. "And this came with the envelope."

Taking the note, Griff read the brief message. His brows snapped together, his stern features becoming downright grim. Almost as if he was personally bothered by the words.

At last he lifted his gaze to study her face, his dark eyes smoldering with an odd intensity.

"Whoever sent these wanted you to believe they were from a dead serial killer," he said, an edge in his voice.

She chewed her bottom lip. "That was my first assumption, too."

He blinked, as if surprised by her words. "And now?"

Her gaze moved to stare out the French doors at the sunlit patio. It looked so bright and cheery. The complete opposite of the darkness that seemed to spread through her as she forced herself to consider the purpose of the envelope.

If it was another serial killer trying to gain her attention, then there was no reason to imitate Neal Scott. Usually each monster had their specific method of murder. It was always a ritual that had meaning to them. An intimate connection to their victim.

But by replicating the deaths from her book, and sending the proof to her, it seemed to indicate that this was as much about her as the victims.

A shudder raced through her.

"No, I think it was to taunt me," she said in a low voice.

"Why?"

She struggled to put her fear into words. "I don't know, but it feels . . ." Another shudder shook her body. "Personal."

She thought she heard him suck in a sharp breath. "You suspect it's someone you know?"

She gave a quick shake of her head, refusing to even contemplate the idea. Wasn't it bad enough to receive pictures of dead women without the horrifying fear that the killer might be a personal acquaintance?

"No," she said. "But I think they read my book and it touched a nerve."

"Or inspired them," he pointed out.

Her lips pressed together. She wasn't going to apologize for her work. Why should she? She'd told the story of American predators and the women who were left vulnerable in a society that should protect them.

If it offended people, then tough luck.

She jutted her chin, holding his searing gaze. "Can you tell anything about the victims?"

He tapped the tip of his finger on the desk, his expression impossible to read.

"Young. White. Blond hair," he said.

She rolled her eyes. She didn't need a computer genius to figure that out.

"Are they really dead?"

"They look dead, but I'm not a doctor."

"Your computer can't tell?"

"No."

She hissed in exasperation. She now knew that the pictures had been taken within the past few weeks, which ruled out that they were victims of Scott. And she knew that the truck with at least one victim had been in the area of I-70.

But she'd been hoping for more.

She still didn't know if the women were truly dead, or if it was some elaborate hoax meant to freak her out.

She needed more.

"Then is there anything we can use to identify the women?" she abruptly demanded.

There was more tapping with his finger on the desk. Tap, tap, tap.

"What is it you think that I do?" he demanded.

She frowned. She didn't know exactly what he was asking.

"You create software that helps law enforcement catch the bad guys," she at last said, referring to the astonishing program he'd created that had allowed the FBI to predict where Dr. Franklin Hammel would attempt to snatch his next victim. They'd managed to catch him in the act.

"Exactly. I create the software." He deliberately paused. "The information that gets put into that software comes from the authorities."

It was his condescending tone—like he was talking to a particularly stupid child—that was the breaking point.

Enough.

Carmen had known when she'd hopped on the plane that it would be a long shot. Griffin Archer didn't like her. Didn't trust her. And apparently felt as if he had no reason to treat her as anything more than an unwanted intruder.

"So what you're saying is that you won't help me."

He frowned. "I'm saying that I *can't* help you."

"Fine." She folded her arms around her waist. It was the only way to hide the fact her hands were shaking with suppressed emotions. "Can you give me copies of the enlarged pictures?"

"Sure." He hit a button on the keyboard and there was a sound from a printer cleverly hidden behind a potted plant.

"Thanks." Carmen moved to grab the sheets of paper, stuffing them into her purse. "I'll leave the originals here," she said as she turned back to meet his guarded gaze. "I'm sure the cops will be more willing to look at them if they come from you."

"I have a few contacts in the FBI that might be interested," he assured her.

"Perfect." With her spine stiff and her chin high, Carmen marched across the room.

"Wait." He surged to his feet. "Where are you going?"

Well, that was a hell of a question, wasn't it?

A pity she didn't have an answer.

"Merry Christmas, Griffin," she muttered.

She walked through the door, and then out of the house.

She'd figure out where she was going when she got to the airport.

Chapter Five

December 22, Kansas City

Hunter was invisible.

It was a trick he'd learned when he'd been very young.

He didn't scream and demand attention like other kids. He didn't stand out at school or in sports or the arts.

Instead, he would fade into background.

It allowed him to see the world from the eyes of a predator.

In the shadows he could detect the weaknesses of others. He peeked through windows. He listened at doors. And collected secrets like other boys collected girlie magazines.

Then he would strike.

Without warning. Without morals.

"Beware the Jabberwock, my son! The jaws that bite, the claws that catch!"

Now he waited once again in the shadows, watching his prey as she stood in line to collect her keys for a rental car. The crowd ebbed and flowed around him, never giving him a second glance. Neither did the woman who shifted her small overnight bag from hand to hand, her expression one of weary impatience.

Excitement bubbled through him.

It wasn't sexual. No. This was sweet anticipation.

She was close enough he could see the sheen of gold in her tumble of curls. And the soft curve of her breast beneath her sweater. It was too far to make out the clear blue of her eyes, or to see the dimples that dented her cheeks when she smiled, but he smothered his flare of frustration.

All good things come to those who wait.

Those were words his mother had whispered in his ear, never understanding what she was teaching him.

So he had waited. Years. And years.

His dark thoughts were interrupted as his phone suddenly vibrated. Keeping his gaze locked on his quarry, he pulled it out of his pocket and pressed it to his ear.

He already knew who was calling.

"What is it now?" he demanded, his voice edged with annoyance. His disciple, who'd taken the name Butcher, had called three times in the past two days.

It'd been his own idea to create secret names. Just like the killers from *The Heart of a Predator*. He not only liked the thought of being called Hunter, but it'd helped to solidify his hold over the others. He'd created them. Molded them out of lumps of meaningless clay into killers with a true purpose.

Now he controlled them.

"I found her," a childish voice breathed. Butcher was in his twenties, but acted more like a boy just entering puberty.

Stunted. Both intellectually and emotionally.

His parents had thrown him away, but Hunter swiftly recognized a weapon when he saw one.

It had taken years to hone the fool into a suitable disciple, but now Butcher was loyal beyond question and willing to perform any task demanded of him.

No matter how depraved.

"Good for you," he said, his voice low and soothing. Not

for Butcher, but to keep any passerby from glancing in his direction.

Invisible.

Incapable of replicating Hunter's Zen-like calm, Butcher was babbling with a hectic eagerness.

"She's lovely," he assured his mentor. "Not too tall, and soft in all the right places."

"She's blond?" Hunter asked. It was one of his three requirements.

Their prey must be young, white, and blond.

"Of course," Butcher said, his voice edged with impatience. "When do I get to squeeze her?"

"Soon," Hunter said, distracted as the woman completed her paperwork and took the keys that were handed across the narrow counter.

There was a buzzing silence in his ear before Butcher spoke the words that had presumably been hovering on the tip of his tongue.

"Executioner says we shouldn't have to wait."

Hunter's jaw tightened. The older disciple had never been as easy to control as the others. They'd known each other from the beginning. From the days before he'd established the Kill Club, and he often resented taking orders. Thankfully, the man wouldn't be a problem for much longer.

"Remind him what happens when people piss me off," Hunter warned, casually strolling toward the nearest door as the woman headed for an exit on the other side of the rental desk.

Butcher sucked in a sharp breath, perhaps remembering the sight of Hunter casually putting a bullet through the head of the thug who'd tried to carjack him in Memphis. It'd all been over in less than a split second, with the young man crumpling onto the road with half his skull missing. Hunter had even run over the limp body as he drove away. More as a lesson for the men in his car.

Don't screw with him.

"It's hard to wait," Butcher at last whined.

Hunter stepped into the frigid morning air, quickly crossing to the short-term parking lot. The cost was nothing less than criminal, but the placement allowed him quick access to his car.

"You could spend the next fifty years waiting in a jail cell if we're not careful," he reminded the younger man, shivering as he reached his boring tan sedan and slipped inside.

He switched on the engine, his gaze focused on the woman who was climbing into a shuttle bus that would take her to the car she'd just rented.

There was a crackling on the cell phone, as if Butcher was pacing from room to room.

"When are you coming to Baltimore?" the younger man asked.

Hunter smiled. He'd actually been on his way to join his disciples when the hacker he'd blackmailed into keeping electronic track of his private muse had contacted him with the information that she had just purchased airline tickets to Kansas City. He'd been instantly intrigued.

Was it possible she'd discovered that one of the kills had taken place in this area?

It seemed unlikely, but then again, what other reason could there be for her to fly to Kansas City?

The desire to toy with his prey in person was too tempting to pass up, so he'd made a swift U-turn and headed straight for this airport north of town.

"Soon," he said in soothing tones, putting his car in gear and driving to the exit of the parking lot. Once in position he watched the shuttle as it came to a halt and the woman stepped out. "First I have to make sure our last party is cleaned up and the garbage buried deep enough it will never be found."

There was another pause. "Is Assassin with you?"

A smile twisted Hunter's lips. It had been a sweet relief to press his gun to the side of Assassin's head and pull the trigger. The disciple had been weak. A fool who craved the thrill of the hunt without the spine to accomplish the final deed.

But like all his followers, he'd served his purpose.

If the authorities managed to locate the abandoned farmhouse in the middle of Kansas, they would discover the bodies of the five prostitutes tossed into the basement and Assassin in an upstairs bedroom with a bullet in his head. Any cop would assume that he was responsible for the deaths and had taken his own life out of guilt.

Murder/suicide.

A convenient way to close the case.

"No." He laced his voice with surprise. "He isn't in Baltimore?"

"No one has seen him since we left Kansas City," Butcher said.

"Odd. I'm sure he'll show up," Hunter said, anticipation curling through the pit of his stomach as he watched the woman climb into a white SUV. "He might have decided to spend Christmas with his family."

"I suppose," Butcher said slowly, as if not entirely convinced.

"I have to go." Hunter ended the call and tossed his phone on the seat beside him.

His prey was backing out of the parking place and heading toward the exit.

The hunt was on.

The December day was what weathermen called "blustery" and what people who actually had to be out in it called "shitty."

The late morning sky was hidden by a thick layer of

clouds that hung low and ominous, drizzling ice and spitting out the occasional flake. At the same time, the wind was zipping over the flat plains at a speed that picked up the recently fallen snow that coated the ground, swirling it around the parking lot like frozen tornadoes.

Welcome to winter in the Midwest.

Carmen grimaced, pulling her rented SUV into the parking lot of the Fairview Hotel.

The one-story L-shaped building had seen better days.

Her gaze skimmed over the structure that was miles from the nearest town. The white paint was peeling, like a snake sloughing off its skin. The doors that had once been a bright yellow had faded to a dull mustard color. At the far end, a small brick diner had been added with a large window that blinked with a neon sign that said OPEN.

Parking in front of the office next to the diner, Carmen climbed out of the SUV and shivered. The cold was more cutting here than in the mountains. Or maybe her brief trip to California had reminded her that there were places where you didn't have to worry about your face freezing when you stepped outside.

She entered the office and closed the door behind her.

The space was cramped and coated in the sort of cheap paneling that was popular in the sixties. The carpet was a weird orange color and the ceiling had dark splotches that had accumulated over the years from a leaking roof.

But the two wooden chairs in the alcove that made up the lobby had been recently polished, and there was the faint scent of bleach in the air.

The place was at least clean.

Moving toward the narrow counter, Carmen waited for a heavyset woman to heave herself out of a recliner that was set in front of a small TV.

She had salt-and-pepper hair that was scraped from her round face, and she was wearing a sweater in a shocking shade of pink with matching polyester pants. She looked like a grandmother from a Hallmark movie.

There was a gold tag pinned to ample bosom that told Carmen the woman was named Blanche and that she was the owner of the fine establishment.

"Need a room?" Blanche asked with a hopeful smile.

"Yes."

"A single?" The woman glanced toward the window that offered a view of the parking lot.

"That will be fine."

Blanche grabbed a pencil and the old-fashioned reservation book that was set on the counter.

"How many nights?"

"Just one. At least for now," Carmen said, digging in her purse for her wallet. She pulled out her credit card, handing it to the woman, who was looking at her with an odd expression. It took Carmen a second to realize that a woman traveling alone didn't stay in random hotels for unspecified amounts of time. "It depends on the weather," she hastily added.

The woman gave a nod. People in Kansas understood the fickleness of nature.

"If it does turn bad, I can let you keep the same room," she said, her voice dry. "This isn't exactly a hot spot for the holidays, so I don't expect we'll have a sudden rush of guests."

"This time of year I assumed a lot of people would be on the road," she said.

Blanche shrugged. "They are, but travelers prefer to stop at a place that is part of a hotel chain. They're always looking for reward points or free breakfast or Wi-Fi. It gets harder every day for regular folks to run a decent business."

Carmen offered a sympathetic smile. The older woman had a worn demeanor. Like running a mediocre hotel fifty miles from the nearest city was grinding away her soul.

"I prefer a place with some character," she smoothly lied.

The woman shrugged, no doubt sensing she was being

patronized. "Thankfully, most of our customers are truckers. All they're looking for is a clean bed, a big parking lot, and a nearby café that's open twenty-four seven."

Carmen leaned against the counter in a subtle gesture of encouragement as the woman ran her credit card and filled out the register book.

"You know, I remember a friend of mine who stayed at a hotel in this area a couple of weeks ago," she said, trying to sound as if she'd just been struck by the memory. "He mentioned that there was some trouble with someone stealing a semi from the parking lot. Was that here?"

Immediately the woman was on the defense, her cheeks flushing a dark red.

"I can promise you that this hotel is very safe." She pursed her lips. "You should hear what happens to people who stay in Kansas City. Criminals break right into their rooms."

Carmen held up a hand. "I'm sorry. I wasn't trying to imply the hotel was dangerous. I was just wondering if they'd caught the thief."

Blanche's broad shoulders twitched. She looked like a hen who was trying to smooth her ruffled feathers.

"The truck was found a few miles away, so I don't think anything ever came of it."

"How weird." Carmen tried to look confused. "Why would someone steal a truck and then just abandon it?"

"The cops assumed it was the work of some teenagers acting like fools," she said, her voice tight with remembered annoyance. "Or maybe someone who thought they could steal the truck only to find out how hard them things are to drive."

"What did you think?" Carmen pressed.

The woman shoved Carmen's credit card across the counter, her flush deepening.

"I thought it was a bunch of crap," she snapped.

Carmen blinked at the fierceness of the woman's words. "Excuse me?"

"The driver who lost his truck was stomping around and cussing while the cops were upsetting our guests. Then they started pointing the finger at my husband, because the camera in the parking lot is just a fake." Her expression was pinched, like she'd just sucked on a lemon. "It was a very unpleasant experience, let me tell you."

"Yes, I can imagine," Carmen sympathized, swallowing a sigh as the woman yanked open a drawer and pulled out an old-fashioned key.

If Blanche had any information about the truck's disappearance, she would have happily shared the information with the cops, or anyone else who asked. Anything to make certain that no one could blame her or her husband for the theft.

"Your room is in the middle. There's a small fridge and extra blankets, but if you need anything else just let me know."

"Thanks." She pasted a smile on her lips and turned to head out of the office.

She would go back later that evening. There was a good chance the husband would be taking the night shift. He might have more information.

For now, she intended to get a few hours' sleep. She'd spent the entire night waiting in the Phoenix airport for her connecting flight. She was exhausted.

The snow had picked up speed while she'd been inside. With a grimace she opened the door of the SUV and grabbed her overnight bag. Her room was just down the sidewalk. It would be more trouble than it was worth to move the vehicle.

Slamming shut the door, she locked it and then turned to

hurry past the row of mustard-colored doors. Intent on reaching her room before her eyes froze shut, she didn't notice the dark form that appeared from the edge of the hotel until she heard footsteps crunching through the layer of ice coating the sidewalk.

The stranger was hunched forward, as if trying to make himself a smaller target for the icy wind. Something that might have been easier if he wasn't wearing a puffy black parka that looked three sizes too large. Hands were stuffed in his coat pockets. A heavy stocking hat was pulled low, and his face was buried in the scarf that was wound in a deep layer of cashmere around his neck.

She stepped to the edge of the walkway as he neared, but at the same time his foot slipped on the frigid pavement and he lurched to the side.

He bumped into her with enough force to make her lose her balance, but before she could fall, his hands shot out to grab her arm. She felt a pressure, as if he was holding her too tight.

She jerked her arm free, ignoring his muttered apology as she hurried to unlock her door and step into the room. With more force than necessary she slammed shut the door and slid home the deadbolt.

The encounter had thoroughly unnerved her. She wasn't sure why. She was at a hotel, so strangers were bound to be scurrying around. And it was slick enough that anyone could lose their footing.

Still, she couldn't halt the sudden tremors that raced through her body.

She switched on the light and dropped her bag and purse onto a chair that was near the window nearly hidden behind heavy curtains. The dim bulb battled against the gloom that shrouded the cramped room, revealing the double bed that was covered by a worn blanket and the pressboard dresser holding a TV that was older than Carmen.

Not exactly the Ritz, but once again she noticed the scent of polish and bleach that assured her it had been recently cleaned.

That was good enough for now.

She reached to unzip her coat, frowning at the pain that burned through her upper arm. She peeled off the heavy garment and allowed it to drop onto the shag carpet. Then, she lifted her arm to discover what was wrong.

Her breath hissed through her teeth as she caught sight of the blood staining the sleeve of her sweater.

Damn.

She'd been cut.

Griff wasn't a fan of traveling during the holidays. He was even less a fan after endless hours of crowded airports, planes stuffed with cranky children, and a drive through a raging snowstorm from Kansas City to the small hotel on I-70.

More than once he told himself to turn around and go home.

Why ruin his Christmas by chasing after Carmen Jacobs? It wasn't like she was any of his business, thank God.

But after she'd left, he'd been unable to scrub the image of her pale, worried face from his mind. There had been a brittle tension that had hummed around her body, and shadows beneath her eyes. She was truly worried.

He'd tried everything. A hot shower. Lunch out with a beautiful woman who'd hinted she wouldn't mind spending a lazy afternoon in his bed.

At last annoyed with his inability to enjoy his day, Griff had driven home and stomped into his office. Maybe if he sent the photos on to his FBI contact, he could shove Carmen out of his head.

Collecting the Polaroids, he'd been in the process of stuffing them into a padded envelope when he was struck by a chilling thought.

After spreading the pictures across his desk, he'd studied them for a long time. Then he'd grabbed a book off his shelf and flipped to the page he wanted.

Suddenly any attempt to dismiss Carmen and her worries was shattered. Damn. He needed to warn her what he'd found.

He'd tried a dozen times to call her, only to have his messages go straight to voice mail. No surprise. She hadn't been very happy with him when she'd left.

He would have to track her down the hard way.

Contacting his friend in the FBI, he'd sent the pictures with an overnight carrier service and then settled in front of his computer to work his magic. With ruthless precision he hacked into Carmen's privacy, discovering the credit card purchase of an airline ticket from Los Angeles to Kansas City.

Shit. It was worse than he expected.

She'd not only ignored his advice to return to her home, but the stubborn woman was heading to the precise spot the killer had struck just two weeks ago.

Calling himself all sorts of an idiot, he'd shoved some clothes in a bag and headed to the airport for his hellish journey.

It was near three o'clock the next afternoon when he'd pulled into the icy parking lot of the Fairview Hotel. He'd already done another hack into Carmen's credit card to make sure she was actually staying there.

Entering the office, he'd discovered that the middle-aged woman in the office was easily distracted with one simple request for directions to the nearest gas station. While the woman was plucking a roadmap from a wire rack hung behind the counter, Griff easily managed to peek at the registration book.

Carmen Jacobs, Room 7.

With a vague thanks for the directions, Griff left the office. A part of him was relieved he hadn't had to resort to knocking on each door, while another part was furious that anyone could have discovered where she was staying.

And that she was there alone.

Moving the four-wheel-drive truck that he'd rented at the airport, he parked it directly in front of Carmen's room. Reaching across the seat, he grabbed his backpack and climbed out. Then, with long steps he moved through the snow that continued to drift from the sullen sky. With a frown, he glanced toward the distant security light that was blinking off and on.

It was no wonder a thief had targeted this hotel.

One surveillance camera that even a rookie could tell was a fake. One light pole that left most of the parking lot shrouded in shadows. And one manager on duty who no doubt fell asleep behind the desk by ten o'clock.

With a shake of his head, he lifted his hand and rapped on the door. Silence. He rapped again. And again.

Was she out? Maybe she'd walked to the nearby diner to get a late lunch.

But what if—

He was in the process of reviewing the wide variety of evils that might have befallen a young woman on her own when the sound of steel scraping against steel warned him the deadbolt was being pulled aside. A second later the door was opened a half inch to allow Carmen to stare out at him in blank shock.

Had she been expecting Santa Claus?

"Griff ?" She shook her head, as if he was a figment of her imagination that would disappear in the swirling snow. "What are you doing here?"

He stepped forward, hoping there might be some heat leaking through the narrow opening.

"Right now I'm freezing my bal—" He bit off his words. "Are you going to let me in?"

She scowled. "Now?"

He shuddered as a blast of wind nearly knocked him off his feet.

"The sooner the better."

For a long minute she debated, clearly wanting to slam the door in his face. At last she pulled it wider.

"Fine." She gave a wave of her hand. "Come in."

"Very gracious," he drawled as he stepped into the cramped room.

She shut the door behind him with a force that was just below a slam.

"You're lucky I didn't make you get on your knees and beg."

He watched as she marched to stand in the center of the room. She was wearing a short terry cloth robe that allowed him a stunning view of her legs, and her hair was tangled around her flushed face.

Heat pooled in the pit of his stomach. She looked deliciously disheveled. As if she'd just crawled out of bed.

"Were you sleeping?" he asked, trying not to glance at the bed that was only inches away.

She hunched a shoulder. "It was a long trip."

He snorted. A long trip? Did she endure an elderly woman poking her in the ribs with her knitting needle? Or a kid kicking the back of her seat for three hours straight?

"No crap," he muttered.

She took a step backward, as if wanting to put some

space between them. A futile effort. The room was the size of a closet.

"How did you find me?"

He turned away to toss his backpack on the chair and pulled off his leather coat. He needed an excuse to hide his expression, since there was no way he was confessing that he'd used his hacking skills to track her down.

It didn't look like she was hiding a weapon beneath the skimpy robe, but better safe than sorry.

"I knew you would try to track down information on the women in those pictures," he instead said. "You're like a dog with a bone when you decide on a goal."

She released a short laugh. "Thanks a lot."

He shrugged, laying his coat on a nearby chair. "It's true."

Griff sensed her gaze burning a hole in the side of his head. "Okay, I'll concede I can be stubborn, but you couldn't have known I'd be at this hotel."

He turned back to meet her suspicious gaze. "Where else would you go?" he asked. "It's the only place you know for certain the killer was at."

She jerked, a strange expression touching her face. "The killer? Does that mean you believe me?"

He considered his answer. Only a fool would encourage her to continue her investigation. On the other hand, he needed her to understand that if the pictures were real, she was in danger.

The kind of danger that got people dead.

"I believe someone sent you those pictures," he finally said. "And that there's a good possibility those women were murdered."

She clutched her hands together, her knuckles white with tension.

"Did you send the pictures to your FBI contact?"

"This morning before I headed to the airport."

"What did you find out?"

His lips twisted at her impatience. "Nothing yet. The pictures won't arrive until tomorrow," he pointed out in dry tones. "Plus, when I called my contact I was reminded that it's the holiday season. My ears are still ringing." He grimaced. "And not from 'Silver Bells.'"

She blinked. As if shocked that he might have a sense of humor.

To be fair, it surprised most people. Apparently, computer nerds weren't supposed to be funny. At least not ha-ha funny.

"Then why are you here?"

He held her gaze. "I noticed something in the pictures when I was packing them up to send to my contact."

"Noticed what?"

"The women were all blond."

"So?"

He stepped toward the chair, unbuckling the straps on his backpack to pull out the book he'd stuck in before leaving his house.

"I was looking at Neal Scott's victims," he said, swiveling back to Carmen as he flipped through the pages to find the pictures that had been included at the end of the chapter.

"You have my book?"

He glanced up to discover Carmen looking at him with an odd expression. On cue, he felt a flush crawl beneath his skin.

"It was a present," he said, silently assuring himself that it was close enough to the truth. He'd used a gift certificate to buy it at the local bookstore.

"Of course."

He ignored the disbelief in her voice, moving to stand at her side. He held the book so she could see the pictures.

"Scott's victims had one thing in common, right?"

She frowned, as if he'd just asked her a trick question. "They were all prostitutes who worked at truck stops."

"Exactly," he said. "They were all various ages and ethnicities."

"If you read my book, then you know that I thoroughly researched the victims," she said, not bothering to hide her impatience. "There was no obvious connection. They were all from different towns, they all worked different truck stops, and they had different pimps. As far as I could tell they'd never met one another."

"So if there is a copycat killer out there who is following Scott's pattern, then his victims should look like this." He tapped the tip of his finger on each picture of dead women. "Young, old, black, brown, and white."

"What's your point?"

He tossed the book on the rumpled bed and returned to his backpack. Reaching in, he pulled out the photocopies of Polaroids she'd left on his desk.

"Look at the newest victims," he said, moving back to stand at her side.

Reluctantly accepting the papers he shoved in her hand, she glanced down at the pictures.

"I'm not sure what I'm looking for."

He once again pointed to each picture. "They're all young, they're all white, and they're all blond."

She stilled, her gaze locked on the pictures. Even in the dim light Griff could see her face lose a shade of color. Then, sucking in a deep breath, she gave a shake of her head.

"It could be a coincidence," she said. "A lot of hookers bleach their hair."

"Carmen." Before he could halt the impulsive gesture, he reached to cup her chin in his palm, tilting back her head to meet his worried gaze. "They all look like you."

Chapter Six

Carmen cleared the lump from her throat. "There might be some similarities," she conceded.

"Too many," he said.

She wanted to argue. There were millions of women in the world. And a huge number of them were young, white, and blond. It could be that simple.

But as soon as he'd pointed out the obvious, a familiar chill had snaked down her spine.

She hadn't consciously associated the women with herself. It had been more of a vague sense of dread that she hadn't wanted to accept.

Now, however, Griff had made sure she couldn't ignore the ugly suspicion any longer.

She dropped the photocopies on the bed and folded her arms around her waist. Having Griff standing so close, staring at her with such genuine concern, was unnerving.

Perhaps because she was still feeling raw after she'd traveled to California to plead for his help. Or because he was the last person she'd expected to see.

Or because she was acutely aware that her hair was a rat's

nest, and her robe was wrinkled, and there was a distinct possibility there was drool on her chin.

Not the way she wanted any man to see her. Let alone this one . . .

She slammed her mind shut on her ridiculous thoughts, glaring at Griff, who was watching her with a searching gaze.

"Okay, I'll agree it's creepy," she said. "That still doesn't explain why you're here."

The lean, chiseled face was impossible to read in the muted light. "I wanted to warn you that I think you might be in danger."

"You could have called."

"I tried."

With a frown she glanced toward the nightstand, then she grimaced. Oh yeah. After she'd stumbled into the shower to wash off the blood dripping down her arm, she'd felt like a zombie. She had a vague memory of leaving the bathroom and pulling on her robe before she'd collapsed on the bed.

She hadn't even thought about plugging in her phone. Which meant that the battery was probably dead by now.

She glanced back at Griff. "Why would you care?"

"You came to me for help."

"And you turned me away."

He frowned, as if he didn't want to be reminded that he'd been less than encouraging when she'd been on her knees pleading for his help.

"Are you saying you don't want me to stay?" he demanded.

She pivoted away. She wanted to tell him to march his very fine ass out the door and return to California. He'd had his opportunity to be a part of her investigation and he'd refused.

But she wasn't stupid.

She had many talents, but Griff was a tech god. And she

suspected that he had the ability to tap into law enforcement resources. The sort of resources she didn't even know existed. Plus, she was still jittery from the weird encounter with the stranger.

On cue, Griff reached out to grasp her upper arm. His touch was light, but it was enough to press against her tender wound.

A sound of distress was wrenched from her throat before she could squash it. Instantly Griff released his grip and Carmen started to blow out a breath of relief.

Then her eyes widened when she felt the belt of her robe being undone so Griff could peel the thin material off her left shoulder.

"Hey." She glanced around in shock, her hands lifting to keep the robe pinned to the upper curve of her breast as he continued to tug the material down her arm.

Not that Griff was interested in her naked body. Instead, he was unwrapping the layers of tissue paper that she'd stuck to the thin cut to sop up the blood that had thankfully stopped leaking in the past couple of hours.

"What the hell?" he rasped.

"It's nothing," she said, taking a step back.

His gaze continued to study the gash that marred her pale skin.

"That's a knife wound," he growled.

Her brows lifted in surprise. Was he psychic?

"How can you tell?"

He reached to pull up the faded Green Day T-shirt that he had tucked in his jeans.

For a second, Carmen's mind went blank. The hard ripples of his abs were sculpted to perfection. She liked her men to be lean rather than bulked up with muscles. It was no wonder she'd been physically attracted to him from the minute she'd seen him jogging on the beach.

Thankfully unaware of the unwelcome lust that sizzled

through her veins, Griff pointed to the long scar that angled from his hip bone across his lower stomach. There were pinpricks of paler skin that attested to the fact that he'd been stitched up by a doctor who was more worried about speed than skill.

"What happened?" she demanded.

He shrugged. "My neighbor decided he wanted my bike when I was twelve. I disagreed. He ended the argument by slicing my stomach open."

Carmen abruptly sat on the end of the bed, her knees feeling weak.

Delayed shock.

"Mine isn't nearly so dramatic," she said, relieved when her voice didn't shake at the memory of the stranger grabbing her arm.

"What happened?" he asked.

She wrinkled her nose. "I'm not really sure."

"Carmen."

"I mean it." She tilted back her head to meet his fierce glare. "I'd just checked in to the hotel and was walking to my room when some man bumped against me," she explained. "I didn't realize I was really hurt until I took off my coat."

His jaw tightened, his dark eyes flashing as if he was personally angered that she'd been injured.

"Was he a guest?"

She shook her head. "I don't think so. I didn't see him coming out of a room."

"Did he go into the office?"

"I'm not sure." She shivered. "I was in a hurry to get into my room and lock the door."

"Did you notice any cars in the parking lot?"

She closed her eyes, forcing herself to remember back to the moment she'd arrived at the hotel.

"There was a pickup and a compact car parked at the far end of the hotel," she said, picturing what she'd seen as she'd pulled to a halt in front of the office. "And I think there were a couple cars near the café. I didn't notice any other vehicles."

He moved to pull aside the heavy curtain, glancing out the window.

"The SUV near the office belongs to you?" he asked.

"Yeah. I rented it at the airport."

"The pickup and the compact car are still here," he said. "I can run the plates, but I doubt the man who attacked you would have been stupid enough to be staying here." Allowing the curtain to drop back into place, he returned to stand directly in front of her. "What about the man? Did you notice anything?"

She paused, searching her mind for anything that might help. Then she grimaced. The memory was blurred. Like a Monet painting where nothing was quite in focus.

"No. It was freezing and I was in a hurry," she admitted. "Besides, he was wearing a huge parka and a stocking hat, plus he had a scarf wrapped around most of his face. I could pass him on the street and not recognize him."

She braced herself for the typical male response. The roll of his eyes. The patronizing smile that said *Of course a woman was too emotional to recall details of her attack.*

Instead, his expression was one of sympathy, as if he completely understood her inability to recall specific details.

"You're sure it was a man?"

The question made her pause before giving a firm nod. That was the one thing she was certain of.

"Yes."

"White? Black? Hispanic?"

"He had his head lowered, and with the scarf I really couldn't see more than a sliver of his face, but I think he was white."

"Height? Weight?"

She reached up to wrap the robe tighter around her body as a cold shiver shook her.

"He was hunched over and wrapped in a puffy coat, but I would guess that he was average height and weight."

Another nod before he was leaning down to pick up the coat that she'd dropped next to the chair. He ran his fingers over the sleeve until his fingers located the slash that penetrated the thick layers of fabric.

"The blade must have been sharp," he said, speaking more to himself than her.

"Sharp enough to ruin my favorite sweater," she tried to tease.

He dropped the coat, his expression tight. "This isn't a joke, Carmen."

She pursed her lips. "I know that."

"Do you?" Without warning he was kneeling in front of her, reaching up to grasp her hands in a tight grip. "There's a very good chance that you were cut by the lunatic who sent you those pictures."

She tried to be angry at his chiding. She wasn't a child.

But his skin was warm and his touch was easing the anxiety that churned deep inside her.

"If it was the killer, then why didn't he just slice my throat instead of my arm?"

"Because he isn't done with you."

The soft words hit her like a sledgehammer.

A ruthless blow that she instinctively tried to avoid.

"If he was the killer, he could have forced me into a car or even into one of the hotel rooms," she said.

He made a sound of impatience. "Are you trying to convince yourself that this was some random attack?"

"Yes."

"Why?"

"Because I'm scared."

The grip on her fingers tightened. "Good."

"Good?"

"You should be scared," he assured her. "You need to go home and lock your doors."

She jerked her fingers free. She'd spent her entire life being told to hide from the monsters that lurked in the shadows.

Don't go looking for trouble, Carmen . . .

The words of her grandmother whispered through her mind.

A fine idea in theory, but life had taught her that those monsters didn't stay in the shadows. They pounced without warning, destroying her life.

"And then what?" she demanded. "Wait for him to sneak into my house and kill me in my sleep?"

His jaw tightened. "Let the authorities deal with it."

"Which one?" She surged to her feet, glaring down at him. "The deputy who called me a liar? Or your FBI contact who will look at the pictures when he manages to clear his desk of every other case he's working on?"

"She," he muttered in distracted tones.

"What?"

He slowly straightened. "The FBI agent I contacted is female."

"Of course she is," Carmen said with a roll of her eyes.

Griff looked confused. "Does it matter?"

Yes. It did matter. But Carmen didn't have a clue why, so she pasted a smile to her lips.

"Of course not."

He heaved a sigh. "You're not going home, are you?"

Griff did everything in his power to keep his thoughts from straying to the woman who was standing naked in the shower just a few feet away.

A herculean task, considering the thin walls of the hotel allowed him to hear the splash of the water and catch the scent of lemons that laced the humid air. What man wouldn't be imagining his fingers running over her slender curves, which were damp and slick with soap? Or pressing her against the wall of the shower and wrapping her legs around his waist?

Grimly he headed out of the room. He had hopes the frigid air would clear the fog of lust from his brain. And he needed to get his computer bag, which he'd left in the passenger seat. While he was out he also took the opportunity to stroll down the icy walkway, snapping a picture of the two vehicles at the end of the hotel before returning to Carmen's room.

He could hear the hair dryer coming from the bathroom as he booted up his laptop and used his phone as a hotspot for the Internet. Then he quickly typed in the license plate numbers of the two vehicles in the lot, along with the names of the hotel owners. He might as well run a search on them. The fact that the truck had been stolen from their lot, and the killer had been there at the precise moment to attack Carmen . . .

His brows snapped together.

How had the killer known that Carmen would be there?

Dumb luck? Griff shook his head. He didn't believe in luck. Or coincidence. Or random chance.

He might have followed her, but how likely would it be he could have gotten a last-minute flight on the same plane?

While he was sitting on the edge of the bed, Griff's fingers flew over his keyboard as he pulled up a program he'd designed for the FBI and typed Carmen's name into it. The software would allow him to monitor Carmen's online identity. If anyone searched her name or tried to break into her accounts, he would be notified.

He'd just finished his task when Carmen returned to the

room. Her face was rosy from the heat of the shower, and her hair was a mass of golden curls that defied her attempts to smooth them as they tumbled past her shoulders.

She looked unbearably young and vulnerable.

At least until her eyes narrowed at the sight of his computer gear, which was spread across the bed as well as the small dresser.

"Make yourself at home," she muttered.

He closed the laptop and rose to his feet. "Actually, I was thinking we should go somewhere to have dinner."

She started to frown, but then she realized just what he was saying.

"Maybe a truck stop?" she asked.

"First a drive."

"Okay." She moved toward the door where she'd left her shoes. Sliding them on, she reached for her coat. She grimaced as she ran her finger over the cut in the sleeve. "I don't suppose the truck stop will have any jackets for sale."

Griff ground his teeth together at the vivid reminder that she'd been injured.

What was the point in dwelling on how easily she could have become one of the victims? Carmen Jacobs was determined to finish this crazy quest of tracking down the person responsible for sending her the pictures.

Nothing was going to stop her.

"If you want I could drive you into Kansas City. There should be a local mall still open," he said, trying his best to keep the frustration out of his voice.

He wasn't entirely successful, as her expression tensed with wariness. Did she suspect that he was considering the viability of hauling her back to his home and locking her in his house?

Or better yet, he could handcuff her to his bed . . .

"Maybe after dinner." She interrupted his dangerous thoughts. "I'm not really much of a mall person anyway."

On cue, his gaze lowered to the gray sweatshirt she was wearing. It had a picture of the Grand Canyon on the front. No doubt she'd picked it up at the airport during her layover. His lips twitched as he recalled the clingy spandex she'd worn when he'd first seen her on the beach months ago, and then the fuzzy sweater she'd been wearing yesterday.

Her taste leaned more toward sex kitten than frumpy tourist.

Who could blame her? She was a smart woman who knew how her gorgeous curves affected poor men's brains.

"You can't convince me you don't love clothes," he said.

A small flush stained her cheeks as his gaze slowly returned to her face.

"I prefer the vintage shops," she said, looking oddly flustered as she slid her arms into her coat, careful not to scrape the sleeve against her wound. "There was one in the small town near my grandparents' place and I worked there during the summer months."

He tugged on his own coat and grabbed his laptop before moving to pull open the door.

"Your grandparents had a horse farm, didn't they?" he asked, sticking to the info that had been revealed in the bio at the back of her book.

He wasn't ready to tell her that he'd done a full background check on her after he'd realized she'd tried to trick him.

Her past had been traumatic, to say the least.

He desperately wanted to ask her questions, but he sensed she would shut down as soon as he tried to pry.

Proving his point, she grabbed her purse and stepped past him, refusing to meet his gaze.

"We can take the SUV," she said.

"Wait." He pulled shut the hotel door, making sure it automatically locked. "Let's take the truck."

She jerked her head toward him, her brows lowering. "Why?"

"It has four-wheel drive."

The icy breeze tugged at her curls. "And I suppose you have to drive?"

He shrugged. "Not if you want to."

"No fight for dominance?"

"Nope." He shoved his hand into the front pocket of his jeans to pull out the keys. He tossed them to her. "It's been years since I've driven in the snow. Plus, I want to run some searches."

She caught the keys with an exaggerated expression of surprise.

"Astonishing."

He climbed into the passenger side of the truck, tucking the computer on his lap and keeping the hot spot open on his phone so he could have Internet access.

"My manhood isn't based on whether I'm the one behind the steering wheel," he told her as she climbed in beside him and turned on the engine.

It was true. He'd been a scrawny kid living in a tough Chicago neighborhood with a mom who was a cop. He was never going to be big enough or mean enough to survive. So he had to be smart. Really, really smart.

Carmen's defensive expression eased as she headed toward the exit of the parking lot.

"Which way?" she asked.

"West," he said.

She turned onto the narrow road, crunching over the ice before she reached the nearest ramp to veer onto the highway. The plows had been out to scoop off the worst of the snow, leaving narrow paths in the middle of the lanes. Carmen held on to the steering wheel with a tight grip, cautious enough to keep them at a sensible speed as they traveled through the gathering dusk.

It was just five o'clock, but night was already crowding in.

"Are you going to tell me where we're headed?" she asked.

Griff turned his attention to his laptop, pulling up the file he saved.

"I want to see the spot where the truck was abandoned," he said.

"Oh. That's a good idea."

"I do have them on occasion," he said dryly.

"Hmm." She reached to flip the heater on high.

"The police report says they found the truck abandoned six miles west of the hotel."

"At least the snow has stopped," she said.

He glanced up to survey the passing scenery. White. White. And more white.

"My feet are still going to get wet." He swallowed a sigh. "I didn't pack any boots."

"Do you own any?"

"No." He hadn't bothered buying boots since he'd moved to California. He glanced at her feet, which were covered by a pair of tennis shoes. "What about you? I thought you were staying in the mountains?"

She shrugged. "I didn't bother to pack them."

He returned his gaze to his computer, keeping his tone light. "Do you own the cabin you were staying at?"

There was a long pause, as if she wanted to ignore his question.

"No, I just rented it for the holiday season," she at last admitted.

"Alone?"

She sent him a quick glance. "Why do you assume I was alone?"

A strange tension clenched his stomach. As if the thought of her with another man was distressing.

"If you had a lover with you, he would never have allowed you to travel away from the cabin without him," he said, feeling the heat of her glare.

"I don't need a man to tell me what I can or can't do."

"Plus, he would have punched the deputy in the nose who assumed you sent those pictures to yourself for a publicity stunt, and you would be busy trying to bail him out of jail," he continued smoothly.

She released a grudging laugh. "You are . . ."

"Adorable?" he suggested when she struggled to find the right word. She rolled her eyes. "Why a cabin?" he asked.

She shrugged. "I prefer to spend the holidays someplace where I can have some peace and quiet."

"Me too."

She shot another quick glance in his direction. "Do you have any family?"

He grimaced. It was his turn to feel the barriers come up. His past might not have hit the scandal pages, but it had been far from perfect.

Still, he knew that if he ever wanted her to open up, he would have to share at least a few details.

"My father and his second wife live in Texas." He shrugged. His only contact with them was a Christmas card that had arrived the week before. It was sitting unopened on his desk. "Or maybe it's Florida now," he admitted, having a brief memory of the return address. Seemed like it had Miami typed on it instead of Austin. "They move every year or so."

She slowed as a car whizzed past them, throwing up a slush of salt and ice that smeared their window. She hit the wipers.

"You're not close?" she asked.

He snorted. That was the understatement of the century.

"No, we're not close. My only real family is my grand-mother. She lives in Iowa, but she's spending the holidays with her sister in Arizona." A genuine smile curved his lips. "She called me yesterday to say that she won seventy-two dollars at bingo. She couldn't have been more excited if she'd hit the lotto ticket."

"What about your mother?"

"Dead."

He heard her breath catch. "I'm sorry."

He pointed toward the mile marker that was listed in the police report.

"The truck was found just ahead," he said, eager to change the conversation. "Why don't you pull off the road at the rest area?"

She slowed, turning onto the narrow road. The rest area wasn't much more than a couple of picnic tables and a small brick building that housed the bathrooms and a vending machine.

She parked and they both glanced around. "There's not much here."

Griff nodded, his gaze skimming over the snowy landscape still visible despite the deepening shadows.

"A perfect place to dump the truck," he said. "There's no exit ramps nearby. No businesses. No houses. No tourist attraction that might encourage a passerby to take pictures to put on social media. Or for the cops to have a license reader set up." He grimaced. If he was going to abandon a vehicle, this was the exact spot he would choose. "Nothing but empty fields as far as the eye can see."

"The killer must have had someone pick him up."

"Yes." Griff nodded. She was right. The killer had to have a way to dump the truck and then get away. A partner? Damn. That was disturbing.

"Do you think the women were murdered here?"

He shoved away the nasty fear there might be more than one person out there hunting women. Speculation wasn't going to help.

Right now he had to concentrate on digging up as much concrete information as he could.

"I can't say for sure, but according to the report, the truck was left on the shoulder of the highway. If I was the killer, I would be afraid someone might stop to see if I needed some help." He waved a hand to the small rest area. "If I was searching for someplace to kill my victim, or to dump the body, I would choose someplace less visible."

She gave a slow nod. "So where could you kill five women without being noticed?" She paused, her fingers tightening on the steering wheel. "The truck stop."

"That would be my guess," he agreed. "No one would think twice about a semi parked in the back of a lot reserved specifically for truckers. They wouldn't even notice a woman climb into the back trailer with a man."

She shifted the gear stick and eased out of the rest stop. "Where's the nearest one?"

"Another five miles west of here," he told her.

Pressing the gas pedal, Carmen had them back on the highway and headed west.

Chapter Seven

Carmen decided truck stops possessed a weird gravitational force.

They sucked in passing motorists, luring them in with platters of greasy food and hot coffee, and then spun them back into the cold with bloated bellies and the buzz of caffeine.

Tonight, however, the large restaurant and attached fuel station were eerily empty. The threat of more snow kept most travelers off the road, while the professional truckers were too anxious to get home for Christmas to linger over their meals.

Leaving Griff to speak with the manager about any strangers who might have been hanging around the night the truck was stolen, as well as any arrests that had been made in the area for prostitution, Carmen headed into the restaurant area, interviewing the handful of diners.

They'd all been eager to speak with her once they'd recognized her as the famous author they'd seen on the cable news shows. They all had a story they just knew would be perfect for a book. And they were all willing to offer her the rights, as long as they got a cut of the profits.

But not one of them had been in the area two weeks ago.

Or knew a trucker by the name of Lee Williams who'd had his semi stolen.

Certainly, none of them had any knowledge of prostitutes who worked the parking lot.

Taking a table, she'd waited for Griff, not surprised to discover that the manager denied any existence of illegal activities happening in or around the parking area.

Dead end.

To compensate for her disappointment, Carmen ordered the Trucker's Special, which included a stack of pancakes, hash browns, scrambled eggs with onions and green peppers, a pile of crisp bacon, and a slice of cantaloupe.

It was enough food to feed a small tribe, so she left the cantaloupe. No need to be a pig.

They climbed into the pickup and drove back to the hotel in silence. It wasn't until she'd parked in front of her room and turned off the engine that she at last heaved a frustrated sigh.

"Well, that was a colossal waste of time," she muttered.

Griff unbuckled his belt and swiveled in the seat to face her. The security light was barely bright enough to make out more than his silhouette, but suddenly she was conscious of his close presence.

The rich, male scent of his cologne that laced the air. The soft sound of his breathing. The prickle of heat that was a tangible force between them.

He leaned toward her. Did he share her acute awareness?

"Not entirely," he said in soft tones. "You did manage to consume an impressive number of pancakes."

Carmen's lips twitched. She'd always had a huge appetite. It was something she enjoyed without apology.

"I was hungry."

"Hmm." She could feel his gaze skim down her body. "I'm still not sure where you put them."

"You sound like my grandfather." She told herself the

shiver that raced through her was from the cold that was already creeping into the pickup. "He used to claim I ate more than his farmhands."

Griff's arm draped along the top of the seat, his fingers reaching out to brush her cheek.

"You were close to him?"

"Yeah." The pang of grief had her retreating into her familiar shell. "Are you going back to California tonight?"

He stilled, one of his fingers tracing the line of her jaw. "Are you returning to your home?"

She turned her head to study the hotel.

She could stay here and hope the killer tried to approach her again. Not the most pleasant thought. Or she could return to her cabin in the mountains and worry that there might be a monster under her bed. An even less pleasant thought.

Or she could return to the small horse farm that belonged to her grandparents. A place she hadn't seen in months.

She gave a shrug. "I haven't decided."

"Then I'm staying."

She turned her head, trying to make out his expression in the shadows.

"I don't need a babysitter."

"What about a friend?"

"What?"

"Do you need a friend?"

Her breath lodged in her throat, a strange warmth curling through the pit of her stomach.

"Griff."

His fingers brushed a stray curl behind her ear before he was pulling back and shoving open the door.

"Let's get inside," he said. "It's freezing out here."

"Stubborn," she muttered as she climbed out of the truck and followed behind him.

"You know there's a saying about a pot calling the kettle black."

She pulled the key out of her purse and stuck it in the lock.

"I'm determined, not stubborn," she informed her companion, pushing open the door.

"There's a difference?"

"Of course."

She reached in to flip on the light, then stepped into the cramped room. It was at least warm.

In the process of walking forward to give Griff the space to enter behind her, she abruptly froze.

A protective arm wrapped around her shoulders as Griff tucked her close to his body. "What's wrong?" he demanded.

She lifted her arm to point toward the vase of flowers that was placed on the nightstand next to the bed.

"Look."

She felt Griff tense as he took in the three blood-red roses that were a vivid splash of color in the otherwise drab room.

With a slow movement he laid his laptop on the chair near the door. Then, giving her shoulders a comforting squeeze, he lowered his arm and headed into the bathroom. He did a quick search before opening the closet to make sure no one was lurking inside.

Only then did he slowly approach the flowers. "Did anyone know you were staying here? Someone who might send you an early Christmas gift?"

Carmen wrapped her arms around her waist, giving a sharp shake of her head.

"No one."

He sent her a brief glance. "Not even your publicist? The one who forwarded the pictures to you?"

Another shake of her head. "No one."

He returned his attention to the flowers, leaning forward to read the card that was stuck on a plastic holder.

"Until we meet again. The Professor," he read out loud.

Carmen hissed, feeling as if she'd just been hit with a sledgehammer.

"Oh my God," she breathed.

"The Professor." He turned his head, studying her horrified expression with a searching gaze. "That's one of the killers you profiled in your book, isn't it?"

She licked her lips, struggling to think through the instinctive fog of fear that clouded her mind.

"Yes. Dr. Franklin Hammel," she said, her voice hoarse. "He's the one your program helped to capture."

"I wasn't given any details about the case." He studied her with a steady gaze. "The software was designed so any agency could put in data from a specific suspect and use it to predict their movements. Tell me about him."

"He was an unemployed English professor who was obsessed with Edgar Allan Poe. He kidnapped coeds from college campuses in Baltimore and held them captive before he would dispose of their bodies with a copy of Poe's 'The Raven' lying near the body."

She grimaced, recalling the time spent with Hammel. Behind the protective glass that had separated them, he'd looked like a slug. A big, bulbous head that was shaved smooth. His long face, and the lanky body that'd been covered by a white T-shirt and white pants.

Unlike the other killers he hadn't tried to manipulate her with sob stories of painful childhoods, or protests of innocence. The Professor had been an arrogant, self-absorbed psychopath who'd believed that his superior intelligence assured him the right to abuse women. They were, after all, lesser beings in his mind.

"Carmen?" Griff's soft voice penetrated the macabre memories.

She shivered. The room felt like an icebox. "When I interviewed him he told me that he was searching for his perfect muse," she said. "No woman could give him the satisfaction he needed to create his masterpiece."

His jaw tightened. "Where is he?"

"North Branch Correctional Institute, dying of prostate cancer," she said. Hammel had already known he was sick when he'd agreed to speak with Carmen.

She assumed that's why he'd been so candid during their interviews. It was his last gasp to obtain the fame that had eluded him in his literary endeavors.

Griff nodded. "So he's probably not responsible for sending you flowers."

"No." Another shiver raced through her. "It has to be the copycat killer."

His attention returned to the vase of flowers. "Why roses? Why not a copy of 'The Raven'?"

Carmen considered for a long minute. Various possibilities shuffled through her mind before a sick dread twisted her stomach into a knot.

"He's telling me he's going to Baltimore," she rasped.

Griff frowned. "How?"

"The Poe Toaster."

"Toaster? Wait, I've heard about him," Griff said. "It's some mystery person who goes to Poe's grave on his birthday, right?"

She nodded. "Yes, the person cloaks themselves in black and makes a toast at the original gravesite with a glass of Martell cognac, and then leaves the bottle along with three red roses."

He immediately followed her train of thought. "The grave is in Baltimore?"

"Yes."

Pulling out his phone, he moved around the vase in a semicircle, taking pictures of the flowers as well as the card from a dozen angles.

"I need to let Nikki know," he said.

"Nikki?"

"Nikki Voros." He turned the phone and tapped on the screen, sending the photos into cyberspace. "She's my FBI contact."

Carmen didn't protest. He could contact all the FBI agents he wanted. Hell, she would be happy if he flashed the Bat-Signal.

They could use all the help they could get.

Waiting until he slid the phone back into his pocket, she glanced around the shabby space. A nasty chill inched down her spine.

"Do you think the killer was in this room?"

His eyes darkened, then without warning he was moving to grasp her hand.

"Let's find out," he said.

Carmen found herself tugged out of the hotel room and back into the frozen night air.

"Where are we going?" she demanded.

"To speak to the manager," he said.

She scurried to keep up with his long strides, her gaze darting around the nearly empty parking lot. Was the killer somewhere out there watching them? Savoring the fear that he was creating?

Keeping close to Griff's side, she stepped into the office. She grunted at the suffocating temperature. Did the manager hope to convince any stray traveler that whatever the hotel might lack in elegance it made up for in sheer heat?

There was a loud creak as the reclining chair was pushed upright and a large male form wrestled its way out of the cushions to shuffle toward the counter.

The night manager was a man in his late fifties with a small fringe of gray hair and a large, soft body that moved at the pace of a drunken snail. His round face was wreathed in a welcoming expression, although there was a hint of pain in his pale eyes. As if the mere task of standing made his bones ache.

"Evening, folks," he said in a hearty tone. "Can I get you a room?"

Carmen stepped forward. The room was in her name. Which meant she would have to take the lead in questioning the manager.

"Actually, I'm already a guest," she said. "I'm Carmen Jacobs in room seven."

"Oh, yes." His gaze shifted to Griff. "And you, sir?"

He wrapped an arm around Carmen's shoulders. "I'm with the lady."

Despite her raw nerves, Carmen felt a blush stain her cheeks. Not at Griff's implication that they were lovers. But at the pleasure that the mere thought stirred deep inside her.

"I see." The man heaved a disappointed sigh. "Is there something you need?"

"I want to know if you let anyone into my room," she said. "I recently returned to discover that someone had left me roses."

The man scowled before he gave a snap of his fingers.

"Oh, right," he said. "There was a deliveryman who came about an hour ago. I tried to have him leave the flowers at the desk. I don't like entering a guest's room, but he insisted that the person who'd ordered them had been very specific that the flowers be given directly to you, Ms. Jacobs." The man's face twisted, as if he'd just bitten into a lemon. "The driver all but implied he thought we couldn't be trusted to see that you received them."

Carmen frowned. Had the killer masqueraded as the deliveryman?

Griff pulled out his phone. "Do you remember the name of the flower company?" he demanded.

"Yep." The man began sorting through a messy stack of

papers. "I made them leave a card in case something wasn't right."

He finally located a black business card that was embossed with gold lettering and handed it toward Carmen.

"I'll check it out." Griff reached out to pluck it out of her fingers. He was dialing the number as he paced away from the desk.

The manager cleared his throat. "Did I do something wrong?"

Carmen sent him a strained smile. "I'm just trying to find out who sent the flowers."

The older man shrugged. "Some secret admirer, no doubt."

Carmen's mouth went dry. "That's what I'm afraid of."

Chapter Eight

Ten minutes later they were back in Carmen's hotel room.

Griff had reached the flower shop listed on the business card and had a confirmation that yes, they'd received an order earlier that day for the roses to be delivered to Ms. Jacobs at the hotel. Yes, it had been a man. Yes, he'd insisted the flowers be delivered directly to Ms. Jacobs's room. Yes, he'd paid by credit card and added a hefty bonus to ensure the delivery was made despite the icy roads. And yes, the driver had been with the store for the past six years.

Which meant that it wasn't the killer who'd entered the room.

Ignoring the manager's curious stare, Griff hustled Carmen out of the office and back to her room. If the killer had left a paper trail, Griff could follow it.

Or at least that was his assumption.

As he sat on the edge of the bed with his laptop balanced on his knees, his confidence took a severe nosedive.

Shit.

It had been a simple matter to trace the invoice for the red roses to a credit card. And to discover that the mystery person tormenting Carmen was not only cruel, but fiendishly clever.

"The flower shop is legit, but the credit card is bogus," he growled.

She moved to stand next to the bed, her face pale in the muted light.

"How can you be sure?"

His jaw clenched so hard his teeth ached. "The name on it is Frank Hammel."

She jerked in shock. "It couldn't be the real one."

He gave a decisive shake of his head. It wasn't impossible to manipulate the world from behind bars. But Frank Hammel wasn't a part of a Mafia organization, or the member of a loyal gang. From what Carmen had told him the man was a loner, like many serial killers, without connection to friend or family. Plus, there was no way he could possibly have known that Carmen was at this hotel. Not when his computer search had just revealed the older man was lying comatose in a hospital bed.

"No, it wasn't Hammel."

She wrapped her arms around her waist. "It's just another part of the game."

"Yes." He set aside the laptop and rose to his feet. "We need to find someplace for you to stay where you can be protected."

She tilted her chin, her features settling into a defiant expression.

"I'm going to Baltimore."

Baltimore? Had she lost her mind?

"No way," he snapped. "That's exactly what the maniac wants. You need to go to a safe house."

"I'm not going into hiding while innocent women are being stalked and killed."

"What do you expect to accomplish if you go to Baltimore?"

She blinked. Apparently, she hadn't thought that far ahead.

"I'll go to the police," she at last said.

He held her mutinous gaze. "What do you expect them to do?"

"I don't know." She gave a frustrated lift of her shoulder. "Put out extra patrols. Maybe warn women not to walk alone near a college campus."

He reached out to grasp her upper arms, as if worried she might bolt out the door and drive to Baltimore tonight.

She was stubborn enough to take that risk.

"You can call them," he told her. "From a safe house."

She sent him a frustrated glare. "And just where is this mythical safe house?"

"You could stay with me." The words were flying out of his mouth before he even realized he was thinking them.

Her eyes widened with shock. "Griff—"

Seemingly in the grip of some sort of madness, Griff didn't try to explain his offer for her to share his home. Instead, he kissed her.

Just like that.

He had a brief memory of when he was seven years old. An older boy had dared him to jump off the fire escape of their apartment building. He hadn't allowed himself to think about the consequences. He'd simply climbed onto the edge of the iron railing and leaped into the Dumpster below.

This was the same thing.

One second he was watching her lips part, and the next he had them covered in a kiss that blazed with a need he'd been battling for hours. Hell, maybe for months.

She tasted just like her scent implied. Crisp, clean, and a little tart.

His arms wrapped around her tiny waist and he hauled her hard against his body. She grasped his shoulders, her lips parting in silent invitation.

He didn't hesitate. Dipping his tongue into the warm temptation of her mouth, he allowed his hands to slide beneath the hem of her sweatshirt. She shivered, but she didn't make any move to pull away.

Griff made a sound deep in his throat. He'd fantasized about this woman a hundred times, but reality was so much better than his dreams.

Her lips were softer. The curve of her hips beneath his searching hands was sweeter. The tentative stroke of her tongue against his was even more erotic.

He was instantly hard and aching.

With a low groan, he turned his head to brush his lips over her heated cheek.

He heard her suck in a raspy breath. "What are you doing?" she demanded.

He nuzzled his mouth against her temple, savoring the citrus scent of her skin.

"Convincing you to come to California with me," he said.

She released a shaky chuckle. "You have a lot of faith in your kisses."

"It's not faith, it's fate," he corrected in thick tones. "I knew it would be like this from the first minute I saw you standing on the beach."

He felt her stiffen.

"I'm sorry I wasn't honest from the start. I thought . . ." Her words trailed away on a sigh. "I don't really know what I thought. I just wanted to meet you so I could try to convince you to let me interview you. Then I kept putting off telling you the truth."

"The past is gone," he said. "This moment is all that matters."

For a blissful minute she snuggled against him, all soft and warm and yielding. But even as his fingers stroked up the curve of her back, her hands moved to press her palms against his chest.

"Wait," she muttered. "You're not going to distract me."

Griff swallowed a curse. As much as he wanted to toss the

woman on the nearby bed and forget the world outside the tiny hotel room, he needed to be certain she wasn't going to do something crazy as soon as his back was turned.

He lifted his head to glare down at her upturned face. "You can't go to Baltimore."

Something that might have been pain tightened her features. "If I don't, and women start turning up dead, I'll never be able to forgive myself."

His lips parted, only to snap shut.

He wasn't a psychiatrist, but he knew what this was about.

Carmen hadn't been able to save her mother all those years ago. Now she refused to have any more deaths on her conscience.

December 23, Kansas

Carmen managed a few hours of sleep. She'd offered the bed to Griff, but he'd refused, instead grabbing a spare blanket and pillow and lying on the floor near the door.

She tried not to feel guilty at the fact he had to be miserable on the nasty carpet.

She'd told him to go home. After an hour of arguing about her trip to Baltimore, she'd pointed toward the door and ordered him back to California. But he'd stubbornly refused to go.

Instead, he'd settled on the ground and turned his back to her.

End of conversation.

By seven the next morning they were both up and dressed. Griff had run to the nearby diner for coffee and doughnuts while she showered and put on the same clothes.

At some point she was going to have to hit a store. Or a laundromat.

In the meantime, she was on her second cup of coffee and her third doughnut as she paced the floor while Griff silently worked his magic on his computer. At last he glanced up from the bed, his expression impossible to read.

"There's nothing."

She frowned, trying not to notice how very fine he looked in his flannel shirt and faded jeans. His dark hair was rumpled and his jaw was dark with his unshaved whiskers.

Deliciously male.

"There has to be something," she insisted.

He glanced up from the laptop. "The only tickets available would mean flying from Kansas City to Detroit to Atlanta to Baltimore. Over ten hours with layovers. That's always assuming there's no delays, which would be a miracle." He glanced toward the window where the snow was beginning to flutter from the gray sky. Big, puffy flakes that looked pretty until they were coating the runway. "It will be faster to drive."

"You're kidding?"

He shrugged. "It's the holiday season."

She couldn't argue. Finding plane tickets this close to Christmas was like mining for gold.

She blew out a frustrated sigh. "Fine. I'll drive."

His eyes narrowed. "*We'll* drive."

"Griff." Her protest was cut short by a sharp *ding, ding, ding*. She blinked, her gaze lowering to the computer he had perched on his knees. "What was that?"

His slender fingers were already flying over the keyboard. Like a piano virtuoso. If it was her, she'd already have busted the keys. She tended to treat a computer like it was an old-fashioned typewriter, smashing her fingers against the letters as if she could somehow transfer her emotions to the words on the screen.

Maybe it had something to do with being a journalist.

"Someone just tried to hack into one of your accounts," he said.

She felt a stab of surprise. "How do you know?"

"I'm using one of the programs I designed to alert us if anyone attempts to trace you in cyberspace," he said. "I filtered out the random searches. You're a celebrity, so your name gets a lot of traffic."

She ignored his reference to being a celebrity, moving to settle on the bed next to him.

"So what triggered the alarm?"

"It looks like a search on your credit card," he said, his gaze on the computer screen as files flashed by at a speed that made her dizzy.

"Identity theft?" she demanded, already searching her mind for what she had to do to cancel her card.

What a pain.

"No." He lifted his head, his expression tense. "I think the stalker is using your credit card to follow your movements."

She sucked in a sharp breath. She'd used her card to buy her plane tickets. And then again to rent the car that brought her to this hotel.

"That's how he knew I was coming to Kansas City?"

Griff nodded. "It's the easiest explanation."

She grunted at his offhand words. Hacking into some-one's credit card account was easy? Clearly, he didn't under-stand the real world. Most people could barely get online to check their own account, let alone break into someone else's.

"Which means he has to have some expertise with com-puters," she pointed out.

"Or hired someone who does," he said, returning his at-tention to the computer. "Damn," he muttered.

"What's wrong?"

"Whoever did it managed to block me from tracing them."

A nasty fear battled with the doughnuts and coffee in the pit of her stomach.

"So we can't figure out who tried to hack my account?"

"Not without some effort. And time we don't have." She could feel him stiffen, his breath hissing loudly through his clenched teeth, as if he'd been struck by a sudden thought. "Wait."

She studied his grim profile. "Griff?"

He scowled at the screen. "When the flowers were sent to you, the order should have alerted me."

She leaned closer, pressed against his shoulder as he closed out the open files and started a fresh search for new ones.

"That's quite a program," she said, not entirely comfortable with the knowledge he could keep track of her with the press of a button.

"Creating software to siphon intel from cyberspace is like creating a net to catch a specific fish," he said, his tone distracted. "Too tightly meshed and it scoops up everything, including the trash, and buries anything of interest. Too loose and the intel slips away."

Her discomfort spread from a personal level to a more universal unease.

She wasn't a crazy conspiracy theorist, but she wasn't naïve. She knew that the technology Griff created could be abused by people with too much authority and not enough integrity to accept a personal right to privacy.

"How big can you make the net?"

"As big as it needs to be."

"That's a lot of intel."

As if hearing the edge in her voice, Griff turned his head to send her a faint smile.

"Yes. Which is why the program that I lease to law enforcement has a few tweaks."

She studied him with a lift of her brows. "What sort of tweaks?"

"If you want to cast a large net, then it only works for a limited amount of time before the information is automatically dumped," he explained. "Or you can do a targeted search for a lengthier amount of time."

She gave a small nod. "Absolute power."

"Corrupts absolutely," he finished.

They shared a long glance, and Carmen felt that odd tug of fascination toward her companion. Not the awareness of a woman for a handsome, successful man. That was easy to explain. This was a sensation of catching a peep of that brilliant mind of his and wanting to climb into his lap and just talk for hours. Days. Years.

That was . . . weird.

And more than a little unnerving.

"So why didn't your program get triggered?" she forced herself to ask.

He leaned toward the computer screen, his brow furrowed.

"I'm going to find out." His fingers again flew over the keys and suddenly the image of an invoice from the flower shop filled the screen. "Here it is," he murmured, quickly scanning the order. He grunted as he pointed toward the top of the invoice. "That's the reason."

From Carmen's angle, it was impossible to read the tiny print.

"What happened?"

"They put your name in wrong," he said. "It's listed as Carrie Jacobs, not Carmen."

Carrie?

Carmen surged off the bed, goosebumps spreading over her skin like frost across a window.

"What did you say?"

He lifted his head, his body going still as he caught sight of her expression.

"It was typed in as Carrie." He set aside the laptop and rose to his feet. "What is it?"

Someone walking across her grave.

She shook her head, desperately trying to dislodge the thought.

"Nothing," she said, her voice an octave too high. "I'm sure it was just a mistake."

"You don't look like you've seen a ghost just because of a mistake," he said.

She sucked in a deep breath before slowly releasing it.

It didn't help. Her stomach remained tied in a painful knot and her mouth dry.

"When I was young, I was called Carrie," she admitted.

Griff stepped toward her, his tension filling the air with a tangible sizzle.

"By who?"

She shrugged. "Everyone. It wasn't until I went to live with my grandparents that they insisted I go by Carmen."

Chapter Nine

December 23, Baltimore, MD

Joy sensed she was being watched.

It'd started two days ago. She'd taken on extra hours at the small community college where she worked as a janitor. During the Christmas break there was always a frenzy of activity to polish floors, paint walls, and tidy up the campus before the students returned. It wasn't a dream job, but it paid the rent on her cramped trailer, and more importantly, it gave her a steep discount on the night classes she was taking.

She wasn't going to be a janitor forever.

Nope. She intended to be a medical lab technician.

Her future was upwardly mobile and far away from the sort of crappy life her mother was trapped in.

Which was what made the sensation that there was some pervert out there keeping tabs on her all the more annoying. She didn't have the time or interest to deal with the creep.

With a shiver as the morning air sliced through the fabric of her secondhand coat, Joy turned in a slow circle. Her eyes took in the narrow road that had been plowed during the night, piling the snow into a ridge along the sidewalk.

The white clapboard buildings next to her were silent, the residents either at work, or students who'd gone home for the holidays.

Overhead the sky was a sullen gray that bled into the misty fog that surrounded her. The sort of morning a person wished they lived on a tropical beach.

Someday . . .

There was no one in sight, but Joy had the heightened senses of a girl who'd spent her entire life surrounded by rough, aggressive men who were eager to take advantage of any weakness.

"I know you're there," she called out, her hand slipping into her coat pocket. She never left home without her handy-dandy can of pepper spray. "Hello," she called again. "Step out where I can see you or I'm calling the cops."

There was the crunch of footsteps on snow, then a dark form appeared from a nearby alley.

Joy frowned. The stranger looked to be in his mid or early twenties with a heavy jaw and sleepy eyes. He was short and stocky beneath his parka, with dark hair that was cut short and stuck up with cowlicks at the back. He had small, dark eyes and skin that was oddly yellow, as if he was jaundiced.

Weird.

He held up a gloved hand, and a nervous smile twitched around his lips.

"Wait," he said, moving slowly forward.

Joy took a step backward. No need to panic. It was broad daylight on a public street. Right?

"Who are you?" she demanded.

His lips were still twitching with a nervous smile as he approached.

"Josh." He held out his hand. Like she was actually going to shake it.

She took another step back. "Why are you following me?"

"I wasn't following you."

She made a sound of disgust. "Yeah, right."

Something flashed through his eyes. "This is a public street. Just because I was walking behind you doesn't mean nothing."

Her fingers tightened on the pepper spray. "Look, I'm not stupid. You weren't walking behind me. You were hiding in the alley."

He hunched his shoulders. "Okay, maybe I wanted to see you."

"Ew." She wrinkled her nose. He reminded Joy of her oldest stepbrother. The sort of boy who was always trying to get a peek of her in the shower, or fingering through her underwear drawer. "You're a creeper."

"Don't call me that." His expression became petulant.

"Why not? It's true."

"I was just trying to work up my courage to talk to you."

"Men who want to talk to me don't hide in the alley."

"I'm shy."

She rolled her eyes. "Shy?"

"I am." He continued to move toward her, his movements slow and lumbering like a sloth. "Can we just talk?"

"No. Stay back," she said.

"Please."

She brought the pepper spray out of her pocket, holding it out in warning.

"I said stay back, you perv."

"Why do you call me names?" He scowled, but he continued forward. *Crunch. Crunch. Crunch.* His footsteps sounded unnaturally loud. "That's not very nice."

"I'll spray you."

He stopped right in front of her. Close enough she could catch the foul scent of his breath.

Coffee and stale cigarettes.

Gross.

"There's no need to be a bitch," he groused.

Her upper lip curled in disgust. "God. Jerks like you make me sick."

"He told you not to be a bitch, Carrie," a voice whispered directly in her ear.

Joy parted her lips to scream, belatedly realizing that the *crunch, crunch* she'd been hearing hadn't come from the man standing in front of her. But before she could make a sound, a gloved hand clapped roughly over her mouth and she felt a pinprick at her neck.

Instantly her brain went fuzzy.

Shit. She'd been drugged.

The man who called himself Josh moved in close, watching her features slacken with the concentration of a child watching an ant being fried beneath a magnifying glass.

Strong arms wrapped around her from behind, catching her as her knees went weak. Her last thought was . . .

They have the wrong woman. My name's not Carrie.

December 23, Missouri

Griff had a firm understanding of his strengths. And his weaknesses.

He had an above-average intelligence. He could outrun most casual joggers without breaking a sweat. He could coax a computer to do anything he wanted.

But people . . .

He was usually clueless.

With Carmen Jacobs, however, he seemed to sense exactly what she was feeling. Which was why he kept her busy with the need to check out of the hotel and to return her SUV to the rental agency. He kept his truck for the long drive. He also insisted that she purchase a plane ticket to Baltimore.

If she was being electronically monitored, he wanted

whoever was watching her to think she was going to spend the next twelve hours traveling from airport to airport.

By the time she'd regained command of her shaken composure, they were already heading along I-70 to Louisville.

"I still think we should go to Baltimore," she complained, sitting stiffly in the leather seat as she studied the crowded highway that stretched in front of them.

It was two days until Christmas and everyone was anxious to get to their destination.

He risked a quick glance at Carmen, taking in her tense profile.

He sympathized with her urge to try to track down the stalker. The thought that there was a potential killer out there hunting more women made his gut twist with dread.

But he wasn't going to let her charge into an obvious trap.

Besides, he couldn't dismiss the flower order. It might have been a typo, but he didn't think so.

From the beginning the stalker had tried to establish an intimate connection with Carmen.

If he was just a random whackadoodle who'd been inspired by her book, there would have been no need to send her the pictures. Or follow her to Kansas City. Or send her the flowers.

This was personal.

"We could chase shadows. I'm sure that's what the bastard wants," he said. "Or we can try to figure out who he is."

She clicked her tongue. "I don't know why you're so convinced that it's someone from my past."

He slowed as a car raced past him, spraying snow and ice and rock salt onto his windshield.

"Who else would call you Carrie?" he demanded.

"It could have been a clerical error," she insisted.

Griff's hands tightened on the steering wheel. He didn't

miss the edge in her voice. This was about more than her need to track down the killer.

She didn't want to go back to Louisville.

"I assume your real name is Carmen?" he asked. There was no use in demanding to know why she was reluctant to go home.

Carmen would tell him when she was ready. And not a second before.

"Yes," she said. "My mother was an amateur opera singer who loved Bizet's *Carmen*. She was determined to name her first daughter after the opera." There was a brief hesitation before she continued. "My father agreed with the understanding that I would be called Carrie."

"He wasn't an opera fan?"

"Actually, that's how they met," she said, her voice strained. "His parents were sponsors of a small community theater and my mother was performing. I remember my father telling me that it was love at first sight."

"So why Carrie?"

"My father thought Carmen made me sound too adult. He wanted me to stay his little princess."

"It sounds like he loved you very much," he said in low tones.

She gave a short, humorless laugh. "Not hardly. My father didn't know how to love."

Griff resisted the urge to tell her that she wasn't the only one with a father who didn't know squat about loving a child.

Right now this was about Carmen and who might be tormenting her.

"Tell me about your family."

There was a rustle of fabric as Carmen wiggled out of her coat. He heard a hiss of pain as the movement jostled the wound on her upper arm. Anger flared through him. When he found the bastard responsible for attacking her, he intended to make sure there was some serious payback before he was handed over to the authorities.

"My grandmother died when I was twenty and my grandfather passed two years ago," she said as she settled back in her seat.

"They weren't your only family, were they?"

He risked a quick glance to catch her momentary confusion.

"Oh," she at last said. "My father has a younger brother, my uncle Lawrence."

It was obvious she didn't consider the relatives on her father's side as part of her family.

Not surprising after what had happened.

"What do you know about him?"

He could sense her confusion. "You can't imagine that he's involved."

"Humor me," Griff said. He didn't know if he suspected an actual member of her family or not. He just needed a place to start. "Is he your father's only sibling?"

"Yes. My father was a few years older, so when his parents were killed in a plane crash, he became Lawrence's guardian until he was old enough to go to college."

"They were close?" Griff asked.

"I think so," she said, the words hesitant, as if she'd never given thought to her uncle or his connection to her father. "They inherited my grandparents' business and ran it together."

"What sort of business?"

"A chain of hardware stores," she said. "There were several of them spread across the state of Kentucky."

Griff nodded. He'd known that her parents had been wealthy. The fact that they'd been a part of the elite Louisville society had made their deaths all the more scandalous. But he hadn't known how they'd made their money.

"The brothers were equal partners?" he demanded.

"I guess." She drummed her fingers on the console that separated the bucket seats. A visible indication of her discomfort. "My father took care of the finances. I'm not sure exactly what my uncle did, but he traveled a lot. My cousins used to come stay with us when he was out of town."

Griff's interest in Lawrence Jacobs went up several notches.

"Did your cousins stay with you because his wife traveled with him?"

She gave a firm shake of her head. "No. My aunt Viola was . . ." Her words trailed away as she dredged up ancient memories. "I think my mother used to say 'delicate.' I'm not sure what that meant, but she didn't want to take care of Matthew and Baylor when my uncle was gone."

"Two boys?"

"Yes."

Another spike of interest. "Younger than you?"

"No, both of them were older." She paused to consider. "I think Matthew is five or six years older and Baylor around four," she finally said. "Lawrence married right out of college. My dad was a confirmed bachelor until he met my mother. She was ten years younger than him."

"Is your uncle still in Louisville?"

"I lost track of them after—" She bit off her words, clearing her throat before she continued. "After I moved in with my grandparents."

Griff frowned. He needed to make sure he understood the situation.

"You haven't had any contact at all?"

"No."

"What about your inheritance?"

"What inheritance?"

Her tone was genuinely baffled. Hadn't she been the least curious about the fortune that should have been hers?

"Do you know what happened to your parents' property?" he pressed. "Or the money from the business?"

He heard her shifting in her seat, as if she was increasingly agitated by his questions.

"My grandparents refused to discuss anything to do with my father or his family."

Griff was distracted as a car zoomed past with the windows rolled down and blaring "Jingle Bells." He slowed, assuming the driver had already been indulging in some pre-Christmas spirits.

Ho. Ho. Ho.

"Are there any other relatives?" he finally asked.

"None that I can remember." Her tone was deliberately stripped of emotion. Griff got it. He had the same habit. When you were without a family, you pretended that you were happier alone. Sometimes you even believed it. "My mother was an only child," she added.

Griff nodded. The family seemed like a good place to start. But he wouldn't let his swelling dislike for an uncle and cousins who didn't seem to have made an effort to reach out to the orphaned Carmen blind him.

Right now he needed to gather as much intel as possible.

Later he would decide who and what needed to be further investigated.

"What about close friends?" he asked.

"Of my parents?"

"Yes."

There was a long silence as she tried to sort through her childhood memories. He wondered if she had any happy ones. A strange emotion tugged at his heart.

"None that stand out," she finally announced. "There were a lot of parties and weekends spent at various people's homes."

His lips twitched. The life of the rich and powerful.

"What about you?" he asked. "Did you have anyone you spent time with?"

"I had a group of friends from school."

"Any boys?"

"No." She gave a firm shake of her head. "I was sent to a private girls' school."

Griff felt a stab of relief. That narrowed down the possibilities.

"What about the neighborhood?" he asked. "Any boys who used to hang around more than you wanted?"

Again with the shake of her head. "Our estate was on the edge of town, so there weren't any close neighbors."

His brows pulled together as he thought of his childhood in Chicago. With only his mother's income as a cop, they'd lived in apartments that weren't in the worst part of the city, but certainly weren't the best. They'd been crammed next to their neighbors like sardines in a can.

"No kids at all?"

"My cousins on occasion," she said, then she made a tiny sound. "Oh, and the housekeeper's son. I'd almost forgotten about Ronnie."

"You had a housekeeper?"

"Yes." He could feel her curious glance. Like she didn't understand how anyone could be surprised they had a servant. "Ellen Hyde."

"Did she live in?"

She nodded. "Ellen had an apartment above the garage."

"Was she married?"

She took a minute. "I don't know if they were married, but there was a man who lived with her," she finally said. "His first name was Andrew, but it seemed like he had a different last name."

"Did he work for your parents?"

"Yeah. He helped around the house doing odd jobs. Sometimes he'd drive me to school."

The unknown servant was put on Griff's mental list of suspects.

"What about the son?"

"Ronnie?" Her tone was dismissive. "He was usually somewhere around the estate."

"Were you friends?"

"Not really."

"Because he was the housekeeper's son?"

She made a sound of annoyance at his question. "Because he was older than me. And a boy," she said in sharp tones. Clearly, she didn't like being accused of being a snob. "He spent a lot more time with my cousins."

Ronnie went on the suspect list.

"Is there anyone else from your childhood?"

"None." She flopped back in her seat, clearly done with the conversation. "I'm telling you that going to Louisville is a waste of our time."

"It's a place to start," he said, his attention focusing on the thickening traffic as they neared the suburbs of St. Louis.

He sounded more confident than he felt.

After all, he was clinging to the fact that her name had been written incorrectly on an invoice. He could very well be chasing shadows.

But he did have one comfort no matter what happened.

Carmen wasn't going to Baltimore.

Not even if he had to drive her all the way to California and lock her in his bedroom.

Chapter Ten

Hunter wasn't entirely satisfied.

The four women looked perfect. They were all neatly arranged on the basement floor. They all had copies of "The Raven" prominently placed on their chests. They had their hair brushed and were all wearing white robes. They looked like angels that had simply laid down to go to sleep.

The perfect muses.

It wasn't until a person peeled back the robes that it would be obvious they'd been brutally raped and beaten to death.

Still, the pictures he'd just taken didn't fully capture the glory of his staging.

Maybe it was the nasty basement. He'd let Slayer locate the row of abandoned homes where they could stash the bodies. It wasn't until he arrived that he realized they were used by the local drug addicts to smoke their meth. It not only meant the bodies would be found quicker than he wanted, but that the cellar floor was littered with beer cans, used needles, and condoms.

Disgusting.

Or maybe it was the lack of decent lighting. The one

narrow window was boarded over, leaving the space bathed in shadows.

He gave a shake of his head, tucking the pictures in the pocket of his heavy parka. He should have posed the women upstairs before he'd had his companion carry them down the rotting staircase, but they would have to do.

He didn't have time to make changes. His schedule was already tight.

A shame since he'd had a text from his informant that Carrie was on her way to Baltimore. It would be delicious to stay and toy with her, but he had to get home for the holidays. He couldn't risk having people asking where he was, or why he wasn't around for Christmas.

He'd drop the pictures into the mail. Maybe to her house. She'd eventually find them, right? Or maybe her PR person again.

But first he had business to finish.

Stepping back, he watched as the younger man paced around the women, his square face even more jaundiced in the fluorescent light.

Butcher was still eager, even after he'd spent the morning abusing his female. Clearly, his bloodlust was escalating.

A good thing his expiration date had just arrived.

"They look so peaceful," the younger man said, his movements jerky.

Hunter took a step back, a tiny smile playing around his lips. There was no reason he couldn't have a little fun before he rid the world of one more monster.

"Do you think so?" he asked.

"Yes." The younger man's hands twitched, blood still staining his fingers. A messy, childish monster. "Death must be a relief," he continued.

Hunter released a low chuckle. "I doubt they thought it

was a relief. They screamed and pleaded as if they wanted to live. Even after we'd all had our turn with them."

Butcher turned to face him, his too-wide brow furrowed. This wasn't part of the game. The younger man liked to be comforted after the violence.

"Their lives are miserable, right?" he demanded. "That's what you said. They flaunt their bodies and tempt men to do bad things. It's not like we would want to hurt them if they didn't beg for it."

Hunter pursed his lips, refusing to soothe the man's swelling distress.

"Completely their own fault, hmmm?"

"It is." He stomped his foot. Like a petulant child. "You said—"

"A tale begun in other days, when summer suns were glowing," he softly quoted.

"What does that mean?"

"Do you believe everything you're told?" Hunter demanded, his expression mocking.

"I'm not stupid."

"Actually, you are," he assured his companion. "Unbelievably stupid."

The younger man flinched, his eyes filling with tears. Hunter had been able to manipulate his companion with the approval he so desperately craved. Withdrawing that support was like a knife in the heart.

"Why are you being so mean?" he asked.

Hunter strolled forward, his hand reaching into the pocket of his coat. He'd already ensured his favorite pistol was tucked in there. Loaded and with the safety off.

"I think we all must occasionally be honest with ourselves," he drawled. "You, my friend, are a butcher in name and deed." He nodded his head toward the dead women who lined the floor. "Just look at your handiwork."

Butcher hunched his shoulders. "It wasn't me. We all did it."

Hunter reached out with his toe to lightly touch the nearest body. The female had been his. Not very satisfying, but his side trip to the hotel in Kansas had meant that he hadn't had the same opportunity as the others to choose a proper victim.

Sacrifices, sacrifices.

"Yes, so much easier as a group, isn't it?" he asked in soft tones.

Belatedly sensing the danger that prickled in the stale, nasty air, the younger man took a sharp step backward. His gaze darted around the gloom.

"Where is everyone else?" he demanded.

"It's the holidays, my dear boy." Hunter closed the space between them. It wasn't really necessary. He was an excellent shot. But it was so much more satisfying to witness death up close and personal. "It would look suspicious if we weren't home."

"What about Assassin?" The man licked his dry lips. "You said he was coming to join us."

Hunter smiled. "I'm afraid he was detained."

The younger man's frown deepened. Maybe he didn't know what *detained* meant. Or maybe he realized that he wasn't getting out of the cellar alive.

"Where is he?"

"He decided he wanted to stay with our previous victims."

"What does that mean?"

Hunter considered before he confessed the truth. Why not? It wasn't like the man was going to have the opportunity to tell anyone.

"I shot him in the head and left his body in the farmhouse. Eventually he'll be found."

Butcher gasped in shock. "Why?"

"Because he was a weak link." Hunter pulled the gun out of his pocket and aimed it at his companion. "Just as you are."

"No." The man held up his hands, as if he could stop a bullet with his fingers. Idiot. "We're a team. You said so."

Hunter snorted. "I say a lot of things I don't mean."

"But you need me." With an awkward movement, the younger man lowered himself to his knees, his expression pleading. "I'm your friend."

"You are my scapegoat."

Hunter pulled the trigger, drilling the bullet right between the man's eyes. Blood and brain matter splattered across the back wall before the man toppled to the side. Hunter shook his head, his ears ringing as the shot echoed in the small space. Then, leaning down, he pressed the gun into the dead man's hand.

The cops would eventually realize that this was more than a meth head who'd gone on a crazed shooting spree. But it would give him time to drive to the airport.

Rising to his feet, he gazed down at the man he'd trained to become a killer.

"Merry Christmas, Josh."

He stepped over the corpse and headed for the stairs.

His work here was done.

December 24, Louisville, KY

Carmen sat next to Griff as he drove the truck through the nearly empty streets of the fancy Louisville suburb.

The morning had dawned with a crisp, pure beauty. The clouds had given way to reveal a brilliant blue sky and the golden wash of sunlight. Even the icy breeze had been dulled to a bearable chill.

It wasn't balmy, but it wasn't the brutal cold they'd left in Kansas City.

So why was she shivering?

It was a stupid question.

She might have spent the past twelve hours trying to ignore the fact she was in the city she'd sworn never to step foot in again, but she couldn't completely fool herself.

Thankfully, last night she'd been so exhausted, she'd barely had the energy to stand next to Griff as he'd checked them into the suite at the fancy hotel. A distant part of her brain had acknowledged he'd no doubt had to call in a few favors and paid a fortune to get them a room on such short notice. Another part had whispered that she was beginning to rely on this man's capable ability to take care of her. But the numerous concerns that stewed inside her had been muted by her fuzzy weariness.

She didn't want to worry about being home. Or the fear that there was still a serial killer out there somewhere. Or her snowballing dependency on Griffin Archer. She wanted to sleep.

So that's what she did.

Crawling into the guest bed in the elegant penthouse suite, she'd pulled the covers over her head and allowed the darkness to overwhelm her.

Unfortunately, she couldn't hide in the bed forever. Not when Griff was knocking on her door at an ungodly hour to say that breakfast had been delivered.

She shuffled out to find a large tray of food waiting next to the window that offered a stunning view of Louisville, as well as several plastic bags that were filled with mounds of clothing from the downstairs boutique. Pulling them open, she discovered that there was everything from casual jeans to an elegant cocktail gown.

To face her family, she chose a sleek black pencil skirt and sapphire silk top. Both fit to perfection. Griff chose a pair of black slacks and a cream cable-knit sweater. More perfection.

A dangerous warmth flared through her heart. Griff had not only remembered her voracious appetite, but he'd sensed that she needed the sort of expensive clothing that would be worn by her relatives.

Like putting on a layer of armor.

Then, in silence they'd ridden the elevator down to the parking garage and taken off in the truck.

Less than half an hour later, Griff was pulling to a halt in the circle drive in front of the two-story white antebellum house with black shutters. The wide front porch was framed with four fluted columns and sweeping steps that led to the double oak doors. The surrounding grounds were swaths of closely trimmed grass with ancient trees that had been there long before George Rogers Clark had created the first settlement that had eventually become Louisville.

It was all graceful lines and elegant pride.

Exactly what a Southern home should be.

But the mere sight of it twisted Carmen's stomach with dread.

Next to her, Griff released a low whistle. Like most people he could only see the surface beauty. Not the rot that was hidden beneath the superficial charm.

"This is where you grew up?"

She gave a stiff nod. "Yes."

"Nice."

"I prefer my grandparents' farmhouse."

Griff switched off the engine of the truck, wrapping them in silence. The house was only a few miles from downtown Louisville, but it might as well have been a hundred.

In this neighborhood there were no sounds of honking horns, or buses rattling over potholes. Certainly, there weren't any wailing sirens or chatter from pedestrians as they hurried to work.

Nope. The only sound allowed here was the occasional purr of a large engine as the Jags and Porsches zoomed past the outer road.

"Obviously, your uncle didn't share your lack of appreciation for your childhood home," Griff said, his gaze skimming over the porch that was larger than most apartments. "I did a quick background check. He moved in the day after your parents' funeral."

She resisted the urge to sigh. She couldn't remember being particularly close to her uncle or cousins, but she couldn't make herself believe they were cold-blooded serial killers.

Of course, her father had obviously been unstable.

Maybe it ran in the family.

She gave a sharp shake of her head, trying to dislodge the horrible thoughts.

"The estate has belonged to the Jacobses for a couple generations," she explained. "He probably felt it was his duty to move in."

"Hardly a duty," Griff protested.

"A big house and lots of grass doesn't equate to happiness," she said, her tone sharp.

Griff reached to grab her fingers, giving them a small squeeze. "Are you ready for this?"

"Not really."

He leaned toward her, wrapping her in his warm, masculine scent.

"If you want to go back to the hotel, I can—"

"No." She sucked in a deep breath. The sooner they could eliminate her family as suspects, the sooner they could return to the hunt. "I just want to get this over with."

He lifted her fingers, pressing them to his lips. A tingle of heat spread through her body, easing her shivers.

This man clearly had a magic touch.

A renegade image of allowing those enchanted fingers to explore her naked body seared through her mind.

"I'm going to be with you every step of the way," he murmured. "I promise."

The urge to lean forward and snuggle against his chest was shockingly strong. As if her body had suddenly developed a mind of its own.

With a silent curse, she pulled away from his light grasp, and unbuckled her seat belt. By the time she'd shoved open the passenger door and crawled out of the truck, Griff was at her side, firmly grabbing her elbow.

Did he think she might bolt?

Or was he hoping to offer her strength to face her family?

The thought was almost as unnerving as the lust that continued to heat her blood. She'd put a lot of effort into making sure she didn't need anyone.

For anything.

Still, she didn't pull away. She didn't ask herself why not.

Together they climbed the shallow stairs and crossed the planked floor of the front porch. Griff reached out to press the bell, ignoring the heavy gold knocker.

Several minutes passed before the door was slowly tugged open to reveal a middle-aged woman in a starched uniform.

Carmen felt a stab of surprise, realizing that she'd been expecting Ellen to open the door. Ridiculous, considering how many years had passed. The woman could have retired. Or moved from the area.

"May I help you?" the servant asked, her round face flushed as if she'd been forced to run from the back of the house.

Griff took charge. "Miss Jacobs is here to see her uncle."

The color in the woman's cheeks darkened with confusion as she shot a brief glance in Carmen's direction.

Had the housekeeper heard the horror stories? Or did she recognize Carmen from her book? Either way the woman took a hasty step backward, waving them through the door.

"Please come in," she said, waiting for them to enter the foyer. "I'll tell Mr. Jacobs you're here, if you'll wait in the salon?"

She led them across the marble floor and Carmen's gaze moved over the walls that were painted a pale peach with crown molding at the top. On one side of the open space a staircase formed a half crescent as it soared toward the second-floor landing. At the back was an opening that led toward the rest of the house.

The servant turned to the right to enter a long room with the same peach walls. There was a bank of windows that offered a view of the front drive, and a large fireplace that had a marble mantel. The floor was wide wooden planks polished to glow beneath the chandelier that hung from the medallion in the center of the high ceiling.

The furniture was created more for style than comfort, with a narrow sofa and matching love seat. The tables were low and delicate with a plethora of ceramic figurines arranged on frilly doilies.

Carmen felt Griff flinch, no doubt worried about whether the sofa would hold his weight and if he could cross the room without knocking over any figurines. But as the house-keeper left the room, she found herself pulling away from his side so she could circle the room.

Now that she was actually in the house, the memories that she'd spent the past fourteen years trying to bury suddenly burst free. Like a dam fracturing beneath the force of flood waters.

Her fingers touched the mantel. There'd once been silver framed pictures there. Of her at her piano recital. Of her parents' wedding. Of her mother performing *Carmen*. The silver frames remained, but the pictures were of people she barely recognized.

The pictures, however, were the only thing that were different.

Captured by her memories she headed toward the door. Her fingers continued to touch familiar objects. The table with the crystal vase where her mother kept the flowers her father would bring her after he returned from a business trip. Out into the foyer where Carmen would whoosh down the curved staircase by sliding on the banister. She crossed the marble floor to head down the hallway.

The memories came faster and faster.

Some of them good. The sound of her mother singing as she moved through the house. Her father tossing Carmen in the air to make her giggle. Birthday parties for her, and grown-up parties for her parents with expensively dressed guests who'd drifted through the house like glittering ghosts.

And some of them bad. The chiding from Ellen when Carmen dragged in mud on her clean floors. The torments from her older cousins who'd once locked her in the wine cellar for an entire day. And the shouting between her parents. When she was young she'd thought they were arguing because they enjoyed the drama.

In retrospect, she accepted that her father had been possessive of his young, beautiful wife. And quick to anger when he feared she might be pulling away from him.

Maybe that was the reason . . .

Her mouth went dry as she passed by the hidden door that held the coat closet. A brutal cold filled her veins as her feet continued to carry her forward. Just as they had that fateful night.

Step. Step. Step.

She thought she heard someone say her name, but it was difficult to hear. As if she was underwater.

Her hands were shaking as she finally entered the kitchen.

It was a newer addition to the main house, with lots of sunlight and stainless steel appliances. Once upon a time it'd been Carmen's favorite room in the house.

Now her memories tinted it in red.

Blood red.

"Carmen." Strong fingers wrapped around her upper arms, giving her a small shake.

She blinked, struggling to come back to reality. Desperately she clung to the sight of Griff's lean, handsome face as he leaned toward her.

"Nothing's changed," she said, the words coming out like a croak.

His brows drew together, his expression worried. "You mean the furniture?"

"The furniture. The artwork." She shuddered, sucking in a deep breath. "It even smells the same. Like my dad's pipe."

"Carmen, I'm sorry." His arms slid around her, tugging her against his chest. "I know this is difficult for you."

She remained stiff in his arms, but she didn't try to pull away.

"You know what happened here?" she demanded.

He nodded. "I read a few articles."

She wasn't surprised. Griff probably had done a complete background search on her as soon as he realized she'd deliberately approached him on the beach.

"Then you know that fourteen years ago my father shot my mother and then killed himself." Her gaze lowered to the tiled floor. "In this room."

His hand slid up and down her back in a soothing motion. "Were you here?"

She gave a slow nod, feeling beads of sweat form on her brow. It was weird. She could remember exactly what she'd done on that fateful day. She'd gone to a friend's house for a birthday party. They'd played in the pool, rode horses, and giggled over boys. She'd come home after dinner and gone straight to her room. A few hours later she was sound asleep.

After that, things got . . . fuzzy.

"I was asleep upstairs," she said, her voice low and strained. "The first shot woke me. I didn't know what it was. I thought someone had broken a window. It frightened me."

His fingers threaded into her hair, combing through the golden curls.

"What did you do?"

"I crawled out of bed and went to find my mother." It'd been a warm night, she abruptly recalled, but she'd been shivering as she'd silently crept through the dark house. "I looked in my parents' bedroom, but it was empty. So I came downstairs."

He pressed his lips to the top of her head. "You're safe now."

Her hands lifted to lie against his chest, taking strength from the feel of his strong arms wrapped around her.

"I started to go toward the living room where my parents usually watched TV at night. Then I turned to go to the kitchen."

"Why?"

She tilted back her head to meet his dark, steady gaze. "What?"

"Why did you come to the kitchen?"

Oh. Her brow furrowed. Why did she?

She tried to battle through the fuzz.

"I think I heard something," she finally decided, allowing herself to feel the floorboards beneath her feet that creaked as she moved, and the lingering scent of pipe tobacco that hung in the air. "A voice, maybe," she said, then gave a shake of her head. It hadn't been a conversation. "Or my father's cry," she at last concluded, still not satisfied. "I was just outside the doorway when the second shot went off."

His hand splayed on her back as he lifted his head to stare down at her with dismay.

"You didn't come in here, did you?"

"No." She grimaced. "The sound was so loud I ran back down the hall and hid in the coat closet. That's where the cops eventually found me."

"I'm sorry."

"So am I." She released a shaky breath. "I was a coward."

"Coward?" He sent her a confused glance. "You were just a child."

The guilt that churned deep inside her bubbled to the surface, searing against her nerve endings like acid.

"If I'd come in here instead of running away—"

"You'd have what?" he sharply interrupted. "Spent the rest of your life tormenting yourself with the image of their bodies?"

She hunched a shoulder. "I could have called nine-one-one right away. My mother might have been saved."

He jerked, as if struck by a sudden thought. "Who did call the cops?"

She hesitated, sorting through the thoughts. At last she concluded that she'd never been told who'd been responsible for the call.

"I assume it was Ellen," she said with a shrug. "I really don't know."

"Was anyone else in the house?"

She glanced toward the window, a wrenching sadness making her feel as if she weighed a thousand pounds.

"The cops asked me the same question, but I really didn't know. I'd been gone all day and I went straight to my room when I came home."

Perhaps sensing she was reaching the edge of collapse, Griff slid his fingers beneath her chin and turned her face back.

"Look at me." He patiently waited for her to meet his gaze. "There's nothing you could have done to change what happened that night." He leaned so close their noses were nearly touching. "Nothing."

She pulled back. It was the same thing she'd told herself a thousand times.

She still didn't believe it.

"How can you be so sure?"

There was a long silence, as if Griff was weighing something in his mind.

"Because I was just five feet away from my mother when she was murdered," he said. "Sometimes fate decides to be a real bitch, but blaming yourself doesn't help anyone."

The air was pressed from her lungs as she studied his grim expression.

"I didn't know," she murmured, even as she silently wondered if she had somehow sensed that tragedy had struck his life.

It might be why she'd felt so drawn to him from the beginning. A shared sense of loss that few people could understand.

"Like you, it's not something I talk about."

She slid her hand across his chest to rest it over the rapid beat of his heart. She sensed how much it cost him to speak about the past. And she knew he was only doing it to ease her own emotional roller coaster.

"What happened?" she asked.

"My mother was a cop in Chicago."

She blinked. She didn't know why that surprised her. It certainly explained Griff's decision to concentrate his computer expertise on catching criminals. Still, she found herself staring at him in amazement.

"Really?"

"Yeah." A small, bittersweet smile touched his lips. "She grew up in a small town, and no one, including my grandparents, thought she'd last more than a few weeks in the big city, but she loved it. And she was good at it."

There was no missing his pride in his mother.

"She was killed in the line of duty?"

His pride was replaced with the same aching grief that haunted her.

"No, she was out of uniform." There was a short pause before he forced out the words. "I'd just gotten an A on a quiz and she'd promised me I could have anything I wanted for dinner. I told her that I wanted to go to the pizza joint that was just down the street from our apartment building."

She raised her hand to lightly touch his cheek. "Was it just the two of you?"

"It was." His eyes grew distant as he became lost in his memories. "My dad had walked out when I was just a baby. He wanted a wife who'd stay home and take care of him and his kids, not a woman who was dedicated to her career."

She wrinkled her nose. Jerk.

"Did the shooting happen on the street?" she asked.

He shook his head. "No, we were in the restaurant waiting for our order when a man came in to rob the place."

"Oh, Griff." She cupped his cheek in the palm of her hand, her heart twisting with sympathy.

"It might have been just another robbery, but the man was high on crack, and when a waiter came out of the kitchen the movement startled him." She felt the tremor that shook his body. "He started shooting around the room."

"And your mother was hit?"

"Everyone screamed and fell to the floor." His lips twisted. "Everyone except my mother."

Carmen could visualize the scene. The panic. The cries for help. The frantic attempts to get low to the ground.

And the woman who was trained to react during times of crisis.

"The cop," she said softly.

"Always the cop." His jaw tightened. "She charged forward

and took the man down. His weapon discharged and caught her in the chest."

She flinched. "And you watched it happen."

"Yes." His voice sounded far away. "I was angry for a long time."

"No one would blame you," she assured him. "I hope they put the bastard away for life."

He gave a shake of his head. "I wasn't angry with the shooter."

"You weren't?"

"He was a pathetic junkie who had no idea what he was doing," he said. "I was angry with my mother for not saving herself like everyone else in the room. And with myself for not stopping her."

Her heart melted. Not just with sympathy for a boy who'd watched his mom die. But with gratitude.

His story hadn't only assured her that she wasn't alone in her grief, but his words forced her to consider her own anger. And how she'd allowed it to taint the memories of her childhood.

It hadn't all been bad. In fact, most of her younger years had been filled with happiness.

She should cherish those times. Not try to suppress them.

"Your mother couldn't have done anything else," she said. "That's the reason she became a cop."

"I'm learning to accept that." His gaze swept over her face. "Just as you have to accept there was nothing you could have done to protect your mother."

"Thank you," she breathed.

He lowered his head to press his lips against her forehead. "I promised I would be at your side."

She briefly leaned against him, accepting that the walls she used to protect herself were crumbling.

"Where did you go after your mother died?"

"To my father."

"That must have been difficult," Carmen said, instantly regretting her stupid words.

"That's one way of putting it," he said dryly. "We were complete strangers, and to make matters worse, he had a new family. I was little more than an unwelcome intruder into their home."

"I'm sorry."

"I survived. I had my computer. And every summer I spent a few weeks with my grandparents."

"And now you have Rylan?" she said.

A smile instantly curved his lips. "Yes. And his new wife, Jaci. They're a part of my family now."

She was happy for him. She truly was. Griff clearly deserved to be surrounded with loyal, supportive friends. But she was also just a little envious.

Unlike Griff, she hadn't reached out to create a new family. Instead, she'd convinced herself that it was better to keep herself isolated.

If you didn't care about anyone, they couldn't hurt you.

Her lips parted, but before she could speak there was the sound of sharp footsteps. She turned to watch her uncle march into the kitchen, his face familiar despite the deepened lines and touch of gray in his light brown hair.

"I don't know who you think you are, but—" His angry words dried on his lips as his eyes abruptly widened. "Carrie? Is it really you?"

Chapter Eleven

Griff allowed Carmen to pull away, his gaze locked on the man he assumed was Lawrence Jacobs.

He reminded Griff of a square. A short, broad body that was currently clothed in a casual sweater and charcoal slacks. A block-shaped head with brown hair dusted with silver, and blunt features. His eyes were a pale blue that remained cold as they stared at his only niece.

He looked like the kind of guy who went around telling everyone how important he was.

"Hello, Lawrence." Carmen filled the sudden silence, her voice steady.

Griff smiled with pride while Lawrence managed a grimace.

"My dear. This is such a surprise," he breathed.

Carmen shrugged. "I happened to be in town and it seemed rude not to stop by."

"Of course. Of course." Lawrence cleared his throat, his gaze shifting to Griff. "And you are?"

Griff stepped forward and held out his hand. "Griffin Archer."

Lawrence clasped his fingers in a firm grip, his expression puzzled.

"Why is that name familiar?"

Griff pulled his hand free and stepped back to stand next to Carmen.

"I own a tech firm."

"Archer," Lawrence said slowly, and then he snapped his fingers. "Tyche Systems, right?"

Griff nodded. Tyche Systems was the corporate branch of his business. It was more lucrative than the government contracts, but not nearly as interesting.

"Yes."

A restless greed flared through the older man's eyes. No doubt his brain was busy trying to decide how he could take advantage of Griffin Archer standing in his kitchen.

"We just installed your latest security software for our office."

"Good to hear."

Easily sensing Griff's lack of interest in discussing business, Lawrence returned his attention to his niece. He pasted a stiff smile to his lips, shifting uneasily.

The older man was clearly nervous.

But why?

A question that Griff fully intended to have answered before he left Louisville.

"Yes, well. What a pleasant surprise." Lawrence glanced over his shoulder. "Your aunt will be down shortly. Preparing for the holidays has been exhausting for her."

Carmen's smile was equally strained. "Are Matthew and Baylor here?"

Lawrence turned back, his fingers drumming against the side of his leg.

"They have their own apartments in Louisville, but we're expecting them to spend the next couple of days here," he said. "It's a family tradition."

An awkward silence filled the kitchen. Griff folded his arms over his chest, saying nothing. He wanted to get

Lawrence alone before he asked the questions that were on the tip of his tongue.

"The house hasn't changed much," Carmen finally said.

"No." Lawrence glanced around the kitchen. "I wanted to keep it the same. It's all I have left of my parents." He paused, then continued. "And Stuart."

Stuart Jacobs. Carmen's father.

She flinched, but with a grim determination she maintained command of her composure.

"You have a new housekeeper," she said.

Lawrence nodded. "Unfortunately, Ellen died last year," he said. "Cancer."

"I'm sorry to hear that."

"So were we." The older man's tone sounded more annoyed than regretful. "We've had a devil of a time trying to replace her. I believe the current woman is our third in the past six months."

Griff glanced toward Carmen in time to catch her grimace. Clearly, she was disgusted by the man's selfish reaction to his servant's tragic death.

"Is Andrew still here?" she asked.

"Yes, thankfully. He tends to the grounds and acts as our chauffeur when we need him."

Carmen nodded, pretending to scour her memories. "Didn't they have a son?"

"Yes." Lawrence shrugged. "I really don't know much about him."

Griff believed him. Lawrence was the sort of man who would consider the housekeeper's son beneath his notice.

Before Carmen could ask another question, there was the light sound of footsteps. Griff glanced toward the doorway to watch as a thin, waiflike woman wearing one of those designer dresses that looked plain but cost a thousand dollars drifted into the room. Her skin was pale and her dark auburn hair was pulled into a knot at the back of her head. Her eyes were unfocused.

A medicated zombie.

"Ah. Here's Vi," Lawrence said in bluff tones, moving to wrap an arm around his wife's narrow shoulders. A warning? "Look who's come for a visit. Little Carrie." His gaze returned to Carmen. "Although you're not so little now, are you?"

Vi didn't seem particularly joyful at the reunion. Instead, she blinked, looking confused.

"Why on earth are you standing in the kitchen?"

Carmen gave a lift of her hands. "I was just looking around my old home."

There was another awkward pause, and then Vi managed a quick smile that didn't reach her eyes.

"What a nice surprise. We should have some coffee," she said, as if she'd just been struck by divine inspiration. "Or tea if you prefer."

"Not here." Lawrence forced out a chuckle. "We'll go into the salon and be served like civilized people."

Vi nodded. The obedient zombie.

"If you want," she said, turning to head out of the kitchen. "This way."

Lawrence remained. "I'll find the housekeeper and get her started on the coffee," he said.

Carmen remained in the center of the kitchen, her expression hard with determination. Griff, however, captured her gaze and gave a nod of his head toward the door. Viola Jacobs would be much more likely to speak openly if she was alone with Carmen. Besides, this was a perfect opportunity to force Lawrence to answer his questions.

Carmen hesitated, as if trying to decide if she was going to insist on being the one to interrogate her uncle. She was the journalist, after all. Then she heaved a resigned sigh.

Clearly, she sensed that her uncle was too jumpy in her presence to let down his guard. For now, she'd have to content herself with trying to drill through her aunt's medicated haze.

Waiting until Carmen disappeared through the door, Griff glanced toward the older man.

"If you don't mind I'd like a tour around the estate," he said, the words more a command than a request.

Lawrence frowned. "There's not much to see. My family didn't invest in more than a few acres of land. Just enough to keep their private stables."

Griff spread his hands. "I'm just looking for an excuse to stretch my legs, to be honest," he said. "You know how it is after a couple days of traveling."

The man hesitated. He obviously wanted to say no. For whatever reason, he was unnerved by the return of his niece and wanting to get rid of them as quickly as possible.

But he was a businessman. And he wasn't willing to insult Griffin Archer, famous entrepreneur and current darling of Nasdaq.

"Certainly. I'll have a word with the housekeeper and grab my coat." He nodded his square head toward the door. "I'll meet you on the back terrace."

Griff exited the house and strolled across the wide veranda. His brows lifted at the magnificent sight that spread before him.

There was the usual sunken garden that was bedded for the winter, as well as a pool and tennis courts, but it was the rolling grounds that captured his attention. A layer of frost coated the pastures and the distant hills, shimmering like diamonds beneath the morning sunlight. It emphasized the quiet peace that surrounded the estate, reminding him of his grandparents' farm.

Beautiful.

Fifteen minutes passed before Lawrence at last joined

him on the terrace. The older man had pulled on a leather coat and managed to compose his expression into a polite mask.

Griff had seen the same expression a hundred times, in a hundred boardrooms.

The professional business face.

"Would you like to see the old stables?" Lawrence led Griff toward the steps without giving him time to answer. "I've had them converted into a garage."

Griff quickly followed the man off the terrace and with long strides was walking at his side.

"This is a lovely estate," he said.

"Yes." They used a pathway that circled the edge of the driveway and headed toward the long, white single-story building that was near the old paddocks. His steps were slow and deliberately casual. Just two men strolling together. "Carrie said that she was in the area, but she didn't say why," he at last spoke the words that had no doubt been trembling on his lips.

Griff shoved his hands in the pockets of the new trench coat he'd bought at the shop in the hotel. At some point he needed to get home so he could pack a suitcase. He'd rather spend the money for a plane ticket to California than to face the holiday shopping madness trying to buy new clothes.

"We didn't have any firm plans for Christmas, and Carmen mentioned that she hadn't been home in years," he said. "I convinced her that it was time for a visit."

"Ah." The fake smile remained firmly in place. "Wonderful."

"I'll admit that I was curious when Carmen told me that not one of her father's relatives have ever made an effort to contact her," Griff said, covertly watching the man at his side.

Lawrence's profile tensed, his hands clenching into fists. But with an admirable composure, his steps never faltered.

"She didn't tell you about Stuart?" Lawrence demanded, his gaze locked on the building just ahead of them.

"I know what happened to her parents."

"Then you should realize that her grandparents took her away and insisted that we have no contact with her."

Griff made a mental note to ask Carmen if she'd ever discussed the shooting with her grandparents. Did they have a reason to fear Lawrence might be as violent as his older brother Stuart?

"And you agreed?" he asked.

"Carrie had suffered enough," Lawrence smoothly pointed out. "The last thing we wanted was to remind her of what she'd lost."

They left the pathway to crunch over the graveled driveway that ran in front of the old stables.

"Very admirable," Griff said, his tone deliberately insincere. "But even if you were reluctant to visit her, I would assume that your lawyer would have insisted on a few visits."

"Lawyer?" Lawrence sent him a wary frown. "What are you talking about?"

Griff arched a brow, as if surprised by the question. "Carmen's inheritance, of course. She might not know much about business, but I do. She should have received a quarterly account of her share of the family funds."

The man scowled, trying to look suspicious. Instead, he looked nervous as hell.

"Just what is your interest in my niece?" he asked in gruff tones.

Griff refused to rise to the bait. He'd long ago earned more money than he could ever reasonably spend. No one in their right mind could accuse him of being a gold digger.

"She's in my care," he said. "I'll do whatever necessary to protect her."

"In your care?" Lawrence snapped. "What does that mean?"

"Exactly what I said. I intend to protect her."

"Against what?"

"Anyone who might think they could hurt her." His eyes narrowed with a silent warning. "Or take advantage of her."

Lawrence flattened his lips, quickening his steps as he reached the front of the stables.

"Here we are," he muttered, punching in a series of numbers on the keypad that was set next to the newly installed steel door.

Griff waited until the man had stepped inside and turned on the lights before he followed him. It wasn't that he was afraid. Even if Lawrence was responsible for terrorizing Carmen, he wouldn't be stupid enough to kill a respected businessman at his own home. Especially not a businessman who also happened to have connections to the top law officials in the FBI, CIA, and Homeland Security.

No, he was watching the man's jerky motions. It revealed an anxiety that was hidden beneath the practiced smile.

At last stepping through the door, Griff allowed his gaze to travel around the stables.

The long, narrow room maintained the original wood plank walls and vaulted ceiling with open beams, but the old stalls had been gutted and the floor covered with a cement slab to accommodate the six Corvettes that were in various stages of being restored.

"Nice," Griff said, as he walked toward the nearest car, a 1968 Rally Red Corvette convertible. "You work on them?" he asked.

"No." Lawrence stepped next to him. "My older son Matthew tinkers with them when he's around."

Griff sensed the man's eagerness to change the conversation. Which made him all the more determined to find out what the man was hiding.

"Do your sons work for the family business?" he asked.

Lawrence muttered a curse before turning to face Griff.

"I think you have a misunderstanding about the business, Archer."

"Do I?" Griff shrugged. "It seems fairly straightforward. One business. Four heirs."

"Not one business," the older man denied. "Two."

"What does that mean?"

Lawrence folded his arms over his chest. In the bright overhead lights, the wrinkles that carved his face were even more apparent.

"You're an entrepreneur," the man said.

"I am."

"Then you realize that the business landscape is constantly shifting and reforming."

Griff rolled his eyes. It was the sort of mumbo jumbo they taught in business school.

"I assume you have a point?"

The square face reddened. Griff sensed the older man would have given him a tongue-lashing if he had been just a random boyfriend of Carmen's. Or God forbid, one of his employees.

"As I'm sure you know, my brother and I inherited a lucrative chain of hardware stores."

"Yes."

"They'd been started by my grandparents and provided a comfortable life for our family. Unfortunately, by the mid-nineties the big-box home improvement stores had cut into our profits," he explained. "I could see then that it was only a matter of time before we were driven completely out of business."

Griff gave a slow nod. Later he would check the financial history of the company; for now he was more interested in what was making Lawrence so jumpy about Carmen's unexpected arrival.

"And your brother?"

"Stuart was older than me and had been deeply instilled

with a sense of family loyalty," Lawrence said. "He refused to accept that we had to close down at least half of the stores before we went into the red."

It was all perfectly logical, but the words sounded rehearsed.

"What did you do?" he asked.

Lawrence turned away, strolling toward the yellow Corvette that had the hood up and the engine pulled out and spread across the concrete floor in little pieces. Someone was ambitious to think they could put the thing back together.

"I continued to work with Stuart, but I started investing my money in the larger stores," Lawrence at last admitted.

It took Griff a second to decipher what the man was telling him.

"You invested in the competition?"

Lawrence's back stiffened, his tone defensive. "It wasn't competition. We were the past and they were the future. I had to think of my family."

Griff's lips twitched. Lawrence clearly wasn't the sort of man to go down with the ship. Instead, he scurried off like a rat and joined the enemy.

"Did your brother know?"

"I can't be sure." The older man's voice was muffled. "Toward the end he was overwhelmed with the fact we were headed for bankruptcy. I think that might have been part of the reason he . . ." There was a small pause, as if he was searching for the right word. "Snapped. He feared that he'd failed our parents."

"Hmm."

Lawrence abruptly turned, glaring at Griff. "There was nothing left of the business after I'd paid for the funerals."

Griff deliberately glanced toward the window that offered a view of the house, which had to be worth several million dollars.

"And what about this estate?"

Something flared through the pale eyes. A dangerous anger. Like a dog protecting his favorite bone.

"It belongs to the Jacobs family," he said.

"And Carmen isn't a Jacobs?"

With an abrupt motion, Lawrence was heading back toward the door. Griff assumed that meant the question-and-answer session was at an end.

"We should get back," Lawrence announced. "Vi will be wondering what happened to us."

Griff offered a meaningless smile, strolling along the line of cars until he reached the door at the far end of the stables.

"What's in here?" he asked, halting in front of a steel door set in the back wall.

"Nothing."

Shrugging off his mother's training on good manners, Griff grabbed the knob and shoved open the door.

A dark unease settled in the pit of his stomach as he studied the long, narrow room painted a bright white. Directly across from him was a glass case filled with a dozen different guns. Everything from a Sig Sauer to M16 rifles. At the far end of the space were two targets that were cut out in a human shape.

"A shooting range," he said, not needing to feign his surprise.

"My sons and I enjoy a little target practice," Lawrence snapped, at the end of his patience.

"An interesting hobby," Griff murmured, closing the door and crossing to join Lawrence.

They walked back to the house in silence.

Chapter Twelve

Carmen tapped her fingers on the carved arm of her chair. Frustration bubbled through her as she watched her aunt glance toward the doorway for the hundredth time.

The older woman had barely said more than ten words since they'd taken their seats in the salon. Not that Carmen hadn't tried.

She'd asked her aunt a dozen questions about the house and what she'd been doing over the past fourteen years. Then when the tea tray had arrived, she'd tried to encourage her aunt to discuss the upcoming holidays and the parties she was attending.

Nothing.

It was as if the woman's body was in the room, but she'd left her brain upstairs. Maybe in a jar with water, like it was dentures needing a good soak.

A pharmaceutical lobotomy.

Suddenly the words that she'd heard her father whisper when speaking about her aunt Vi made perfect sense.

"I can't imagine what is keeping Lawrence," the older woman breathed, aimlessly twisting a lace handkerchief between her heavily jeweled fingers.

"Griff is probably wanting to look around," Carmen said, silently hoping Griff was having better luck than she was.

Vi turned back to Carmen. "Why?"

"He's never been to this area before."

A slow, disturbing blink. "More tea?"

Carmen hid her shudder. "Not for me, thanks." She continued to tap her fingers, accepting she was going to have to be more direct. Subtle probing was getting her nowhere. "Tell me about Matthew and Baylor."

More blinking. "What about them?"

"I haven't seen my cousins since I was twelve years old. I'm just curious."

The older woman took a minute to dredge through her brain fuzz.

"They both graduated from college and live in Louisville," she finally announced.

"How nice." Carmen smiled. "What are they doing with their lives?"

"Doing?"

Good. God. "Are they working?"

"Oh well, they work for Lawrence." Vi gave a vague wave of her hand. "I'm not sure exactly what they do."

"Are they married? Do they have kids?"

"No."

Carmen grimaced. She wasn't sure if the woman would have noticed if there'd been a couple weddings and a dozen kids.

"At least they live close enough for you to spend time with them," she forced herself to say.

"Not really. They're both very busy," Vi said. "And they travel a lot."

Carmen's fingers tightened on the arm of her chair. "Travel where?"

"All over."

Vi's eyes drifted back toward the door and Carmen knew

she'd lost her again. She sighed. It was like trying to scoop water out of a bucket with her bare hands.

Rising to her feet, she aimlessly wandered across the room, glancing out the window that offered a view of the side garden. When she was very young, her mother would set up a table in the garden so they could have a tea party with her dolls.

The memory was interrupted as she caught sight of a car pulling past the house to halt in front of the nearby garage. She stepped closer to the window, craning her neck to watch as a man climbed out of the vehicle.

He was average height and looked slender beneath his leather coat. His hair was a sandy blond and tousled from the breeze. She guessed his age to be late twenties.

"Who is that?" she asked.

There was a rustle of expensive silk as Vi shifted in her chair, but she didn't bother to rise to her feet.

"Excuse me?"

Carmen's gaze remained locked on the man who had moved to open the trunk of the car.

"Someone just arrived."

"It could be one of the boys," Vi said. "Or maybe Andrew."

Carmen frowned. The man was glancing toward the garage, not the main house, but he was too young to be Andrew.

"Is Ronnie around?" she demanded.

"Who?"

Carmen rolled her eyes. Of course her aunt didn't recognize the name. She was no doubt lucky to remember her own.

"Andrew's son."

"Oh. I suppose he comes to visit his dad, but I haven't seen him."

Carmen turned back to study Vi's blank face. "He doesn't

live in the area?" she asked. Blink, blink, blink. Carmen shook her head. "Never mind. I'll be back."

Grabbing the coat that she'd draped over the back of her chair, Carmen allowed her distant memories to lead her out of the room and down the hallway to a side door. Stepping into the small garden, she crossed the paving stones at an angle, managing to intercept the young man as he neared the side of the garage that led to the private apartment.

"Ronnie?" she called out.

The man halted, seeming to pause before he slowly pivoted to watch her hurry toward him.

"Can I help you?"

Close up, Carmen could make out the thin features. The narrow nose and tight slash of a mouth. His cheekbones were high, and he had pale blue eyes that were surrounded by sandy lashes. His skin was pale and pocked with old acne scars.

Her gaze lowered to take in the cheap coat, and the worn overnight suitcase he was carrying in one hand.

"I'm Carmen Jacobs," she said in bright tones. "I used to live here with my parents."

His brows drew together. "Carmen?"

"Carrie," she added.

"Carrie." The pale eyes widened. "Of course. I haven't seen you in forever."

"It's been a while." She glanced toward the bag in his hands. "Are you visiting your family?"

"Just Andrew," he said. "My mother passed last year."

Carmen didn't have to fake her pang of sympathy. From what she could remember, Ronnie had been very close to his mother. She also remembered he'd always called his father Andrew. Maybe because he wasn't his real father, or just because the two didn't get along.

"I heard. I'm so sorry."

He offered a pained grimace. "She was sick for a long time. It was a blessing, really."

Carmen nodded. "It's still hard."

"Yes."

"Do you live in the area?"

Ronnie shook his head. "No, but Andrew insisted I come back for Christmas. The past year has been difficult for him." He glanced from her to the looming mansion. "Are you moving back to Louisville?"

She couldn't entirely squash her shudder. Even after fourteen years this place haunted her dreams.

"No. Just passing through."

His gaze remained on the big house, as if wondering why anyone would walk away from such luxury. Understandable. Looking at the wealthy from a distance always made it seem as if they lived golden lives.

You had to be beneath the roof to realize they were just as messed up as everyone else.

"I suppose you're having Christmas with the family?" he finally asked.

"That's the plan." She shrugged. "Although, I have to admit that they really don't feel like they're my family after all these years."

His lips flattened as he returned his gaze to her face. "Blood is blood, no matter how many years pass."

What did that mean? Carmen didn't have a clue. She pasted a meaningless smile on her lips.

"What have you been doing with yourself? Did you get married and have a family?"

"No, not yet."

"Where do you live now?"

"Here and there," he said. "I like to travel around."

Carmen hesitated. Was he being deliberately vague? Or was he naturally awkward around women?

"That's nice. I've been traveling myself." She made her tone casual. "In fact, I just drove here from Kansas City."

She carefully watched his expression, looking for any hint that she'd struck a nerve.

There was nothing.

"It must have been cold there," he said, his expression unchanging. "I heard there was a snowstorm in the Midwest."

"There was. Did you have to drive through it?"

"No."

Stalemate. Carmen reverted to her journalistic skills. It was possible Ronnie was trying to hide something. On the other hand, there were people who simply didn't like to talk about themselves. At least not directly.

She needed a new approach.

"It's been several years, but I still remember when you were young and you helped me sneak cookies from the jar your mother kept on top of the fridge," she said.

His wary expression eased. "It didn't seem fair to keep them out of reach."

Carmen wrinkled her nose. "She probably knew I'd eat the whole batch if I could get my hands on them," she said with a laugh. "I had a terrible sweet tooth."

His thin lips moved in a ghost of a smile. "Not the whole batch. I usually stole a few for myself," he admitted.

"Do you have a job you can do from home?"

He gave a lift of his shoulder. "I do construction, and gardening when I can find a job."

"Like your dad."

An indefinable emotion darkened his eyes. "I guess you could say that."

Her lips parted. She wanted to probe deeper into his travels, but before she could ask, the door at the top of the stairs was pulled open and a short, heavyset man with silver hair stepped onto the landing. He was wearing a faded muscle shirt and a pair of jeans, with bare feet.

Andrew.

"Ronald," the man called down, barely glancing at Carmen.

"I should go," Ronnie muttered.

"It was good to see you," Carmen said as Ronnie hurried toward the stairs.

"You too," he said without glancing back.

Carmen released a frustrated sigh. Could Ronnie be the one tormenting her?

He hadn't seemed to recognize her, but that could be an act. And he'd admitted he was more or less a drifter, which meant he could have been traveling around the country killing women and terrifying Carmen.

But why?

Their paths had crossed when they were young; they lived on the same property, after all. But Ronnie had never been aggressive. And as far as she could remember she'd never done anything that would anger him.

Lost in her thoughts, she was caught off guard when her uncle suddenly stepped into the garden, closely followed by Griff.

"Ah, there you are, Carrie," the older man said, his expression strained.

Carmen briefly wondered if Griff had caused her uncle's tension. Probably. For a man who seemed so cool and collected, Griff had a unique ability to get beneath a person's skin.

"Done with your tour?" she asked.

"Yes." Lawrence cleared his throat, his hands shoved in the pockets of his coat. "I'm afraid we have plans for today, but you'll come to lunch tomorrow? We'd love to spend some time with you."

Carmen resisted the urge to roll her eyes. It was perhaps the most insincere invitation she'd ever received.

"I wouldn't want to intrude," she said.

"No intrusion." Lawrence managed to force the words past his stiff lips. "I insist."

"We'd be happy to join you," Griff smoothly agreed. "Until then we're staying at the Regal downtown."

Griff didn't try to draw Carmen into conversation as they drove toward the center of town. Her face was pale, her eyes dark with the wounds he'd forced her to reopen.

Leaving the truck in the hands of the uniformed valet, he wrapped his arm around Carmen's shoulders and led her through the double glass doors. They angled across the expansive lobby that was festively decorated for the holidays, and hit the bank of elevators.

A few minutes later they were safely enclosed in the privacy of their room.

Griff moved to the desk near the window that overlooked the city and opened his computer. Behind him he could sense Carmen wandering around the large suite that was designed in muted shades of tan and brown. It was an old-school hotel that had once catered to the wealthy travelers, and later to businessmen who demanded the finest accommodations.

The elegance of a bygone era remained, along with a solid masculinity that was rare in newer hotels.

At last her aimless circles led her to stand next to his shoulder.

"What are you doing?" she asked.

He pulled up one of the programs he'd helped to create for Interpol and typed in the name Lawrence Jacobs.

"Running a trace on your uncle's finances."

"Why?"

"I think he's hiding something," Griff said. "And I want to know what it is."

"Even if he is, that has nothing to do with the pictures I received."

Griff typed in the names of the cousins. "Don't be so sure," he warned.

Carmen made a sound of impatience. "You met him. Do you really think he's a serial killer?"

Griff straightened from the computer and turned to face his companion.

She was staring at him with blatant frustration. Which was better than the bruised expression he'd seen earlier, but still not what he wanted to see.

Months ago he'd encountered a pretty woman with a glorious smile standing on the beach. She'd been confident, flirtatious, and captivating. Granted, she'd been trying to trick him into an interview, but he wanted that woman back.

"I think he's a clever businessman who has the morals of a shark," he said, reaching out to unbutton her coat.

She allowed him to gently tug off the outer garment, but she was clearly distracted by his claim.

"That still doesn't make him a murderer," she said.

He tossed her coat on the nearby sofa, his gaze never leaving her upturned face.

"We still don't know that there've been any murders," he said, prepared for her protest. Reaching out, he touched a finger to her parted lips before she could blast him with her outrage. "Please, Carmen, hear me out."

Her face flushed, but with an effort she gave a small nod. "Fine."

He took a step closer, his fingers brushing through her curls, which had been tangled by the winter breeze.

"What if your uncle decided that he didn't want to share his inheritance with his niece?"

His question caught her off guard. "What inheritance?"

His lips twisted. For all of Carmen's acute intelligence and undoubted success, she could be remarkably naïve. No wonder her family had been so eager to take advantage of her.

The knowledge stirred his deepest protective instincts. Something that should probably worry him.

"The business. The estate. Probably stocks and bonds," he told her. "It could be in the millions."

Her eyes widened. "If I had a million-dollar inheritance, I would know about it."

He brushed a curl behind her ear before allowing his fingers to trace the delicate line of her jaw.

"How?" he asked. "Your grandparents cut off all contact with the Jacobses. It would be simple for Lawrence to take control of your share."

"But wouldn't there be lawyers involved?"

That had been Griff's first thought as well. If there was as much money involved as he suspected, there was no way there weren't a clutch of lawyers eager to become Carmen's advocate. It would mean a fat payroll for them. Then he remembered that she would have been a minor at the time.

"Not if your uncle had been named as executor of your father's will," he said. "Lawrence would have had full rights to make decisions for you and your inheritance. And since your grandparents had forbidden any contact, it would have been difficult for anyone to warn you that you were being denied your share."

"Okay." She gave a grudging nod. "That seems reasonable, but I still don't get the connection to those horrible pictures."

He cupped her cheek in his palm, knowing his words were bound to hurt Carmen. It didn't matter if she was close to her family or not; they were all she had left. Now he suspected they might be her worst enemies.

It was bound to cause even more damage to a woman who'd suffered more than her share of tragedy.

"For the past fourteen years you were either concentrating

on your studies or consumed with your research on your book. You didn't have the time for or interest in reconnecting with your family."

"True."

"There's also the fact that you were relatively powerless," he said.

She jerked, instantly offended. "Powerless?"

"Your grandparents were no doubt fine people, but they weren't rich," he said, his thumb tracing the full curve of her lower lip.

"No," she agreed. "They lived a simple life."

"Then they both were gone and you were a struggling journalist."

"Okay." She glared at him. "But that doesn't make me powerless."

He belatedly realized how important it was for Carmen to deny the idea she was helpless. He got it. Like him, she'd been incapable of saving her mother. And now she was at the mercy of some unknown lunatic.

She was clinging to her fierce need to be in control of her life.

"You're right," he murmured softly, his gaze sweeping over her face. "You, Carmen Jacobs, are a very dangerous woman."

A tiny tremor shook her body as she easily heard the sincerity in his voice.

She was dangerous. He'd known that from the first day. And even after he'd discovered she was trying to use him, she'd lingered in his mind.

He told himself it was because he was furious that she'd played him for a fool, but he'd always known that was a lie.

She'd lingered because she was special.

Dangerous.

She drew in a slow, deep breath, as if trying to break free of the sensual spell that was weaving around them.

"Finish your theory," she commanded.

He suppressed a smile. His body was tense with anticipation, but he made no effort to press his advantage. He wasn't sure when it'd happened, but he'd already decided that Carmen was going to be a part of his life for the foreseeable future.

They had all the time in the world to explore the heat that sizzled between them.

"My theory is that you haven't been in a position where you possessed the support or finances to battle against a tribe of expensive lawyers."

She slowly nodded. "Not until my book hit the best-seller list."

"Exactly. Now you have money, plus connections to the press that offer you leverage if Lawrence tried to intimidate you," he continued. "It wouldn't be nearly as easy to turn you away if you started snooping into the past."

She took a long time to process his words, the pain that he'd been expecting slowly spreading across her pale features. Griff's fingers brushed over her cheek, his heart twisting with regret.

Then, with the courage that had allowed her to endure the death of her parents to become a strong, successful woman, she squared her shoulders.

"Even if he's stolen millions from me, that wouldn't turn him into a psychopath."

"He wouldn't have to be a psychopath. Not if the pictures were faked," he reminded her.

"What would be the point?"

He hesitated, not wanting to hurt her further. "Being stalked by a lunatic would keep you distracted."

She stiffened, her eyes narrowing. Her instinctive ability to read people was clearly warning her that he wasn't being fully honest.

"That's not why you think Lawrence did it."

"No." He shrugged, silently conceding she wouldn't stop digging until he revealed what was troubling him. No wonder she became a journalist. "I think it's for his protection."

She studied him in confusion. "What are you talking about?"

"I think your uncle wanted to make sure that if you ever decided to show up and start asking uncomfortable questions he would be able to get rid of you."

She went perfectly still, as if she'd been frozen into place. A minute ticked past. Then another. Griff's hand traced the curve of her neck, feeling the moment that she swallowed her horror and forced herself to accept the danger she was facing.

"You mean that he might try to kill me?"

"Yes," he said bluntly. "It would no doubt be a last resort, but your uncle strikes me as a man who plans ahead. In the event he had to dispose of you, he'd make sure it couldn't be traced back to him."

He heard her breath catch, but she grimly refused to flinch. Instead, she considered his hypothesis.

"With pictures of supposedly dead women?"

"If something happened to you . . ." He was forced to halt and clear the lump from his throat. Silently he reminded himself that no one was going to be allowed to hurt Carmen. Not on his watch. "The first thing the cops would suspect would be a jealous lover."

"I don't have a lover."

His fingers lightly touched her lips. "Not yet."

"Griff," she breathed.

With an effort, he forced himself to concentrate. This was too important for him to be distracted.

"Once that was ruled out, the cops would look to see who would benefit from your death."

"Lawrence," she said.

"That would be my guess," he agreed. "It wouldn't take

long for the cops to learn that you are related to the wealthy Jacobs family. The last thing your uncle would want is a bunch of detectives rummaging around his finances and asking inconvenient questions. He would need to make sure they were too occupied to consider the money angle."

She nodded, her quick mind capable of leaping to his inevitable conclusion.

"So, if I turned up dead, everyone would assume I was killed by the psycho who was sending me pictures," she said. "The man I am publicly chasing."

He lowered his hand, grabbing her fingers in a tight grip. "It would be a cunning plan."

"Cunning?"

He gave her fingers a squeeze. "You know what I mean."

She started to nod, only to stiffen as if she was struck by a sudden thought.

"What about the person who cut me in Kansas City?" she demanded, her hand lifting to touch her upper arm. "I would have known if it was Lawrence."

He arched a brow. "Are you positive?"

"I . . ." She released a harsh breath. "No, I can't be sure."

"There's also your cousins," Griff added, his voice tight with anger at the reminder she'd been injured. "Or he could have hired someone in the Kansas City area to drive to the hotel and wait for you. And it would have been easy to send the flowers. Except he didn't realize that you no longer went by Carrie."

"That would explain Lawrence's surprise at seeing me." Her expression hardened as she accepted there was a possibility that her only remaining family wanted her dead. "If he's monitoring me, he would think I was flying to Baltimore."

"Yes."

They both fell silent as they considered the thought of Lawrence coldly plotting the murder of his niece, then Carmen pulled away from him to wander toward the window.

"God. He would have to be sick," she breathed.

He moved to stand behind her, his hands resting on her shoulders. He desperately wanted to comfort her.

"Greed can be a form of sickness," he said. "I've met people who would lie, cheat, and sell their own mother for money."

She shuddered beneath his hands. "How long will it take to get the information you need?"

"It could take hours," he said, then he grimaced. If Lawrence was truly clever, he probably had several layers of bullshit that Griff would have to dig through to get to the pertinent details of his business dealings. "Even days."

"What should we do until then?"

Heat scorched through his veins, hardening his body with a painful need.

"I have a few ideas," he assured her, lowering his head to nuzzle the side of her neck.

She stiffened before she released a soft sigh and melted against his chest. He parted his lips, allowing his tongue to touch her soft skin.

A hint of citrus and warm woman exploded in his mouth. Delicious. His hands skimmed down her arms before he grabbed her hips and tugged her even closer.

Although she was inches shorter than him, she fit against him perfectly.

His lips moved to the hollow just beneath her ear, his arousal pressed against her lower back. He could stand there all day. Just holding her in his arms.

She angled her head, allowing him greater access. His arms tightened, his lips skimming to the base of her neck. Okay, holding her was fantastic, but there was a bed just through the nearby door . . .

A low purr interrupted the silence, and Griff swore

beneath his breath as Carmen instantly pulled out of his embrace.

"What's that?" she demanded, turning to glance around the room.

"The worst timing in the history of the world," he muttered as he crossed the floor to snatch up the hotel phone.

He didn't know why the front desk would be contacting them, but he assumed it had to be important. A minute later he'd replaced the phone and turned to meet Carmen's curious gaze.

"Well?" she demanded.

"It seems we have a guest waiting for us downstairs," he told her.

She frowned. "Who?"

"Your cousin. Baylor Jacobs."

Chapter Thirteen

Carmen concentrated on their surroundings as they stepped off the elevator.

The hotel truly was lovely. Built in the English Renaissance style, it had long, arched arcades and towering ceilings with hand-painted plaster reliefs. She could easily imagine long-ago travelers in elegant clothes as they moved across the marble floor.

At her side, Griff placed a hand on her lower back as they walked down the second-floor gallery. The heat of his skin seared through the fabric of her skirt, offering a welcome reminder that for the first time in a very long time, she wasn't alone.

The fuzzy sensation was destroyed the second she caught sight of the man seated at a table near the arched opening that overlooked the lobby below.

Baylor Jacobs. Her cousin.

He'd changed. It'd been fourteen years since she'd last seen him, after all, and the pudgy teenager with an overbite and a constant scowl had thinned down, while the protruding teeth had been modified until they were barely noticeable. The wonders of the modern orthodontist.

His dark brown hair was sternly slicked back and he wore an expensive suit that was designed to convey the impression of success. His eyes, however, remained the same.

They were a pale hazel, with a cold, flat stare that had always reminded Carmen of a snake.

That hadn't changed.

An unreasonable anger speared through her as she watched him rise to his feet at her approach, his lips pressed into a flat line.

She was a part of his family that had been estranged for years. Surely, most normal people would at least pretend to be pleased at the opportunity to be reunited with her?

Instead, his expression was hard with blatant suspicion.

He wasn't looking at her as if she was his long-lost cousin. He was looking at her as if she was the enemy.

A strange, corrosive disappointment joined her anger in a toxic brew that bubbled in the pit of her stomach.

Out of the corner of her eye she caught sight of Griff sharply turning his head to study her tense profile. As if he could sense her emotional turmoil. No surprise. From the beginning he seemed to possess an uncanny ability to read her moods.

In contrast, Baylor Jacobs was holding out his hand, completely impervious to her chilly expression.

"Carrie," he said, his lips stretching even farther.

Definitely snakelike.

"Carmen," she corrected, ignoring his hand.

"Carmen, of course." He lowered his hand, turning to study her companion. "And you must be Griffin Archer."

"I am."

"Thanks for agreeing to meet with me." Baylor waved his hands toward the small table near the scrolled iron banister. Griff moved to pull out her chair, giving her shoulder a light squeeze as she sat down before he took his seat beside her.

Baylor settled across from them, nodding toward the glossy menu. "Drink?"

Carmen shook her head. "No, thank you."

Baylor cleared his throat. "You haven't changed. You still look just like your mother," he said.

Carmen's chin angled upward. She had a sudden memory of Baylor stealing her doll and tossing it down the well. One of several times he'd made her cry.

The truth was, she'd never liked her cousin. Either one of them.

"Actually, I've changed a lot. Especially over the past couple of years," she said, her words a warning. "I'm not the little girl you remember."

He visibly struggled to make his expression friendly. She wondered how much an effort it was.

"Yes, congratulations on your book," he said. "I hear that it's been quite a success."

"You haven't read it?"

"Not yet," he admitted. "But I've seen it in airports."

Carmen forced herself to take a deep breath. The day had been stressful, on top of a week that had been epically stressful. She was losing focus of why they were in Louisville.

This wasn't a trip down memory lane. She was here to discover if anyone in her family was responsible for sending her those horrid pictures.

"Nice to know the book is on the shelves," she said, studying her cousin's pale face. "If you've been in airports, that must mean you travel?"

He blinked, as if caught off guard by her question. "I'm expected to check on our stores on a regular basis. I'm usually on the road or in the air several days a month."

Which meant no one would have noticed if he'd taken a quick trip to Kansas City.

"After a year of being in one hotel after another, I'll be glad to settle at home," she said.

"And where is that?"

It was her turn to blink. "What?"

"Where is your home?"

"I have my grandparents' farm."

"And that's it?"

She arched a brow. She already knew where this was going. The question was whether she wanted to try to steer the conversation back to Baylor's recent travels. Then she realized it was even more important to learn why he was clearly suspicious of her. And just how desperate he might be to get rid of her.

Either to protect himself, or someone close to him.

"Why are you asking?" she demanded.

He leaned forward, resting his forearms on the table. At the same time his bland features lost their battle to look anything but grim.

She sensed the gloves were about to come off.

"I could try to pretend I'm here out of cousinly affection, but we both know it would be a lie," he said, proving her suspicion right. "And I'm not very subtle. My older brother was gifted with all the charm in the family."

She deliberately glanced over his shoulder. From below, the sound of children's laughter echoed through the air.

"Where is Matthew?"

"I assume my brother is still in bed. He usually spends the holiday season stumbling from one drunken gala to another." A genuine aversion flared through the hazel eyes. "He's very good at parties, but not so good about getting to work on time."

So. If Baylor was covering for someone, it wasn't his older brother.

She was pretty sure he'd throw Matthew under the bus just for the fun of it.

"So you were elected to come and speak with me?" she asked.

He pretended to look confused. "Elected?"

"Uncle Lawrence called you, didn't he?"

Baylor sat back, straightening the cuffs of his crisp white shirt. Carmen recognized the ploy. He needed time to think of his answer.

"He came to the office, and I could tell that he had something on his mind," he at last said.

"Me?"

"Your unexpected arrival," he clarified.

Her lips twisted. She could almost see her uncle jumping into his car and racing to his office to warn his sons that the sky was falling.

Just like Chicken Little.

"He wasn't happy to see me?"

"Of course he was," Baylor lied with smooth ease. "My father was heartbroken at the loss of his brother and sister-in-law. And it only made matters worse when your grandparents cut off all contact with you."

She snorted. "But."

"Excuse me?"

"I sense a 'but,'" she said. "You know. Uncle Lawrence is happy to see me, but . . ."

A flush stained the pale face. "He *is* happy."

Carmen arched a brow. "But."

"But he is curious why you would choose this moment to travel to Louisville."

She felt Griff reach beneath the table to lay his hand on her knee. A silent warning not to give away the fact that they were in town for more than a family reunion.

She shrugged. "I have a few weeks before my next book

tour starts. And it's the time of year most people want to visit their family."

He studied her with his snake-gaze, clearly not comforted by her explanation.

"And that's all? Just a long overdue reunion?" he demanded.

She looked confused. "What else could it be?"

There was a long silence before Baylor turned his attention to the man seated next to her.

"My dad mentioned a conversation with you, Mr. Archer."

"Griff."

"Griff," Baylor stiffly agreed. "My father said that you were interested in the family business."

Griff shifted in his seat, angling forward. A subtle gesture of dominance.

"Carmen is a part of your family, whether you want to recognize her or not."

Baylor's fingers stopped their drumming and clenched into a fist. "She is certainly a part of the family. A most welcome part."

Carmen rolled her eyes. "Again with the *but*," she muttered.

Baylor ignored her. Was he one of those men who thought women should be seen and not heard? Or did he assume Griff was the one pressing Carmen to try to claim her inheritance?

As if he wasn't worth billions.

"But not the business. That was created by my father out of the ruins of the original stores." He sent a brief glance toward Carmen. "I'm afraid that there's nothing left of your father's inheritance."

"And the house?" Griff demanded.

A darkness filled the hazel eyes. "It is always given to the eldest son. A feudal system, but that's how the will was set up by my grandfather."

Carmen didn't need to read minds to know what her

cousin thought about the house being handed over to his brother.

"So you'll be left in the cold?" she prodded. "Just like me."

His jaw hardened. "Someday I'll build my own estate."

"I'm still not sure why you insisted on this meeting," she said, veering back on topic. So far she hadn't learned anything of interest. Time to shake things up. "If you wanted to convince me I have no right to your money, you could have waited until Christmas lunch. Then the whole family could have all banded together to make me feel like a gold digger."

Baylor stiffened, and then he tried to look contrite.

"I'm sorry, I'm not doing a very good job with this."

"Maybe I shouldn't be a job," she pointed out. "Maybe I should just be your cousin."

He released a heavy sigh, his expression difficult to read in the shadows of the arch.

"Carrie—"

"Carmen."

"Carmen," he forced himself to say. "I'm sorry. Father was worried you might be here to cause trouble and I promised that I would have a word with you. I realize now that this was all a mistake." He studied her face, as if judging whether she was going to accept his apology. "Can we start over?"

Intent on Baylor, Carmen gave a small jump when a shadow fell over the table and a hand landed on Baylor's shoulder.

"I can see I'm too late," a male voice drawled. "You've already managed to piss everyone off, haven't you, bro?"

Carmen glanced up at the man who'd silently appeared next to her.

Matthew Jacobs had a vague resemblance to his younger brother, but everything about him was . . . more.

His features were more finely carved, his hair was a rich mahogany and tousled in a way that made him look like some woman had just run her fingers through it. He had a shadow of whiskers on his square jaw and he was wearing a pair of faded jeans and a silver cashmere sweater. His green eyes glittered with a roguish sense of humor. But when he smiled, he abruptly reminded Carmen of a shark.

All pearly white teeth and ruthless hunger.

She shivered, wondering if it was her imagination that was causing her to look at her own family like they were dangerous animals.

"Matthew, what are you doing here?" Baylor demanded, roughly knocking his brother's hand off his shoulder.

"Cleaning up your mess, as usual," Matthew said, his gaze never wavering from Carmen.

"You—" Baylor halted, before he cleared his throat and attempted to disguise his obvious dislike for Matthew. "Carmen, you remember my brother?"

"Of course," she said. "Hello, Matthew."

"Exquisite," he said, his gaze skimming over her face before his interest turned to the silent man at her side. "And Mr. Archer."

"Please, call me Griff."

"Griff," Matthew agreed, holding out his hand. "This is quite an honor. My brother will tell you I'm not much of a businessman, but even I've heard of you."

Griff rose to shake hands before sliding back into his seat, his arm moving to rest across her shoulders. She didn't mind. Confronting her cousins was just as difficult as she'd expected it to be.

"I'm not sure if that's good or bad," he said.

"Good for you, and bad for me." Matthew flashed his shark smile. "Once the word that you're in town gets around you'll be inundated with invitations, and I'll be a forgotten has-been."

"I'm not here to party," Griff said.

Matthew shrugged. "No, according to my frantic father and bumbling brother, you're here to steal away our fortune."

"Matthew," Baylor snapped, his face flushed.

Carmen broke into the looming squabble. "I assume you've come here to ask the same questions?"

Matthew raised a hand to press it to the center of his chest in a gesture of sincerity.

"No, I'm here to welcome my cousin to our home," he assured her. "I'm very happy to have you here, my dear, and I personally hope you'll consider staying so we can have a proper reunion."

She hid her grimace. Matthew had a slick charm that she'd encountered too many times during her book tour.

"I plan to come to lunch tomorrow," she told him.

"Good. Perhaps if you stay a few more days we could plan a proper celebration—"

"I thought you were skiing in Aspen after Christmas?" Baylor interrupted.

Matthew snapped his fingers, as if he'd just remembered his plans.

"That's right." He sent Carmen a regretful glance. "I'm afraid I already have my reservations."

"Please don't change them on my account," Carmen said, her interest captured by his casual words.

"We'll still have tomorrow," Matthew said.

"Do you travel a lot?" she asked.

Matthew shrugged. "Sometimes for business." There was a loud snort from Baylor. Matthew chuckled. "Mostly for pleasure," he admitted.

"I've been crossing the country for the past year." She offered an encouraging smile, as if she was fascinated by his journeys. "I'm surprised we've never bumped into each other."

"Actually, we were in the same city. At least for a few hours," he surprisingly told her.

Her heart missed a beat and she felt Griff stiffen at her side. "Really?"

"Yes. I was in Chicago for the opening of a friend's night-club when I saw you on the local television station talking about your book."

Carmen frowned. Her book signing in Chicago had been over six months ago.

"Why didn't you contact me?" she asked.

His smile remained, but she sensed a sudden wariness. He was hiding something.

"I thought about calling the station to get your number, but I was afraid they would think I was some weirdo." He lifted his hands in a dismissive gesture. "And besides, I wasn't sure you would even want to see me."

With a sharp motion, Baylor was on his feet. Was he afraid that Carmen could sense Matthew was lying?

"We should go," the younger man announced.

Matthew scowled. "We haven't had a drink yet."

"I'm sure if we checked your blood alcohol it would be over the limit from last night," Baylor mocked.

Genuine annoyance tightened the older man's handsome features. "You nag like a wife. It's no wonder I've never wanted to get married."

Baylor grabbed his brother's arm, sending Carmen an impatient glance.

"We'll see you tomorrow," he said.

Her lips twitched. It was difficult to imagine how he could have made the words sound less enthusiastic.

"I can't wait."

Chapter Fourteen

Dusk came early. Along with it was a brisk breeze that made Hunter shiver as he paced along the edge of the lake. Not the sort of night anyone wanted to be out walking, but it was the only way he could be assured of privacy.

He needed to think. And revise his plan.

The last thing he'd expected was for Carrie to travel to Louisville. She was supposed to be in Baltimore, following the clues he'd so conveniently left for her. It should have taken her days. Even a week.

That would have given him time to do his duty here, and then travel to his next location to complete the next act in his ongoing drama.

His first impulse had been to kill her.

He had a feral desire to lay her in a nearby field, her golden curls spread around her head like a halo. Her eyes would be wide with wonderment as he revealed himself to her. Then, he would slowly slide a knife into her heart.

In the garden of memory, in the palace of dreams . . .

He would watch her blood seep into the ground. *His* ground.

And he would be free. Free of the past. Free of his nightmares.

But even as his dark desires had tried to lure him into a hasty finale, he'd resisted temptation.

There were still games to be played, he'd sternly reminded himself. And women to be savored. Not to mention a couple loose ends that needed to be tidied up.

No. He would have to wait. Which meant that his timeline was screwed. Pulling the phone from his pocket, he prepared to start making the necessary calls.

At the same time, he glanced around at his surroundings, a wistful regret tugging at his heart.

"It's no use going back to yesterday, because I was a different person then," he whispered.

December 25, Louisville, KY

Griff rose early. It wasn't just that he'd wanted to sort through the vast amount of information his program had managed to collect overnight. Or the fact that he'd been awake since five o'clock with his body clenched with a frustrated desire.

The information, after all, could wait. And he'd made the conscious decision after returning to their room yesterday not to pursue the erotic awareness that sizzled between him and Carmen.

Being in Louisville was draining her spirit. He'd seen it in the slump of her shoulders and her weary expression as she'd wandered around the room.

When she came to his bed, he wanted her warm and willing and whole.

Nope, the reason he was up at the crack of dawn had been to make sure that the surprise he'd put into motion yesterday had arrived.

Dressed in a pair of black slacks and a charcoal sweater, he headed down to the lobby. Thirty minutes later he had a slender package tucked in his pocket and a tray loaded with coffee, scones, and pots of jam and cream.

He'd just returned to the room and crossed to set the tray

on the low coffee table when a noise had him turning toward the guest bedroom.

Carmen.

Instant awareness heated his blood as his gaze skimmed over her damp curls and her rosy cheeks. His attention lowered to her slender body, which was covered by a terry cloth robe.

She'd clearly just stepped out of the shower, and her citrus scent filled the room.

"Merry Christmas, sunshine," he murmured.

She appeared momentarily flustered, as if she'd forgotten what day it was, and then she was moving toward the tray with brisk steps.

"Has your computer program found anything?" she asked.

"We can discuss it later," he assured her, watching with pleasure as she filled a plate with three scones and a large dollop of cream. He didn't know where she put the food, but he loved knowing that he could provide it for her.

Like he was some primal animal.

She took a large bite of the scone, unaware of his weird thoughts. Then she gave a shake of her head.

"No, I'd rather concentrate on our investigation."

He arched a brow. "It's Christmas."

"And I'm about to spend it with the family I never wanted to see again, in a house where my parents died," she reminded him in dry tones.

He grimaced. She had a point.

"Okay."

He crossed the room to the desk next to the large window. Sliding out the leather chair, he took a seat and pulled up the program he'd used to investigate Lawrence Jacobs's finances.

A silence filled the room as he sorted through the vast amount of information he'd already managed to gather. Most of it he deleted. He was more interested in the past than the current accounts.

At last he heaved a frustrated sigh. "So far it looks like Lawrence was telling the truth about the family business. It was running in the red before Lawrence closed the stores and sold the properties to pay off the creditors," he told her.

She sat aside her empty plate and leaned over his shoulder. Instantly he was surrounded by her warm scent.

"And the estate?" she asked.

Griff cleared his throat, trying to pretend he wasn't reacting to her like a hormonal teenage boy.

"Your grandfather's will is written to make certain that house is to be passed to the oldest son."

She moved back, turning to pace toward the large windows. "So my uncle has no reason to try to get rid of me."

Griff grimaced. He truly believed the stalker had some connection to her past. But so far it was nothing more than gut instinct.

He needed proof before he could try to involve the authorities.

"I'm continuing to search," he assured her, his brows tugged together as he skimmed over Lawrence's private bank accounts. "Your uncle managed to use a large influx of cash to purchase three new big-box stores after your father's death, but the accounts are so tangled together that it's impossible to unravel where the money actually came from without more information."

She heaved a rueful sigh. "We should have gone to Baltimore."

Rising to his feet, Griff moved to stand next to Carmen, who continued to admire the view. Who could blame her? The morning sun was bright in the cloudless blue sky, while a layer of frost added a glittering beauty to the buildings that curved along the edge of the Ohio River.

A perfect Christmas morning. A damned shame they were going to waste the day with the Jacobs family.

"Before you start any 'I told you so's,' I have something for you," he said.

Clearly surprised by his soft words, she turned to face him. "For me?"

He pulled the long, narrow package from his pocket and handed it to her.

"For you."

She studied the gold paper that was neatly wrapped around the box and the tiny bow.

"Where did you get this?"

"Do you ask Santa Claus where he gets his gifts?" He reached to tuck a curl behind her ear. "It's Christmas magic."

"But I didn't—"

"Shh." He leaned down to press a kiss to her lips. "Just open it."

She wavered for a minute, then, lowering her gaze, she ripped off the paper and pulled the top off the box.

Griff stepped closer, watching as her face softened with shocked pleasure at the sight of the gold bracelet with antique charms that was nestled into the ivory satin.

"Oh, Griff." She lightly touched a charm in the shape of a seashell with a dusting of tiny diamonds. "It's perfect."

Satisfaction raced through him. He'd contacted a friend who owned one of the most exclusive antique stores in L.A. He'd told him he wanted something unique. A special gift for a special lady. Then he'd paid an obscene amount of money to have it shipped overnight on Christmas Eve.

And it had been worth every penny.

"Good," he murmured softly.

She lifted her head, her expression oddly vulnerable. "I mean it," she insisted. "This is exactly what I love."

His lips twitched as he reached into the box to pull out the bracelet.

"Does that surprise you?" he demanded, fastening the ends of the chain around her slender wrist.

The tiny charms filled the air with a tinkling sound as they moved, Carmen's eyes wide with an emotion he didn't understand.

"I think it frightens me," she said.

Griff threaded his fingers through hers, tugging her until they were just an inch apart.

"Why?"

Her lips twisted into a rueful smile. "Because in a few days you know more about me than most people who've been my friend for years."

He lifted her hand, pressing her fingers against his mouth. He didn't doubt for a second that she was telling him the truth. She kept herself so closely guarded it was almost impossible for people to ever know the true Carmen Jacobs.

The thought that he was one of the very few to ever be allowed past her defensive walls humbled him.

"I intend to know you even better before this day is over," he assured her in husky tones.

A flush of awareness touched her cheeks. "Griff."

With a low growl he dropped her hands. Now wasn't the time to start something they couldn't finish.

"Get dressed and we'll go to your family lunch," he forced himself to say. "The sooner we eat, the sooner we can leave and enjoy the rest of our day."

She glanced down at the charm bracelet around her wrist before sending him a wary frown.

"You said I was dangerous, but I suspect I'm an amateur when it comes to you, Griffin Archer."

She turned to hurry back into her private bedroom, closing the door firmly behind her. Left alone, Griff pivoted to look down on the city that was still enjoying a sleepy Christmas morning. He didn't feel dangerous.

He felt . . .

Hell, he didn't know.

And, if he was being honest with himself, he didn't want to waste his energy trying to figure it out. Not when he needed to focus his attention exclusively on protecting Carmen.

An hour later they'd left the hotel and driven across Louisville to pull to a halt in front of the house.

Turning off the truck's engine, he pocketed the key and turned to study his companion.

She looked beautiful. Of course. Her curls tumbled to her shoulders with a shimmer of gold. Her skin was as smooth as silk, and her eyes as blue as the winter sky.

She was wearing the same skirt from yesterday with a soft red sweater that clung to the slender curves of her body.

His heart skipped with a familiar jolt of awareness.

It was ridiculous. He'd been in her constant company for three days. This giddy awareness that blasted through him each time he glanced in her direction should be gone.

Or at least dulled to a manageable zap that didn't make him feel like he was being struck by lightning.

He gave a faint shake of his head, forcing himself to concentrate on her tense expression.

"Ready for this?"

She wrinkled her nose, unhooking her seat belt as she shoved open the passenger door.

"Like you said. The sooner we eat, the sooner we can leave."

She slipped on her coat and crawled out of the truck, heading toward the door. Griff was moving to catch up to her brisk strides when a shadow appeared from the side of the house.

"Carrie."

Carmen whirled around to face the man with a narrow,

pock-marked face and pale eyes. Ronnie Hyde. The son of the housekeeper that Griff had seen Carmen speaking to when he'd returned to the house with Lawrence.

Griff muttered a curse as he hurried to Carmen's side and wrapped his arm around her shoulders. Some protector he was.

He hadn't even noticed the man lurking in the shadows.

"Good morning, Ronnie," Carmen said.

"I was hoping I could catch you before you went inside," Ronnie said, ignoring Griff as if he wasn't standing directly in front of him.

"Do you need something?" Carmen asked.

The pale eyes darted toward the house before returning to Carmen.

"I thought you might walk with me to the lake."

Griff felt Carmen stiffen in surprise. "Now?"

He gave a jerky nod. "I have something I think you should know."

She didn't hesitate. "Okay."

"Carmen," Griff growled. Even if she wasn't being harassed by a mysterious stalker, he wouldn't let her waltz off with this man.

Not only had it been years since she'd known him, but he had a furtive quality about him that Griff didn't like.

"This won't take long," Ronnie promised, continuing to act as if Griff was invisible.

"Fine." Griff tugged Carmen tight against his side. "I'm coming with you."

No doubt sensing the sudden tension that sizzled in the air, Carmen swiveled her head, glancing from one man to the other.

"I don't think you were introduced yesterday," she at last said. "Ronnie, this is Griff Archer. Griff, this is Ronald Hyde."

Ronnie didn't hold out his hand. Neither did Griff.

Mutual dislike at first glance.

"What I have to say is private," Ronnie said, his gaze returning to Carmen, although the challenge in his voice was directed at Griff.

Griff answered. "She isn't going anywhere without me."

Ronnie flattened his lips, once again glancing toward the house.

"I suppose I don't blame you," he muttered. "It's true there are vipers in the garden of evil."

Griff narrowed his eyes. "Are you talking about the Jacobses?"

The man hesitated. Carmen reached out to lightly touch his arm, as if worried that he might change his mind about offering whatever information he'd planned to share with her.

"You can trust Griff."

The narrow face tightened before Ronnie was hiding his disappointment. He'd clearly hoped he could spend some time alone with Carmen. Then, with a stiff nod, he turned to lead them around the corner and between the house and the six-car garage.

In silence they passed through the side garden, circling around the pool at the back of the house. And then stepped onto the flagstone pathway that led to the lake that shimmered in the distance.

Ronnie dropped back to walk at Carmen's side, seemingly convinced that they were out of earshot.

"After your father shot—" Ronnie snapped his lips together, his face staining with color.

Griff felt Carmen jerk, but her expression remained encouraging.

"Go ahead, Ronnie," she urged.

"After you left Louisville with your grandparents," he corrected himself. "And the new Jacobses moved in, my mother decided I should live with my aunt."

Griff sent the younger man a startled glance. That seemed extreme.

"Why?" he demanded.

Ronnie's gaze remained locked on Carmen. "I didn't know at the time," he said. "It wasn't until she was diagnosed with cancer that she revealed the truth."

Carmen looked genuinely sympathetic. Griff could tell that she'd been fond of the family housekeeper.

"What did she say?" she asked.

Ronnie shoved his hands into the pockets of his light jacket, his hair disheveled by the winter breeze.

"First, can you tell me what you remember of that night?"

Griff's brows snapped together. "What the hell?"

Carmen reached out to grab his hand, giving his fingers a warning squeeze.

"Nothing more than being woken by the first gunshot," she answered, her voice carefully bland. "I was walking toward the kitchen when the second shot sent me scurrying to the closet where I hid until the cops found me." Her head tilted to the side as she studied the man walking next to them. "Why are you asking?"

"That night my mother had been at choir practice," Ronnie said. "She'd just pulled into the driveway when she heard the gunshot. She ran into the kitchen and found your parents already dead. She looked for you and when you weren't in your bedroom she was terrified you'd been kidnapped."

"Oh." Carmen looked startled. "I never thought about that."

"When you were found in the closet it became obvious that it was a murder-suicide," Ronnie continued, sending Carmen a small grimace. "I'm sorry."

Griff's temper snapped. Had the jerk lured Carmen into this conversation just so he could poke at her ancient wounds?

"Do you have a point?" he snapped.

"Griff," Carmen chided.

"Yes, I have a point." Ronnie glanced toward Griff, his eyes glittering pale and cold in the bright sunlight, and then the gaze swiveled back to Carmen. "My mother told me that after she'd discovered what your father had done, she assumed it was because he thought your mother had been unfaithful."

Carmen's breath hissed between her teeth. "Are you saying my mother had an affair?"

"No." Ronnie held up a slender hand. "But everyone knew that your father was very possessive of his young and beautiful wife. Even I overheard him yelling at a deliveryman who he thought was staring too long at your mother."

Carmen's chin jutted to a stubborn angle. "That doesn't mean she was unfaithful."

"It was the only reason my mother could conceive your father would do such a thing, but she changed her mind," Ronnie hastily assured Carmen, no doubt sensing she was about to bring an end to the painful conversation.

Griff wished she would. He didn't trust this man.

Of course, right now, he didn't trust anyone.

"Why?" Carmen demanded.

"After Lawrence moved into the house my mother realized that the Jacobses' family business had been near bankruptcy for years," Ronnie said. "She also discovered that your uncle had been badgering your father to sell everything." There was a dramatic pause as Ronnie came to a sudden halt. "She overheard Lawrence saying that he regretted pushing your father over the edge, but that his death had rescued the family from catastrophe."

Carmen lifted her hand to her lips, her face paling at Ronnie's sudden claim.

"You're not implying that my uncle—"

"No," Ronnie hastily interrupted. "My mother didn't say

that Lawrence pulled the trigger, but she did believe your uncle deliberately harassed your father, driving him to the point of suicide."

Carmen stepped closer to Griff, as if unconsciously seeking his support. He wrapped his arm around her waist and tucked her tight against his side.

"Why?" she asked. "So he could inherit the company? It was already bankrupt."

Ronnie stepped closer and lowered his voice. As if one of the ducks who were floating on the nearby lake might be eavesdropping.

"At first my mother wasn't sure, but she'd suspected that the new Jacobses didn't have the same morals as your parents," Ronnie confessed. "Which was why she sent me away in the first place."

Griff's opinion of Ronnie's mother went up several notches. Obviously, she was determined to protect her son from the influences of Lawrence, as well as the Jacobs brothers, Matthew and Baylor.

Smart woman.

"And later?" Carmen asked.

"Later she was cleaning your uncle's private study and she knocked off a stack of papers," Ronnie told them, a tight smile curving his lips. "When she placed them on the desk she realized that they were from a life insurance policy."

Carmen frowned. "Most people have life insurance."

Ronnie leaned forward, anticipation shimmering in his cold, blue eyes.

"This was in your father's name," he said, his voice a mere whisper. "And had you listed as the beneficiary."

Griff sucked in a sharp breath. Not at the man's theatrical style. Ronnie Hyde was clearly a drama queen.

Nope, it was his own stupidity that took his breath away. Why the hell hadn't he considered a life insurance policy when he'd discovered the influx of cash into Lawrence's bank account?

It was the most obvious explanation.

Beside him, Carmen gave a bewildered shake of her head. "I don't remember my grandparents mentioning anything about a life insurance policy."

"I doubt they were ever contacted," Griff said, glancing toward Ronnie. "Do you know the amount?"

Ronnie's smile widened. "My mother said it was three million dollars."

"Shit."

At Griff's low curse, Carmen turned to look at him with a puzzled frown. "What is it?"

"We need to go back to the hotel," he said.

She blinked. "Now?"

"Yes."

"What about Christmas lunch?"

He grabbed her hand, hurrying back toward the truck. "It was just canceled."

"Thank you, Ronnie," she called over her shoulder.

"I'm sorry if I ruined your family reunion," he called back.

"I'm not," she muttered. "Families suck."

Griff didn't argue.

Chapter Fifteen

Carmen paced the floor of the hotel, the soft jingle of her bracelet the only noise to stir the silence.

They'd been back in their private room for almost two hours. Since then Carmen had called her aunt to make their excuses for Christmas lunch, and changed her skirt for a comfortable pair of jeans.

Now she had nothing to do but watch Griff work on the computer and consider the accusations that Ronnie had delivered in a soft whisper.

A three-million-dollar life insurance policy.

It sounded like an outrageous sum for most people, but not for someone in her father's position. He would have wanted to ensure his wife and daughter could continue to live in the lifestyle they were accustomed to if something happened to him.

And she wasn't particularly shocked by the thought that her uncle might have found a way to steal the money that should have been hers.

But would he actually go the extreme measure of sending her the photos? Or following her to Kansas City?

That seemed less convincing.

Still, if they could find proof that he'd taken the life insurance policy and confront him with the evidence, then he wouldn't have any reason to continue to harass her.

His sins would be exposed.

Time passed and she called down for room service when her stomach began to rumble in protest. Within half an hour, a waiter was wheeling in a tray loaded with hot turkey, mashed potatoes, gravy, and two pieces of pecan pie.

Griff offered a smile as she placed a plate next to the computer, grabbing it to eat with a distracted expression. She took her own food to the chair that she pulled in front of the window.

A rueful smile touched her lips. This wasn't the best Christmas she'd ever had. On the other hand, it wasn't the worst.

She at least had pie.

Finished with her meal, she returned the plate to the tray. She was just considering a nap when Griff abruptly rose to his feet and stabbed his fingers through his hair.

"Damn."

"What's wrong?" she demanded, even as she knew exactly what was bothering him.

"I can see the cash, but he's run it through a dozen different accounts over the years," he growled. "It makes it almost impossible to pinpoint the exact source of the income."

She bit her lower lip. "So we don't have any proof?"

He shook his head, his expression hard with frustration. "What we need is a copy of the policy." His brows snapped together, as if he was struck by a sudden thought. "Did your father have a safety-deposit box?"

She gave a lift of her hands. "If he did I'm sure my uncle would have already cleaned it out."

Disappointment rippled over his face. "So all your father's financial records could have been destroyed."

"Yes." A similar disappointment speared through Carmen.

Not that she particularly cared about the money. Wait. That wasn't entirely true. Three million dollars was nothing to sneeze at. But she needed to know if her family was responsible for the pictures of those women, or if there truly was a demented killer on the loose. Unfortunately, she didn't have anything of her father's. "Wait," she breathed.

Griff stepped toward her. "What is it?"

"When my grandparents came to pick me up they packed up my mother's personal belongings. Including a small safe that she always kept in her closet."

"You're sure?"

"Yes." She grimaced, her stomach twisting as if she was once again that lost teenage girl who needed a tangible reminder that she'd had a mother who'd loved her. "One day I crept into the attic of my grandparents' house to see what was inside, but it was locked and before I could get it opened my grandfather found me." She shook her head, her arms wrapping around her waist. "I'd never seen him or my grandmother so upset. At least not since my mother's funeral."

He reached out to grasp her hand, instinctively sensing that she needed the comfort of his touch.

"Do you know why?"

"I just assumed they didn't want to be reminded of my mother's life in Louisville. Now I don't know," she confessed. "It might have contained my father's legal papers."

"Is the case still there?"

"Yes."

Even after her grandparents' deaths she hadn't had the nerve to go into the forbidden attic. No doubt a psychiatrist would tell her that she was in some sort of denial at the horror of her past. Carmen preferred to think of herself as a survivor.

Simple as that.

"How far is the house from Louisville?" Griff asked.

"Around three hours."

He glanced toward the window. It was shortly after noon, and the sun was high in the clear blue sky, bathing the city in brilliant sunshine.

"How do you feel about a field trip?"

She didn't hesitate, already heading to her bedroom to grab her coat and purse.

"I'll drive."

Within fifteen minutes they were headed away from the hotel and out of town. Carmen was behind the steering wheel of the truck, roaring through the nearly empty streets. Next to her, Griff was busy with the open computer on his lap while he made a dozen phone calls.

She tried not to eavesdrop, but she could tell a couple of the calls were to people he wanted to help him find out more about her uncle's finances, plus a request for his neighbor to pick up his mail. Then he had several calls to family and friends, wishing them a merry Christmas.

His low chuckles as he spoke into the phone were a stark reminder that she didn't have anyone waiting for her call.

No family. No friends who were waiting with bated breath by the phone.

A familiar emptiness formed in the pit of her stomach. An emptiness she'd been battling since the night her parents died. Then, with a mental slap, she brought a sharp end to her bout of self-pity.

If she wanted to create intimate relationships, she couldn't remain so guarded. She had to lower her barriers and allow people into her heart, as well as her life.

She shot a quick glance toward the man seated next to her.

He was the reason she was feeling so lonely. And why she suddenly ached to form something deeper than a transitory affair.

So did she have the nerve to do something about it?

She cleared the strange lump from her throat as he held the phone away from his ear and gave a shake of his head.

Carmen could hear the sounds of his friend's voice warning of dire consequences if he didn't get his ass to Missouri to spend a few days.

Pressing his thumb to the screen, Griff ended the call and tossed the phone onto the dashboard.

"It sounds like you're in trouble," she said, and then she grimaced.

Nothing like pointing out the obvious.

"Mmm." Griff's attention locked on the open computer balanced on his lap. "Rylan was disappointed that I won't be joining him and Jaci for the holidays."

"You know, you should go."

"Stop," he interrupted without ever glancing in her direction.

Carmen rolled her eyes, taking the exit off the highway and turning onto the narrow county road.

"Are you bossy with everyone or just with me?" she demanded.

"Everyone." He paused, pretending to consider her question. "Although I make a special effort with you."

"Thanks," she said in dry tones.

"No problem."

His lips twitched as he focused on the computer. She didn't know what he was doing, but she decided it must be fascinating since he didn't say a word for the next thirty miles.

It wasn't until she made another turn, this one onto a narrow gravel road, that he lifted his head to glance around.

His brows arched as he caught sight of the vast, rolling meadows that were occasionally framed by long white fences and wrought iron gates. In the far distance there were whiffs of smoke coming from the chimneys of farmhouses hidden behind clumps of trees.

The people who lived in this area didn't have mansions or elegant stables. These were working farms where men wore coveralls and rubber boots and the women had never once attended a Kentucky Derby party.

"When you said the house was in a rural area, you really meant rural," he said.

She made the last turn onto the tree-lined drive that led to her grandparents' home.

"We already went through the last town of any size," she said, wincing as they hit a pothole that should have been fixed two years ago. "The next town is forty miles north of here."

His gaze narrowed as she halted in front of the white clapboard house with green shutters. The roof was sharply peaked with a dormer window above the covered porch. At the far end was a red brick chimney that was starting to crumble. Yet another item on her to-do list.

"You stay out here alone?" Griff abruptly demanded.

"Not very often," she told him. "The last year I've been spending most of my nights in a motel room. Before that I was in college finishing my masters in journalism and a couple years traveling to the different prisons to do the interviews for my book."

His tension seemed to ease. "Why do you keep it?"

She wrinkled her nose. It was a question she'd asked herself a hundred times.

Maybe a thousand.

"Because letting it go would be admitting my grandparents are never coming back," she confessed.

She sensed Griff stiffen at her blunt honesty. As if she'd struck a nerve.

"I get that," he breathed, his gaze moving over the untamed meadows that were coated in a thin layer of ice. The temperature had steadily fallen as they'd driven north. "It's beautiful."

She nodded. It was beautiful. But more importantly, it was home.

The place where she'd always been loved. And protected.

That made it worth a lot more money than the family mansion on the edge of Louisville.

"Peaceful," she murmured.

"Yes."

She parked and switched off the engine. Then together they slid out of the truck and headed toward the house. They'd just stepped onto the front porch when Griff reached out to lightly touch her shoulder.

"Stop," he murmured, his gaze locked behind her.

She turned to glance toward the road that continued past the house.

"What's wrong?"

He pointed toward the deep ruts she could see carved into the mud. The low hedge that framed the yard had hidden them from view when they'd first pulled up. Now that they were standing on the porch, it was easy to see that someone had pulled onto the soft shoulder directly in front of the house.

"It looks like someone got stuck," Griff said.

Unease crawled over her skin, like a spider scurrying over its web.

"It's not that unusual," she said, trying not to push the panic button. She'd seen ruts before, right? It didn't mean there was a bogeyman lurking in the shadows. "The roads are terrible."

Griff scowled. "Do you have mail delivery?"

She shook her head. "No. I have a PO box. And most of my professional correspondence is sent to my PR firm in New York."

He stepped to the edge of the porch. "Where does the road go?"

"It comes to a dead end at the old stables just past the barn," she told him, pointing toward the clump of trees that hid the outbuildings from view.

His jaw tightened. "So there's no reason for anyone to be out here."

She shivered even as she tried to ignore the dark dread spreading through her heart.

"It could have been one of the neighbors," she said, trying to reassure herself as well as Griff.

He sent her a sharp glance. "Why would they be here?"

"My family has owned this property for over a century. And everyone loved my grandparents." She nodded toward the house. "Since people know I spend a lot of time traveling they come by and check the property for me."

Clearly unimpressed with her logic, Griff held out his hand.

"Give me your keys," he commanded.

Carmen took a sharp step back. She had grudgingly accepted that she needed help. And that Griff was the person she wanted at her side.

But she wasn't going to be patted on the head and set in the corner like she was some empty-headed doll.

"It's my house," she said.

His expression hardened into stubborn lines. "I check it out first, or we call the local cops to do it."

She suspected her expression was equally stubborn. "We go together."

"Carmen."

"I promise to huddle behind you like a good girl," she told him.

His brows snapped together. "I want to keep you safe."

She knew that. Griff Archer was truly one of the good guys. But that didn't stop her from feeling a pang of annoyance at his patronizing tone.

"I can protect myself," she informed him.

"Not if someone has a gun."

She snorted. "Like you could dodge a bullet?"

He leaned toward her, allowing her to catch the warm scent of his skin.

"No one is trying to kill me," he growled.

She rocked onto her tiptoes, touching the ends of their noses together.

"I said you can go first."

He muttered a curse, stepping back as his gaze swept the barren meadows and thick lines of trees that hid them from any neighbors.

No doubt he was deciding that there was no good option in such a remote area. He couldn't deposit her in a crowded café while he went to check on the house. Which meant that she was either left alone in the truck, or she went with him.

"Fine." He reached to pluck the key from her fingers. "Let's do this."

He unlocked the door and shoved it open. They stepped into the shadowed living room, instantly surrounded in a stale gloom. Out of habit, Carmen moved to pull open the heavy drapes, allowing the sunshine to spill through the window.

The darkness was dispersed to reveal the worn carpeting that had faded to a dull brown, and the furniture that was covered with the plastic that her grandmother insisted was a necessary protection. Carmen wasn't sure what posed a danger to the sofa and chairs, but she hadn't dared to remove the stiff coating. She'd been afraid the cushions might disintegrate if they were exposed to air.

She had added a flat-screen TV that was set on the mantel, and bought a new lamp, but those were the only changes that had been made in the past thirty years.

"Does it look like anything has been disturbed?" Griff asked her, his gaze sweeping over the tidy room.

"No."

He led her into the narrow kitchen that had the usual linoleum floor and white-painted cabinets. She crossed to the built-in china cabinet and squatted down to pull open the bottom drawer.

"My grandmother's silver is here," she said, opening the velvet-lined case where the silverware was kept, along with a matching sugar bowl and creamer. She closed the drawer and straightened to peer through the glass of the china cabinet. The antique dishes and figurines were still there, covered in a light layer of dust. "There's really nothing else that might have been worth any money."

He poked his head into the mudroom, which led to the back porch. "Is there a basement?" he asked.

"No." She waved a hand toward the window over the sink, which offered a view of the backyard. There was a large mound at one end of the lawn with a wooden door. "There's a root cellar where my grandmother kept the vegetables she canned, but it doesn't connect to the house."

"Where's the attic?"

She turned to leave the kitchen, only to roll her eyes as he darted in front of her, clearly still concerned that there might be some madman lurking in shadows.

"Through the living room and to the right," she directed, following him into her grandparents' bedroom.

It was a large room, with windows that overlooked the front yard. The wooden floors had been worn over the years, but the planks had been lovingly waxed and polished by her grandmother. The sturdy furniture had been carved by some distant ancestor, and probably weighed as much as a bulldozer. Which meant that it'd been hauled into the room a hundred years ago and never moved. There was a worn quilt spread across the mattress and homemade drapes that framed the windows.

A bitter sense of pain sliced through Carmen. Her grandparents had been all she had. Now they were gone. It didn't seem fair.

Sensing Griff's steady gaze, she gave a faint shake of her

head and crossed the floor toward the narrow door at the back of the room. Someday she was going to have to come to terms with her loss. Otherwise this place was going to end up another rotting farmhouse that would collapse into oblivion.

Grabbing the rusty doorknob, she tugged on it. Then tugged again, and again.

"Sorry," she muttered, when the door abruptly flew open with a cloud of dust. She coughed, waving her hand in front of her face. "This hasn't been opened in years. After I moved in my grandfather converted the loft of the barn into a storage area. That's where they put most of the stuff from the attic."

He moved next to her, peering at the steep flight of wooden steps.

"What stuff?"

"Christmas decorations. Old pots and pans," she said. "And every work of art I ever brought home from school, including the turkey I made out of dry macaroni."

His lips twitched. "You made a turkey out of macaroni?"

"Don't scoff. I'm multitalented."

"I believe you." He paused before sending her a questioning glance. "Are you going up?"

Her brows lifted in surprise. "You'll let me go first?"

He shrugged. "There might be bats."

She rolled her eyes before heading up the stairs, which were too narrow for more than one person at a time. The man was willing to go into the house first when he thought there might be a killer waiting for them, but he was afraid of a bat?

She reached the planked floor of the attic, but before she could move into the thick darkness that shrouded the space, she felt Griff's arm wrap around her waist.

"Is there a light?" he demanded.

"There's a bulb hanging from the rafters with a string attached to it," she told him.

"Hold on," he said. "I'll find it."

There was the squeak of old boards as Griff moved cautiously forward. Then Carmen heard a faint click before a small circle of light appeared in the center of the room.

She was on the point of moving to join Griff when he abruptly muttered a curse.

"What is it?" she demanded.

"Someone's been in here," he said, pointing toward the floor where there was a smudged outline of footsteps in the dust. "Look."

"Crap."

Without giving Griff time to protest, Carmen pushed past him to hurry toward the boxes that had been neatly stacked at the back of the attic. She was forced to hunch over as the slanted roof threatened to smack her on top of the head. By the time she reached the boxes she was bent almost double.

Dropping to her knees, she pressed her fingers to her lips. Each of them had been tugged open and the contents spilled across the wooden planks.

Clothes, shoes, a locked jewelry box, and a stack of letters that were tied together with a frayed ribbon.

With gentle care she folded her mother's belongings and tucked them back into crates with hands that weren't quite steady. Then, tugging off the ribbon, she opened one of the letters and angled it to catch the muted light.

Her heart clenched. The letter was addressed to her mother and the words were an outpouring of love and desire that brought a blush to Carmen's cheeks. Quickly skimming to the bottom of the page, her heart gave another clench. The letter had been written by her father.

She trembled, carefully folding the fragile notepaper and tucking it back into the envelope.

What had happened?

How had her father gone from a man who blindly adored

his young wife to someone who could end her life with a shotgun?

It didn't make any sense.

Barely aware that a tear was trickling down her cheek, Carmen felt an arm wrap around her shoulders to tug her against the broad strength of Griff's chest.

"I've got you," he murmured softly, brushing his lips over the top of her head.

Carmen sniffed, then blinked back her tears. Now wasn't the time to try to deal with her father's tangled motives for pulling the trigger. Or the pressures that might have led him to such a desperate act.

For now, she just wanted to get out of the dusty attic.

"I'm okay," she assured him.

His lips touched her brow, then the tip of her nose before he was turning toward the boxes.

"Can you tell me if anything is missing?"

"The safe," she said without hesitation. It'd been the first thing she'd noticed.

He muttered a curse before he was nodding toward the envelopes she clutched in her hands.

"What are those?"

"Love letters." The words came out as a croak.

His arm tightened around her before he was pulling back and urging her away from the boxes.

"Let's get out of here," he said.

She allowed herself to be pulled across the floor and down the stairs. They moved in silence, both brooding on the fact that there had been unmistakable footsteps in the attic and now the safe was missing.

Someone had been at the farmhouse to steal her parents' private papers.

She shook her head in bewilderment. It seemed that Griff had been right. This wasn't about a copycat serial killer. It'd been nothing more than a disgusting trick by her family to ensure that they could protect the three million dollars they'd stolen from her.

Trying to come to terms with the knowledge that her wretched family were all a bunch of greedy psychopaths, she barely noticed when Griff strolled toward the window, his expression distracted.

Pacing from one end of the ugly carpet to the other, she finally came to an abrupt halt. Walking in circles wasn't going to solve her troubles.

"What now?" she asked.

He slowly turned to face her. "If someone got their car stuck in the road, who would they call to get pulled out?"

"If they were local they would just ask a friend with a tractor to come and help."

"And if they weren't local?" he pressed.

She considered, then gave a shrug. "I suppose they would call the garage in town. I'm pretty sure they have a tow truck that they could send out."

He pulled his phone from his pocket. "Do you have a number?"

She nodded toward the small desk in the corner of the room. Her grandfather had been an old-fashioned man who refused to be dragged into the current century. He'd never turned on a computer, preferring to write out checks for his bills at the end of each month. And he'd never had a cell phone, maintaining his landline until the day he died.

"I'm sure my grandfather has an old phone book that would have the number," she said, her brows pulling together. "But it's Christmas. There won't be anyone there today."

"Damn," he breathed, shoving the phone back in his pocket. Once again he glanced out the window, this time angling his head to study the sky, which was painted with deepening shades of lavender and peach as the early dusk settled over the landscape. "How do you feel about spending the night here?"

Carmen paused. This was the only true home she'd ever had, and now it'd been violated by some unknown intruder. Had the sense of peace she felt when she came here been ruined forever?

After a pause, she released a small breath of relief.

She didn't feel afraid. Or apprehensive. Not like she did when she'd entered her parents' old home.

No. She felt angry.

She seriously wanted to find out who'd dared to break in and toss around her mother's belongings like they were trash. Then she wanted them thrown in jail for a very, very long time.

She met Griff's watchful gaze. "Actually, I'd like that."

"Good." His expression eased, as if he'd been prepared for a battle that hadn't happened. "I want to see if we can discover who made the tracks in your driveway before we return to Louisville. I'll run into town and get something to eat."

She wrinkled her nose. The nearest town had one small grocery store that was locked up tight by five o'clock and a gas station that sold milk and bread.

"I doubt anything will be open, but I always keep food in the freezer," she said. "And there will be a few bottles of wine in the root cellar."

A slow, wicked smile curved his lips. "Perfect."

Carmen forgot how to breathe.

Chapter Sixteen

December 25, Rural Indiana

Dinner turned out to be a frozen pizza and garlic bread that Carmen had pulled from the freezer along with a bottle of Merlot that Griff had found in the cellar.

For a man who was accustomed to being wined and dined in some of the finest restaurants in the world, it should have been a huge disappointment. Instead, it was the best meal he'd ever eaten.

A part of his enjoyment was their surroundings. He'd lit a fire from wood he'd found stacked in the barn, and laid out a blanket on the floor in front of the cheery blaze. Outside, the moonlight frosted the ground in a shimmer of silver, making it look like a picture on the front of a Christmas card. He'd even pulled out a few decorations to add a festive air.

Holly was hanging from the mantel, an elf was perched on a shelf, and a tiny tree that played "Jingle Bells" when he plugged it in was set in a corner.

The largest part of his enjoyment, however, was solely due to his dinner guest.

Carmen fascinated him in a way that no other woman ever had.

It wasn't just her beauty. Or her feminine charm.

It was her cunning intelligence. Her wary vulnerability. And her persistent determination to pierce through his natural reserve to discover the man he kept hidden from the world.

Eating pizza in front of the fire, she managed to coax him to talk about his childhood. Something he never did. Not even with Rylan. He told her about the Sunday afternoons that his mother insisted they spend together. They would choose some new activity, like visiting the zoo or attending a Cubs baseball game, or just walking along the edge of Lake Michigan. It didn't really matter what they did, as long as they were together. He even told her about visiting his grandparents' farm, where he would sleep beneath the stars and dream about becoming an astronaut.

Once dinner was done, he poured the last of the wine into their glasses and tossed the paper plates into the fire. Then, scooting toward her, he brushed a golden curl behind her ear before he allowed his fingers to trace the curve of her throat.

"I forgot to ask about the cut on your arm," he murmured. "Is it healing?"

Her cheeks were lightly flushed, her eyes as brilliant as sapphires in the firelight.

"It's fine," she said. "It wasn't very deep."

He gave a tug on the scooped neckline of her sweater, pulling the knit material over her shoulder to reveal the thin line of red that marred her pale skin.

She was right, it wasn't deep. And it didn't look like it was infected. Still, the sight of it made fury burn through him like a corrosive acid.

"When I get my hands on the son of a bitch who hurt you—"

His threat was cut short when Carmen pressed a finger to his lips.

"No," she murmured softly.

"No?"

"Not tonight."

He studied her upturned face. The wide, impossibly blue eyes. The narrow blade of her nose. The lush lips.

Heat swirled through his body that had nothing to do with the nearby fire.

Allowing his hip to press against her side, Griff used the tips of his fingers to trace her lovely features.

She felt delicate beneath his touch. Fragile. Utterly feminine.

For too long she'd been out of his reach.

First he'd feared that she was merely using him to further her fame. And then he'd been overwhelmed by his fierce need to protect her.

Tonight, however, was different.

They were alone in the middle of nowhere, with the doors and windows locked up tight. Including a window in the mudroom that Griff had discovered didn't have a latch. He suspected that was how the intruder had managed to get into the house and steal the safe. Now it was firmly nailed shut. No one else was going to be sneaking in.

But even as he savored the feel of her skin, warm and satin smooth beneath his touch, he sensed that she kept a part of herself locked away. He understood her need to protect her heart. She'd been through hell. But that didn't halt his increasing need to break through the invisible walls that surrounded her.

Why?

There was only one answer.

He wanted more than her body. He wanted her mind. Her heart. Her trust.

His hand moved to trace her full lips, his erection hardening as desire blasted through him with a sharp-edged need.

"You take my breath away," he whispered.

He was braced for her to pull away. She might be sexually attracted to him, but he knew she was feeling raw and vulnerable from the past few days.

He wouldn't blame her for being reluctant to become intimately involved.

With anyone.

But even as he watched a hint of uncertainty flare through her eyes, she released a slow breath. Then, snuggling closer, she slid her hands beneath his sweater. The soft tinkle of her bracelet was like music to his ears. She hadn't taken it off since he'd placed it around her wrist. The knowledge warmed his heart in a way he couldn't fully explain.

"I could say the same," she assured him in soft tones.

Griff hissed at her touch. Raw, delicious heat jolted through him. It felt like he was being branded.

Claimed by this woman.

Tangling his fingers in her golden curls, he lowered his head and kissed her. Electricity zapped him, a thousand watts of sheer pleasure sizzling between them.

He heard Carmen's soft gasp. A smug satisfaction raced through him. Apparently, he wasn't the only one who was shocked by the sheer power of their attraction. A mere kiss wasn't supposed to scorch through you like wildfire.

"You've haunted me for months," he muttered against her lips.

"Haunted?" She tilted her head back, studying him with a darkened gaze. "That doesn't sound very nice."

"It wasn't," he assured her in a gruff voice. "I've endured more restless nights and cold showers since I met you than I have in my entire life."

Her fingers skimmed over his chest. "Are you sorry I approached you on the beach?"

"Hell, no," he rasped.

Another kiss. He used the tip of his tongue to trace the seam of her mouth, groaning in appreciation when her lips parted to allow him to fully taste her sweetness.

At the same time, he lowered his hands to find the hem of her sweater. Then, with one smooth motion, he was tugging the fuzzy material over her head. With a flick of his hand the sweater was tossed onto a nearby chair.

He locked his gaze on the frilly bra, taking a second to appreciate the lacy concoction before it was joining the sweater on the chair.

His breath hissed between his teeth as he lifted his hands to cup the soft swell of her breasts.

There was another blast of desire, and unable to resist temptation he lowered his head to suck the tip of one breast between his lips.

Her nails dug into his chest, her back arching. "Griff."

"What about you?" he demanded, circling the hardened peak with his tongue.

"What?" Her voice was distracted as she trembled beneath his teasing strokes.

He kissed a path to her other breast.

"Are you sorry you approached me?"

She arched against him, her head tilting back to allow her curls to tumble down her back in a blaze of gold.

So beautiful.

"I'm not sorry," she assured him. "I knew from the beginning we could make a great team."

His hands lowered to unfasten her jeans, pulling them down her legs along with the tiny wisp of fabric that served as her underwear.

"Team—I like the sound of that," he murmured. "Of course, I get to be the coach."

Her lips twitched, her eyes dark with desire. "Why do you get to be the coach?"

"Because I have the right equipment."

She released a startled laugh that turned to a groan as he used the tips of his fingers to trace her slender curves. At the same time, he allowed his gaze to take a lingering survey of her naked body.

He released a slow breath. She was just as exquisite as he'd known she would be.

Firelight danced over her skin, revealing the soft, rounded breasts tipped with rosy nipples. The curve of her waist that flared to the slender width of her hips. And the trim legs that were the perfect length to wrap around his waist once he was buried deep inside her.

Obviously, it's true. Great things do come in small packages.

As much as he wanted to spend the next few hours simply appreciating her beauty, there were things he wanted to do more.

The sooner the better.

Kicking off his shoes, Griff stripped and allowed his clothes to drop to the blanket.

Carmen's eyes widened as she took in the sight of his hard, flagrantly aroused body. He smiled, using her distraction to his advantage as he pressed her back against the blanket.

She instinctively grabbed his shoulders, her hair a golden halo around her flushed face and her eyes glowing with passion. A lethal tenderness squeezed his heart. She looked young and vulnerable and utterly edible.

Yes, edible.

The thought passed through his mind as he tugged her legs gently apart and then moved to kneel between them. Carmen held out her arms in invitation, then blinked, momentarily confused as he remained on his knees, his gaze roaming over her silky pale skin.

"Is something wrong?" she demanded.

"Everything is perfect," he assured her.

Holding her gaze, he gently pushed her legs apart, allowing him access to her most intimate secrets.

Her lashes fluttered, but at last she gave a small nod and he leaned forward so he could settle between her legs. The sweet scent of her teased at his nose, and with a low groan, he angled his head to run his tongue through her moist heat.

Carmen made a choked sound of bliss, her fingers threading through his hair as her toes curled into the blanket.

Griff took that as an open invitation to continue his taste test. He plunged his tongue inside her body before tormenting her clit with short, relentless strokes.

Her fingers tightened in his hair, her breath coming in soft pants.

She felt like velvet beneath his tongue, her soft moans music to his ears.

A beautiful symphony.

"Griff, I want to feel you inside me," she rasped.

He allowed himself one last, lingering taste before he was reaching out to grab his jeans. With fingers that weren't quite steady he pulled out his wallet and located the condom.

A minute later he had it rolled on and was moving up to brace himself over the top of her. Gazing down, he studied her with a need he didn't entirely understand.

Lust, he knew all about.

But this. This was so much more.

"Let me in, Carmen," he growled.

A smile curved her lips. The smile of a siren.

She reached down to circle his arousal with her fingers, positioning him at the entrance to her body.

"I'm not stopping you," she told him.

"I don't mean your body."

Holding her gaze, he slowly pressed himself deep inside her. There was a shocked moment as they both adjusted to the shattering bliss. She was hot and wet and tight around his erection. They groaned in unison.

Like a rising crescendo in their glorious symphony.

Holding her gaze, he started to move. Slowly at first, then gaining speed as her legs wrapped around his waist and her fingers tangled in his hair.

"Griff," she muttered, her breath coming in small pants.

He leaned down, kissing her with a maddened sense of urgency.

"Let me in," he demanded.

Carmen woke to find herself tightly wrapped in Griff's arms. He'd made love to her twice more before he'd added wood to the fire and found a blanket to wrap over them. Then, they'd fallen into an exhausted slumber.

A perfect, glorious night.

One that Carmen didn't regret for a minute.

His gentle caresses. The slow, delicious kisses. The feel of his hard body covering her as he thrust deep inside her.

But even as she savored the memory of their sizzling passion, a part of her shied away from the words he continued to whisper in her ear.

Let me in.

She knew what he was asking. And she knew the danger if she gave in to his demands. She'd accepted that she could trust him with her life. And even her body.

But her heart?

That was something she didn't allow anyone to touch.

Which was why she wiggled out of his arms and headed toward the shower as soon as she woke. She wasn't in the mood for any postmortems.

Thankfully, her panicked flight clearly warned Griff not to press the issue. After his own shower they shared a breakfast of frozen waffles. Not the finest meal, but at least she had plenty of hot, black coffee.

Once they were done eating, Carmen shuffled through

her grandfather's desk until she found the number for the local auto shop.

The owner answered on the seventh ring. In this area a small business didn't have secretaries. Or answering machines. On the other hand, the owner easily remembered being called to haul a stuck vehicle out of the road.

Five minutes later she ended the call and turned to meet Griff's curious gaze. He was standing near the window, his lean face bathed in the pale, winter sunlight. Her stomach clenched, raw desire blasting through her.

Obviously, one night in his arms wasn't enough.

Not nearly enough.

"Well?" he demanded, thankfully unaware that she was imagining the pleasure of urging him out of his sweater and jeans so she could run her fingers over his naked body.

She gave a shake of her head, forcing herself to concentrate on her recent conversation with the mechanic.

"You were right," she told him.

She half expected a smug reaction. Instead, he merely nodded. Griffin Archer was a man who was used to being right.

"Someone called to be pulled out?"

"Yeah."

"Did you get a name?"

"John Smith." She held up her hand. "And, before you ask, he paid in cash."

Griff's jaw tightened with frustration. "Of course he did. What about a description?"

She grimaced. "Average height and weight. Nothing that made him stand out."

"Hair color?"

"He was wearing a hat."

Griff took a step toward her. "Did he at least get his license number?"

She shrugged. "No, but he did say that he was driving a white Ford Focus."

Griff made a sound of disgust. "What do you want to bet it was a rental?"

Carmen heaved a sigh. "Another dead end."

He drummed his fingers on the side of his leg, his expression distracted as he tried to consider the best way to track down the intruder.

"I'll run a search through the car rental agencies in Louisville," he said. "We might get a lucky hit."

"The mechanic said he came out the day before Thanksgiving," she told him. "He remembered because he had to pull out two other cars who were in the area for a funeral."

"So it happened before you received the photos."

Her brow furrowed. "Do you think that's important?"

Before he could answer there was the buzzing sound of a phone on vibrate.

"Hold on," he murmured, pulling his cell out of his pocket. He glanced toward the screen, his lifted brows indicating surprise. He turned to walk into the kitchen, his phone pressed to his ear.

Carmen stiffened, something that might have been jealousy slashing through her. She was certain she'd heard a female voice as Griff had strolled away. Was it his lover? Did he have a woman back in California?

With a sharp shake of her head, she dismissed her childish urge to think the worst. She was terrified of being betrayed. Which meant it was easier to find a reason to push people away than to trust they might be sincere.

But not even her damaged heart could believe that Griff could have spent the night making love to her and then calmly taken a call from another woman. He no doubt had plenty of faults, but he wasn't a jackass.

At least not a deliberate jackass.

Almost as if wanting to prove her point, Griff returned to the living room, still holding the phone in his hand.

"That was Nikki," he said, his expression tense.

It took a second for Carmen to place the name. "Your FBI contact?"

"Yes."

"What did she want?"

"She needs us to meet her at her office in Chicago."

Carmen frowned. "The FBI office?"

"Yep."

A hard knot of anxiety settled in the pit of her stomach. As far as she knew, Griff hadn't been in contact with the agent since he sent her the Polaroids.

"Why?"

He shoved the phone in the front pocket of his jeans. "She refused to tell me any more over the phone."

She licked her lips, which were suddenly dry. "That can't be good."

He moved toward her, his hands framing her face so he could tilt it back, forcing her to meet his steady gaze.

"We don't know anything yet," he said in firm tones.

"Do you think—"

He bent his head, halting her words with a brief, searing kiss.

"I think it doesn't do any good to speculate," he insisted.

He allowed his hands to drop and turned to begin gathering their few belongings, which were spread around the room.

His motions were brisk, confident. But Carmen hadn't missed the unease smoldering in his eyes.

He was just as afraid as she was that they were about to discover those photos weren't just a hoax.

Chapter Seventeen

December 26, Rural Indiana

Griff insisted on driving. He didn't want Carmen behind the wheel when she was distracted. Especially not when a light snow had fallen during the night, covering the roads in a layer of ice.

It also prevented him from spending the next three hours brooding on Carmen's reaction to their night of hot, endless passion.

He hadn't expected her to leap around the house with sheer joy. Had he? He grimaced. Okay. Maybe he'd expected a leap or two. They'd set off fireworks during the night, for Christ's sake. That deserved recognition.

But one glance at her panicked expression as she'd scrambled out of his arms had warned him that Carmen wasn't ready for a heart-to-heart.

He hadn't even dared to give her a good-morning kiss.

A fact that gnawed at him like a pit bull with a bone.

He'd never thought of himself as affectionate. He liked to touch women when they were in his bed. A lot. But he'd never been a man who'd been into public displays of affection. Women who were forever kissing him and snuggling close when they were walking down the street, or eating in a restaurant, were more annoying than charming.

Now he wanted nothing more than for Carmen to lean across the cab of the truck to lay her head on his shoulder. Or to place her hand on his leg as they traveled through the back roads to reach the I-90.

Good Lord. He was turning into one of those kissy-face sort of guys.

Rylan would never let him hear the end of it.

His dark thoughts were interrupted half an hour into their silent drive. Slowing the truck, Griff studied the bridge that looked like it had been built by the early pioneers. Narrow planks set over a rusty frame with nothing on the side. The locals might feel comfortable with the sketchy construction, but he wasn't nearly so trusting.

Not when the entire thing was slick with ice.

Coming to a halt, he reached toward the GPS that was built into the dashboard.

"What are you doing?" Carmen asked, blinking as she glanced around.

"I'm looking for an alternate route," he said. "There has to be a state highway nearby."

She nodded, leaning forward as if she intended to help him. At the same time there was a sudden squeal of tires. Startled, Griff glanced in the rearview mirror. The road had been empty for miles. The last thing he'd expected was some jerk racing over the icy pavement like he was at the Indy 500.

Watching the heavy SUV thunder toward them, his annoyance abruptly transformed into fear. This wasn't a teenager with more horsepower than sense. Or a local who'd lost control of their car on the ice.

Whoever was driving the SUV was headed straight

toward them. At a speed that meant that the driver had no intention of stopping.

Griff had less than half a second to make his decision. There was no way to avoid the impact, but he could do his best to keep them from being slammed over the edge of the steep bank and into the icy river below.

"Brace yourself," he snapped, shoving the truck into four-wheel drive and gunning the engine as he turned the steering wheel sharply to the side.

The wide tires spun on the ice, fishtailing the back of the truck so when the SUV slammed into them it sent them spinning into the ditch instead of forward and off the bridge.

Carmen cried out, grabbing the dashboard to absorb the majority of the impact. Griff clutched the steering wheel and continued to smash his foot against the gas pedal. The tires churned through the mud, slogging them slowly forward into a nearby field.

Griff glanced over his shoulder, seeing the SUV come to a halt, the front bumper half hanging off and the headlights busted. There was a brief hesitation as the attacker was no doubt considering whether to pursue them into the field. Then, with another squeal of tires, the SUV was backing down the road at a reckless speed.

Griff cursed as he realized the damaged bumper was hiding the license plate. And worse, the angle of the sun reflected off the windshield, meaning he could only catch a shadowed outline of the driver.

Once certain that the SUV wasn't planning another round of bumper cars, Griff stomped on the brakes and put the truck in park. Then he swiveled in his seat to study Carmen's tense expression.

That'd been close.

Too close.

If he'd attempted to cross the bridge, the slightest tap

from behind would likely have sent them spinning over the edge and into the river.

An icy fury detonated through him. Not only at the mystery driver who'd tried to ram them into the river. But at himself for not paying attention to their surroundings.

He'd allowed the empty roads to lull him into a false sense of safety. A near-fatal mistake.

"Are you okay?" he demanded, his voice harsh with a toxic combination of fear and anger.

"I think so." She released a shaky breath. "Some people shouldn't be allowed to drive when there's ice on the road."

"That was no accident."

Griff heard her suck in a startled breath. "You think they deliberately tried to hit us?"

"I think they tried to kill us," he corrected.

There was a shocked silence as Carmen glanced over her shoulder at the empty road, then toward the icy bridge. It didn't take her long to realize how close they'd come to disaster.

Her face paled, but she turned back to confront him with a determined expression. Her courage tugged at his heart, even as it made his gut twist with dread.

There was no way he was going to be able to convince her to find a place where she would be safe until this was over.

"Did you see the driver?" she asked.

He shook his head. "The sunlight was reflecting off the windshield. I couldn't see more than a shadowy figure behind the steering wheel."

Disappointment darkened her eyes. He knew that it must feel like fate itself was trying to prevent her from discovering the identity of her stalker.

"Should we call the police?"

He considered their options before giving a shake of his head. The local cops would dismiss it as an accident caused by the slippery roads. Besides, they wouldn't have the manpower or the training to locate the SUV. Griff would bet good money that it was already stashed in a hidden location until it could be repaired.

"We'll report it to Nikki when we see her," he finally said. "She'll have more resources."

Carmen shivered and he reached to switch the heater on high. He ached to pull her into his arms and comfort her, but he'd already failed Carmen once by letting down his guard.

It wasn't going to happen again.

He allowed his gaze to roam over the empty field before returning to the rearview mirror to keep watch on the road.

"It had to be one of my family, right?" Carmen demanded. "But how would they know we're here?"

He considered her question. "They might have suspected we'd discovered the truth of the insurance money," he at last suggested. "The logical place to search for evidence would be your grandparents' home."

"The evidence they already stole," she muttered.

His jaw tightened. It didn't matter if the actual policy was missing or not. Eventually he would be able to track down the insurance company and get a copy of it. What pissed him off was the knowledge that the bastard had intruded into Carmen's home. How could she ever feel safe there again?

"True," he agreed. "Or someone might have followed us from the hotel."

She released a shaky breath. "This is insanity."

"You're not going to get an argument from me," he said in dry tones, giving one last glance around before he shoved open the door of the truck. Even if he wasn't one hundred percent certain that the attacker wasn't waiting down the road for them, they couldn't stay there all day. "I'm going to check the truck."

He climbed out, grimacing as his feet sunk into the

muddy field. His shoes would be ruined. No big loss. But his wet socks were going to make the drive to Chicago uncomfortable.

Moving down the side of the truck, he bent to examine the crumpled metal where the SUV had slammed into them. The impact had dented the side panel just behind the wheel, and a section of the tailgate, but the damage was mostly cosmetic. Now the only worry was whether he could get the thing out of the muddy field.

Oh, and whether there was still a crazed killer on the road who wanted them dead.

Climbing back into the truck, he shut his door and pulled on his seat belt.

"Well?" Carmen demanded as he ensured they were still in four-wheel drive.

"I'm glad I got the insurance, but it's okay to drive," he assured her, pressing his foot on the gas pedal.

The wheels began to spin, spraying mud and chunks of cornhusks behind them. Seconds later, they caught traction and lurched forward. Griff wrapped his fingers tightly around the steering wheel, turning them in a wide arc that took them back to the road.

Then he veered to the left. He still wasn't going to cross the icy bridge. They would have to find another way to Chicago.

Carmen remained locked in her dark thoughts as they reached the interstate and headed north. How had her life descended into chaos? Each day seemed to bring a new attempt to terrorize her. If not outright kill her.

On top of that, she was still reeling from her less than spectacular homecoming. It was hard to be all warm and fuzzy when you suspected your remaining family had stolen three million dollars from your inheritance and were now conspiring to keep you from discovering their treachery. By any means necessary.

It wasn't until Griff pulled the truck to a halt in a half-empty lot that she realized they'd already driven into Chicago, and were parked in front of the FBI headquarters. She narrowed her eyes as the early afternoon sunlight reflected off the large glass building.

Although it was a weekday, the manicured grounds that surrounded the area appeared empty. She guessed the agency was running with a skeleton staff during the holiday season.

Not waiting for Griff, Carmen unhooked her seat belt and slid out of the truck. She'd been too distracted to consider why they'd been driving to Chicago. Now she pressed a hand to her stomach, trying to ease her sudden tension.

She'd taken fewer than a half dozen steps when Griff was at her side, his arm wrapping around her waist. She leaned closer to his solid form. She told herself that she wanted the heat from his body. The wind was frigid as it howled around the street. But if she was being completely honest, she'd admit that the feel of him pressed against her side offered a welcome sense of security.

She wrinkled her nose, but she didn't try to pull away from his tight grip.

Even Lois Lane depended on Superman every once in a while, right?

In silence they walked up the pathway and stepped through the front entrance. Carmen glanced around the long, narrow lobby. Like the exterior, glass seemed to be the major focal point. Glass wall, a glass crescent-shaped front desk, and polished marble floors.

It was all very shiny. And cold.

They moved to the front desk, where a man demanded their IDs. Then, before he could question them further, the sound of heels clicking against the marble echoed through the lobby.

"I expected you a half hour ago," a crisp female voice said.

They both turned to watch the agent who walked toward them with the brisk steps of a woman in complete charge of herself and her surroundings. She was dressed in dark slacks and a snowy white shirt that should have looked severe. Instead, it gave her a sleek, elegant appearance. Her hair was a light shade of red, shimmering like copper in the sunlight, and smoothed into a knot at the base of her neck. The style emphasized the perfect oval of her pale face and the bright green eyes that were surrounded by thick black lashes.

Carmen felt an instant stab of envy. This agent was the tall, sophisticated sort of female she'd always wanted to be. Not to mention she had the expression of a true ball-buster.

"We had some troubles," Griff said, moving toward the woman.

Carmen watched as they shook hands. Friendly, she decided, with none of the awkwardness that came from previous lovers.

"What kind of trouble?" the woman demanded, her gaze moving toward Carmen.

"First, let me introduce you to Carmen Jacobs," Griff said in firm tones. "Carmen, this is Special Agent Nikki Voros."

Carmen moved to stand at Griff's side. "Special Agent," she murmured.

Nikki offered a brief smile. "Please call me Nikki." The green gaze snapped back to Griff. "What trouble?"

Griff sent Carmen a rueful glance. He was clearly used to the agent's one-track mind.

"Someone tried to ram us off a bridge."

"You're sure it was deliberate?" the agent pressed. "The roads are slick."

"It was deliberate."

She gave a small nod, pivoting on her heel. "Come with me."

Griff reached to grasp Carmen's hand, giving her fingers a reassuring squeeze as they followed Nikki out of the lobby and down a hallway.

"Her bark is worse than her bite," he assured Carmen.

"No, it's not," Nikki denied, pushing open a door to lead them into a small conference room. "Although I'm not a complete bitch." She moved across the silver carpet toward a cabinet set against the glass wall. On the top was a tray with a stainless steel coffeepot and cups along with several bottles of water. "Would you like something to drink?"

Carmen shook her head, slipping off her coat. Griff took it from her, and hung it next to his on the hooks near the door.

"Nothing for me."

"I'm fine," Griff said.

"Please have a seat." Nikki waved a hand toward the rectangular table in the center of the room. It was made of smoked glass and steel with five chairs arranged around it. Nikki moved to sit at the head of the table where there was a file folder, along with a pad and pen already neatly arranged.

Griff instinctively pulled out a chair for Carmen next to Nikki. She moved to sit down, her gaze briefly skimming over the room.

There was a flag on a stand in one corner, and a whiteboard on the wall next to the door. On the opposite wall there was a framed map of the United States.

It was all very austere, she decided.

Waiting until Griff was settled next to Carmen, Nikki folded her arms on top of the table.

"Now tell me what happened," she said, her gaze locked on Griff.

In clipped tones he told Nikki about stopping at the icy bridge and then the SUV ramming them from behind. Nikki grabbed her pen, making quick notes.

"So you didn't see who was driving or get a license number."

"No," Griff said.

"Do you know someone who might want you to be at the bottom of an icy river?" Nikki asked.

Griff hesitated before heaving a rough sigh. "I have a few guesses. But no proof."

"I'll see if I can get any video from the area that might have caught the SUV so I can pull a plate," she told Griff. "I assume you'll be checking out the rental agencies?"

Griff nodded. "And the local auto shops," he added. "The driver will need to get the damage to his vehicle repaired before he can drive it on the highway."

Nikki abruptly lifted her hand. "Don't tell me how you get your intel."

Griff shrugged, and Carmen's gaze once again darted around the room. This time she realized they were being monitored by at least one camera. Maybe more.

"Wouldn't dream of it," he assured her.

"Once we have proof of who is responsible we'll contact the police," Nikki said, her attention shifting to Carmen. "Until then, I'd like you to tell me everything you can about the pictures that were sent to you."

Carmen clenched her hands in her lap, trying to match the other woman's cool composure.

"Why?"

"I promise to explain my interest, but first I'd like to hear about the pictures." Nikki offered a smile. It was as perfect as the rest of her. Straight white teeth, and just the right amount of professional charm.

She probably practiced in front of the mirror, Carmen thought. Then she heaved a small sigh. She was being a bitch because she felt grubby and tired and scared out of her mind.

This woman was an FBI agent. Exactly the person she'd desperately wanted to get involved in the investigation.

She wasn't going to waste this opportunity because she was jealous.

Trying to match Griff's ability to share the pertinent points without getting bogged down with unnecessary detail, she told the woman about the package left on her porch, and the fact that it had been sent to her PR firm under a false name. She also made sure to point out the cops had refused to believe that the pictures were anything more than a publicity stunt, so she'd asked Griff to help her.

"A smart choice," Nikki murmured, scribbling notes on her pad.

"Not so smart," Griff disagreed. "I managed to trace the freight in the back of the freezer truck, but I let Carmen travel to Kansas City alone."

Nikki lifted her head. "Did something happen?"

"I was cut on the arm," she admitted.

"By who?" Nikki demanded.

"I'm not sure." Carmen reached up to touch the wound, which remained tender. "The man was bundled in winter clothing and I didn't notice I'd been hurt until I was in my room."

Nikki stared at her as if trying to process why anyone would randomly slash a woman's arm, before giving a slow shake of her head.

"Strange," she murmured. "What about the flowers?"

Carmen blinked at the abrupt question, but then she remembered that Griff had sent photos of the roses to this woman.

"They were waiting when I returned to my hotel room. I didn't see or speak with the deliveryman."

Nikki's gaze flickered toward Griff before returning to Carmen. "Sounds like a gift from a lover."

Carmen shook her head. "They were from the same person who sent me the Polaroids."

"How can you be sure?"

"Because they were a clear warning that the killer was going to Baltimore."

Nikki set down her pen, laying her palms flat on the table as she leaned toward Carmen.

"Why Baltimore?"

"That's where the second serial killer in my book hunted his prey," Carmen said. "He was called the Professor."

Nikki once again grabbed her pen. "I haven't had the opportunity to read your book. Why don't you give me a quick overview of the killers you profiled?"

Carmen hid a wry smile. The fact that this woman hadn't read the book was probably a good thing. Carmen had spent an entire chapter detailing the FBI failures that allowed two of the killers in her book to remain on the streets.

"There are five of them," she said.

"Why five?" Nikki asked.

Carmen shrugged. "They were the only ones who would agree to be interviewed."

"And that's the only reason you chose them?"

Carmen frowned in confusion. "I'm not sure what you're asking."

"You didn't have a personal connection to them?"

Personal connection? Carmen's brows snapped together. What was the agent implying? That Carmen's past was littered with friends who just happened to be serial killers?

"No," she snapped. "I hadn't met any of them until the actual interviews."

Nikki held her gaze, almost as if she was judging whether Carmen was lying. Then she gave a small nod and scribbled something on her pad.

"Did any try to stay in contact after you were done with the interviews?"

Griff reached to lay his hand over Carmen's fists, which

were clenched in her lap. His touch was warm, soothing. Reminding her that Nikki wasn't the enemy.

Carmen forced her stiff muscles to ease.

"Not that I know of," she said. "I didn't give any of them my personal contact information." The original interviews had been set up while she was still in college, so she'd had all the original correspondence sent to her professor's office.

Indifferent to Carmen's attempt to remain reasonable, Nikki tapped her pen on the pad.

"Tell me about the killers," she said. The words were a command, not a request.

Griff gave her fingers another squeeze, but this time Carmen was prepared for Nikki's brusque style.

Instead of bristling, Carmen settled back in her seat and focused her mind on the men who'd become woven into the fabric of her life.

"The first was Neal Scott," she told Nikki. "He was called the Trucker by the reporters for the obvious reason he drove a semitruck with a freezer trailer. He chose his victims from prostitutes who worked the truck stops along I-70. He would rape and kill them with a crowbar. Then he would keep the last victim hidden in his truck until he could find a new one."

Nikki made several notes before she returned her gaze to Carmen.

"Number two?"

"The Professor," Carmen said without hesitation. The sooner she finished with Nikki's questions, the sooner she could learn why they'd been summoned to Chicago. She had to assume the FBI agent had a damned good reason for demanding they drive three hours to meet with her. "His real name was Dr. Franklin Hammel. He was an out-of-work English teacher in Baltimore who was obsessed with Edgar Allan Poe."

Nikki glanced toward Griff. "You mentioned him when you sent me the pictures of the flowers in Carmen's hotel room."

Griff nodded. "His name was used on the credit card."

A shudder shook through Carmen. All the men she'd interviewed had been monsters. But Franklin had truly terrified her. He had no remorse. No regret. As far as he was concerned, he was a creative genius who had the right to do whatever he wanted. And if he ever escaped from jail he wouldn't hesitate to kill again.

"He would snatch girls from the local campuses and use them as his muse," she said.

Nikki sent her a quick glance. "Muse?"

"He raped and beat them for inspiration."

"Nice," Nikki muttered.

"When they no longer satisfied his creativity, he would strangle them and leave them with copies of Poe's stories on their chests and a bottle of cognac next to their bodies," Carmen continued, deliberately blocking the memories of the women she'd seen in police photos. She still had nightmares.

Nikki's fingers tightened on her pen, revealing she hadn't been completely hardened by her job. She still reacted to the horror humans could inflict on one another. Then she gave a motion of her hand, indicating that she wanted Carmen to continue.

"Number three?"

"The Morning Star," Carmen said, referring to him by the name she'd given him in the book. "Harlan Lord. He would hunt for his victims up and down the West Coast. He usually chose older women who reminded him of his mother."

Nikki glanced up, her expression curious. "How old?"

Carmen understood the woman's surprise. Most people assumed that serial killers always hunted young, beautiful women, or men, who could fulfill their sexual fantasies.

"Between forty and sixty," Carmen said. "His mother was some sort of religious fanatic who brutalized him when he was young. He showed me scars on the bottom of his feet where she tried to burn out the demon in him." She paused. It'd been difficult during her interview not to feel sympathy for what he'd endured. At least until she'd read the autopsy reports. He'd been a vicious killer. "So in turn, he would burn his victims on the beach at sunrise to cleanse his sins."

Nikki jotted down more notes. "Go on."

Carmen released a sharp sigh. She was trying to be patient. She truly was. But rehashing the crimes of men who were either dead or locked in jail didn't seem the best use of their time.

"Wouldn't it just be easier to read the book?" she demanded.

Nikki lifted her head, her expression impossible to interpret. "Right now I just want a brief idea of the killers and their victims."

Carmen muttered a curse beneath her breath. She'd always thought that she was stubborn, but next to Special Agent Voros she was an amateur.

"Number four was Rob Merill, who was known as the Clown, although he wasn't one." Her voice was clipped. "He actually was the owner of a small carnival that traveled through the South. He never sexually assaulted the women he kidnapped, but he always shaved their heads before he would drown them in the dunking booth and dump them at a local junkyard." She held the agent's gaze. "He told me he wanted to humiliate them like they used to humiliate him."

Nikki gave a small nod. "And the last?"

"Mike Clayborn, Mr. Clean," Carmen said. "He was a rancher in Montana who would lure male lovers to his remote home and dispose of them in barrels of bleach. Most of his victims were undocumented workers who no one would ever report as missing."

Nikki was silent as she studied her pad, which was covered with hasty notes. Then she lifted her head and stabbed Carmen with a suspicious glare.

"They don't appear to have anything in common beyond the fact that they were all ruthless killers." She leaned forward. "And in your book."

Griff abruptly wrapped an arm around Carmen's shoulders, even as his free hand landed on top of the table with a sharp bang.

"Okay, Nikki," he growled. "What the hell is going on?"

Chapter Eighteen

December 26, Chicago, IL

Griff glared at his friend with a smoldering impatience.

He'd met Nikki in college. She'd been a fellow computer geek, and equally uninterested in the typical activities that consumed most of their fellow students. Parties. Spring break. More parties.

They'd bonded over writing computer code, and once she'd told him that she intended to head to Quantico after she graduated, he'd realized that they were soul mates.

Or at least they should have been.

She was perfect for him. The only problem was that they were *too* much alike. Both quiet, introverted, obstinate. And there was the fact that there hadn't been a physical spark between them.

They'd ended up more like brother and sister than lovers.

Which was why their relationship had lasted even after they'd graduated and moved on to their separate careers.

At this moment, however, he wasn't feeling very friendly. In fact, he was wishing that he'd demanded to know exactly why Nikki had insisted they come to Chicago.

If it was just to harass Carmen, he intended to walk out the door.

As if sensing she'd been even more insensitive than usual, Nikki dropped her pen and sat back in her seat with a rueful grimace.

"After you sent me the envelope with the pictures, I put out the word I was interested in any women who'd been killed by a blow to their right temple."

Griff felt Carmen stiffen beneath his arm. "You got a call?" she asked.

Nikki gave a nod. "Christmas morning a young man in rural Kansas was enjoying a ride on his new four-wheeler when he stopped at an old farmhouse to get out of a sudden snowstorm."

Griff studied Nikki's pale, perfect face. He'd always thought it ironic that she was one of the most beautiful women he'd ever known, but she cared the least about attracting the attention of the opposite sex. Right now, he was more concerned with the tension etched on her delicate features.

A bad feeling settled in the pit of his stomach.

He'd gone to a great effort to convince himself the Polaroids that had been sent to Carmen were some sort of elaborate hoax.

It fit the evidence, right? The name on the invoice for the flowers in Kansas City. The rumor that there was a missing three-million-dollar insurance payout. The safe that had been stolen from her grandparents' home.

And, if he was being honest with himself, he would have to admit that he'd latched onto the suspicion with more haste than common sense.

He understood how to battle against a greedy businessman.

A few hours with his computer and he could prove that Lawrence was a thief. From there it would be a simple matter to pressure the man into admitting he'd been harassing

Carmen. And to force a promise he would never trouble his
niece again.

Simple.

But a serial killer. Griff shook his head. He had software
that had been specifically created to help the authorities
track the patterns of a killer, and where he might strike next.
But it could take months, or even years, to actually capture
the lunatic.

How the hell could he keep Carmen safe?

But as much as he wanted to cling to his hope that this
was all a hoax, he wasn't stubborn enough to stick his head
in the sand. If Carmen was being stalked by a killer, he had
to take action to protect her.

"How many?"

Nikki's lips tightened. "All five."

Griff's breath hissed through his clenched teeth. "Have
you compared the photos to the bodies?"

"I got the images faxed to me this morning from the medical examiner's office," Nikki told him. "It's not official, but
they looked like a match to me."

Carmen made a small sound of distress, her fingers lifting to press against her lips.

"So they were real," she breathed.

Nikki nodded. "Yeah."

"God." Carmen shook her head, her face pale and her
eyes wide. "I'd just convinced myself that the pictures had
been faked."

Griff tightened his arm around her shoulders. He needed
to feel the delicate warmth of her body. To reassure himself
that she was safe.

At least for now.

"That was my mistake," he admitted.

Nikki glanced from Carmen to Griff, easily sensing the
tension that prickled in the air.

"What mistake?"

"I traced the invoice from the flower delivery," he told his friend.

She held up a hand. "Again, don't tell me how."

Griff didn't need the warning. He had no intention of revealing that he'd hacked into the accounts of the flower shop.

It was strange. He'd always been a law-abiding citizen. Not only because his mother was a cop, but the computer software he created along with Rylan was capable of great harm if used without restraint.

As he'd told Carmen when they were in Kansas City, power corrupts. Absolute power corrupts absolutely. He could do immeasurable damage if he didn't possess rock-solid ethics.

But his determination to discover who was stalking Carmen overrode even his deepest-held convictions. He would do whatever necessary. Even if it meant breaking a few laws.

"Carmen's name was listed as Carrie Jacobs."

Nikki folded her hands together on top of her notepad, her attention fully focused on them. Griff knew her formidable intelligence was sorting and calculating every word they spoke.

Like the most sophisticated computer.

"Is that significant?" Nikki asked.

Carmen answered. "I haven't been called Carrie since I left Louisville when I was twelve years old."

Nikki arched a brow, glancing back at Griff. "You thought this lunatic might have a personal connection?"

Griff reluctantly removed his arm from around Carmen. He'd always been a man who had perfect focus. Rylan used to tease him that a nuclear bomb could go off and Griff would never notice if he was working on a project. But that was before Carmen.

Now just the warmth of her body or a whiff of her citrus scent was enough to destroy his concentration.

He had it bad.

With an effort, he cleared away the distractions. Then he quickly told Nikki about meeting with Lawrence Jacobs, and his suspicion that the man was hiding something from them. But it wasn't until he revealed what Ronnie Hyde had told them about the life insurance policy and the house-keeper's suspicion that Carmen's father had been driven over the edge by his brother that Nikki looked intrigued.

"Three million dollars is a lot of money," she agreed.

Carmen gave a sharp shake of her head. "Not enough to kill five women," she said.

"You'd be surprised," Nikki said, her tone edged with anger. As if she could offer a list of creeps who'd been will-ing to murder for financial gain.

And she probably could.

"Are you taking the lead on this?" Griff asked his friend.

Nikki shook her head. "I'm going to the crime scene, but my presence will be in an unofficial capacity."

Griff frowned in confusion. Serial killers were usually handed off to the feds.

"Has it moved up the chain?" he guessed.

"Nope." Nikki's expression was carefully bland. Which meant that inside she was seething with frustration. "There was no chain at all."

"The locals are in charge?" Griff rasped in disbelief. Nikki nodded. "Why?" he demanded.

Nikki hesitated, as if she was debating whether to share privileged information. Then she gave a small shrug.

"Because the women weren't the only ones found in the house."

The sunlight poured through the glass wall like liquid gold, but it was devoid of warmth as it spilled over the three people seated around the table.

Not that any amount of sunlight could actually combat the icy fear that was forming in the pit of Griff's gut.

"The owners of the farmhouse?" he asked.

"No. A man," Nikki said in clipped tones. "He was shot in the head. An apparent suicide."

Carmen blinked in confusion. "I don't understand."

Nikki reached to flip open the manila folder that was next to her notepad. Griff suspected it was more an opportunity for Nikki to decide how much to share, rather than any need to review the case file.

At last she lifted her head, speaking directly to Carmen.

"The local detectives searched the house and found the women neatly laid side by side on the basement floor. And in an upstairs bedroom they found a man with a gun in his hand and a hole in the side of his head." She tapped her finger on the file. "The cop's conclusion is the man killed the women then brought them to the house to hide them. But once he'd seen them laid out together he'd suddenly developed a conscience, and unable to bear his guilt, he decided to kill himself."

Griff made a sound of disgust. He'd never heard such a stupid theory. Serial killers didn't have consciences. They hunted and slaughtered their prey without remorse. That's what made them serial killers. And the only reason they would ever consider ending their life was because they were about to be captured.

He didn't bother expressing his opinion of the cops. Nikki was as aware as he was that their explanation of what happened was full of crap.

"Do they have a time of death?" he instead asked.

"Not yet. The autopsies will take a while," Nikki said. "By the times the bodies were found they were completely frozen."

There was a tense pause as the horror of what was found in the farmhouse crashed over them. Seated hundreds of miles away in an FBI office, it was easy to forget they were talking about young women who'd been brutally murdered and stashed in an abandoned house like unwanted trash.

It was finally Carmen who broke the silence. "Why are they so convinced this man is the killer and not just an unlucky witness?"

"They already ran his fingerprints and identified him as—" Nikki once again glanced at the file folder, her gaze skimming to the bottom of the top page. "Archie Darrell. Do you recognize the name?"

Carmen flinched, her brows snapping together. "No. Should I?"

Nikki flipped to the next page. "He started out as a petty thief who spent his childhood in and out of juvie. From there he graduated to sexual assault. He was sent to a mental facility when he was twenty."

Griff leaned forward, trying to catch a peek at the file. He didn't doubt for a second that Nikki would keep vital information from them. Right now she was an FBI agent. Not his friend.

"Why wasn't he sent to prison?" he asked.

"According to the police report he was delusional when they arrested him. He claimed to hear voices and was convinced that the woman he'd raped was Jezebel from the Bible. The judge ruled that he was unfit to stand trial." Nikki shuffled through the stack of papers. "He disappeared from the hospital over two months ago."

Jezebel? Griff grimaced. It was possible that it was nothing more than an act. But it was equally likely that he was truly unhinged.

Carmen curled her hands in her lap, but she didn't flinch. She'd spent the past few years listening to stories from killers that would make most people lock themselves in their home and never leave.

"Why would you ask if I knew him?" she demanded.

Nikki flicked a quick glance toward Griff, as if silently warning him to brace himself.

The icy ball in his stomach doubled in size.

Nikki spoke directly to Carmen. "After Archie Darrell escaped from the hospital, they searched his room. They found a copy of your book along with several pictures of you."

Griff swore beneath his breath, wrapping his arm around Carmen's waist as she abruptly leaned back, as if in need of his support.

"How did he get pictures of me?" Carmen's words came out as a shaky whisper.

Something that might be sympathy flickered through Nikki's green eyes, but her expression remained hard with determination. The perfect FBI agent.

"They think that the pictures were sent to him, but they had no way to trace his mail."

Carmen fell silent, her head turning to burrow in the hollow of his shoulder. The air itself felt heavy. As if Archie Darrell's sickness was managing to leak from the file folder.

Carmen, however, wasn't hiding from the truth. Instead, she was absorbing and processing what Nikki had just told her. At last she tilted back her head, meeting Griff's worried gaze.

"There's more than one killer," she rasped. "There has to be."

Surprisingly, Nikki gave a sharp nod of agreement. "That was my thought as well," she said. "I don't believe for a minute that the man committed suicide. If he was overcome by guilt, why would he go upstairs and lie down on a rotting mattress before putting the gun to his head? And where was his car? He didn't walk to the farmhouse carrying five dead women."

Griff tried to visualize the scene. The abandoned house. The victims laid neatly in the basement. The dead man upstairs with a bullet through his brain.

"If he had a partner, the two of them might have had a falling-out," he suggested. "Or Archie Darrell might have become so unstable he was a liability to the sick collaboration."

"Agreed." Nikki pressed her lips into a tight line. Her frustration was almost a physical force. "Unfortunately, the cops are eager to avoid mass panic at having to admit there might be more than one killer stalking women. It's far easier to reassure everyone that the madman is dead and that the public can go back to enjoying their holiday."

Without warning Carmen was leaning forward, her hand slamming on top of the table with a burst of fury.

"And what happens when the killings continue?"

Nikki didn't recoil at Carmen's outburst. Instead, a grim smile curved her lips.

"Then I'm no longer there as a professional courtesy," she told Carmen. "I'll take charge of the investigation."

Carmen scowled in frustration. Griff didn't blame her. He might have full faith in Nikki's talent as an agent, but that meant nothing if she wasn't allowed to do her job.

"So until then, we have to wait around for the killer to strike again?" Carmen's voice was harsh.

"No. I might not be the primary investigator in Kansas, but that doesn't mean I'm not able to follow my own leads." Nikki picked up her pen and flipped the page on her notepad. Then, settling her forearms on the table, she studied Carmen with a fierce intensity. "It's clear to me that you're somehow connected to these killings, Ms. Jacobs. I want to know everything about you."

Carmen's scowl deepened. "But—"

"Carmen." Griff interrupted her protest, giving her fingers a squeeze. He'd seen that expression on Nikki's face. Right before she'd spent the night disassembling her ex-boyfriend's prized motorcycle down to the last screw after she'd caught him with another girl. "You might as well get comfortable."

* * *

Despite the fear that churned through her like a toxic sludge, Carmen did her best to answer Nikki's questions. Even the ones that were intrusive, or downright stupid.

Of course, it'd taken more than one silent reminder that Nikki was doing her job. The woman could be downright abrasive. But having the vast resources of the FBI helping to track down the mystery killer, or killers, might make the difference between life and death.

And not just for herself.

If the maniac truly intended to imitate the killers in her book, then there were a lot of women in danger.

She had to do whatever possible to stop him.

It was after four when they at last returned to the truck waiting in the parking lot. By mutual agreement they drove straight to Louisville, stopping long enough for a quick meal at a fast food restaurant before they were back on the road.

Carmen's thoughts were too distracted to conduct a conversation.

She'd been right from the beginning. There was a serial killer out there. Probably more than one. And the lunatics were using her book as some sort of twisted inspiration.

Already five women had died. How many would be dead before the nightmare was over?

And was her name on the list?

It was after nine by the time they were crossing the hotel lobby and taking the elevator to the upper floor. She unlocked the door and stepped inside before she reached to flip on the light. As she was about to step out of the way so Griff could enter the room, Carmen's attention was caught by a white square on the carpet.

She bent down. "You must have dropped something when we were leaving yesterday," she said.

Griff abruptly brushed past her. "Wait," he commanded.

He was too late. Carmen had already grabbed the paper. Straightening, she felt the slick gloss beneath her fingers. It wasn't a note as she'd first thought. It was a postcard.

She turned it over, puzzled at the picture printed on the front. It looked like one of the cheapo postcards you picked up in a gift shop when you were on vacation. This one had an image of the ocean lapping against an impossibly white beach. The gentle waves reflected the sun that was just cresting the horizon and the words SURF AND TURF were stamped across the top in a large font.

There was nothing to show exactly where the picture had been taken. Just a typical sunrise over the water.

Sunrise.

Carmen reached to grasp Griff's arm. Once when she'd been helping her grandfather around the farm, she'd gotten too close to the edge of an old well. The soft ground had crumbled beneath her feet, sending her tumbling into the dank darkness. This felt just like it.

The terror. The sensation of falling through the air. And the jolting pain as she hit the bottom.

"Oh my God," she breathed.

Griff turned so he was standing directly in front of her. "What is it?"

"The Morning Star." She shoved the postcard into his hand. "The killer is going to the beach."

He studied the happy ocean scene, his lips tightening. Then he pulled his phone out of his pocket and took a picture of the postcard.

No doubt he would be sending it to Nikki.

Then he moved across the room. "I'll put it into the mail tomorrow morning," he said. "Nikki might be able to use her magic to get prints or DNA."

Carmen watched as he took the seat in front of the desk, booting up his laptop.

She moved to stand at his side, not sure if it was curiosity that sucked her across the room or his gravitational force field. Somehow over the past few days, she'd come to depend on having him near.

A knowledge that should have terrified her. Instead, she laid a hand on his shoulder, savoring the heat that seeped into her palm and through her body.

She didn't realize until that moment just how cold she was.

"What are you doing?" she asked.

"Using my own magic," he told her, his fingers flying across the keyboard. "The hotel has to have security cameras."

Carmen raised her brows. "You can break into their security system?"

"I prefer to think of it as borrowing their video for a short period of time," he informed her.

She watched as the computer screen was filled with the image of the hotel lobby. He really did break into the security system.

He touched the keypad and the image shifted to the empty restaurant. Another touch and she could see the kitchen.

She shook her head, caught somewhere between admiration and wry amusement. She hadn't realized what a formidable enemy Griff Archer could be when she'd blithely plotted to lure him into helping her with a new book. Otherwise she would never have tried to cross his path.

"No wonder Nikki didn't ask you any questions," she murmured.

Griff's attention remained locked on the screen. "This could take a while," he warned.

Accepting that she couldn't help, Carmen reached into her purse and pulled out her phone to plug it in. She didn't bother to glance through the dozens of messages. The details of her upcoming book tour would have to wait, along with the numerous invitations to speak around the country.

She didn't have the energy to concentrate on anything

beyond catching the bastards who were killing innocent women.

Pacing from one end of the hotel suite to the other, Carmen racked her brain for any memory that might give her a clue. There was her family who hated her, but it seemed a stretch to think they could brutally kill five women. And later, there'd been a few boyfriends. None who had seemed unstable, although who knew? It was impossible to look at someone and know that they might be capable of murder.

There'd also been men during her college years. A few lovers, several friends, and two professors who had been her mentors.

Again, it was impossible to think of them as psychotic killers.

She'd moved to stare out the window when Griff broke the silence that filled the hotel room.

"I got it," he said, leaning toward the computer screen.

Carmen's heart skidded to a halt. Was it possible they had caught the killer on camera? That this might all be over?

She hurried to stand directly behind Griff, leaning over his shoulder as he replayed the security footage to share what he'd seen.

The image of the hallway outside her hotel room came into focus, the camera obviously hidden in the ceiling only a few feet from her door. The video ran for a few minutes without any movement, and then a shadow fell across the carpeted floor.

Carmen leaned even closer, her hands grabbing Griff's upper arms to keep her balance. On some level she was aware of the hard muscles beneath her fingers, and the intoxicating scent of his male cologne, but her focus remained centered on the video.

The shadow lengthened, a pair of shiny, black leather shoes appearing first, followed by long legs covered by black slacks and then a uniformed jacket. Seconds later, the young man was in full view of the camera as he halted in front of her door.

The man looked from left to right before he squatted down and shoved something under the door.

The postcard, Carmen acknowledged. It had to be.

With another quick glance to see if he was still alone, the man straightened and hurried back down the hallway, turning the corner and going out of the range of the camera.

Carmen frowned. The man's round face and shaggy brown hair seemed vaguely familiar. As if she'd recently passed him in the street. But he certainly wasn't someone she actually knew. Not now, and not in the past.

She would swear to that.

Her breath hissed between her clenched teeth. The video had just created more questions than answers.

"He's one of the porters," Griff said, rewinding the video once again to study the man. He pointed toward the fitted jacket with the hotel emblem stitched onto the lapel.

Carmen straightened and stepped back, disappointment curdling through her. "That's why he seemed familiar."

Griff abruptly rose to his feet, turning to face her with a grim expression.

"I saw him when we first checked in and then again in the lobby when we arrived tonight," he said. "I'm going to have a word with him. You stay here and lock the door behind me."

He was headed toward the door with long strides. Carmen briefly considered going with him. Griff wouldn't be happy, but he couldn't actually force her to stay behind.

Then she gave a shake of her head. Griff was capable of tracking down the young man without her assistance. And she suspected that he might use more than his winning personality to get the information he wanted. She wouldn't be much help in a physical confrontation.

Besides, she had things to do.

Whatever they did or didn't discover from the porter, she was convinced that at least one of the killers intended to follow in the footsteps of the Morning Star. Which meant that he was headed to the West Coast.

With a flurry of activity, Carmen locked the door and then moved through the hotel suite, packing her clothes and then heading into Griff's bedroom to gather his belongings. They were both in need of a laundromat, or a shopping mall, but for now she was more interested in heading to the airport.

She was finished and had returned to her task of pacing the carpet when she at last heard a soft tap on the door. She hurried forward, taking the time to check through the peephole to make sure it was Griff on the other side.

Clicking back the deadbolt, she waited for him to walk past her, his bleak expression revealing that the meeting hadn't gone as well as he'd hoped.

Still, she had to know. "What happened?"

Griff turned to face her, his hands shoved in the front pockets of his jeans.

"He denied knowing what I was talking about, at least until I threatened to haul him to the security office," he said, his dark eyes burning with a smoldering fury.

Carmen studied his lean face, a strange pang tugging at her heart. It was more than just his sheer male beauty. It was the fierce determination that was etched in his features and the clenched muscles of his hard body.

In just a few short days this man had become her rock, her self-appointed protector. Someone she could depend on after years of being on her own.

The question that whispered in the back of her mind was whether he would still be there after the danger was gone.

"And then?" She forced herself to concentrate on far more important matters.

"Then the porter admitted that some man approached him when he was taking his cigarette break. I guess the management doesn't let the employees smoke near the hotel, so he always goes to the parking lot down the street," Griff said. "The man paid him fifty bucks to slide the postcard beneath the door. He didn't see any harm in it, so he took the money."

"Did he get a description?"

Griff shrugged. "Medium height, wearing a long trench coat with a scarf around his neck and a hat."

"Of course he was." Carmen rolled her eyes. She felt more resigned than disappointed. She'd already prepared herself for the fact that the killer was too clever to reveal his identity to the hotel porter. "He couldn't tell you anything helpful?"

"Nothing more than the fact that he'd talked to a fellow porter who'd been approached by the same man earlier in the day," Griff told her. "That porter refused."

Her brows drew together. She sensed there was a reason he mentioned the first porter, but she didn't understand how it could help.

"Did he recognize the man?"

Griff shook his head. "No, but he spoke with the first porter at ten in the morning."

"So . . ." Her impatient words died on her lips. Her eyes widened as she realized just what he was saying. "Oh."

He nodded, his lips pulled into a humorless smile. "Exactly. He couldn't have been the person who tried to run us off the road. Not unless he's capable of being in two places at one time."

Carmen muttered a curse as she pressed her fingers to her aching temples.

"I feel like I'm on a hamster wheel, running as fast as I can but never moving forward."

He stepped toward her, wrapping her tightly in his arms.

"I'm not going to let anything happen to you." She felt his lips brush the top of her head. "I swear."

She leaned against him, trying to absorb his strength. A chill was crawling over her skin, like an icy breath from the grave.

Or perhaps a warning that she was running out of time.

"We have to go to California," she said softly.

"I couldn't agree more," he shocked her by saying.

She tilted back her head, studying him with suspicion. What was going on? She'd expected him to fight her tooth and nail.

"You agree?" she demanded, assuming this was some sort of trick.

His hands framed her face, his expression hard with resolve.

"We're going to my house and you're staying there until Rylan can join us," he said, the tone offering no room for compromise. "By then Nikki will hopefully be on the case and we can track down the bastards and put an end to this nightmare."

She held his gaze. They were going to California. That's all that mattered for now.

Once they got there, she would decide how she was going to lure the killers out of hiding.

"Whatever you say," she meekly agreed.

Chapter Nineteen

December 27, California

It was just after midnight when Anita King trudged through the dark streets of Oxnard.

She'd worked a double shift at the local diner. This time of year the regular customers were out of town, or staying home with family to eat leftovers. Which meant she had to work twice as hard for the tips she needed to pay the rent this month.

A few years ago, the endless hours on her feet wouldn't have bothered her. But she wasn't thirty anymore. Hell, she wasn't even fifty. Now each step jarred her knees that ached from arthritis, and her shoes cut into her swollen ankles.

Which was why she'd decided to take the shortcut instead of remaining on the main thoroughfare.

Most nights she was happy to take the longer path. The price of aching feet was worth paying to delay the moment she had to walk through the door of her apartment.

She grimaced, hitching her purse strap higher on her shoulder.

It hadn't always been that way, she thought with a nostalgic pang of regret. She'd come to California forty-five years ago. She'd been young, barely seventeen, with big blue eyes and a girl-next-door beauty. But she hadn't just been another pretty face.

She could sing, and dance. She'd worked every summer to take tap lessons. And she could act. But after a few small roles, and one local stage production of *Annie Get Your Gun*, she'd made the classic mistake. The one thing certain to bring an end to her dreams. She'd fallen in love.

She'd played at being a sophisticated woman of the world, but the truth was, she'd remained that naïve girl from Nebraska. So when she'd gotten pregnant, she'd never considered the idea of getting rid of the baby. Instead, she'd demanded the handsome young actor who'd knocked her up put a ring on her finger.

No big surprise that the marriage had barely lasted long enough for her to give birth. By the time she'd returned to their cramped apartment with the baby her husband had already flown the coop.

Anita had been a single woman raising a baby without any training to earn a decent living. She should have returned home. Her parents wouldn't have been happy, but they would have taken her in. Instead, she'd panicked and seduced the young man who worked at the local deli counter. He'd been blinded by her beauty and it'd been easy to lure him into a quickie marriage before he could consider whether he was ready to take on a wife and child.

She grimaced. Unlike her first husband, Earl had done the honorable thing and stayed married to her even after the passion had faded, but Anita knew that somewhere deep inside him, he'd nurtured a small resentment. And that resentment had destroyed any hope that they could build a decent marriage.

Instead of marital bliss, they'd spent forty years bickering and sniping at each other. They fought about the kids. The finances. The shattered dreams.

Her blue eyes had dimmed, her long red hair had faded to a weary peach fuzz. And instead of gracing the silver screen, she was delivering hash to the late-shift workers.

And then the stroke had left Earl in a wheelchair.

And she was stuck.

Again.

Her gloomy thoughts matched the gloom that surrounded her as she walked past the brick buildings with their front windows boarded over and covered with graffiti. At one time the area was ravaged by gangs, but now even they had abandoned the place.

What remained was an eerie husk of a shell that used to be bustling with life.

Like her, she thought with a humorless smile.

Lost in her dark thoughts, Anita was caught off guard when a vehicle rounded the corner and a pair of headlights momentarily blinded her. Coming to a halt she blinked. There were white dots that were floating in her eyes. Until her vision cleared she wasn't going to risk continuing down the sidewalk that was cracked and pitted with holes. The last thing she needed was a twisted ankle.

When she opened her eyes again, it was to discover a white van had pulled along the curb right next to her.

Instinctively she took a step back as the window rolled down, her hand dipping into the pocket of her jacket. She never left her house without her Taser. Diamonds might be a girl's best friend, but fifty thousand volts of electricity was a woman's best defense.

The dome light came on in the van, revealing a nice-looking man with a charming smile.

"Excuse me," he called out.

Anita eyed him with hard-earned suspicion. She wasn't stupid enough to think that a man could be trusted just because he was good-looking and was wearing expensive clothes.

They were usually the worst.

"What?"

"I'm looking for Java Central."

She frowned. It sounded like a place that would be in L.A., not Oxnard.

"I've never heard of it," she told him.

He pointed to the empty building behind her, his expression sheepish in the dim light.

"My GPS shows that it should be right here."

"Don't know what to tell you." She turned to continue walking down the sidewalk.

"Wait," the man commanded, allowing the van to roll along the curb next to her. "This is really important. I'm supposed to meet my future in-laws there. My fiancée will kill me if I'm late."

Her lips twisted in a sour smile. Young love. What a bunch of hooey.

Her steps never faltered. "Look, I never heard of it. Ask someone else."

"Maybe if you'd look at the directions that she texted me, you would recognize where I went wrong."

"Yeah, right," she muttered. Even when she first arrived in California she wouldn't have been naïve enough to let a stranger on a dark street lure her toward his car.

"Please."

She halted long enough to send him an exasperated glare. She wasn't naturally rude. But after a day of hustling to serve people who assumed she was at fault with everything from the speck of dirt on the plate to their soggy fries, she was tired. Bone-deep tired.

"No," she said in sharp tones. "Just call your fiancée and ask her."

On the point of walking the short distance to the end of the street, Anita caught a movement out of the corner of her eye. She gave an awkward jump to the side, assuming that it must be one of the nasty homeless people. They were forever squatting in doorways and leaping out to demand money when she least expected it.

But even as her fingers tightened on her purse, the shadowy stranger lifted his arm. Was he holding something?

It looked like a hammer.

With a small gasp she raised her hands, holding them in front of her face as the man swung the object directly toward her head. Like that was going to help.

At the same time, she was aware that the man in the van was just sitting there. Watching.

Which could only mean one thing.

The two men had been working together. The man in the van had kept her distracted as she walked right toward her hidden attacker.

What she didn't know was why.

One glance at her waitress uniform and ragged coat that she wore over it would tell a robber that she didn't have much money. Especially for men who clearly weren't in need of pocket change. And it wasn't like she had a dozen enemies who could pay for a hit on her. She went from her crappy apartment to her crappy job and back to her crappy apartment. That was her life.

Sad? Sure. But not the sort of existence that made someone want her dead.

She was still mulling over the baffling attack when the hammer connected with the top of her head. Pain exploded through her brain and she shrieked.

She couldn't think. At least not clearly. Instead, her most primal instincts took control and she fell heavily to the ground, bending forward to burrow her head in her arms. Blood dripped down her cheek, the stench of old cement and piss wafting from the sidewalk. She braced herself for another blow, but astonishingly it never landed.

For a long minute there was nothing but the loud rasp of the man breathing. He sounded as if he was excited by her crouched body. Or maybe it was the tiny whimpers that were escaping from her lips. Then she felt hands gripping her upper arms and she was yanked to her feet. Before she could brace herself, she was roughly shoved into the back of the van.

Anita groaned, the shocking pain in her head making her fear that her skull had been cracked. Not that it mattered, she supposed dully, listening to the van door slam shut. She might not know why the men had taken her, but she did know she wasn't going to live to see the morning.

She was wrong.

The sun was just cresting the horizon when she died.

December 27, California

Carmen rarely lazed in bed.

She was an early riser who liked to get as much accomplished as possible before lunch. Her grandparents had been firm believers in the early bird getting the worm, and their tradition had been passed on to her. Even after she'd left home and moved on campus.

Her roommate had bitterly complained at being stuck with a morning person, but Carmen had ignored her whining. She had goals to achieve. And she wasn't going to do that by lying in bed.

This morning, however, she made no move to throw back the covers and dash toward the shower.

It could be because they'd spent hours in various airports trying to get to California. By the time they'd landed at LAX she'd made a firm promise to never, ever travel during the holiday season again.

Or it could be because she still wasn't sure how she intended to search for the killers. It was one thing to fly to California. That was a straightforward goal. Now that she was here, she didn't have a Plan B.

But more than likely, her reluctance to leave the bed was directly related to the man who was holding her tightly in his arms.

When they'd arrived last night, they'd stumbled up the stairs toward the bed. She'd had a brief glimpse of a large loft with rustic paneling and wooden beams on the ceiling. There were wide French doors that opened directly onto the balcony with stairs that led down to the garden. And an attached bathroom that was as large as some people's apartments.

She'd barely had enough energy for a brief kiss before they were asleep.

Now she turned onto her side and pressed her face into Griff's chest. He was wearing nothing more than a pair of loose boxers, while she'd stolen one of his T-shirts to slip over her undies.

It felt good to have their naked limbs entwined, with his lips brushing lazy kisses over her face.

Warm. Safe. Unbearably erotic.

As if equally bemused by the tender moment, Griff released a deep sigh.

"Is this a dream?"

His chest rumbled as he spoke, his heart thudding with a steady assurance beneath her ear.

"You haven't opened your eyes," she pointed out. "It might be a nightmare."

"Mmm." His hands skimmed down the curve of her backside and beneath her thin T-shirt. "Nothing that feels this good could be a nightmare."

She shivered in pleasure, even as her predictable fear of intimacy had her instinctively trying to push him away. Figuratively, if not literally.

"You have to admit your holidays would have been a lot more peaceful, not to mention safer, if I hadn't forced you to help me."

He abruptly rolled her onto her back, his heavy body covering her. Bracing his hands on the mattress, he gazed down at her with eyes that blazed with an unnerving intensity.

"First of all, no one forces me to do anything I don't want to do," he growled. "Just ask Rylan. He's been moaning about my pigheadedness for years."

Carmen blinked at his harsh tone. Had she touched a nerve?

She studied his lean, beautiful face. With his dark hair tousled and his jaw emphasized by the shadow of his morning beard, he looked far more primal than usual.

Her hands lifted to rest against his chest. She liked the feel of his heat beneath her palms. And the steel hardness of his chiseled muscles.

Of course, his muscles weren't the only thing steel hard, she realized as he settled between her legs. Her breath caught with excitement as his arousal pressed against her.

With an effort, she tried to remember what she was saying.

"You didn't want to get involved," she finally managed to mutter.

"I didn't want to admit just how much I wanted to help you," he corrected, his dark gaze lowering to her lips. "Which was why I sent you away, only to use the first excuse I came across to follow you to Kansas City. I already knew that once I gave in to temptation there was no going back."

He had followed her. Even though she'd tried to use him. And since then, he'd done nothing but try to protect her.

Another chunk of the wall surrounding her heart cracked and crumbled away.

"I suppose I should confess as well," she said.

His eyes lifted to meet her gaze. "Confess what?"

Carmen blushed, feeling weirdly vulnerable. "That I didn't try as hard as I could have to find a cop who would believe me," she told him. "Instead, I decided you were the only one who could help me."

He kissed the tip of her nose. "And you were right."

"I might have been right, but I've put you in danger."

He frowned at her low words. "Don't."

Her hands slid up his chest to grab his shoulders. "It's the truth."

His lips stroked over her cheek, pausing to nuzzle the corner of her mouth.

"We're in this together."

Together. She waited for the predictable surge of panic at the implication that they were a couple. But it didn't happen. Maybe because she was already overwhelmed by a more tangible fear.

On some level she'd realized that she was putting Griff at risk by asking for his help. But they'd been constantly on the move, always one step behind the killer, so it'd been easy to minimize what she was asking of him.

But alone in Griff's house, which he'd obviously spent time and effort to transform into a home that reflected his preference for quiet serenity, she was acutely aware of the danger.

"If something happens to you, I'll never forgive myself," she breathed.

He stilled, as if caught off guard by the sincerity throbbing in her voice. Then he tangled his fingers in her curls, pressing a swift kiss to her lips.

"Then we need to make sure nothing happens to me," he said, his lips tracing a path of destruction down the side of her throat.

Coherent thought began to slip away from Carmen. She'd

never realized how sensitive her skin could be. The merest whisper of his breath, the warm brush of his lips, the raw sensation of his body pressing her deep into the mattress.

It all combined to stir her desire to a fever pitch.

She wrapped her arms around his neck, her fingers tangling in his soft curls.

"How do you propose to do that?" she asked.

His lips lingered over the pulse that pounded at the base of her throat.

"The simplest answer is that we stay here," he pointed out.

"In your house?"

"In my bed." He paused, and then he corrected himself. "*Our* bed."

The unexpected vision of waking every morning in this bed, with Griff's strong arms wrapped around her, seared through her mind. Her heart missed a beat.

The image was fully formed, in vivid detail. No doubt because it'd been the starring feature in her dreams for months.

"For how long?" she asked.

"I'm thinking . . ." He deliberately hesitated, his lips tracing the neckline of her T-shirt. "Forever."

Her heart missed another beat. This one wasn't solely caused by his shocking words. She never took a man seriously when he was lying on top of her.

But because his hands were slowly moving down her body and slipping beneath the shirt, her toes curled as darts of pleasure ricocheted through her.

"A nice thought, but hardly practical," she husked.

He chuckled, pressing kisses along the prominent line of her collarbone.

"You know me better than that, Carmen," he said, his fingers hooking around the elastic top of her undies. "I could program our world so we would have everything we need delivered directly to the door."

Her breath was released on a low hiss as he tugged the panties down her legs and tossed them onto the floor.

"I would laugh, but I think you're serious."

He gazed down at her, his eyes dark with an intoxicating glow of desire.

"Never more serious," he assured her, ridding himself of his boxers with swift efficiency.

Then he was once again settled between her legs, the thick hardness of his erection pressing at precisely the perfect spot.

She struggled to think. She had something important to say. Didn't she?

It finally came back to her.

"We can't just ignore the fact that there's a serial killer out there."

He bent his head to kiss her with a fierce passion, as if willing her to push away all thoughts of the lunatics who were tormenting her.

"That's a job for the authorities," he rasped against her lips.

"But—"

Another demanding kiss. "Let them do their jobs."

He was probably right. What could she possibly do? She didn't know where the killers were, or how they intended to hunt for their next victims. She didn't even know how they connected to her.

But logically understanding she wasn't responsible for the deaths of unknown women didn't ease her desperate sense of guilt.

She had to do something. Anything. Even if it was only to make herself feel better.

"You know I can't," she breathed in rueful tones.

She expected anger. Or at least impatience for her stubborn refusal to concede defeat. Griff, however, allowed a slow, wicked smile to curve his lips.

"Ah." Without warning, he grasped the hem of her T-shirt and yanked it over her head. "A challenge," he growled.

Her lips twitched. It still enchanted her when she caught a glimpse of Griff's playfulness. She'd spent so long fantasizing about his male beauty and his clever mind that she'd forgotten his quirky charm.

"Challenge?" she questioned, her hands smoothing over his chest, her bracelet tinkling.

"You assume I can't distract you." He lowered his head. "I intend to prove I can."

His tongue stroked over her tightly furled nipple. She moaned. The pleasure that streaked through her was so intense it bordered on pain.

Clearly inspired by her reaction, he did it again. This time his stroke was rougher, more insistent.

Her back arched, her nails digging into his flesh.

"Are you distracted?" he demanded, blowing a warm breath over the wet tip of her breast.

She shuddered, her legs parting to allow the tip of his arousal to slip toward the entrance of her body.

"I might be a little distracted," she breathed.

He reached toward the small table next to the headboard, grabbing a condom and quickly slipping it on.

"I want you a lot distracted," he warned her.

Matching his action to his words, Griff used his hands and mouth to create havoc with her ability to think clearly.

White-hot desire seared through her. His touch was magic, creating sparks of hunger that had her legs wrapping around his waist in a silent plea.

"Griff," she muttered, her fingers threading into his hair as his lips stroked over her flushed face.

He lifted his head, holding her gaze as he slowly sank into her welcoming heat.

"Let me in, Carmen," he commanded, demanding far more than just access to her body.

"Yes," she whispered, offering him precisely what he desired.

December 28, California

The dune that overlooked the isolated beach wasn't perfect.

Sure, there was a view of the ocean, but it was almost a mile away. Not as satisfying as being directly next to the water. And while the driftwood that he'd piled to build the large pyre was impressive, there was too much brush and undergrowth around the area to properly see the three women who were balanced on top.

Hunter grimaced, taking a few pictures despite the thick shadows. The sky was just beginning to lighten, splashes of deep purple and burnt orange reflected in the waves. The Polaroids wouldn't be great, but they would have to do.

Returning his camera to the backpack he'd left at the edge of the small clearing, Hunter glanced impatiently toward the nearby trail. Executioner was supposed to be here waiting for him when he arrived half an hour ago.

Not that Hunter was entirely surprised he was late.

The man had always been the most challenging disciple. He was a narcissist who hated taking orders. On the other hand, the man had enough brains to realize that he needed help if he was ever going to achieve greatness.

Each day that passed, however, he was becoming harder to control.

A good thing that his "use by" date had just arrived.

On cue, the short, slender man strolled down the trail and entered the clearing. The darkness had lightened enough that Hunter could make out the thin, sharply carved features and the dark hair that had been stylishly cut short on the sides and left to flop over his brow. Executioner liked to think he was a cool hipster. Just like he wanted to think he was smart.

Both were self-delusions.

He folded his arms over his chest. "What took you so long?"

The man shrugged. As if he was the one in command, not just another disciple.

"You told me to clean out the hotel room and stash our stuff in the warehouse before meeting you," he drawled, then waved a hand toward the beach where a black-and-white truck was parked near the water. "Plus, the entire area is crawling with cops. I almost decided not to come at all."

Hunter's temper flared, but with an effort he forced himself to smile. *Soon*, he silently promised himself. But first he wanted to make certain that the man understood just how easily he'd been manipulated by a superior predator.

"Don't tell me that you're losing your nerve?" he mocked.

"No." Executioner curled his lips. "Just my patience."

"What's that supposed to mean?" Hunter demanded.

The man conjured a derisive expression. As if they were true rivals.

Idiot.

"So far you've expected the rest of us to take all the risks while you enjoy the rewards."

Hunter took a step forward. "We've all enjoyed the rewards. Or have you forgotten your handiwork?"

The man glanced toward the waiting pyre, his attention lingering on the three women.

The one with frizzy peach hair had been Executioner's choice despite Hunter's insistence that they find a blond. He said that the woman reminded him of his aunt Sheryl. A nagging bitch who'd been his babysitter when he was young. He confessed he'd always wanted to choke the woman until her lips stopped flapping.

He didn't add that he'd always wanted to tie her up and rape her until her screams filled the air with sweet music, but it'd been obvious in his enthusiasm.

An ugly flush stained the man's face. "I've forgot nothing. Including the fact that I was the one who had to spend an entire week freezing my ass off in Kansas researching the perfect truck stops to snatch the whores, and another week in Baltimore looking for a dump site." He flicked a glance over Hunter. "And what have you done?"

Hunter couldn't deny the man had been useful. Unlike the others, he was capable of completing tasks without constant supervision. But that didn't mean he was going to let him think he was anything more than a tool that he'd used for his own goals.

"What am I supposed to do," he told the man. "Fulfill my destiny."

"What destiny?"

"To become a god."

"A god?" The man released a stunned laugh. "You really are nuts."

Hunter's eye twitched. How had he ever thought this fool as being worthy to become his disciple? He should have left him to rot in the institution.

"I created you," he said in harsh tones.

His companion snorted. "Bull. Shit."

Hunter stepped forward, his eyes narrowed. "Who were you before I allowed you to become a member of our Kill Club?" he demanded. "A nothing. A nobody."

"You don't know anything about me."

"I know you were a sniffling, pathetic loser who failed at his attempt to rape and murder his own sister." His lips twisted. He'd done his research before using his contact in the outside world to reach out to him. Executioner had been a very naughty boy who'd been found in the woods behind his house with his sister. He had her staked to the ground, and beside her was a grave he'd dug to toss her body in. Only the fact that he was fourteen and the son of a wealthy banker had kept him from being thrown into prison and never seen again. Instead, he'd been like Hunter. Quietly stashed into a place their families could forget about them until they were properly rehabilitated. "They caught you with your pants down. Literally."

The flush darkened, his shoulders hunching even as the disciple tried to remain defiant.

"She wasn't my first."

"Liar." Hunter took another step forward. He could catch the scent of cigarettes and the bottle of bourbon the man had been drinking after they'd finished killing the women. It made his nose flare with disgust. Only the weak needed the crutch of nicotine and alcohol. "You were a wannabe and I gave you what you needed. Direction. Courage. Freedom." He deliberately paused. "I made you my disciple."

Executioner took an instinctive step back before he realized what he was doing. Stiffening his spine, he glared at Hunter.

"You tried to turn me into a spineless ass-kisser like the rest of your groupies."

He shrugged. There was no arguing with his logic.

"There are leaders. And there are followers," he said. "I'm a leader."

"Well, I'm done following," the man snapped. "We torch the bodies, then go our separate ways."

Hunter slipped his hand into his pocket. He wanted to play with the man, but already the sun was beginning to crest the horizon. Time was running out.

"Executioner, or should I call you Lou?" he mocked. "You're hurting my feelings."

"You don't have any feelings."

"You're wrong." Hunter took another step forward, and then another. Until he was standing a mere inch from his companion. Killing should be an intimate thing. Something that he could savor. "I feel anticipation."

The man scowled. "Hey, back off."

Hunter stood his ground. "Haven't you wondered what happened to your companions?"

"Not really." Like most narcissists, this man was incapable of thinking about anyone but himself. Hunter hadn't worried for a minute whether he would start to question the disappearance of the others. "I assume that they got tired of your stupid game and moved on. Just like I'm going to do."

Hunter pulled his hand out of his pocket, revealing the pistol he had clutched in his fingers.

"I suppose you could say they moved on," he agreed with a low chuckle.

The disciple glanced toward the gun, then back at Hunter's wide smile. He looked more baffled than terrified.

"What are you doing?"

Hunter gave an exaggerated roll of his eyes. "I suspected that you weren't very smart, but even you should realize what I'm doing."

He pointed the weapon directly against the man's forehead. It seemed to at last prove that he wasn't screwing around.

"No, please," the man rasped, lifting his hands in surrender. "You were right. I'm nothing without you."

Hunter smiled. He could almost smell the fear in the air.

This was what he craved. The control. The knowledge that he was in absolute control of life and death.

"I'm your god," he breathed.

The man nodded, sweat dripping down his face. "Yes."

"The sea was wet as wet could be, the sands were dry as dry," he quoted softly. *"You could not see a cloud, because no cloud was in the sky."*

Executioner frowned in confusion, but before he could speak Hunter squeezed the trigger.

The gunshot echoed through the nearby canyon, making Hunter's ears ring. He preferred to kill with his hands. Not only was it more satisfying, but a gun had the tendency to attract unwanted attention.

On the other hand, if you wanted someone dead, there was nothing more efficient.

And he wanted his companion dead.

Stepping back, he watched as the man tumbled forward, revealing the impressive hole in the back of his head. Any doubt of whether it was a survivable wound was answered. No one could live with most of his skull blown open.

In fact, Hunter was fairly certain he was dead before he hit the ground.

With a grimace, he circled the lifeless body and grabbed the man's ankles, pulling him until he was next to the pyre. Then, grabbing the red plastic container he'd left next to his backpack, Hunter sprinkled his disciple with gasoline.

The pungent smell clung to the air as he tossed the empty container onto the top of the pyre. A reminder that he needed to be careful as he shoved his hand into his pocket and pulled out the lighter.

Using his thumb to strike a flame, he leaned toward the large pile of kindling he'd stacked at the bottom of the pile. There was a loud swooshing sound as the dry wood instantly caught fire.

Nothing like a California drought, he acknowledged as he scurried away from the sparks that were already dancing on the breeze.

Within minutes the flames had grown into an inferno, easily destroying the bodies. At the same time the sun moved above the horizon, spilling golden rays across the beach. Not perfect timing, but close enough.

Turning, Hunter moved to grab his backpack and hurried up the trail. As much as he might want to linger and enjoy the sight, he wasn't a fool. The state park authorities were always on the lookout for fires. They would be swarming to this area the second they caught sight of the smoke.

Besides, the smell was hideous.

Once he reached the top of the trail, he moved across the nearly empty parking lot. He halted at the small compact car that Executioner had rented when he reached California. He didn't think the man was smart enough to suspect that he might become a victim, which meant he might have left something behind that would reveal their identities.

He grabbed the sheet of paper from the rental agency and Executioner's suitcase before he closed the trunk and crossed the lot to the white van waiting near the exit. He climbed directly into the back and tossed the case across the narrow space. He'd dispose of it later.

"Took you long enough," the driver complained, starting the engine.

Hunter didn't bother to glance in his direction. Like his other disciples, the man would grouse and complain, but in the end, he would do as he was told.

"I had some unfinished business."

"Can we go?"

"Yes." A shiver of anticipation curled through the pit of his stomach. "It's time to take our game to the next level."

Chapter Twenty

December 28, California

Griff woke early and slipped out of bed. He was careful not to wake the woman curled beneath the blankets beside him.

Standing next to the mattress he studied her tangled blond hair and pale face. After a day being forced to pace the floor, the poor woman had been unable to sleep. A fact that might have pleased him, since she'd turned to him for comfort more than once during the night. But he hated the knowledge that she was tormenting herself with guilt.

It was after five in the morning before she at last stopped her tossing and turning and fell into an exhausted slumber.

Now she was oblivious as he bent down to brush a light kiss over her curls and headed into the bathroom.

By eight o'clock he'd made coffee and was waiting for Rylan to pull into the driveway. He opened the door and, barely waiting for his friend to step across the threshold, grabbed him for a fierce hug.

Just having Rylan back in California was a huge relief.

"Thanks for coming, man." He pulled back, leading his friend into the kitchen.

"No thanks necessary," Rylan said, slipping off his

jacket to reveal his casual shirt and jeans. The younger man studied Griff with obvious concern. "You've always been there for me."

"True." Griff forced a smile as he poured Rylan a cup of hot coffee and crossed back to hand it to him. Together they leaned against the counter. "I remember getting out of bed at three in the morning to pay off your bar tab so you didn't get the crap beat out of you."

Rylan chuckled, a portion of his tension subsiding at Griff's teasing.

"Hey, we'd just made our first big score," he reminded Griff. "I thought we should celebrate."

Griff arched a brow. They'd been seniors together in college since Griff had managed to finish in three years rather than the traditional four. At the time, Griff had completed a school project that created a computer program that could perform facial recognition at twice the speed as any other. Rylan had been confident that he could sell the program.

And he had.

For a ton of money.

When the first check had come in, Rylan had headed to the local hangout and gotten plastered along with half the student body.

Griff, on the other hand, had put his money in the bank and gone to bed early. His way of celebrating.

Just a wild and crazy dude.

"We?" he demanded.

Rylan tried to look innocent. "I drank several toasts in your honor. I swear."

Griff sipped his coffee. "And the night you decided to sneak into the Rapson headquarters and got arrested? That was another three-o'clock-in-the-morning phone call."

Rylan shrugged. "I was trying to prove to them that they

had a shitty security system. If you'll remember I managed to score us a twenty-thousand-dollar project."

Griff's lips twitched. He'd been furious when Rylan had phoned from jail. They'd been in California less than a year and Rylan had been determined to get a contract from the corporation that owned more than a thousand storage units throughout the state. When they refused to believe there was anything wrong with their current system, Rylan had sneaked his way into their headquarters, telephoning the CEO of the company from his own office.

The president had predictably called the cops, who'd hauled Rylan to jail.

Thankfully, the board members of the corporation had been impressed by Rylan's ingenuity, and not only dropped all charges against him, but also rewarded them with a hefty contract.

"Fair enough." Griff's smile faded as he set aside his mug. "I just want you to know I appreciate your sacrifice. This was supposed to be your family time with Jaci and your father."

"Don't worry about it." Rylan waved aside his words. "To be honest, it wasn't that great a sacrifice. Jaci was about to start baking five dozen chocolate chip cookies, and she was giving me a look that said she was expecting me to help."

"I thought she was cutting back on her catering business?"

Rylan grimaced. Griff understood that his friend didn't object to Jaci working. She was an artist in the kitchen. But he had insisted that she try to slow down. She'd been burning the candle at both ends for years trying to make ends meet.

"She has," Rylan said, his expression frustrated. "But that doesn't stop every church, club, and local charity from calling her whenever they have a potluck dinner to raise money."

"So you get to be her sous-chef?"

"Sometimes I wash dishes," Rylan said dryly. "And other times I get to keep Riff and Raff from causing complete chaos."

Griff laughed. The thought of his sophisticated, charismatic friend spending his days with his hands in dishwater and corralling Jaci's gigantic mutts was mind-boggling.

"A year ago you were walking the red carpet with a pretty starlet and planning to spend the holidays skiing in St. Moritz," he said.

Rylan's features softened. "There's no place I'd rather be than spending the night in that small farmhouse with Jaci in my arms."

"Amazing."

"It is," Rylan agreed. "Once you find the right woman all your priorities will change."

Just a week ago Griff would have felt a stab of envy. What man didn't want to find a lover and companion he could spend the rest of his life with?

Now he just smiled.

"I've already discovered that," he said.

Rylan frowned. "Carmen?"

"Yes, Carmen."

There was an awkward pause before Rylan cleared his throat. "Do you remember our conversation when I came back to tell you I intended to marry Jaci?"

Griff nodded. He'd been standing in the kitchen when Rylan announced his intention to return to Missouri and live with Jaci, although he'd promised that he would travel back to California on a regular basis. Griff had been genuinely happy for his friend, but he'd also known that Rylan's protective instincts had been in hyperdrive when Jaci's life had been threatened.

"I warned you that a man shouldn't make important decisions in the heat of battle," he said.

Rylan eyed him, as if he was trying to bore deep into Griff's brain.

"You were right. It wasn't the time to make any big decisions."

"Then why didn't you take my advice?"

"Because I love Jaci. And I've known her my entire life." He said the words as if they were undeniable facts. "You barely know this Carmen Jacobs."

Griff narrowed his gaze. He didn't need to know Carmen since she was riding a tricycle or making macaroni art. There'd been an undeniable connection between them from the beginning.

"I know her well enough to give my life to protect her."

Rylan parted his lips, no doubt intending to continue the argument. Then he caught sight of Griff's expression and he instead heaved a small sigh.

Rylan never bothered fighting losing battles.

"It's not going to come to that," he promised.

Griff glanced toward the wide opening that led toward the staircase. For now, Carmen was safely tucked in his bed. But he wasn't stupid enough to think that she was going to be willing to remain locked in this house forever.

A day, maybe two, and she was going to insist they do something to try to find the killer.

"I hope not," he muttered.

Rylan reached out to squeeze his shoulder. A silent promise that Griff wasn't alone.

"I called in some favors while I waited for my flight," the younger man told him.

Griff had expected no less. "And?"

"The California Bureau of Investigation has promised to send agents to assist the local cops," he said. "If the killer . . . or killers . . . hope to mimic the Morning Star, they'll have to bring the bodies to the beach at some point."

Griff shoved his fingers into his hair, frustration bubbling through him.

"Assuming that they intend to copy the killers in the book."

Rylan frowned. "I thought that was your theory?"

Griff paced across the floor. He couldn't shake the sensation that he was missing something. Like they had all the pieces to a puzzle, but they'd put it together wrong.

"It's a theory, but so far the only real evidence we have is the pictures that were sent to Carmen, and the bodies that were found in Kansas," he said. "They both point toward one of the killers she profiled, and there were the flowers that were sent to her hotel room. Still . . ." His words trailed away as he gave a shake of his head.

"Is there something else you want me to do?" Rylan demanded.

"I don't know. I—" His words cut off as the phone he'd stuck in his front pocket suddenly vibrated. Pulling it out he felt a surge of hope as he saw the name on the screen. "Speak of the devil," he breathed.

"Who is it?"

"Nikki." He pressed the phone to his ear and paced into the living room. "Tell me you got the bastard."

His brief optimism was immediately squashed. Nikki not only denied any leads on the killers, but she revealed that he had even more reason to worry about Carmen. With a terse good-bye, he slid the phone back in his pocket and called out for Rylan to follow him.

He was in his office and seated at his desk when Rylan hurried to join him.

"What happened?"

Griff fired up his computer, his hands unsteady as he typed on the keyboard.

"Carmen's PR firm received another packet of photos," he said.

Rylan sucked in an audible breath. "Like the first ones?"

"Yeah," Griff said. "This time they realized that it might be important and opened it. Once they saw the pictures they sent them straight to the FBI, who contacted Nikki. She's on the way to Baltimore."

Rylan grabbed a chair and set it next to Griff. He leaned forward as Griff clicked into his e-mail.

"Why Baltimore?"

"Because the bodies that went with those photos were found early this morning by a homeless man."

Rylan stiffened. "How many?"

"Four," Griff said. "And it gets worse."

"Tell me."

"Nikki didn't go into many details, but she did say that the women had been laid side by side, like those in Kansas. And all the women were strangled and left with copies of Poe's 'Raven' on their chests."

Rylan's jaw tightened, but he didn't look surprised. Of course, he dealt more directly with the law officials who used their products. Including agencies that battled against terrorists.

There were few things left to shock him.

"Just like in Carmen's book," he said.

"Not exactly," he corrected. "Nikki said after the cops sent her the preliminary photos from the crime scene that there were a few obvious differences."

"What differences?"

"They were all blond."

It took a second before Rylan muttered a curse. "Just like Carmen."

"Yes."

An ugly dread clouded his mind, bringing with it visions of dead women who looked like Carmen.

Christ. It didn't make any sense. There were dozens of true crime books written every year. Maybe hundreds. Why would the killers become obsessed with Carmen? Was there some personal connection? Or just an unlucky trick of fate?

The unanswerable questions spun over and over, churning the acid in his stomach. If he didn't end up with an ulcer, it would be a miracle.

"Is there more?" Rylan thankfully interrupted his dark thoughts.

Griff nodded. "There was a man who was in the same abandoned house. He had a gunshot to the head just like the one in Kansas."

Rylan wrinkled his brow, trying to piece together the relevant details with what they already knew.

"So this time there were four women, not five."

Rylan gave a slow nod. He hadn't really considered the change in M.O. Was it important? A part of a pattern? Or had they been interrupted before they could get the fifth victim?

"That's what the cops told Nikki."

"And what about the man? Do they think he's one of the killers?"

Griff turned his attention back to the computer, scrolling through his messages.

"She just got an ID on him. She said she sent me the file," he said.

Easily finding the e-mail, he opened it to find a rap sheet attached.

"Josh Lucroy," he read out loud. He studied the fuzzy picture of a guy with a square face and dark hair that needed to be combed. He had small eyes and looked half asleep. There was nothing that indicated he might be a ruthless serial killer. His gaze lowered to his arrest report, annoyed when he realized that it was official. Which meant that his juvenile records were sealed. The arrests didn't show up until he turned eighteen. "Looks like he got picked up for peeking in windows. And exposing himself in a park." His gaze skimmed over the petty crimes, moving to the bottom of the list. "Christ. He set a homeless person on fire."

Rylan grimaced. "Sounds like a real charmer."

Griff clicked to the next page. He'd expected information on the trial. Instead, there was an official form from a court-appointed psychiatrist.

"He was found mentally incompetent to stand trial."

"What happened to him?"

It took a few minutes to search through the file and discover Josh Lucroy's final destination.

"He was put in an institute." Griff paused. He felt a tug of recognition. Something to do with the first man found. "Wait," he muttered, pulling up the search he'd done on Archie Darrell.

"What is it?" Rylan asked.

He quickly read through his notes, locating what had been teasing at the edge of his mind.

"The man who was found dead in the house with the first women was put in an institute as well."

Rylan laid a hand on the desk as he bent sideways to read the screen.

"The same one?"

Griff cursed beneath his breath. He'd leaped to the conclusion that it would be the same institute. Which would mean they could narrow down possible suspects. Perhaps even find a connection to Carmen.

Of course, that would have been too easy.

"No," he growled, his voice harsh with frustration.

Rylan gave his shoulder a squeeze. "There could still be a connection."

With an effort, Griff sucked in a deep breath and released it with a low hiss. Now more than ever he needed to keep his emotions under firm control.

"True." He concentrated on his computer, sorting through his programs until he found the one he wanted. "I'll run a search to see if the two had any contact before they were put away, and then I'll find someone I can talk to at the hospitals. They might have a way to trace any correspondence he sent and received." He was struck by a sudden thought. "Plus, I want to know if they found anything that might relate to Carmen in his room."

Rylan sent him a curious glance, but before he could ask why the man should have information connected to Carmen, his phone buzzed. He pulled it out of his pocket and glanced at the screen.

"Jaci?"

"No. My contact at the California Bureau of Investigation." Rylan frowned as he rose to his feet and pressed the phone to his ear.

Griff surged out of his chair and watched his friend as he paced toward the window. Five minutes later Rylan ended the call and turned back, his expression grim.

Griff clenched his hands at his sides. "Did they find something?"

"Yeah." He walked back to stand next to Griff, his voice pitched low enough it wouldn't carry. Clearly, he didn't want Carmen to overhear if she happened to be awake. "They just finished investigating a suspicious fire."

"On the beach?"

"On a dune, just twenty miles south of here," Rylan corrected. "Which is why they didn't see anything or anyone until too late. They were concentrating their efforts closer to the ocean."

A nausea rolled through his gut. They were too late. Again.

"Bodies?" he demanded.

Rylan nodded. "Three women and one man. They're too badly burned to know more than that."

Griff drummed his fingers on the desk. They hadn't been exactly on the beach, but it couldn't be a coincidence that the victims had been burned. The killers had copied the Morning Star, just as they'd feared.

So, did that mean they were about to move on?

About to track down a copy of Carmen's book, Griff froze. He'd been too focused on the fact that the killers had already struck to chew through the few facts they had.

"Wait," he murmured. "You said there were three women and one man?"

Rylan nodded. "That's what my contact said. I'm not sure if they've fully processed the scene, so I guess it's a possibility they might find more bodies."

Griff didn't think so. He was beginning to see the pattern.

"They went from five women to four women to three women," he said.

Rylan hesitated before he realized what Griff was saying. "Right. And each time a man was shot through the head and left with the bodies."

"It sounds like some weird cult," Griff muttered. "They kill women and then themselves."

"And the cult is growing smaller," Rylan pointed out, abruptly squaring his shoulders. "I want to take a look at the crime scene."

"Can your buddy get you past the local police?"

Rylan's lips twitched. "You know me well enough to realize that a few cops aren't going to stop me."

Griff glanced over his shoulder. "I can't leave Carmen."

"I've got this," Rylan assured him.

"Thanks, Ry."

He shrugged. "It's what partners do." He started across the room only to halt and turn back to face Griff. "After I leave I don't want you to open the door until I get back," he commanded. "I don't care if it's someone waving a badge. Whoever is doing this has managed to kill twelve people and move across the country without getting caught. They're smart, and they're organized. I don't want you becoming the next victim."

"Don't worry, I don't trust anyone," Griff assured him, following his friend out of the study and to the front door. He waited there as he watched Rylan slip into his rented car and drive away.

Only then did he close the door and lock it.

Rylan was right. Whoever was responsible for the killing spree was either incredibly smart or lucky. Either way, he wasn't going to take any chances.

Pouring himself another mug of coffee, he wandered back to his study and tried to concentrate on scouring for more information on the two men who'd been identified. They had to offer some clue to the killers.

Unfortunately, he found it increasingly difficult to keep his thoughts from straying to the woman who was currently sleeping in a room above him.

He didn't want to disturb her. Not after her restless night. But he needed to assure himself that she was safely tucked in his bed.

Strolling to the back of the house, he was struck at how quiet it seemed. Odd. He'd lived here for years, and he'd always felt comforted by the peace that shrouded his home. Now he realized that he'd already become addicted to hearing Carmen's bright chatter and the sounds of her moving around his house. And the scent of her lemony soap lingering in the air.

The thought that she might eventually disappear and leave him alone in his silent house was enough to make his heart squeeze with dismay. He didn't want the silence. Or the illusion of peace.

He wanted Carmen.

In his life. And in his home.

Reaching the master suite, he eased open the door and

stepped inside. He frowned, coming to a startled halt. He'd left the room shrouded in shadows. Now the French doors had been pushed open to allow the morning sunlight to spill across the empty bed.

Carmen was awake. And instead of coming to find him, she'd chosen to walk in the garden.

Weirdly hurt, Griff headed onto the balcony and down the staircase. His head might tell him that it was perfectly reasonable for Carmen to want to spend time in the beautiful morning air, but his heart wanted her to jump out of bed, anxious to be with him.

Juvenile, but true.

He headed down the flagstone pathway, and his steps quickened as his gaze swept the garden. Where was she?

He didn't think she would leave the yard alone. Even if she was frustrated by her inability to be a part of the hunt for the killer. She was stubborn, not stupid.

He reached the end of his property and circled toward the side of his house. It was possible she preferred the shady terrace. In his haste, he didn't notice the sound of the side gate being pushed open, or the man who strolled up the paved walkway. It wasn't until a male voice interrupted his increasingly frantic search that Griff realized he was no longer alone.

"Morning, Griff."

Glancing to the side, Griff came to a grudging halt. His neighbor was a tall, lanky man with a thick mane of silver hair. Dr. Randall Gregory had been a plastic surgeon to the stars for over forty years before retiring and moving away from the glitz and glamour of Hollywood.

Now he was like Griff. A man who just wanted to live his life without people poking their nose into his business.

Which made them perfect neighbors.

"Randall." He smoothed his features to a polite smile. "Have you seen the young woman who's staying with me?"

The man's heavy brows rose at the unexpected question. "Not this morning. Has something happened?"

Griff shrugged. "Just wondering if she'd wandered out here. I was about to make breakfast."

"Oh." The man gave a lift of his hands. "I can't help you. I just came out myself."

"Okay. Thanks." On the point of turning away, Griff was halted when the man spoke again.

"Hey, I was going to ask if you got your alarm system fixed?"

Griff froze. "What?"

"The security firm you asked to come check your system was here a couple days ago," Randall told him.

"I wasn't home a couple of days ago," Griff reminded the man.

"Yeah. The man came over and said that you told him that I had a key," Randall said. "I didn't tell anyone I had a spare to your place, so I assumed you must have sent him."

"You let him in?"

"Yeah." Randall frowned, a hint of worry settling on his tanned face. "Did I do something wrong?"

Griff wanted to screech in fury. Instead, he forced himself to find out as much information as possible.

"What do you remember about the man?"

"He had on a uniform from a security company." Randall looked defensive. "I assumed you must be having trouble with your alarms."

Griff balled his hands into tight fists. He'd never gone into details about his business or the fact that he was the owner of one of the top security firms in the world. Which meant he would never, ever hire anyone to screw with his high-tech equipment. Now his dislike of casual chitchat was coming back to bite him in the butt.

"Do you remember the name of the security company?"

Randall furrowed his brow, searching his memory. "Residential Alarms," he at last murmured. "Or something like that."

"Did you see what he was driving?"

"Just a plain van. White."

"Christ," Griff breathed.

"Is there anything I can do?" Randall called out as Griff spun on his heel and ran at full speed back into the house.

Griff ignored his worried neighbor as self-disgust blasted through him. He was considered the premier security expert in the world. His talents helped to protect America from terrorist attacks. But he'd been outmaneuvered by one of the oldest tricks in the book.

Jerking out his phone, he dialed 911.

Then he called Rylan.

Chapter Twenty-One

December 28, California

After a year spent traveling from one hotel room to another, Carmen was used to waking up and not knowing exactly where she was. Usually she'd roll onto her back and slowly allow the memory from the day before to fill in the blanks. Eventually she'd figure it out.

This morning it wasn't nearly so easy.

For one thing, she was lying on a hard floor instead of a bed. And despite the gloom that surrounded her, she could tell that she was in a vast space, not an expensive suite.

With a small groan, she lifted a hand to press it against her aching head, trying to pinpoint just what had happened.

She remembered being in Griff's bed. His arms had been tightly wound around her as she'd finally fallen to sleep. And then . . .

Nothing.

She struggled to clear her oddly fuzzy gaze, her confusion only deepening as she focused on the ceiling high above her.

There were a few rays of sunlight that peeked through narrow windows. The rays caught the speckles of dust that danced in the hushed air, and allowed her to catch sight of the heavy iron beams that served as rafters. The sort of beams that were only used in industrial buildings.

Certainly not expensive hotels.

It took longer than it should have, but at last her confusion mutated into fear.

She didn't exactly know how she'd gone from the comfort of Griff's bed to being stretched out on the hard cement floor, but she did know that she was in danger. And that she had to escape.

Sucking in a deep breath, she sorted through the fog in her brain. Her first instinct was to leap to her feet and flee in terror. A smart decision, except for the fact that her limbs felt like they were filled with lead.

Her second instinct was to close her eyes and pretend that she was still unconscious. Playing dead worked for possums, didn't it?

But almost as if to prove that she couldn't run, or hide, the sound of soft footsteps echoed through the silence.

Fear clogged her throat, making it hard to breathe as she forced herself to turn her head. At first she was distracted by the huge stacks of wooden planks that were neatly piled on steel racks throughout the vast, open space. On the far walls were square sheets of plywood and tall posts that didn't fit on the shelves.

It was some sort of lumberyard, she inanely decided. Or warehouse.

Which explained why the place smelled like the inside of her mother's hope chest. A musty cedar odor that was almost overwhelming.

Carmen frowned in confusion. Why would her kidnapper bring her to this place? And why was it empty?

Her confusion only deepened when a slender form appeared from behind one of the long racks and she caught sight of the man strolling toward her.

She easily recognized the thin face and pale blue eyes. Her heart skipped a beat, her mouth dry.

"Ronnie?" she breathed, feeling as if she was in a dream. Or a nightmare.

A smug smile curled his lips. He was dressed in jeans and a chunky sweater that emphasized his wiry body. Not that Carmen was fooled. He could easily overpower her.

She laid her palms flat on the cement and pushed herself into a sitting position. She grimaced. It felt like her brain was sloshing around in her skull.

As if sensing she was incapable of rising to her feet, Ronnie squatted next to her. She caught the scent of smoke. As if he'd recently been standing next to a bonfire.

An unnerving chill spread through her body.

"Are you surprised?" Ronnie demanded.

She licked her dry lips. Surprised? Stupefied came closer to the truth.

Ronnie Hyde. The son of her family's housekeeper. The strange, silent boy who was always sneaking around the house.

Was he mixed up in this madness? Was he one of the killers? It seemed impossible.

"I don't understand."

"You will," he murmured, his words spoken as a promise. "In time."

She scooted an inch backward. It wasn't an attempt to escape. Just a need to put some space between her and the man who looked like her childhood friend, but had grown into a stranger. A dangerous stranger.

"Where am I?" she demanded, the words coming out as a croak.

"At a Jacobs warehouse." His pale gaze swept over her, a muscle twitching at the base of his jaw. As if he was struggling to suppress an emotion that was so big it threatened to engulf him. "I thought it was an appropriate setting for our reunion. And it has the added benefit of being closed until after the New Year."

Her brow furrowed. "This place belongs to my uncle?"

"Yes." His smile twisted. "They managed to use your inheritance to expand the family business. I'm sure they won't mind if we borrow it for a few hours."

Fear was a tangible force as it clawed through her, threatening to paralyze her. With an effort, she forced herself to suck in a deep breath.

Panic wasn't going to save her. She wasn't sure anything could, but she intended to be prepared just in case.

"How did I get here?" she asked.

Ronnie shrugged. "I brought you, of course."

"Why?"

He leaned closer, his breath sour as it brushed over her face.

"Because I wanted us to have some alone time."

Alone time? She took more deep breaths, her gaze darting to the nearby racks in the hopes of catching sight of some sort of weapon. There was nothing. Predictable, of course. But she was suddenly struck by the empty silence that filled the vast space.

They were completely alone.

"Where's Griff?" she harshly demanded.

Anger flared through the pale eyes. "He no longer matters."

Carmen dug her nails into the cement, sheer horror overwhelming her fear. The thought that this man might have hurt Griff was unbearable.

"What did you do?"

"Nothing. At least, not yet." Ronnie shrugged, emphasizing his disinterest in Griff. "If he stays out of my way I don't have any interest in him. If he tries to interfere then I'll get rid of him."

Carmen's breath hissed between her teeth. Oh, thank God. Griff was safe. That's all that mattered.

Then, without warning, an unexpected burst of hope exploded through her.

Griff was free. And by now Griff would have to have realized she was missing. Which meant he would be moving heaven and earth to find her.

All she had to do was stay alive long enough for him to work his magic. Right?

The thought was enough to stiffen her spine. At the same time, she subtly pointed and flexed her feet. She needed to get the circulation flowing through her stiff legs in case she needed to run.

"I still don't know how I got here," she said.

"Because I happen to be very clever," he assured her. "I realized after I saw you at Christmas that I could use your relationship with Griffin Archer to my advantage." He paused, then grimaced. "It interfered in my original timeline, but that couldn't be helped."

She studied his scarred face, considering his words. He clearly hadn't expected her to travel to Louisville, but he'd been willing to use her arrival to his advantage. Just perfect.

"You sent the postcard," she said.

"I arranged to have it delivered," he corrected. "And then I traveled here to prepare for your arrival. Including a visit to your lover's home to ensure I could bypass his security system." He reached out to press his finger to a spot on the side of her neck. A small pain jolted through her. "I injected you with a little happy juice and I carried you out the balcony and through the garden. Simple as pie."

She flinched in disgust at his touch. His fingers felt cold against her skin, clammy. Like a fish.

"Why would you kidnap me?" she rasped.

He frowned, annoyed by her reaction. "You know why."

"No, I truly don't understand," she breathed.

He narrowed his gaze. "Maybe you don't." Without warning

he grabbed her chin and roughly forced back her head. He studied her like she was a bug beneath a microscope. "You look so much like your mother."

She tried to jerk away from him, only to gasp when he squeezed hard enough to send shooting pain through her jaw.

"So I've been told," she managed to say.

He continued to study her. "But you have your father's smile. Or should I say *our* father."

She stilled, all thoughts of murder and mayhem forgotten as she met his gaze. The pale eyes shimmered with an inner emotion Ronnie could barely contain. Anticipation?

"What did you say?" she forced herself to ask.

"Our father," he repeated.

"Our?"

"Stuart Jacobs was my father," he said. "And you, sweet Carrie, are my sister."

Ronnie sat back on his heels, watching the stunned emotions that rippled over her face with avid fascination. Carmen barely noticed. She was grappling with his outrageous claim.

Stuart Jacobs was the father of Ronnie Hyde?

She mentally repeated the words over and over, trying to let them sink into her brain.

They refused to penetrate.

Maybe she was being foolish. After all, her father had murdered her mother. He was obviously capable of any atrocity. Including denying the existence of his own child despite the fact he practically lived beneath his own roof.

But Carmen shook her head. Whatever her father's faults, there'd never been a second when he hadn't been devoted to her. There was no way he would have treated his child with such a cold disdain.

"That's impossible," she muttered.

Ronnie's face settled into sullen lines. As if he was disappointed by her reaction.

"Of course the precious princess would assume it was impossible," he sneered.

She flinched at the venom in his voice. Why hadn't she seen the bitterness that stewed deep inside him?

"My father would never . . ." Her words trailed away as his fingers dug into her face with bruising force.

"What?" he snapped, an ugly flush crawling beneath his skin. "Have sex with a mere housekeeper?"

"He would never have denied his own son," she said, blinking back the tears of pain. She didn't know if Ronnie realized he was hurting her, but she didn't want to give him the satisfaction of seeing her cry. "Unless you're claiming he didn't know?"

Ronnie released his hold on her chin and surged upright. He stared down at her with a brooding expression.

"Let me tell you a story," he said.

She released a silent breath of relief. Not just because the pain in her chin eased, but because the longer the crazy, delusional man talked, the longer Griff would have to find her.

"What kind of story?" she asked in what she hoped was encouraging tones. To her ears it sounded like a squawk.

Ronnie shoved his hands into the front pockets of his jeans, aimlessly circling the small open space. They were at the back of the warehouse in an equipment bay. On each side of them were large forklifts. She assumed they were used to move the heavy stacks of lumber.

Ronnie, however, strolled across the cement like he was an actor crossing the stage. Carmen had a sudden suspicion that he'd desperately longed for the spotlight even when he was hiding in the bushes.

"It's about a young, foolish woman who was born to a poor family," he said with a dramatic flourish of his hands. "She didn't have parents who indulged her every whim.

Instead, she had to go to work when she was just seventeen in the fancy house on the edge of town."

"Your mother?"

"My poor, innocent mother." He sent her another one of those bitter glances. As if he blamed her for his mother's lack of fortune. "She came to the house to work, but she was promptly seduced by the rich owner."

Carmen frowned. She could still remember the way her father looked at her mother. Blatant adoration.

There'd been nothing of that when he was in the same room as the housekeeper. She didn't think the two of them even spoke unless it was for her father to ask Ellen to perform some household task.

Surely there would have been some lingering affection if the two had been lovers?

"Why would she stay if my father took advantage of her?"

His features contorted with fury before he was visibly struggling to control his temper. Long minutes passed, his harsh breath the only sound to break the thick silence.

At last he regained control of his composure.

"This is my story," he snapped.

She used his anger as an excuse to scoot away from his looming form, pressing her back against the wall. Not that she had to pretend to be afraid. Ronnie Hyde was scaring the crap out of her.

"I'm sorry."

As if he was soothed by the sight of her cowering on the floor, Ronnie sniffed and returned to his pacing.

"Once she discovered she was pregnant, she couldn't expect the man to do the honorable thing and marry her," he said, the words falling smoothly from his lips. Carmen suspected he'd rehearsed this speech a hundred times. Maybe a thousand. "She was a servant. A nobody."

"She had his child and stayed on as his housekeeper?" she asked.

He sent her an annoyed glance. "What else could she do? She had to support herself and her child."

She paused. She didn't want to anger him. He was obviously demented. And while she didn't know if he was personally involved with the killings, or why he would be fixated on her, she didn't doubt he would happily bash in her head, just like those poor women in Kansas.

Still, she had to keep him busy with his performance.

So long as he was enacting his grand tragedy, he wasn't doing whatever awful thing he had planned for her.

"Did your mother tell you this story?" she finally asked.

He waved a dismissive hand. "Of course not. She was still infatuated with her lover. She would do anything to protect him."

"Then my father told you?" she breathed in disbelief.

His hands clenched. "*Our* father," he insisted. "And no, he wouldn't never tell me the truth. He pretended I was invisible."

She stared at him in confusion. His pain seemed so genuine, but she didn't understand why he was so certain that he was a Jacobs.

Of course, her brain wasn't functioning at full steam. Perhaps she was missing something obvious.

"So why do you believe my—" The words stuck on her lips. She swallowed and forced herself to continue. "Stuart was your father?"

"It was simple. I always knew there must be a reason my mother refused to talk about my father." A tic pulsed in his jaw, his emotions swaying from self-pity to smug arrogance in the blink of an eye. "It could have been because he was a total loser. After all, she let Andrew hang around. A woman who would invite that lazy prick into her home obviously has no taste in men."

"Andrew was always very kind to me," she said before she could halt the words.

"Like he had a choice?" Ronnie sneered. "You were the princess. I was just the bastard."

She licked her lips. Had Andrew been violent to Ronnie? She couldn't remember seeing any visible bruises or broken bones when they were young, but who knew what went on behind locked doors? It might help to explain why Ronnie had grown up to be a psychopath.

"I still don't understand," she told him.

He came to a halt, his chin tilted to an aggressive angle. "It's simple. I refused to believe that I was the product of some lowlife who couldn't keep his pants zipped." He offered a dramatic pause. "I was special."

"And you decided if you were special you had to be a Jacobs?"

He glared at her, easily sensing her disbelief. Did he assume that she would simply agree with his wild fantasy?

"I suspected it," he said in defiant tones. "And I wasn't alone. There were others who could see my resemblance to Stuart."

"Who?"

He slashed his hand through the air with a sudden burst of irritation.

"It doesn't matter. I don't need anyone to tell me what I already know." A hard smile twisted his lips. "Not after I discovered the letters."

"What letters?"

The glitter of anticipation returned to his eyes as he pointed a finger at her.

"Wait here," he commanded before he was heading out of the bay.

Like she had a choice? The drugs Ronnie had injected into her continued to flow through her bloodstream, making her body lethargic.

There was the sound of a nearby door being pulled open. Maybe an office? She couldn't be lucky enough for Ronnie to actually leave her alone in the warehouse.

With a muttered curse, Carmen leaned her head against the wall. Her brain was spinning and there was a sickness sloshing through her stomach, but she tried to put her scrambled thoughts in order.

She was certain Ronnie Hyde was insane. Just the fact that he'd drugged her and carried her to this warehouse was proof of that.

But what was his connection to the killers? Was he an active participant or just a flunky who was being used by others? He hardly seemed a mastermind criminal.

And what was her connection? Was his obsession with her because he had some crazed notion that they were related? Or did it have something to do with her book?

Ronnie and whoever else was involved had been copying the killers she'd profiled. And what did he intend to do with her now?

The questions swirled round and round, picking up speed until Ronnie suddenly returned. Walking forward with a triumphant smile, he gripped a stack of envelopes in one hand. He continued forward, standing directly next to her as he tossed the envelopes onto her lap.

She warily opened the top envelope and pulled out a yellowed sheet of paper that was stained and wrinkled. As if it'd been handled a hundred times over the years.

"Where did you get these?" she asked.

He hesitated, almost as if he didn't want to answer. "They were hidden in my mother's room," he finally muttered.

There was a strange edge to his voice. As if he was lying.

But why?

With a shake of her head, she concentrated on unfolding the paper. She glanced at the words at the top.

My glorious Ellen.

Ellen. Her stomach clenched. Ronnie's mother. Quickly her gaze lowered to the bottom of the letter.

Your adoring lover, Stuart.

Her father.

Good. God. Was it possible?

Had her father actually had an affair with his house-keeper? Had he allowed her to give birth to his son and then treated them both as servants while he married and had a daughter?

Sickened by the thought, she allowed her gaze to drift down the letter. It took a few lines to realize that the words seemed familiar. Not that she'd ever received a love letter that was filled with poetry about her beauty, or the desperation to stroke his fingers over her silken skin. But still, there was something . . .

Carmen sucked in a shocked gasp.

She knew why this letter was familiar. It was an exact replica of the love letter her father had written to her mother.

With shaky hands she pulled out another letter. She skimmed over the words, easily able to recognize the flamboyant declarations of love. It was another duplicate.

So what did that mean?

Did her father have a copy of the letters stashed in his desk to send to whatever woman he happened to be having sex with?

It seemed the most reasonable answer. Then she paused,

her brows knitting together as she belatedly realized that the letters weren't exact duplicates.

She bowed her head, studying the heavy, sloping handwriting that didn't look anything like her father's light, elegant strokes.

The words might have been copied, but it hadn't been by Stuart Jacobs.

"My father didn't write these," she breathed.

"Liar," Ronnie snarled in fury.

Carmen lifted her head, her lips parted to explain that the handwriting didn't match. But before she could say a word, Ronnie was swinging his hand downward, slapping her face with enough force to send her sprawling across the cement floor.

Even knowing it was a waste of time, Griff searched the house top to bottom for any sign of Carmen. Then he searched again. His brain simply refused to accept that she'd been stolen from his bed.

A great protector I turned out to be, he acknowledged in disgust.

He was in his study running a diagnostic on his security system when there was a knock on his front door.

Griff surged to his feet and raced through the house. He hadn't expected the cops to be so quick. Maybe Rylan had called the chief to insist on swift action.

He yanked open the door, and his eyes widened in shock.

It wasn't a cop standing on the porch. In fact, it was the last person he'd expected to see.

His brain stalled, the electronic impulses firing, but refusing to connect. Pure instinct took over as he reached out to grab the man by his tailored leather jacket. Then, with one mighty heave, he was yanking the unwelcome visitor into the house and slamming him against the nearby wall.

"Where is she?" he growled.

Matthew Jacobs flushed, his eyes wide with shock. "What the hell?"

Griff wasn't fooled for a second by the man's pretense of confusion. There was no way his arrival was a coincidence.

No. Way.

He moved one hand upward, wrapping his fingers around Matthew's throat.

"Tell me," he commanded.

Matthew lifted his hands to grab Griff's wrist, his face flushed. Did he think that Griff was stupid? That he wouldn't connect him to Carmen's disappearance?

"Easy, man," he rasped, making a choked noise of distress as Griff tightened his grip. "Christ. Are you high or just crazy?"

Griff narrowed his gaze. He wanted to keep squeezing until the bastard confessed where he'd taken Carmen, but with an effort he forced himself to study the man's frightened expression.

If he killed him, then he couldn't reveal where they'd taken Carmen. For now he had to play the stupid game.

Matthew was here for a reason. And until the man had gotten what he'd come for, Griff assumed he wasn't going to get the answers he needed.

"Why are you here?"

He hesitated, staring at Griff with a wary anger. Then, perhaps sensing his life was hanging in the balance, he licked his lips.

"My dad sent me to California to check on our warehouse," he said.

Griff frowned. He'd gone through the Jacobses' business records. Now he shuffled through his memories, trying to determine if Matthew was lying. He recalled the list of properties. There'd been seven stores. Three of them in Kentucky, the others dotted around the Midwest. But there'd also been warehouses. One on the East Coast and two on the West Coast.

Which meant there might be one nearby.

"Why are you checking on it?" he demanded, still convinced Matthew was connected to Carmen's disappearance.

"Someone used our private code to enter the office in the warehouse two nights ago."

"So?"

"We have a special code for all our properties that allows us to override the security."

When Griff had met Matthew Jacobs, his first impression was that the younger man was an arrogant douchebag.

His impression hadn't changed.

"Special code?"

"My father doesn't trust anyone," he admitted. "He wanted to be able to enter any store or warehouse without giving notice to the managers or guards he was going to arrive and check out the books, or do a surprise inventory. So each property has a code that overrides the alarms so he can come and go without attracting attention." Matthew gave a lift of his shoulder. "Only three of us have that code. My father, Baylor, and me."

Griff didn't have any trouble believing that Lawrence Jacobs felt it necessary to spy on his employees. He wasn't the sort of man who could earn loyalty. He would have to bully and threaten his staff to keep them in line.

But he wasn't so willing to believe the shallow, self-centered Matthew would jump on a plane and travel across the country just because a private code had been punched into the security system.

They no doubt had guards at the warehouse who could investigate what had happened.

"And that made you travel all the way to California?" He shook his head. "Bullshit."

Matthew's gaze darted from side to side, as if hoping someone might magically appear to distract Griff. When it became obvious that there was no help on the way, he grimaced.

"In my inner pocket."

Griff stared at him with blatant suspicion. "What?"

"Just reach beneath my jacket and pull out the paper."

A trap? Hard to believe that he had anything in his jacket that could be a threat. After all, if he had a weapon he would want to keep it hidden.

Griff's fingers continued to press into Matthew's throat. "You even twitch and I'll snap your neck," he warned.

Matthew froze, a drop of sweat beading on his forehead and sliding down his nose.

"I'd heard that tech billionaires were psychos, but you really are nuts," he muttered.

Griff ignored his babbling. He was far more concerned with patting down his visitor. Only when he was certain that Matthew wasn't hiding a weapon did he slide his hand beneath the expensive jacket. His fingers easily located the folded piece of paper in the inner pocket. He pulled it out and held it in front of Matthew's face.

"What is it?"

"It's the reason I'm here," Matthew said.

Griff made a sound of annoyance. Was the man deliberately trying to piss him off? A dangerous choice. Right now he wouldn't hesitate to crush the man's windpipe.

With one hand he awkwardly unfolded the paper. He could make out a fuzzy image that looked like it'd been taken by a cheap camera and then printed out in black-and-white. With a frown he tilted it toward the morning sunlight that poured through the open door. Finally he could make out what looked like a young man in . . . a lumberyard? There were stacks of wood in the background.

He looked closer and suddenly realized that he recognized the sharply carved profile of the man.

"Is that Ronnie Hyde?" he demanded in confusion. Why would Matthew have a picture of his housekeeper's son in his pocket?

"Once the guard realized our code had been used, but none of us were in California, he pulled the footage from the surveillance camera and e-mailed this image to my father," Matthew said. "We instantly recognized who was sneaking around our property."

First Matthew was in California. And now there was seeming proof that Ronnie was here as well. So what did that mean? Were the two working together?

Ronnie, after all, had steered Carmen toward Indiana with his implication that her uncle had stolen her inheritance. He had to know she would return home to try to find evidence of the life insurance policy. It would have been a simple matter to follow them and wait for an opportunity to strike. Like when they were trying to cross an icy bridge.

He gave a shake of his head. Right now he didn't care why Ronnie or Matthew might want to hurt Carmen. All that mattered was bringing her home safely.

"Where's the warehouse located?" he demanded.

"Around forty miles north of here."

Griff's breath caught in his throat. So close. Could that be where they'd taken Carmen? Or was this a trick to ensure he wasted his time trying to track her to the warehouse? Matthew might have been sent to distract him with false leads while they escaped from the area.

Then again, he couldn't ignore a potential lead.

"Is there a reason for Ronnie to be in the warehouse?"

"Hell, no," Matthew snapped.

"Then why give him the code?"

"I didn't."

Griff allowed the paper to drop to the floor, returning his full attention to Matthew.

"Your father or brother might have asked him to take care of something if he was in the area," he pointed out.

Matthew gave a decisive shake of his head. "I talked with both of them. Not that it was really necessary." The younger man's face twisted into an expression of revulsion. "I can promise you that no one in the Jacobs family would trust Ronnie Hyde to pick up our trash, let alone give him security codes to our properties."

Griff studied him. Either Matthew was the best actor he'd ever met, or he truly loathed Ronnie Hyde. Of course, that didn't mean the two weren't working together, he quickly reminded himself.

Greed often made strange bedfellows.

"You don't like the housekeeper's son?"

"No, I don't," Matthew agreed without hesitation. "And not because he's the son of our former housekeeper. He was always a sneak and a liar who I caught spying on me whenever I visited my uncle Stuart's house." His lips curled into a sneer. "Honestly, he was a freak and I was glad his mother sent him away."

Griff arched a brow. What would Matthew think if he knew that the housekeeper had sent away her son because she thought the Jacobs family was lacking in basic decency?

Probably he wouldn't care. Griff had a suspicion that Lawrence and his sons didn't put a high value on ethics.

"A freak?" he asked.

"Yeah." Matthew grimaced. "He was watching. Always watching. From the bushes or the attic windows. I even caught him taking pictures of my uncle when he thought no one was looking. It was weird. If it wasn't for his stepfather's loyalty to the Jacobs family, he wouldn't be allowed on our estate."

Griff's jaw clenched. Had the creep been spying on Carmen as well? That would explain his obsession with her now.

Of course, Matthew could be lying.

Right now Griff had no intention of jumping to conclusions. He'd spent the last few days chasing after shadows. Carmen couldn't afford for him to make a mistake now.

"Then how did he get the code?" he asked.

"I told you. He's a sneak," Matthew said, his gaze darting toward the paper that had fallen to the floor. "And he has access to our estate. He could have searched my father's office and run across it."

Griff studied the man's flushed face. It would be easy to dismiss the idea that Ronnie could have known he would need the codes to the warehouse. That would mean he'd peered into the future and known that Carmen was going to be traveling to California to stay at Griff's house, so she would be conveniently located for him to kidnap.

Then again, whoever had been sending Carmen the strange clues had deliberately been leading her from one location to another. First to Kansas City and then to Baltimore. And finally they'd left the postcard luring her to California.

So it was possible that he'd been prepared for her arrival long before Griff had entered the picture. And that her presence in his house had merely made it easier for the bastard to find her.

Frustrated fury bubbled through him, his need to be out searching for Carmen an overwhelming compulsion.

"You haven't explained why you traveled all the way to California," he snapped. "You could have called the cops."

His eyes darted to the side. Matthew either didn't want to answer Griff's question, or he was about to lie.

"That was my first thought," he finally said.

"But?" Griff prompted.

The younger man tugged on Griff's wrist, as if Griff might have forgotten he still had his fingers wrapped around the man's throat. Griff didn't budge.

Matthew muttered a curse, accepting he wasn't going anywhere until he'd answered Griff's questions.

"I saw you Christmas morning," he abruptly said.

Griff waited for him to continue. When he didn't, Griff made a sound of impatience. The clock was ticking. Tick. Tock. And with every passing second, Carmen could be slipping further away.

He refused to believe that anything might have already happened to her. His world would shatter.

That simple.

"And?" he growled.

Matthew flinched, easily sensing that Griff was reaching the end of his limited patience.

"And I was in the foyer when you pulled up to the house Christmas morning," he hastily continued. "I was about to open the door when I watched Ronnie lure you away. After that you took off like we had the plague."

Griff narrowed his gaze. If Matthew had watched them drive away, he might have been the one to follow them to the hotel and then onto Carmen's farm.

"Ronnie wasn't the only one who likes to watch," he murmured.

Matthew's lips twisted. "Touché," he murmured. "But I wasn't standing there so I could spy on you. My father was nagging because I'd had a couple of drinks before lunch and I was going to step outside to get away from him. It was the only way to enjoy my brandy in peace."

Griff wasn't impressed. "What happened next?"

"After you left I went out to ask Ronnie what he'd said to you," he said. "I knew it had to be something bad about our family or you wouldn't have left without at least stopping at the house and making a polite excuse to miss lunch."

"What did he tell you?"

"He said he'd settled one score. Then he laughed and walked away." Matthew's jaw tightened and he lowered his gaze. Griff once again suspected that he was trying to hide something. "I didn't know what he meant, but when I saw that he was sneaking around our warehouse, I wondered if he was going to try to settle another score. I wanted to catch him in the act so I could figure out what he was planning."

Griff studied Matthew's lean face, before a portion of his suspicion abruptly eased. Finally. Something that made sense.

He wasn't stupid enough to think that Matthew had rushed to California because Ronnie had used their private code. Why not just call the cops? But if Lawrence Jacobs had any nefarious secrets, he would be desperate to keep them hidden. Undocumented workers. Cooked books. Shortcuts around regulations. And if they feared Ronnie was out here to cause them trouble, they would do whatever necessary to stop him.

Especially if they suspected that Carmen was already snooping into the Jacobs family's business.

"Okay," he said, still far from convinced that Matthew was the harmless boob he pretended to be. "Then explain why you're in my house."

"Are you kidding?" Matthew scoffed. "I'm in here because you grabbed my throat like a madman and slammed me against the wall."

Griff narrowed his gaze. Did the man think he was being funny? If so, Griff wasn't amused.

"Don't screw with me," he snapped.

"Christ." Matthew heaved a harsh sigh. "Since I was

going to be stuck in California for a few days I thought I would stop by and see if you were in town."

"Why?"

A flush stained Matthew's face. "I hoped we could hang out together."

Griff was genuinely baffled. "Hang out?"

"You know, a few red carpet events. Maybe a pool party with some half-naked babes." Matthew grimaced, his gaze darting over Griff's shoulder to the nearby door. "Clearly, I caught you at a bad time. So if you'll just remove your fingers from my throat I'll be on my way."

Griff muttered a curse. Was he an idiot? Griff would rather gouge out his eyes than waste one second of his life "hanging out" with this shallow jerk. Or was this all some elaborate trap.

Only one way to find out.

"Carmen is missing," he abruptly said.

Matthew blinked. He looked genuinely baffled. "Missing? Missing from where?"

Griff ignored the question. "I want you to take me to the warehouse."

"Look, man. I just—"

Griff tightened his grip until Matthew's eyes threatened to pop out of his head.

"Now."

"Yeah." Matthew made a gagging sound. "Great idea."

Chapter Twenty-Two

Carmen knew that she'd blacked out from Ronnie's vicious slap. What she didn't know was how long she'd been out. Certainly long enough for Ronnie to have moved so he was crouching next to her.

There was a strange expression on his scarred face as he watched her. Like a snake who'd just bit a mouse and was watching in pleasure as the venom spread through her body.

It was creepy enough that she pressed her hands to the cement floor and pushed herself to a seated position. Jagged pain shot from her jaw to the back of her head, wrenching a low groan out of her.

Crap. Her head was spinning like she'd been on a three-day drinking spree and her mouth was throbbing.

Reaching up, she cautiously touched her lower lip. It was swollen twice its normal size and so tender she wondered if she needed stitches. With a grimace, she pulled her hand away to study the blood that stained the tips of her fingers.

Ronnie abruptly broke the thick silence. "You shouldn't anger me."

"I didn't mean to," she breathed, resisting the urge to try to find a way to placate her captor.

He was clearly unstable. Which meant there was no way

to guess what might or might not trigger a burst of violence. Right now, all she could do was try to stay alive long enough to hope that help was on its way.

The pale eyes held a hectic light as he glared at her. "Why won't you accept the truth?" he demanded. "I showed you the letters."

She scooted back, using the need to rest her aching head against the wall as an excuse to put some space between her and Ronnie. It might be her imagination, but it felt like an evil aura was pulsing around the man.

She didn't want to be tainted.

"The handwriting doesn't look right," she told him.

Ronnie abruptly straightened, his hands curling into tight fists of frustration.

"You sound just like our father."

"What do you mean?"

"I waited for years to earn the right to be claimed as a Jacobs." He paced across the bay, nearly reaching the forklift before he turned to pace back toward her. "I was the perfect son. Always helping my mother around the house and offering to run errands. I would even follow him when he went on his evening walk. I thought if we could be alone together, he would feel more comfortable confessing where we couldn't be overheard by your mother." He released a sharp, humorless laugh. "He pretended as if he didn't even see me."

Carmen shivered. She'd always thought that Ronnie was sneaky, but she hadn't realized he'd been stalking her father.

She pointed out the obvious. "Maybe he didn't tell you because he didn't believe you were his son."

In three long strides he was back at her side, his hand raised in warning.

"Don't say that."

She cringed, turning her head to the side. "Sorry."

Long seconds passed as he tried to regain command of

his volatile temper. He sucked in a deep breath, his expression defiant.

"Do you think I didn't try to convince myself that he ignored me because my mother had never told him that I was his son?" he demanded. "But then I saw the letters."

Her gaze shifted toward the letters, which were scattered a few feet away. In the gloom they looked like bits of discarded trash. A tangible reminder of broken dreams.

"They didn't say anything about a child," she said in confusion.

He clicked his tongue. As if she was being incredibly stupid.

"No, but they proved that my mother hadn't been just a quickie in the pantry," he insisted, a fleck of spit collecting at the corner of his mouth. "They had a relationship. He loved her."

She once again glanced toward the scattered letters. Did she tell him that they were exact copies of letters that had been sent to her mother?

No. She might not be able to predict what would set him off, but she was pretty sure he wasn't prepared to accept that someone had found the letters that had been written to her own mother and simply copied them. He wanted to believe his mother had been special to his father. Whoever that might be.

"Okay," she forced herself to mutter.

His narrow face hardened, but he accepted her pretense of agreement.

"The letters show they were in a relationship. There was no way he wouldn't have realized that his lover was pregnant and that the baby was his." He pivoted away, resuming his pacing. A manic tension hummed in the air around him. "He was deliberately denying my rightful inheritance."

Carmen jerked, watching him pace toward the forklift at

the end of the bay and back again. Had Griff been right in the first place? Was all this horror and blood about money?

"You want an inheritance?"

He waved a hand, annoyed by her inability to understand what he was saying.

"I want what was denied me," he insisted, lifting his hand to point an accusing finger in her direction. "What you had."

She furrowed her brow. "What did I have?"

"Parents who loved you."

She shrugged. She couldn't argue with that. Whatever had been going on between her parents, it had never lessened their affection for her. She'd spent her childhood confident in the belief that she was a treasured member of her family. Something she'd taken for granted until it had been snatched away from her.

Still, she'd seen how Ellen had been with her only son. She might have been a stern woman, but she'd been devoted to Ronnie. In fact, now that Carmen was older, she could look back and see that the woman had kept him close to her side. Almost as if she didn't want him out of her sight.

"Your mother loved you," she said.

Ronnie slashed his hand through the air. "I wanted the right to my true name," he rasped. "Can you imagine what it feels like to be the one cleaning up dog shit from the yard, or taking out the trash, while the princess is flouncing around in her new dress with a bunch of her snotty friends?"

The animosity spilled out of him, like an infected wound that was suddenly lanced. Clearly, he'd been hoarding his resentment for years.

"If you want my share of the inheritance, I'm happy to give it to you," she said. "You said that I should have three million dollars from my parents' insurance policy. You can have it all."

"I don't want money, I want respect," he snapped. "I want

my father to look me in the eye and tell me that he's proud of me."

An unexpected regret sliced through her heart. She'd spent the past fourteen years refusing to think about her father. It was too painful to try to reconcile the man she'd loved with the man who could murder her own mother. It wasn't until she'd been discussing the past with Griff that she realized she'd locked away the good memories along with the bad. Which wasn't fair to her father. Or her.

"It's too late for that," she breathed.

An odd expression twisted his face. "It wouldn't have been too late," he said, reaching up to rub his forehead. Was he in pain? Or sick? Well, beyond the obvious sickness of being a crazed lunatic. "He just wouldn't listen to me," Ronnie continued, seeming to speak more to himself than her. "If he'd just admitted the truth, then I wouldn't have had to punish him."

Her mouth went dry. That didn't sound good.

"Is that why you kidnapped me?" She pressed against the wall, prepared to try to scramble away. "To punish my father?"

Without warning he chuckled with genuine amusement. Like she'd just told a funny joke.

"You don't know anything," he mocked.

"I already told you that."

"Stupid girl."

Carmen braced herself. Ronnie was becoming increasingly agitated. It was obvious in the jerky motions of his body and the muscle twitching beside his eye. She sensed he was ready and eager to hit her again.

Perhaps worse.

"How did you punish my father?" she asked, hoping to keep him distracted.

He hunched his shoulders, looking oddly vulnerable before he was deliberately stiffening his spine.

"I shot him."

The words left his mouth and for a second Carmen thought it was the sort of delusional boast that a man would make who wanted people to believe he wasn't a spineless coward. He could say he'd hidden in the bushes and used his BB gun to take a potshot at the lord of the manor. It wasn't like her father was around to deny the lie.

Then the world tilted, and she was plummeting through darkness. Images streaked past her. Silvery threads of memory. A young girl crawling out of her bed and slipping through the shadowed house in search of her parents. Of that same girl fleeing in terror at the deafening blast of a shotgun.

Then the images shifted. Now she was in the kitchen where two broken bodies were crumpled on the tiled floor. A teenage Ronnie was standing in the center of the room with a shotgun in his hand, his grinning face splattered with blood.

The image began to crack. And then it shattered. Returning her to the chilled warehouse and the brutal awareness that everything she believed about her past was a lie.

And alone with the monster who was responsible for destroying her life.

"Are you saying that my father didn't commit suicide?" she breathed, struggling to accept his words.

"Of course he didn't." Ronnie shoved his hands into his front pockets. "He was too arrogant to take his own life."

"God." She pressed a hand to her throat. Her heart was doing something weird in her chest. Beating too fast, and then forgetting to beat at all. It made it hard to breathe. "You killed him."

Ronnie scowled, looking like a petulant child. "It's not what I wanted."

She studied him in horror. "Are you trying to claim it was an accident?"

"I wanted him to speak the truth."

She shuddered. He was truly insane.

"Where did you get the gun?"

He shrugged. "I found it while I was cleaning the garage. It was in a cabinet with a box of shells."

She slowly nodded. She had a vague memory of her father warning her never to play around the wooden cabinet. The gun had belonged to her grandfather, who'd been an avid hunter.

"How did you get into the cabinet?" she demanded. "It was always locked."

"I found the key," he said with a vague shrug, although it didn't take much effort to figure out the young Ronnie had been snooping around the house until he found it. "As soon as I had it in my hands I knew I finally had the means to force him to acknowledge me as his son."

She scowled. "By killing him?"

The twitching next to Ronnie's eye accelerated as he gave a wave of his arms.

"No," he sharply denied. "That wasn't supposed to happen."

A mixture of pain and fury erupted through Carmen, briefly muting her fear.

She wanted to tilt back her head and scream. Or better yet, leap to her feet and pound her fists into Ronnie's face. She wanted him to hurt. To bleed like he'd made her parents bleed.

"What did you think?" she asked in harsh tones. "That my father would be overjoyed to confirm the fact that you were his son while you were pointing a gun to his head?"

His jaw jutted. "I wanted him to say the words, but he refused. He even denied that my mother had been his lover." His voice didn't hold one ounce of regret. Or guilt. Just an annoying whine, like he was the victim. "I hated him in that moment."

She glared at him in disgust. "So you killed him."

"I told you it wasn't my fault," Ronnie insisted. "He tried to grab the gun out of my hands. My finger squeezed the trigger in the struggle."

Carmen's hand moved up to touch her damp cheek. She hadn't even realized that she was crying.

"He didn't commit suicide," she whispered, feeling something shift deep inside her. A fundamental truth that determined who she was and who she was yet to become. Then she drew in a shuddering breath, staring at Ronnie with an accusing gaze. "Why did you hurt my mother? She had nothing to do with you."

"She must have been on the back terrace when the gun went off. I didn't even have a chance to try to help our father before she ran through the back door and started yelling at me."

Once again there was no guilt. In fact, he looked aggravated. As if her mother had been an annoying pest that he'd had to eliminate.

She curled her hands into tight fists. "You bastard."

With a blur of motion, Ronnie surged forward, an ugly expression twisting his features.

"I'm not a bastard." He grabbed her hair and slammed her head against the wall. "Don't ever say that again."

Griff held his Glock in his hand as Matthew swerved his car to a halt on a quiet side street. He'd grabbed the weapon before they'd left his house. He had a license to carry a gun, but he rarely had it out unless it was to take target practice with Rylan.

Now he kept it pointed toward the younger man.

Not because he intended to shoot Matthew. At least not yet. But if the idiot was plotting to lead him into a trap, then he wanted him to know he was going to take a bullet to the head.

At the same time, Griff's gaze skimmed their surroundings, taking a full inventory of any potential dangers.

It looked harmless enough. The area was dominated by

square buildings with large windows covered by steel bars and flat roofs. He assumed they were mainly warehouses and small factories. There weren't any local stores or residences. A stroke of luck that kept the midmorning traffic to a mere trickle.

Matthew pointed toward the two-story building across the street.

"That's our warehouse."

Griff frowned, studying darkened windows and the empty parking lot. "Where is everyone?"

"We close down our warehouses between Christmas and New Year's Day." Matthew shrugged. "Dad claims it saves us a bundle in salaries."

The casual indifference in the man's voice made Griff roll his eyes. Griff had built his own empire without any help from his father. Nothing had been handed to him on a silver platter.

Thank God. Clearly, being a pampered rich boy did nothing to encourage ambition.

"You don't handle the budget?" he asked in mocking tones.

Matthew sent Griff a humorless smile. "Numbers give me a brain cramp."

With a shake of his head, Griff turned his attention to the warehouse.

It was a two-story structure, built with red bricks and steel doors. It was old, but it looked as if it'd been kept in good repair. Meaning it wouldn't be easy to enter without alerting whoever was inside.

His attention turned to the cement parking lot, which was surrounded by a six-foot chain-link fence.

"There's a truck parked at the end of the lot," he said, trying to make out the gold emblem painted on the door of the vehicle.

"Probably the guard," Matthew said. "We rent them from a local security firm."

It made sense. The truck looked like a company vehicle. His gaze scanned the street, searching for any sign that he was on the right track.

"No van," he finally muttered.

Matthew sent him a confused frown. "Were you expecting one?"

Ignoring his companion, Griff pulled out his phone. He kept the gun pointed toward Matthew as he hit his top speed-dial number. Seconds later Rylan was answering.

"Hey, Rylan, I have a change of plans," Griff said. "I'm at a warehouse owned by Lawrence Jacobs. I'll text you the address." He grimaced as Rylan spent the next minute questioning Griff's sanity in a voice loud enough to wake the dead. "I'm not alone," Griff grimly assured his friend. "I'm with Matthew Jacobs. He made an unexpected visit to my house. He claims he's here to track down Ronnie Hyde. I'll explain when you get here." There was another furious tirade where Rylan promised to kick Griff's ass as soon as he arrived at the warehouse. Waiting until his friend had to take a breath, Griff intruded into his tirade. "Did you manage to find out anything?"

There was a long pause before Rylan revealed what he'd learned. Griff grimaced at the description of the three women and one man who'd been burned to a crisp, even as he accepted that the deaths were a copy of the Morning Star. The killers were here. And it was very possible that they had stolen Carmen from his bed.

His gaze locked on Matthew's stiff profile. One way or another, Griff was going to find her. Or die trying.

"Do they have any leads?" he demanded into the phone. He hissed as Rylan shared what a witness had claimed to see pulling out of a parking lot near the bluff where the bodies were found. "A white van? Did she get a license plate number? Damn."

Dread crawled through him like a living force. He could

almost feel Carmen's fear. As if she was reaching out to him, urging him to hurry. "Where are you now?" he demanded, his jaw tightening with frustration when Rylan revealed that he was headed to Los Angeles to meet with a contact who had access to a satellite. He hoped they might get lucky enough to have captured a picture of the van leaving the area. A fine idea, but Griff needed him at the warehouse.

"Join me here as soon as you can," he said, ending the connection.

He didn't doubt that Rylan was already leaping into his car and heading his way at breakneck speed. But he wasn't sure that would be fast enough.

"Get out," he commanded, crawling out of the car. He kept the gun at his side, his finger on the trigger. He didn't want some nosy passerby calling the cops because a madman was walking around the streets waving a gun.

He quickly moved around the hood of the car, standing close beside Matthew as the younger man stepped out of the car and slammed shut the door.

"You haven't told me why you think Ronnie would take Carrie," Matthew complained.

Griff ignored the question, his gaze searching the warehouse for the best way to sneak inside.

"Is there a back entrance?" he demanded.

"Through the loading docks," Matthew said.

Griff hesitated. It could easily be a trap. But what choice did he have? He couldn't wait for Rylan. And he certainly had no intention of waiting for the cops.

"Tell me about the security."

"We have basic fire alarms, motion sensors, keypad locks, and we have guards on duty twenty-four seven," Matthew said.

Griff's gaze traced the fence with professional attention. This stuff he understood.

"What about surveillance cameras?"

Matthew lifted his hands in a helpless motion. "I know they're inside. There might be a few in the parking lot. I'm not sure."

Griff made a sound of disgust. Did this man know anything about the Jacobs business?

"What is it that you do for your father?" he demanded.

Matthew arched a brow, a hint of condescension in his expression. "I charm investors and grease wheels when necessary."

Griff's lips twisted. It was easy to imagine Matthew schmoozing with the local authorities, trying to ensure they gave out extra tax breaks and turned a blind eye to any zoning codes that might be inconvenient for the company.

"Yeah, I can imagine you're good at greasing wheels," he muttered, moving so he could press the gun against Matthew's lower back. "We're going to circle the block and enter the warehouse from the loading dock. One wrong move from you and I'll shoot a hole in your kidney," he warned. "Got it?"

"Christ, I should have made Baylor come out here to take care of Ronnie," Matthew groused. "No one would care if you put a hole in his kidney. Or anywhere else."

Assuming that the younger man understood that he was deadly serious, Griff jerked his head toward the corner. He intended to avoid the front of the warehouse and the parking lot. If someone was inside watching the security cameras, he didn't want to alert them that he was there.

They headed casually along the sidewalk, just two men out for a stroll. It wasn't until they'd reached the empty lot at the back of the warehouse that Griff crossed the street to halt behind a stack of wooden pallets.

From his position he could study the two large loading docks. They were tightly closed, but there was a steel door between them. He leaned around the edge of the pallets, searching for any sign of the white van.

Nothing.

So what did that mean? His earlier fear that Matthew had been cleverly leading him on a wild-goose chase while Carmen was being taken far away returned with a vengeance. His fingers tightened on the gun.

If he'd been played, he really was going to shoot the bastard.

Then his gaze caught sight of something near the steps that led to the back entrance. It was long and dark, and at first Griff assumed that someone had thrown out a rolled-up carpet. The longer he studied the object, however, the more he began to suspect that it was something far more sinister than an old rug.

Beside him, Matthew heaved a sigh. As if he found being held at gunpoint a tedious way to spend his morning. Certainly not as exciting as lying beside a pool with half-naked models.

"Are we going in, or what?" the man demanded.

Griff frowned. "Do you see something next to the loading dock?"

Matthew glanced across the empty lot before giving a small shrug. "It looks like a pile of trash."

"No." Griff gave a shake of his head. "It looks like a person. Come on."

Motioning Matthew forward, Griff used his companion as a shield as they slowly crossed the lot. If someone was going to get shot, it wasn't going to be him.

As they neared the building, however, Matthew's pace slowed as the younger man realized that Griff had been right. It wasn't trash that had been tossed out the back door. Instead, a man in a dark uniform was sprawled at an awkward angle on the hard pavement.

"That's one of the guards," Matthew whispered, as if

abruptly recognizing that this wasn't some strange California game that Griff was playing. "Look at his head. It's bleeding."

Griff had already crouched down to inspect the man.

The dark uniform easily identified him as a rent-a-cop. He was middle-aged with thick streaks of gray in his dark hair and a flabbiness that might once have been muscle. His square face was unnaturally pale, emphasizing the nasty gash that split open his forehead.

It looked as if he'd been struck with something narrow. Like a steel pipe. Or a crowbar. Whatever it was, it'd done enough damage to fracture the poor man's skull.

Reaching out, he touched the man's neck. No pulse.

"He's dead," he said in a bleak voice.

"Dead?" Matthew stumbled back, nearly falling on his ass. "Are you sure?"

"Sure enough." Griff straightened, urgency pounding through him. The guard's skin had still been warm. Which meant he hadn't been dead for long. There was still a chance that if Carmen was inside he could save her. "I need you to put your code into the keypad."

Matthew was shaking his head, his eyes rolling like a horse who was about to bolt.

"Hell, no. I'm not going in there," he rasped. "We need to call the cops."

"There's no time," Griff snapped. "Carmen could be inside."

"I didn't sign up for this," Matthew whined.

Griff stepped forward, placing the gun against the man's forehead.

"Consider yourself signed up."

Chapter Twenty-Three

Carmen didn't black out this time, but she wished she had. The pain was so sharp she feared that Ronnie had broken her jaw. At the very least he'd knocked a tooth loose.

Not that the physical pain could come close to the ache of her broken heart.

Cupping her chin, which was covered in blood from her busted lip, Carmen glared at the man who was jerkily pacing from one end of the bay to the other.

"You killed them," she spat out. "I lost everything because of you."

Ronnie gave a dismissive wave of his hand, his previous fury replaced by a weird calm.

"I told you, it was their fault," he said.

Carmen cautiously began to inch her way upright. Her skin prickled with a sense of danger. She didn't know what was going to happen, but she knew she wasn't going to like it.

She needed to be up and ready to run.

"If you truly believed you were innocent, then you wouldn't have gone to such an effort to cover up your crime," she said, still hoping to prolong whatever fate was awaiting her.

"I didn't try to cover it up," he denied, glancing over his shoulder with a scowl. "That was my mother's decision."

Carmen leaned heavily against the wall. She was upright, but her knees felt like rubber.

"Ellen knew what you did?" She didn't bother to hide her surprise.

She'd thought Ellen was devoted to her parents. How could the housekeeper have concealed her son's cold-blooded murder?

"She came in just a few minutes later," he said. "She made it look like my father killed your mother and then himself."

Carmen opened her mouth to protest. Even if Ellen was willing to stage the gruesome scene, why hadn't the cops realized that something was wrong? They had to have done a thorough investigation, right?

Then her lips snapped together. Lawrence Jacobs.

She didn't doubt for a second that he would have swooped in the minute it was discovered that his brother and sister-in-law were dead. He would also have ensured the cops wrapped up the case as quickly and with as little fuss as possible. The last thing he wanted was the scandal to continue to dominate the headlines.

"It wasn't enough that you killed my father? Your mother had to destroy his memory?"

He shrugged. "She wanted to protect me."

"By letting you walk away from a double murder?"

He abruptly pivoted to glare at her with eyes that were glittering with a dangerous light.

"She didn't let me get away with it. She sent me to a psychiatric hospital."

Carmen stiffened, abruptly recalling that he'd told her a bogus story about leaving the estate.

"You lied," she accused. "You didn't go to your aunt's to live."

"The polite term is that I was institutionalized," he said in mocking tones. "I was locked away like an animal."

Did he expect her to feel sorry for him? Not a chance in hell.

"You should have been in prison," she said. "You murdered my parents."

With quick, angry strides he was standing directly in front of her. Carmen flinched, but this time he didn't hit her. Instead, he glared at her, a sneer twisting his lips.

"I should have known you wouldn't understand. And it doesn't matter." He waved his hand, his pale eyes still glowing with a strange light. "I wasted years trying to earn the love of a man who was unworthy. Once I was away from that house, I could finally see clearly."

"See what clearly?"

"You had all been stifling me." He held up his fingers, ticking off the people who he believed had stood in his way. "My mother, with her insistence on treating me like a child. Andrew, with his assumption he could control me with his fists. My father, who treated me like a nobody." His hand dropped and he took a small step back. Carmen released a small breath of relief. Having him so near made her skin crawl with revulsion. "They blinded me to my true worth," he continued, his voice becoming louder. He clearly was enjoying telling this part of his story. "But at the institute I could finally accept my true self."

"I'm happy for you."

He either didn't notice the edge of sarcasm in her voice or decided he was willing to overlook it.

"I didn't have to please anyone. And do you know what I learned?"

"I can't imagine."

"Absolute honesty." He held her gaze, a weird smile curling his lips. "I admitted to myself that I didn't feel guilty for killing my father. Or your mother."

Fury raced through her. He'd destroyed an entire family. Then he'd been allowed to go to a hospital instead of being thrown in jail. And now he wanted to gloat that he was proud he didn't even feel guilty.

But even as her lips parted, Carmen was swallowing her impulsive words. Had she heard a door open? The sound had been faint, as if it was far across the warehouse. But it was enough to send a flare of hope through her.

Maybe Griff had managed to find her.

Or maybe it was a security guard. She hadn't seen one since she'd woken up, but it was possible there was one who was roaming around the huge building.

Either way, she needed to be ready to take advantage of the situation.

She pushed an inch away from the wall, relieved when her knees held her weight. Progress, she decided.

"I thought you claimed you didn't mean to kill them," she said, anxious to keep him talking.

The last thing she wanted was for him to realize they weren't alone and panic. She didn't have to be psychic to know that wouldn't be good for her life expectancy.

"I didn't, but knowing they were dead and that I had the power to end their lives was . . ." Ronnie gave a dramatic pause, a slash of fevered color staining his cheek. "Intoxicating. I wasn't a nobody. I was a predator." His smile widened. "A hunter."

Her mouth went dry. The childish, petulant Ronnie was gone. Standing before her was the animal who'd hunted helpless women and bashed in their heads with a crowbar.

"A hunter?" She took a slow, cautious step to the side.

"Yes. I began to fantasize about pulling the trigger again. Only this time it would be someone who I'd chosen, and spent time stalking before I made my kill."

He shivered. Not with fear, but with excitement. Was he recalling the pleasure of killing those poor women?

She struggled not to gag.

"That's awful," she breathed.

He sent her an annoyed glare. "No, it's truthful. I'd become who I was meant to be. And even better, I found other people just like me."

Like him? That was a horrifying thought.

"In the hospital?" she asked.

He shook his head. "Not the same one as me, but the Internet made it easy to connect with other potential hunters," he revealed. "We created a Kill Club."

Nausea curled through the pit of her stomach. It was . . . insane.

He was insane.

"Kill Club?" She shuddered in horror. "Are you serious?"

"Of course I am."

"What did your . . ." She struggled to force the words past her stiff lips, taking another step to the side. "Kill Club do?"

"At first we exchanged messages on the best way to choose our victims and the most satisfying way to murder them." He studied her closely, obviously savoring her horrified expression. "We even created chat rooms where we could role-play how we would lure our prey into our trap."

She pressed her hand to her stomach, the queasiness continuing to roll through her. What sort of pervert crouched over his computer as he lived out his revolting fantasies? And just how many of them were out there?

"The hospital let you chat with other patients?" she demanded in disbelief.

His features twisted with a smug arrogance. "They didn't know anything that was going on. As long as I didn't cause problems they didn't care what I was doing in the privacy of my room."

She took another step, sliding along the wall. She didn't really know where she was trying to go; she just wanted space between her and Ronnie Hyde.

"I still don't understand what any of this has to do with me."

Amusement sparkled in his eyes. As if he was aware of her covert attempt to inch away, and was enjoying her futile efforts. Like a cat toying with a cornered rat.

"We were enjoying our games, but I knew something was missing. We didn't have a focus for our club." With one long step he was once again directly in front of her, his foul breath brushing over her face. "And then a friend brought me a copy of your book. I was instantly inspired. Because of you, I knew my true calling. I was destined to kill."

Her mouth went dry. She originally feared that the stalker—or stalkers—had chosen her because of the book. Then she'd feared it had been because of her past. And then, because of her family.

Who could have known that all her suspicions had been right?

It was insanity.

"That's not why I wrote it," she said, the words sounding ridiculous.

Ronnie seemed to think so too. His eyes darkened with a strange emotion.

"I don't believe you." He reached up to grasp her throbbing chin. "You're fascinated with death just like I am."

"No," she breathed in horror.

His fingers squeezed, his pleasure visibly deepening as she whimpered in pain.

"Why else would you write the book? You were drawn to the dark side." He leaned down until their noses were nearly touching. "Just like me."

She pressed against the wall, wishing it would open up and swallow her. Anything would be better than being trapped alone with this deranged psychopath.

"I'm nothing like you," she denied, refusing to let him think that she had any connection to his sick fantasies.

"Yes, you are," he insisted, a fine spray of spit coating her face. "We might not have been raised as brother and sister, but we were baptized in blood."

The horrifying vision of Ronnie standing in the kitchen with her parents' bloody and broken bodies lying at his feet once again seared through her head.

Lifting her hands, she shoved them against his chest.

"No!" she screamed.

Ronnie laughed.

He'd spent nearly an hour watching Carrie lie unconscious, anticipating the moment she would open her eyes and realize that he was the one who had been leading her directly into his trap.

He'd anticipated the rush of pleasure he would feel at her fear, and then the glorious horror as he revealed his ability to precisely imitate the infamous killers in her book.

She would have no choice but to marvel at his cunning.

But instead of making his grand announcement, Carrie had distracted him with endless questions about the past.

He didn't want to think back to the gutless boy who'd been desperate for a father. Or remember the times Stuart Jacobs had walked past him as if he was nothing better than a bug.

That had been more painful than the blows from Andrew and the sharp words of disappointment from his mother whenever they caught him spying on the master of the house.

Now, however, he at last had what he wanted.

Carrie was visibly trembling as she stared at him with wide eyes. He could almost taste her fear.

This was the power he'd craved. The ability to prove that he might not carry the Jacobs name, but he was just as capable of greatness.

No, he was *more* capable.

Any idiot could go to business school and run a company.

Lawrence Jacobs was proof of that. The fool didn't even know what was going on beneath his nose.

But Ronnie had created magic out of chaos. He'd taken his violent needs and molded them into purpose, not only for himself, but for other misfits who struggled to find their way in the darkness.

And then he'd found his ultimate inspiration, and he'd known exactly what his fate was destined to be.

"I read your book over and over, studying the killers until I understood the precise manner they stalked their victims and their preference for satisfying their most basic urges," he told Carrie. "And, of course, how they each displayed their trophies."

She licked her lips, her hands continuing to push at his chest.

"You killed those women in Kansas."

He trembled with remembered bliss. For the first time he'd been able to act out the years of fantasies.

He'd hunted for the whore who reminded him of Carrie. He'd stolen the truck and lured her into the back. Then he'd raped her as she screamed in terror. And then he'd bashed in her skull.

It'd been extraordinary.

And watching the other Kill Club members live out their own fantasies had only added to his excitement.

He truly had been a god. A man worshipped by disciples as he determined who would live and who would die.

"Not only in Kansas," he said, slightly disappointed she didn't seem to know about his other trophies. "There are more victims in Baltimore. And here. I have the newest pictures." He squeezed her chin until she cried out in pain. "Would you like to see them?"

Her hands moved to grasp his wrist, her eyes swimming with tears. But she didn't whimper again. Instead, she sucked in a shaky breath, her eyes darting from side to side as she tried to think of how to keep him talking.

His lips twitched. He wondered if she truly thought he was so stupid he didn't realize what she was doing?

Naturally, she was hoping she could distract him so she could try to escape. Or maybe she hoped that someone might appear out of thin air to rescue her.

Whatever. He was willing to play along. Now that he had her in his grasp, they had all the time in the world.

"Were you the one who cut my arm at the hotel in Kansas?" she finally asked.

"I couldn't resist," he admitted. "I'd been watching you on TV, but it wasn't enough. I needed to see you in person."

Her brows pulled together and he was sharply reminded of her mother. Mrs. Jacobs had never liked him. Even when he'd been on his best behavior. He'd always assumed it was because she suspected he was her husband's illegitimate son. Whatever the reason, he'd taken great pleasure in blowing her face off with a shotgun.

"You hurt me," she said.

He allowed his fingers to slide downward, lightly circling her throat.

"A promise for the future," he told her.

She tensed at his unspoken warning, her face draining of color. Still, she didn't give in to panic.

Instead, she met his gaze squarely. "How did you know I would be there?"

He shrugged. "The institute is filled with people who have interesting hobbies," he said. "One of my fellow inmates happened to have some skills at hacking. He also has an addiction to painkillers. I send him a few pills and he keeps track of you."

She didn't look surprised. Almost as if she'd already suspected he'd been using a computer to follow her movements.

"How did you get out of the hospital?" she asked.

"My mother died."

This time he did manage to shock her. Her eyes widened before she gave a slow shake of her head.

"I don't understand."

He released his hold on her chin and stepped back. He didn't want her to see that he still suffered from the loss of his mother.

She'd lied to him. She'd forced him to live with that brute Andrew. And she'd put him in an institute. He should hate her.

But she'd also been the only one to love him. And in her way, she'd tried to protect him. When she'd died, it had stolen his last claim to humanity.

"I was never charged with a crime, so I could have walked away anytime I wanted," he said, turning to the side to hide his expression. "But my mother never trusted my assurance that I was all better and would never hurt anyone again."

"Your mother was right," Carrie muttered. "You couldn't be trusted."

"She threatened to tell the authorities everything if I left the institute," he admitted. "It was her last way of controlling me."

"And then she died."

Ronnie curled his hands into fists, stiffening his spine. His mother was gone. He'd mourned her passing and moved on with his life.

"And I was free," he said, turning back to meet Carrie's wary gaze. "My next step was to help my fellow Kill Club members to escape."

She licked her lips, her gaze shifting over his shoulder. Did she suspect there was a horde of crazed killers hiding in the shadows? Probably.

"How many?"

"Don't worry about them."

She frowned. "Why not?"

He offered a taunting smile, reaching beneath his sweater to pull out a handgun.

"Because I'm killing them."

Chapter Twenty-Four

Griff was crouched behind stacks of shingles, a bead of sweat trickling down his face.

He'd spent the past fifteen minutes inching his way through the shadowed warehouse, which had given him plenty of time to overhear the conversation between Ronnie Hyde and Carmen.

Now a part of his mind was struggling to process the fact that not only had Ronnie been responsible for killing those women and stalking Carmen, but he'd actually murdered her parents. It hummed in the background as he forced himself to concentrate on how he could get Carmen away from the crazed madman and escape without her being hurt.

From a distance he could see that Ronnie was holding something in his hand. Something that could be a weapon. Plus, there were too many towering racks and deep bays to see if they were alone in the warehouse. For all Griff knew there might be a half dozen bad guys lurking just out of sight.

The last thing he wanted was to put Carmen in even more danger.

What he needed was a distraction.

At his side, Matthew was staring wide-eyed, his face

unnaturally pale. Confusion? Or a devious adversary playing his role to the bitter end? It was impossible to know for sure.

Yet another variable to put into the equation.

His companion's lips parted, as if he was about to speak and give away their position. Instinctively, Griff reached to slam his hand over Matthew's mouth. Then, grabbing the man's arm, he hauled him back to the door just a few feet behind them.

He'd expected it to be a janitorial closet. Or maybe a storage room. Instead, a quick glance around gave him a stab of hope.

The security office.

Maybe for once luck would be on his side.

In the middle of the room was an L-shaped desk that was situated to offer a view of the four monitors hung on the far wall. Each screen displayed a black-and-white image of the warehouse as well as the parking lot. There was also a computer on the desk, that he was betting controlled the electronics for the entire building.

Shoving Matthew farther into the room, Griff shut the door and moved to study the monitors.

"I always knew there was something wrong with Ronnie Hyde, but I didn't realize he was batshit crazy," Matthew was muttering, pacing nervously toward the file cabinets before moving to stand directly behind Griff. "Did you hear him?"

Griff continued to stare at the flickering images, searching for any indication there was someone else in the warehouse.

"I heard," he muttered, frustration bubbling through him as he realized the security cameras only managed to capture small, random sections of the warehouse. Whoever had been responsible for setting them up should be fired.

Abruptly Griff grimaced. He'd momentarily forgotten about the dead guard near the loading dock.

"He killed my aunt and uncle," Matthew continued to babble, his voice harsh. "And now he has some sort of psychotic kill club."

Griff pivoted to glare at the younger man. The monitors didn't show enough for him to be confident that Ronnie was working alone. For now he was going to have to trust that Matthew wasn't a traitor.

"I need you to focus," he said.

Matthew sucked in a sharp breath, still clearly freaked out. "God, do you think he's going to hurt Carrie?"

Griff muttered a curse. Was Matthew truly that stupid? Hard to believe.

"That's exactly what he's going to do if you don't help me," he snapped.

Matthew grimaced, struggling to regain command of his composure. He continued to tremble, on the verge of a full-out panic attack, but eventually he managed to meet Griff's fierce gaze.

"What do you want?"

"Is there a back way to get into that part of the warehouse?" Griff demanded.

Matthew furrowed his brow. "I don't know."

Griff raised the gun he still clutched in his hand. "Be careful how you answer."

"Christ, man." Matthew lifted a hand, taking a hasty step backward. "My family owns this place, I didn't build the damn thing."

Griff rolled his eyes, turning away from the younger man.

"Worthless," he muttered, heading toward the desk.

He pulled out the rolling chair and sat down. Then, laying the gun on the desk, he fired up the computer. Matthew was clearly going to be zero help. Whether by design, or just because he was a shallow, vain piece of fluff.

Matthew watched him with a frown, possessing enough

intelligence not to approach the desk. One wrong move and Griff was ready and willing to put a bullet in him.

"What are you doing?" Matthew demanded.

Griff easily found what he was looking for, and after hacking his way into the program, he soon had gained control of the security system.

"We need a distraction," he said, locating the file he wanted and abruptly shoved himself to his feet.

Matthew was staring at him in confusion. "Are you going to set off the alarm?"

"Something better." Griff grabbed his gun and waved it toward his companion. "Come here."

Matthew stiffened. "Why."

"I want you to stay in the office," he said, pointing toward the chair.

"Thank God." Matthew breathed a sigh of relief and hurried to take a seat. Coward.

Griff leaned over the man's shoulder and pointed toward the return button on the keyboard.

"In two minutes I want you to press this," he commanded.

"Why?"

"It will start an override of the sprinkler system," Griff explained.

"You're going to set off the sprinklers?"

"No, you're going to," Griff informed the younger man. "In exactly two minutes. Give me your phone."

Predictably, Matthew blinked at him with bewilderment. Griff wondered if Vi Jacobs had dropped her oldest son on his head when he was young. That would explain a lot.

"My phone."

"Just let me have it," he growled, snatching the phone out of Matthew's hand as soon as the man had pulled it from his pocket. Then, setting the timer for two minutes, he placed the phone on the desk. "When the timer stops, hit the button." He once again pointed toward the return key. He was fairly sure that Matthew had already forgotten what he'd told him just seconds ago. "Got it?"

"Yeah, I got it," Matthew promised.

Griff pointed his gun directly in the younger man's face. "Screw me over and I'll make sure you regret it."

Surprisingly, Matthew didn't cringe in fear. Instead, he sent Griff an angry glare.

"Just go save Carrie," he said.

With no choice but to hope Matthew was capable of performing the simple task—oh, and wasn't plotting to stab Griff in the back—he turned to leave the office.

He scurried along the nearest line of shelves and darted toward one of the forklifts that was parked in the bay. He wanted to be as close as possible when the sprinklers went off.

Peering around the back of the heavy equipment, his gut twisted as he watched Ronnie point a gun directly into the face of a cringing Carmen.

Time was running out.

He glanced up, impatiently waiting for the sprinklers to kick on. Nothing. Seconds ticked past. Then minutes.

Still nothing.

"Shit," he breathed.

Matthew had either bolted as soon as Griff had left him alone in the office, or he was involved with Ronnie.

Right now it didn't matter. He was going to have to take a calculated risk before it was too late.

Casting a frantic glance around, he caught sight of a large wrench that was lying on the cement floor. He bent down, grabbing the tool, which was made of solid steel. Perfect.

He turned to the side and threw the wrench with all his might toward the nearby rack of fencing posts. As he hoped, it hit a stack of wood on the top with enough force to send several posts crashing to the floor. The sound was deafening as it echoed through the warehouse.

It was a trick that'd been used a thousand times in cheesy films, but sometimes the oldies were goodies.

On cue, Ronnie whirled toward the noise, and Griff stepped around the back of the forklift, his gun pointed directly at the man's head.

"Turn around and drop your gun," he commanded.

Ronnie jerked his head to the side, his eyes narrowing as he caught sight of Griff.

"You," he spat out, his features twisting with fury. "I should have killed you."

"You could try." Griff stepped to the side, moving so he could keep his gun pointed at Ronnie but with his back next to the wall.

He grimaced as Ronnie pointed his gun directly at Carmen instead of dropping it.

"Oh, I'm going to do more than try," he taunted. "First you drop *your* gun."

Griff ground his teeth. Did he take a risk and shoot Ronnie with the hope that the maniac didn't squeeze off a shot and hit Carmen?

Or did he put down his gun and pray that he could somehow overpower Ronnie?

It was Carmen who made the decision. Catching both men off guard, she was abruptly hurtling toward Griff at full speed. His heart stopped as the sound of Ronnie's gun blasted through the air, but he managed not to panic. Instead, he reached out to wrap an arm around her waist as soon as she got close enough. Then, using the power he'd developed after years of morning jogs, he leaped to the side, taking Carmen with him.

They landed in a tangle behind the forklift, with Carmen beneath him. Griff risked a quick glance down. Anger instantly thundered through his body.

Her face was already showing deep bruises where Ronnie had hit her, and blood dripped from the cut on her swollen lip. He cursed, his finger tightened on the trigger. He wanted to leap to his feet and start shooting. He wanted Ronnie to be sprawled dead on the floor.

But he possessed an aversion to impulsive actions.

Plus, he still didn't know if Matthew was a traitor and was about to leap out of the darkness.

For now, they were safe behind the forklift. There was nothing but a cement floor beneath them and a thick steel wall behind them. The only way to get to them was around the front of the tractor.

Unfortunately, that meant they didn't have an easy way to escape. For now, they were trapped.

"Are you okay?"

"No." She managed a pained smile. "But I will be."

Despite the danger and the blood that continued to leak from her wounded lip, Griff felt a small flare of relief. She'd been terrorized and beaten by the madman, but her courage hadn't been broken.

"Come out," Ronnie called, his voice thick with frustration.

Griff grimaced, brushing a light kiss over Carmen's forehead before he pushed himself to his knees and inched his way to the edge of the large tire. The forklift sat low to the ground, so he didn't have to worry about a stray bullet ricocheting off the floor and striking him.

"I don't think so."

He reached into his pocket and pulled out his phone. He dialed Rylan's number and set the phone on the ground. It wasn't that he hoped his friend could help. Even with his foot heavy on the gas pedal Rylan was probably still a half hour away. But whatever happened, he wanted to make sure his friend heard exactly what was going on.

Ronnie made a sound of impatience. "How did you find us?"

Griff didn't miss the word *us*. Was the man talking about

Matthew? Or was there someone else in the warehouse? Maybe more than one?

"Does it matter?" he demanded, peeking around the tire to discover Ronnie had taken cover behind a stack of cinderblocks.

"I like to learn from my mistakes," Ronnie called out, his shadow a thin strip of black across a nearby shelf. "It's what makes me such a fine hunter."

Griff frowned. "Hunter?"

Carmen was suddenly crouched beside him. "He killed my parents," she rasped. "And all those women."

Griff kept his gaze locked on Ronnie's shadow as it inched to the side of the blocks. He was angling for a clear shot.

"Tell me how you found me," Ronnie commanded.

Griff hesitated. He needed to provoke the man into making a mistake.

"It was easy," Griff finally said. He didn't know much about Ronnie, but it was apparent that he was consumed with his delusion of grandeur. Which meant the easiest way to rattle him was to prick his bloated pride. "I followed the stench of your cowardice."

The words easily pierced Ronnie's thin skin. "I'm no coward."

Griff made a sound of disgust. "What do you call kidnapping a sleeping woman?"

"Or killing the people who took you and your mother into their home?" Carmen called out.

"They betrayed me. I should have been the one who was treated as the beloved child. Instead, it was you." Ronnie's words held an edge of bitterness. "Always you."

Carmen trembled. Her courage might have survived, but she'd clearly been through enough. She was reaching her breaking point.

"Griff, can we just get out of here?"

Griff shook his head, but he called out loudly, "Sure. Rylan is waiting outside with the cops."

"Bullshit," Ronnie growled. "If there were cops outside I would know."

"I warned them not to use sirens and to park in the back," he tried to bluff.

"You must think I'm stupid." He gave a dramatic pause. "No, wait. You believe I'm a coward."

Griff swallowed a curse. There had to be a reason Ronnie was acting so cocky. Which meant that any hope of finding out who might be involved was over.

They needed to get out of there. But how?

He aimed his pistol and took a shot at the top of the cinderblocks. He couldn't kill Ronnie, but he wanted to freeze him in place.

The sound of the bullet hitting the block echoed loudly through the vast space, splinters of cement filling the air.

"I called you a coward because you are a coward," Griff called out.

"Do you know how many people I've killed?" Ronnie demanded.

Carmen shuddered, but Griff refused to react. It was exactly what Ronnie wanted.

"It's tacky to boast," he instead chided.

"Why? If you have a talent you take pride in it." Ronnie sounded like a petulant child. "Especially such a rare talent."

"Being a nutcase isn't a talent," he deliberately taunted. "It's a perversion."

Ronnie laughed. Apparently, he was used to being called crazy. "'We're all mad here. I'm mad. You're mad.'"

Griff frowned. The words were familiar. *"Alice in Wonderland?"* he at last guessed.

"You know, I've spent months anticipating my reunion

with you. Brother and sister shouldn't be parted from each other."

Carmen glanced toward Griff with a horrified expression. "I'm not your sister."

Ronnie chuckled, pleased he finally had the reaction he was hoping to get.

"I dreamed night after night about you," he told her. "I could actually feel my fingers wrapping around your neck while I watched the life draining from your eyes."

"You're sick," she accused.

"But now I see that killing you is going to give me just as much satisfaction, maybe more," Ronnie said.

Griff could sense Ronnie's perverted pleasure in taunting Carmen.

"As I said, you're welcome to try," Griff growled, desperate to keep the creep's attention focused on him.

Ronnie didn't answer. Instead, the shadow began to move again. Damn. Within a few minutes Ronnie would be in position to kill both of them.

Griff briefly considered his options.

They all sucked.

They could wait there and hope that Rylan magically showed up before Ronnie got into position to shoot them. Or they could try to make a desperate run for it. If they could reach the towering racks, there was a faint hope they could reach an exit. At least as long as they didn't run across any of Ronnie's partners.

Yeah. Really crappy choices.

Bending his head, he whispered directly into Carmen's ear, "When I say 'go' I want you to run toward the front of the bay."

She sucked in a sharp breath. "But Ronnie—"

"I'll distract him," he promised.

She shook her head. "No, Griff. We go together."

"Don't be fools," Ronnie called out, easily suspecting

they were plotting to try to escape. "You don't really think you can get out of this warehouse, do you?"

"You can't stop me," Griff said, his gaze carefully monitoring Ronnie's shadow.

"If I don't, my partner will," Ronnie warned.

Griff reached to give Carmen's arm a reassuring squeeze, his gaze scanning the opening while he strained his ears for any sound of approaching footsteps.

"What partner?" he demanded.

Ronnie released a mocking laugh. "You really are stupid. How do you think I found out about this warehouse? Or managed to get past the security?"

"Shit," Griff breathed. He knew exactly who Ronnie's partner was. Matthew Jacobs. No wonder the damned sprinkler system hadn't been triggered. "I knew I couldn't trust him."

Carmen sent him a worried gaze. "Trust who?"

"Get ready," he muttered, reaching toward the cab of the forklift. Blindly he searched for the key switch on the steering wheel column.

"You might as well give up," Ronnie said, his voice sharp with impatience. "You can't get out of the warehouse. The doors have been locked down. They won't open until the security system has been reset."

Griff ignored the warning. He'd worry about getting out of the warehouse once they were away from Ronnie.

On the point of telling Carmen to run, Griff froze at the unmistakable sound of approaching footsteps. He leaned forward again, peering around the rim of the wheel.

If Matthew moved to stand in the proximity of Ronnie, then his hasty plan might still work. If not . . . they were screwed.

"Enough." The voice cut through the air as the man walked around the edge of a rack and stepped into view. "I'm done playing games," he warned.

Shock jolted through Griff. He blinked, wondering if he was seeing things. Then he blinked again.

Once again he'd been wrong.

Ronnie's partner wasn't Matthew Jacobs.

It was the younger brother, Baylor.

"Baylor," Carmen breathed as she pressed next to him, her hand rising to press against her parted lips.

The young man was dressed in a pair of charcoal slacks and a white shirt. Like he was headed to the office instead of helping a psychotic killer murder his own cousin.

With an effort, Griff shook off his sense of disbelief. Right now it didn't matter if Ronnie's partner was Santa Claus. They needed to escape.

And the only way that was going to happen was if they could cause a large enough distraction.

"Stay next to me," he breathed, switching on the engine to the forklift and with his other hand, pressing down on the gas pedal to send the large tractor rumbling forward.

He heard a shout from Ronnie, and the sound of gunfire, but he and Carmen remained bent low as they jogged next to the forklift. He kept the tires straight, forcing the men to back away. Then at the last minute he grabbed the steering wheel and pulled it sharply to the right. The tractor turned with surprising dexterity, the metal fork slamming into the nearby rack.

The industrial shelving was solidly bolted to the floor, but Griff had factored in the haphazard manner in which the wood was stacked. It was top-heavy enough that such a solid hit sent the ten-foot boards flying through the air.

The wooden projectiles pelted anything in their path, forcing Ronnie and Baylor to dive for cover, just as he'd hoped.

"Run," he barked.

Without hesitation, Carmen was bolting through the opening of the bay and toward a narrow aisle just ahead.

Keeping low, she scrambled through the maze of racks with a speed that came from sheer adrenaline. Griff was just a few feet behind her, his gun held ready.

Moving as silently as possible, considering their rasping breaths and the cement floor that amplified every footstep, they reached the middle of the warehouse. Griff grabbed Carmen's arm to halt her flight. Then, with a jerk of his head, he indicated that they needed to circle back the way they'd just come.

She frowned, but with a trust that warmed his heart, she followed him as he cautiously threaded his way toward the front of the warehouse.

He didn't dare try to make a mad dash toward an exit. Although it appeared that Matthew was an innocent stooge of his brother, he'd been fooled too many times. He wasn't going to risk stumbling into another trap.

They were inching forward when the sound of Ronnie's and Baylor's raised voices forced him to freeze. The two men were just an aisle over. Which meant there was no way he could get to a doorway until they moved.

Muttering every curse he knew, in more than one language, Griff tugged Carmen behind a cart of plywood. It was possible they could fit beneath one of the racks, which might be a better hiding place. But he didn't want to get trapped. If worse came to worst, he wanted Carmen to be able to run while he tried to hold off the men.

Another awful plan.

But the only one he had.

Chapter Twenty-Five

Ronnie was furious.

This was supposed to be his grand finale.

Everything over the past months had been plotted and planned for this specific moment.

And now it was ruined.

All because of Griffin Archer. The bastard. He was going to take so much pleasure in killing him.

Shoving himself to his feet, Ronnie ignored the forklift that was now tangled with metal shelving, and the clouds of dust that filled the air. The mess was Baylor's problem. Not his.

He paused long enough to make sure the safety was off his handgun, and then he headed toward the nearest aisle. Carrie was hidden somewhere in the warehouse. He intended to find her and complete his goal of squeezing the life from her.

But first he was going to blow out the brains of Griffin Archer.

Focused on his lust for blood, Ronnie was oblivious to the shadow gliding through the aisle that was parallel to him. It wasn't until he reached a small clearing that Baylor abruptly stepped around the end of a rack to block his path.

Ronnie frowned. He'd hoped that one of the flying boards had plunked his partner in the head. It would solve the problem of killing him once he was done with Carrie and Griffin.

Then again, he didn't mind being the one to put a bullet in Baylor. There would be a nice symmetry. He was the one who started the Kill Club. He would be the one to end it.

But only after the others were dead.

Ronnie came to a halt, sending Baylor an impatient glare. "Why are you just standing there?" he demanded. "We need to find Griff and get rid of him before he shoots us or finds some new way to be a pain in the ass."

Baylor shrugged, his gun held loosely in one hand as he offered a mysterious smile.

"Actually, there's been a change of plans."

Ronnie's brows snapped together. No one changed his plans. No one.

"What are you talking about?"

Baylor's smile remained as he took a step toward Ronnie. "The problem with the endgame was making sure the authorities believe that all the bad guys are dead."

Ronnie shrugged. He'd already planned for that. Baylor just didn't know that his death was going to be the "endgame."

"The cops are too stupid to figure out anything," he said. "We already proved that."

"So we did." Baylor held out his hand. "But just to be sure, I need to borrow your gun."

Ronnie took an instinctive step backward. "You have your own gun."

Baylor's features tightened, but his smile never faltered. Ronnie had learned over the years that the older man shared many of Ronnie's own talents. Including the ability to hide his true emotions.

"Yes, but when I put a bullet into my brother's heart, I prefer to use your weapon."

"Brother?" Ronnie felt a stab of surprise. "Matthew is here?"

"Yes, I found him in the security office when I went in to change the passcode for the locks. I assume he was trying to figure out how to open the doors."

Ronnie cursed. How many people were waltzing in and out of the warehouse? It was a wonder the National Guard hadn't shown up.

"He's the idiot who led Griffin Archer to the warehouse," Baylor said.

"Oh." Well, that explained how Griff had found him. "What did you do with him?"

"I bashed him on the back of the head," Baylor admitted, his tone revealing zero regret at having wounded his brother.

The lack of empathy convinced Ronnie the older man hadn't been lying about wanting his brother dead.

"You're really going to kill your own brother?"

"That wasn't my intention, but now I realize that I'll never have a better opportunity to have what I deserve." A cold glimmer in his hazel eyes. "The company. The estate. The money. I couldn't have planned it any better."

Ronnie's uneasiness deepened. There was something different about the man standing in front of him.

Of the two Jacobs brothers, Matthew had always been bold and brash and charming, while Baylor was quiet and studious, and watchful. When they'd been young, Matthew would enjoy tormenting Ronnie, and it was Baylor who would whisper in Ronnie's ear how to get back at the older boy. He was the one to urge Ronnie to toss the keys of Matthew's expensive Corvette in the lake. And it was Baylor who'd been encouraging when Ronnie had confessed that he was certain Stuart Jacobs was his father.

Now there was an arrogance in his expression that Ronnie didn't like.

"Planned what?" he demanded.

"First you got rid of my uncle for me."

For him? What the hell was he talking about?

"You know why he had to die," Ronnie argued. "He was punished because he refused to admit the truth."

Baylor shook his head. "Christ, you're the most gullible fool I ever met."

Ronnie stiffened. Enough was enough. How dare this man act as if he was more than a mere disciple?

"Don't say that," he snapped.

"It's true." Baylor's voice held a hint of derision. "I've been using you since you were a creepy kid, trailing behind my uncle like a pathetic stray dog."

Ronnie shook his head. "I didn't trail behind him. My father—"

"He wasn't your father, you moron," Baylor interrupted.

Ronnie's breath was wrenched from his lungs. What was going on? Was Baylor trying to confuse him? But why?

"He was. I have the proof," he rasped. "You saw the letters and said they had to mean that he was my father."

Baylor clicked his tongue, taking a step forward. "Poor Ronnie. I wrote those letters."

Ronnie lifted his gun, waving it toward Baylor. "No."

The man stopped, his gaze on the weapon in Ronnie's hand. Still, his expression remained taunting.

"Yes. I copied them from a stack of love letters I found in my aunt's desk."

Ronnie grimaced. There was a pounding behind his right eye. He should just shoot the bastard. It was what he was planning to do eventually. Right?

But he couldn't squeeze the trigger. Not until he'd reasserted his dominance over the man.

"My mother's name was on them," he reminded his companion. As if that explained everything.

Baylor arched a brow. "A simple enough change."

Ronnie struggled to grasp what he was saying. "Why?"

"Because my uncle was destroying our company," Baylor said. "My father refused to force Stuart out of his position, so I decided to take matters into my own hands."

Ronnie made a sound of disbelief. Baylor couldn't have been more than fourteen or fifteen when Ronnie found the letters.

"You were just a kid."

"A very observant kid," Baylor insisted. His smug tone grated on Ronnie's raw nerves. "I could see that my uncle was on the verge of a mental breakdown. Not only was the business going down the toilet, but he was terrified he might lose his young and beautiful wife if she realized he was a failure. So I did everything in my power to add to his stress."

"Yeah, right," Ronnie scoffed. "What could you do?"

The icy hazel gaze flicked down to the gun in Ronnie's hand before returning to his face. Was he worried that Ronnie was going to shoot him?

He should be.

"I would casually mention to my uncle that I happened to see my aunt in town with a strange man," he admitted, his lips twitched as if he was remembering the pleasure he'd taken in tormenting Stuart Jacobs. "I would move things around his office to make him think he was losing his memory." He paused, studying Ronnie with that annoying smile. "And then I realized that you could provide even more chaos."

"Me?"

"Yes, you," Baylor drawled in mocking tones. "I hoped after I convinced you that you were Stuart's son you would confront my uncle." He deliberately paused. "Preferably in front of my aunt. It was possible she might believe that he had his bastard living above the garage. Can you imagine the trouble it would have caused in their marriage?" He released a low chuckle. "I never dreamed you would actually shoot both of them."

Ronnie clenched his teeth. He didn't believe him. Baylor

couldn't have written the letters. They *had* to be from Stuart to his mother.

After all, they were his proof that his real father wasn't a nameless loser. That Ronnie Hyde was as good as all the snotty Louisville society kids, even if he couldn't tell anyone.

If they were fake . . .

Then his entire identity was a lie.

"If it was just some game to you, then why did you help my mother cover up what I did?" Ronnie asked in a harsh voice. "And why haven't you told anyone that I was locked in an institute instead of living with a relative?"

"It suited me to have people think my uncle was responsible. It not only allowed my father to take over the company, but it got rid of my bratty cousin. My family belonged at the Jacobs estate, but having Carrie around would always mean that my father was being compared to his dead brother. No one can match up to a saint." A cold, calculating smile twisted Baylor's lips. "Plus, I'd discovered you were a valuable tool."

Ronnie shoved aside the fact that Griff Archer was hidden somewhere in the warehouse with a gun. As well as his clamoring need to destroy the woman who'd had the life that should have been his. Instead, he glared at Baylor.

This man had been nothing. A younger brother who'd lived in the shadows of his brother who was better-looking and more charming than Baylor could ever hope to be.

Everyone loved Matthew. No one even liked Baylor.

Until he'd started visiting Ronnie at the institute, Baylor hadn't had any friends. And he certainly hadn't had a purpose beyond his stupid work.

Ronnie had allowed him to share in his dark fantasies. And trained him to become a part of the Kill Club. In return, Baylor had helped him stay in contact with the others. He'd even helped them to escape the various facilities when Ronnie was ready to put his plans into motion. But it'd all been with the understanding that Ronnie was the one in charge.

Now Baylor was trying to change the rules. And undermine Ronnie's confidence by rewriting the past.

Ronnie squared his shoulders. It wasn't going to work.

"I'm not a tool," he snapped.

Baylor flicked a dismissive gaze over him. Like he was some sort of bug that he was contemplating squashing beneath his heel.

"Of course you are," Baylor insisted. "One that I created and nurtured over the years."

Ronnie stepped toward his companion, waving his gun in a wild gesture.

"You're nothing but a cowardly liar."

Baylor remained calm. The smug bastard.

"I suspected one day I might need you again. And I did," he told Ronnie. "Over the years I'd hoped that Carrie would find some nice local farmer to marry and settle down in her grandparents' house. She hadn't any contact with us for years, and there was no need for her to return to Louisville." Baylor heaved an exaggerated sigh. "Of course she had to become a problem. Not only did she not stay at her home, she had to go to college to become an investigative journalist."

Ronnie made a sound of impatience. None of this made sense.

It'd been Carrie's determination to become a journalist that had led her to interviewing the serial killers. And eventually had inspired his own killing spree.

"Isn't that what we wanted?"

"Don't be an idiot," Baylor said with an expression of disgust. "I couldn't have her returning to the family estate, snooping into things that were none of her business."

Ronnie frowned. At first he assumed that Baylor was talking about the murder/suicide of her parents. Why would he worry about that? There was no way for Carrie to learn the truth.

Not until Ronnie was ready to reveal his inner self to her.

Then he wrinkled his nose in repugnance. "You did steal the three million dollars," he said, shaking his head.

His mother had been convinced that Lawrence had been up to something nefarious. And it appeared she'd been right. It was disappointing to think that Baylor was just as shallow as the rest of his family.

For the first time since he'd blocked Ronnie's path, the older man flushed, looking oddly defensive.

"The insurance money should have gone to my father in the first place," he growled. "We needed it to save the company from a bankruptcy that had been created by my uncle's stubborn refusal to listen to common sense." Baylor paused, sucking in a deep, calming breath before he managed to paste his smile back on his lips. "Unfortunately, the law wouldn't understand that it was a business decision."

Ronnie didn't understand either. Who cared about money? It couldn't buy respect. Or greatness.

He had earned those without having a penny in his pocket.

"It was stealing," he accused.

Baylor gave a dismissive wave of his hand, once again in full command of his composure.

"Whatever," he said. "I needed to get rid of her. And you were the perfect stooge to do it. Why do you think I brought you a copy of her book?"

Ronnie hunched his shoulders, the pain drilling behind his eye. He didn't want to hear these lies. They were starting to confuse him.

"You said the book was a challenge from my sister," he muttered. "Our blood was calling to each other and only one of us could come out as the victor."

Baylor gave a loud laugh. "I said a lot of shit," he told Ronnie. "I knew that with enough prodding you would finally give in to your need to kill Carrie. After all, you'd wanted to see her dead since she was just a little girl."

"No." Ronnie shook his head, even as the words struck a painful chord of truth. He had wanted Carrie dead.

She had everything.

And he had nothing.

Baylor stepped toward him, continuing to twist the proverbial knife he'd stuck in Ronnie's back.

"And now, miraculously, you've given me a way to get rid of Matthew as well."

"I didn't have anything to do with stupid Matthew," Ronnie denied.

An ugly jealousy rippled over Baylor's face. "You're right. Matthew is stupid. And lazy. And self-indulgent. If there was any justice in the world, I should have been born the older son," he said, each word coming out with biting force. The hazel gaze shifted toward the nearby security office. Presumably, Matthew was still lying unconscious in there. "Thanks to you I can now make it appear as if he was just another of your partners in crime who ended up dead when you were done with him."

Ronnie's lips parted, but before he could speak, an icy dread snaked down his spine.

Did Baylor know what he'd done with the others? Or was this just another trick to try to confuse him?

Ronnie absently rubbed the painful throb beside his eye. "I don't know what you're talking about."

"Seriously?" Baylor scoffed, smoothly moving forward. Ronnie frowned. When had the other man gotten so close? "Did you think I wasn't aware that we were losing our club members one by one?" Baylor demanded. "I'm sure I was next on the list, wasn't I?"

Ronnie forced a choked laugh. "Of course not," he lied.

Baylor shrugged. "Oh, I'm not complaining. It tied up all the loose ends nicely for me. Now when the cops come, they'll find Matthew with a bullet in his head, along with Griffin Archer, who was unfortunately in the wrong place at the wrong time, and they'll blame the deaths on you. Especially since I'll be sure to use your gun," Baylor said, his words soft as if he was speaking more to himself than Ronnie. "And as for Carrie, we need something special, don't you think? Should I strangle her? It's what you wanted to do."

Ronnie licked his lips. This was all spinning out of control. He was the one in charge. He was the one who decided when and how people died.

Baylor was spoiling everything.

"What about me?" Ronnie winced, aware he sounded like a whining child.

Baylor smiled. A real smile that reached his icy hazel eyes.

"You tragically didn't realize that once Matthew had changed the security locks you couldn't get out of the warehouse without having the passcode." As he spoke, Baylor casually strolled to grab a metal can off a bottom shelf. Turpentine. "You died in the fire you lit to hide your crimes. The police will assume that's the end to the killings and I can walk away. Although once the smoke settles . . ." His lips twitched as he managed to open the can while keeping the gun in his other hand. "Literally. I might create my own Kill Club."

For a second, Ronnie watched as Baylor splashed the clear liquid over the wooden planks piled on a nearby rack. Then the full impact of Baylor's treachery hit like a sledgehammer to his head.

This man hadn't been his friend when they were young. And he hadn't been trying to help when he'd visited him in the institute. And he certainly hadn't been the devoted disciple he'd pretended to be when they'd formed their secret club.

"You used me," he breathed, launching himself forward as a misty red fury clouded his mind. He'd allowed this man to be his most trusted disciple. He'd chosen him to be the last to die. A place of honor. And how had he been repaid for his kindness? Betrayal. "You bastard."

If Ronnie had been in his right mind, he would have just shot the traitor. But his anger consumed him. He desperately needed to feel his fist crushing into Baylor's smug face.

"It's about damned time," Baylor muttered as he easily dodged Ronnie's wild swing and reached to wrench the weapon from his hand.

Then, with an expression of sheer triumph, he pressed the muzzle to Ronnie's temple and pulled the trigger.

Oddly, Ronnie felt nothing. There was a bright flare of light, followed by a distant sound of thunder. Like a storm was approaching. Then his knees went weak and the world was painted black.

Wrapped in a peace he'd never experienced in life, he fell to the floor.

Chapter Twenty-Six

Carmen slapped her hand over her mouth, muffling her scream as she watched Ronnie sway and then tumble onto the cement floor.

Eventually she'd have to deal with everything she'd seen and heard since waking in the warehouse, probably with the help of some nice therapist. Ronnie and his crazy belief he was her half brother. Baylor's cunning treachery. The Kill Club. And the sight of Ronnie lying dead just a few feet away.

But for now, she couldn't give in to panic.

Instead, she peeked around the edge of the cart, watching as Baylor tucked one of the guns into the waistband of his slacks before he reached into his pocket to pull out a disposable lighter.

"I know you can hear me," he called out, clearly speaking to her and Griff. "You might as well come out. Unless you want to be burned alive."

With a casual gesture he leaned down to touch the flame to the floor, which was covered in the turpentine he'd spilled. Fire danced toward the nearest stack of boards.

Griff reached out to grasp her upper arm, tugging her toward the aisle behind them. Blood rushed in her ears as she bent low and followed behind him. Then she silently cursed. She hadn't counted on the fact that her legs would've stiffened up while she'd been crouched behind the cart.

Before she could warn Griff, she was stumbling to the side and slamming into the metal rack. It was enough to jolt a box of nails off the shelf. It hit the ground next to her feet, busting open.

In the silence of the warehouse, it sounded as loud as a bomb going off.

Carmen clenched her teeth as horror spread through her. She'd exposed their presence. Nothing she could do about that. There wasn't anywhere to run. And nowhere to hide.

But even as she resigned herself to the inevitable, she abruptly realized that she could make sure Griff had the opportunity to escape. Not giving herself time to consider the consequences, she straightened and walked directly into the small clearing.

Baylor pivoted to face her, his gun pointed at her as his gaze darted over her shoulder.

"Ah. There you are, sweet Carrie," he drawled, trying to hide his fear behind a smug bluster. "So kind of you to join me."

She curled her lip in disgust. "You bastard."

Circling the edge of the small fire that was thankfully producing more smoke than flames, he moved toward her, his gaze continuing to search the shadows behind her.

"Where is Griffin?"

She shrugged. "He got out through the loading dock."

Baylor released a harsh laugh. "You're not dealing with an idiot. I know your lover would never abandon you." At last reaching her, Baylor wrapped an arm around her neck and stepped behind her, as if hoping to use her as a shield. Spineless coward. Then he pressed the muzzle of the gun to her temple. "Come out or I'll put a bullet through her head," he commanded in a loud voice.

"Don't," she instantly called out. "He'll kill both of us anyway."

Baylor's arm tightened around her neck. "You should have stayed on the farm."

A distant part of her knew she should be terrified. This man might be her cousin, but there was no doubt he was truly insane.

For now, however, she was just so damned angry.

This lunatic had used, abused, and murdered anyone who crossed his path. And for what? Ego? Greed? Perverted lust?

"So you could steal my inheritance?" she demanded, her voice harsh with scorn.

Behind her, she could feel Baylor stiffen. As if she'd managed to strike a nerve.

"It belonged to the family, not some spoiled little brat," he snapped.

"Don't you mean that it belonged to you?"

"I run the business."

She released a sharp laugh. "Does Uncle Lawrence realize he's no longer CEO?"

He used the arm around her neck to steer her toward the edge of the clearing, pressing his back against the nearest rack. Obviously, he realized that Griff was nearby with a gun pointed at his head. And that the second he had a clear shot, Griff would put a bullet through his brain.

Which meant he couldn't kill her, right? Not as long as he needed her to protect his own pathetic life.

"I'm the future," he boasted. "With me Jacobs Hardware can become a worldwide corporation."

"You're as delusional as Ronnie," she charged.

Again she seemed to hit a raw nerve as Baylor sucked in a sharp breath.

"Don't compare me to that pathetic psycho," he warned.

Her gaze skimmed blindly from the smoldering fire

toward the shadows across the clearing as the memory of what she'd overheard seared through her mind.

"Are you saying you didn't kill those women?"

She felt him shrugging his shoulders. "It was necessary to play the game with Ronnie," he drawled. "And I'll admit there's something satisfying in releasing my deepest lusts. It cleanses the soul and allows a man to return to civilized society with a sense of peace."

Nausea rolled through her stomach. She still had nightmares from the pictures that had been sent to her. The thought that her own cousin had been responsible for torturing and murdering those poor women was inconceivable.

Had there been warning signs when he was young? Had he always harbored such wicked lusts? Or had his greed slowly corrupted his soul?

"Ronnie was sick," she breathed. "You're pure evil."

He muttered a curse, the gun pressing hard enough against her temple to leave a bruise.

"Last chance, Griffin," he called out, an edge in his voice warning that he was reaching a breaking point. "One. Two."

Carmen squeezed her eyes shut. In the next few seconds, Griff was going to step into the clearing and be shot. Or she was going to have a bullet rip through her brain.

Neither option was something she wanted to watch.

It never occurred to her that there might be a third option. Not until she felt the raindrops that were spraying over her face.

At first she thought she must be dead. Why would it be raining in the middle of the warehouse?

Then she felt Baylor loosen his grip on her as he stumbled backward.

"What the hell?" he muttered.

Carmen opened her eyes and impulsively did a belly flop onto the hard floor. She landed with enough force to knock the air out of her lungs, but she barely noticed as the blast of a gunshot deafened her.

Blinking through the rain that continued to fall, she turned her head to watch as Baylor's eyes widened. As if he'd seen something surprising. Then a trickle of blood flowed down his nose from the new hole he had in the middle of his forehead.

Carmen grimaced, jerking her gaze away as her cousin started to tumble backward. She didn't need to check to see if he was dead. Instead, she frantically searched for some sign of Griff.

He was standing just a few feet away, his dark hair plastered to his head and his arm slowly lowering, with the gun held loosely in his hand.

He was pale and soaking wet, and he'd never looked more gorgeous. Jumping to her feet, Carmen wobbled across the suddenly slick floor and tossed herself into his waiting arms.

"Griff," she breathed, pressing her face into his damp sweater.

He was alive. They'd survived both Ronnie and her crazy-ass cousin.

"I've got you," he murmured, laying his cheek on top of her head.

She was trembling so hard she was sure her knees were about to collapse.

"Why is it raining?"

He chuckled softly. "It's the sprinkler system."

"Oh." She wrapped her arms around his waist. She dismissed the relentless water drops that fell from the ceiling. And the knowledge there were two dead men in the building. Right now nothing mattered but the fact she was in Griff's arms. "Hold me. Just hold me."

"Don't worry, Carmen, I'm never going to let you go," he promised in low tones.

For long minutes they clung to each other, and then the

sound of footsteps had them awkwardly pulling away to watch a slender man stumble out of the shadows.

Matthew.

He looked as bedraggled as Carmen and Griff, but there was a goofy smile on his face.

"I did it," he announced with obvious pride. "I pressed the button."

Epilogue

Griff did finally manage to join Rylan and Jaci to enjoy the holidays. It was a little belated, but with Carmen at his side, he'd never been so happy.

They'd also traveled to visit his grandmother, who'd smothered them with her special brand of affection. Carmen had slowly lost her pallor and the dark circles beneath her eyes had faded to mere smudges.

Griff wasn't naïve enough to believe that she'd fully recovered from the trauma she'd endured. It might take months, if not years. But he could sense that she was starting to heal.

Best of all, she'd agreed to his demands that she allow him to travel with her during her upcoming book tour, and that when she was done, he insisted that she move into his home in California.

He'd leashed his urge to ask her to make their relationship official. Until she was strong enough to stand on her own two feet, he didn't want to pressure her into something she might later regret. When she walked down the aisle toward him, he wanted to be sure it was because she shared the same overwhelming love he felt for her.

It was three weeks later when she abruptly announced that she'd been in touch with a real estate agent and was preparing to put her grandparents' farm on the market. He'd merely nodded and made a few of his own phone calls. Then, loading their belongings in his rental SUV, he'd driven them from Iowa to Indiana, where a professional moving company was waiting for them at the farm, along with a couple of trusted security guards whom he ordered to remain hidden outside.

Although they'd already spoken with the cops, as well as given their statements to Nikki at the FBI, he wasn't taking any chances.

Ronnie and Baylor, along with their Kill Club, might be dead, but that didn't mean the danger was completely over. He wasn't going to take any chances. Besides, he still had one task to complete before he could whisk Carmen back to California.

Brushing a kiss over Carmen's lips as she directed the movers who were loading the furniture and the boxes she'd neatly packed, he'd promised he would be back by the end of the day and driven away from the farm.

He ignored the speed limit and arrived at the Jacobs Hardware headquarters in Louisville before lunch. Leaving the SUV in a loading zone, he strolled through the entrance, then headed toward the private elevator. He'd already hacked into the security system, which meant he could use his own passcode to unlock the elevator and head to the top floor.

His lips twitched as he walked through the hushed lobby that was decorated to look like an old English manor house. All dark wood and muted lighting.

He crossed the crimson carpet with a roll of his eyes, ignoring the elegant secretary who eyed him with open suspicion. He was wearing casual jeans and a leather bomber jacket and was three days past needing a shave. No doubt she thought he was a homeless man who'd wandered in off the streets.

"Can I help you?" she forced herself to ask, her voice as cold as her beautiful face.

He didn't bother to answer, crossing directly to shove open the heavy walnut door. She called out, but he closed the door behind him and entered the office that matched the reception area.

His gaze landed on the older man who was standing next to the bank of windows that overlooked the river.

Lawrence Jacobs had aged over the past weeks. Griff could see added silver in his brown hair and a stoop to his square shoulders that hadn't been there before. At his entrance the older man slowly turned, his pale eyes widening. Obviously, he'd assumed it was his secretary.

"What the hell are you doing here?" he rasped.

Griff reached to lock the office doors before casually strolling toward Lawrence.

"Clearing up the last of the mess."

The man's face darkened, genuine pain flaring through the pale eyes.

"Mess?" he rasped. "Is that what you call killing my son?"

Griff met his accusing gaze without flinching. He didn't regret shooting Baylor Jacobs. Not when the younger man had tormented Carmen and then planned to kill her.

He'd do it again without blinking an eye.

"Would you rather that he was tried and convicted as a serial killer?" he demanded, strolling forward. "What about your precious Jacobs name?"

The square face paled at the direct hit. They both knew Lawrence would always put the reputation of his business before anything and anyone. Including his own child.

"Tell me what you want," he snapped.

"The papers that you took from Carmen's house."

There was a shocked silence as Lawrence's white face was suddenly tinted with a dark flush. If Griff had doubted his wild theory, he'd just had it confirmed.

Lawrence licked his lips. "I don't know what you're talking about."

"Fine." Griff shrugged, reaching into the pocket of his leather coat to pull out his phone. "We'll let the cops sort it out."

"Wait." Lawrence took a step forward, a fine layer of sweat on his forehead. "If someone was at Carrie's house, then it was probably Ronnie. Or even Baylor."

"That was my assumption at first," Griff admitted.

In fact, he hadn't really thought about that particular incident. Not until he'd been sharing an early-morning conversation with Rylan as they'd sipped coffee and indulged in Jaci's decadent blueberry muffins.

As the words had left his mouth, he'd been hit with a sudden revelation. One he hadn't shared with anyone.

Until now.

"Then I realized that it didn't make any sense," he said. "Ronnie and Baylor were planning to murder Carmen. Why bother stealing anything?"

A nerve twitched next to Lawrence's mouth. Griff wondered if the older man ever gambled. He had a terrible poker face.

"They were clearly unstable," the older man tried to bluff. "Who knows what they were thinking?"

Griff shook his head. "No. They were already on their way to California when someone tried to ram Carmen and me into the river. Which leaves you."

Lawrence cleared his throat, his gaze darting over Griff's shoulder as if wondering if he could make a run for it. At last realizing he was cornered like the proverbial rat, he hunched his broad shoulders.

"You have no proof."

Griff heaved a deep sigh. Had the idiot forgotten that Griff had created an empire with his ability to either locate information or hide it?

"I could find the proof in less than ten minutes," he said, holding up his phone. "Using this."

Lawrence scowled. "How?"

"I would start with the car rental. Even if you used cash I could send a picture of you to the local rental agencies. Someone is bound to remember you," he said with a shrug. "If they don't, then one of the auto body shops close to Carmen's farm certainly will. They're too small not to re- member a stranger coming in. And you most certainly had to get the vehicle repaired before driving it back to Louisville." He paused, allowing his words to sink through the man's thick skull. "I have the power and the resources to discover whatever I want."

Lawrence clenched and unclenched his hands, the sweat starting to drip from his forehead.

"It was a moment of madness," he finally burst out. "I swear I rented the SUV and drove to the farm just to see if Carrie was there."

Griff folded his arms over his chest. "Why?"

"When you walked out before we could have Christmas dinner, I feared that you must have discovered something about the . . ." Lawrence's words trailed away.

Griff studied him with a frown before he realized that the older man didn't want to confess what was bothering him until he was sure that Griff already knew the full extent of his treachery.

"About the insurance policy you stole from your own niece?"

Lawrence flinched. Griff was guessing his unease was more from embarrassment at getting caught than any genuine sense of guilt.

"When I saw you leaving the farm, I decided to follow you."

"So you could kill us?"

"No." Lawrence held up a hand, trying to convince Griff of his sincerity. "I was in a panic. I wanted to see where you were going. I had a crazy idea that I could stop you from talking to the cops if I just explained about the money."

Griff snorted with disbelief. He still remembered his horror as he watched the SUV hurtling toward them, knowing that Carmen might die if they went over the edge.

"You weren't trying to talk to us," he said in a voice that revealed his revulsion toward the older man. "You were trying to shove us into an icy river."

Lawrence hunched his shoulders. "I told you. That was nothing more than a mad impulse. I saw you stopped in front of the bridge and my foot just hit the gas pedal. I didn't even realize what I was doing until I felt the impact."

Griff shook his head. There was no way he was going to let the man act as if attempted homicide was nothing more than a silly prank.

"A mad impulse is buying a jet ski," he said in icy tones. "Or dying your hair purple. It isn't trying to knock off members of your own family."

Lawrence lowered his gaze, studying the tips of his expensive Italian leather shoes.

"I was going to lose everything."

Griff rolled his eyes. Obviously, people who were born with a silver spoon in their mouths had different morals than poor schmucks like him.

"The Jacobs family is quite a work of art," he breathed.

"Don't forget that Carrie is a Jacobs," Lawrence ridiculously reminded him.

"Not for long," he said.

Carmen might not have formally agreed to marry him, but Griff had no doubt that it was going to happen. Although he wasn't the most handsome or charming man in the world, he did possess the sort of grim determination that meant he would never give up until he'd achieved his goal. That's how he'd graduated top of his class despite the loss of his mother and the awkward years beneath his father's roof. And how he'd convinced Rylan to go into business with him.

As far as he was concerned, having Carmen as his wife was as inevitable as the sun rising in the east.

"Why are you here?" Lawrence abruptly demanded.

"I want the papers you stole from the attic."

There was only the slightest hesitation before Lawrence was stiffly moving across the room, looking like he had something stuck up his ass. He halted at the large mahogany desk that had been hand-carved and polished until it glowed in the sunlight that angled through the tall windows.

He pulled open the middle drawer to extract a key. Then crouching down, he used the key to open the bottom drawer.

Moving quickly, Griff was next to the desk, his hand on the gun he had holstered beneath the jacket. He'd learned never to underestimate the depths of evil the Jacobs men were willing to sink to.

Including shooting him in the middle of the elegant office.

But when Lawrence straightened, he was clutching a thick envelope in his hand.

"This is the original insurance policy."

Griff reached to take the envelope, and tucked it in his pocket. He'd hand it to his lawyer when he returned to California.

Right now he was more interested in what Lawrence *hadn't* given him.

"What else?" he demanded, holding out his phone when Lawrence's lips parted in protest. "Unless you want to get the cops involved, don't piss me off."

An ugly anger darkened the older man's pale eyes. He

was used to people who jumped to obey his every command. He didn't like having to be the one taking orders.

Still, he wasn't stupid. He knew that if Griff decided to press the issue he might very well end up in jail. If nothing else, his place in the business world would be over.

Corporate America might be cutthroat, but you weren't supposed to get caught trying to kill off your enemies.

With a grudging expression, he bent over and dug through the bottom drawer. At last he pulled out a folded piece of paper and shoved it toward Griff.

"Here."

Griff took the paper, unfolded it, and studied the letter that was signed at the bottom by Lawrence and a Joseph Conway, Carmen's grandfather.

"What is this?" he demanded.

"I was named as legal guardian for Carrie," Lawrence admitted, his expression as stiff as his voice. "This is a document that hands over that guardianship to Carrie's grandparents."

Griff skimmed through the brief note, realizing it was a handwritten contract that would never have held up in court if Carmen had pressed the issue. His lips curled, fury blasting through him as he realized exactly what he was looking at.

"Christ," he rasped. "You held your own niece hostage to force her grandparents to keep shut about the three-million-dollar inheritance that belonged to Carmen."

Lawrence tilted his chin, trying to pretend he wasn't a total slimeball.

"They didn't want the money, and I needed it for the company."

Griff gave a disgusted shake of his head, tucking away the paper. He wondered if this was the reason Carmen's grandparents had been so upset when they caught her in the attic. They wouldn't want her to realize that her own uncle had been willing to barter her away for three million dollars.

"Maybe if you'd been less worried about money, you

would have realized your brother hadn't killed his wife or himself and would have insisted on a more thorough investigation, instead of trying to sweep everything under the rug," he said, sickened by the very sight of the man who'd failed on so many levels. Most basically, Lawrence Jacobs had failed at being a decent human being. "And that you were raising a cold-blooded killer."

Without warning, the man's brittle arrogance visibly shattered. Releasing a harsh sigh, he scrubbed his face with his beefy hands, looking unbearably weary.

"I know it's too late, but I am sorry," he said in harsh tones.

"Sorry for what?"

"All of it," the older man said, lifting his head to meet Griff's hard gaze. "I should have appreciated everything that Stuart sacrificed for me. He took care of me and the business when he was barely old enough to take care of himself. Instead, all I could do was dwell on how much better I would be if I was in charge." He gave a slow shake of his head. "And most of all I'm sorry that I spent all my time here." He spread his arms to indicate the large office. "I should have concentrated on being a real father and husband." He grimaced. "And I should have protected Carrie."

Griff bit back his words of agreement. Who knew if the older man was genuinely regretful or if he was just hoping to sway Griff into going easy on him. It didn't really matter. As far as Griff was concerned, Lawrence Jacobs could rot in his own nastiness.

"It's my job to protect Carmen now," he said, leaning toward the older man. "And I take my duty very seriously."

Lawrence didn't miss the threat. He took a step back, his expression wary.

"What do you want from me?"

"You can start by paying back the money you stole from her."

Griff watched with pleasure at the shock that rippled over

Lawrence's face. It wasn't that Carmen needed the money. She'd probably hand it over to the nearest charity. But he couldn't think of any better way to punish the older man.

"But I—" Lawrence bit off his words as he caught a glimpse of Griff's warning expression. Griff wouldn't hesitate to call in every favor owed to him by various law enforcement agencies to bury this man in legal troubles. "It will have to be in payments," he agreed in sickly tones.

"Fine, but I'll be keeping track of them," he said.

A drop of sweat trailed down Lawrence's jaw before landing on his gray tailored jacket.

"Anything else?"

"Stay away from Carmen," Griff told him. "If she decides she ever wants to speak with you or Matthew in the future, that will be her choice." As much as he wanted to add that it would be over his dead body before Carmen ever got close to a man who had not only stolen her inheritance, but had tried to ram her into the river, he couldn't force Carmen to forget her only family. Someday she might feel it necessary to heal the past. He would stand at her side, even as he guarded her back. "Got it?" he demanded.

Lawrence gave a slow nod. "Got it."

"And always know that I'll be watching you." Griff deliberately glanced toward the computer on the glossy desk. "One wrong move and I'll nail you to the wall."

With his warning delivered, he pivoted to head out of the office. It was overdramatic, but hey, he had to have a little fun after being forced to waste his entire morning personally delivering his threat.

He wouldn't be nearly so nice if he had to come back.

A few minutes later he was in his SUV, making the drive to the farm at the same breakneck speed. He was hoping to get Carmen to the airport to make their evening flight to California. As nice as it was to spend time with Rylan and Jaci, as well as his grandmother, he was ready to have time alone with Carmen.

Forced to slow as he reached the gravel road, he turned into the driveway. Pulling out his phone he made a quick call to the security team he had hired. Moments later he watched a nondescript sedan appear from the shadows of the hedge and head away from the house.

He climbed out of his vehicle and walked toward the barn where the last of the equipment was being packed into a long trailer. The heavy machinery would be sold at a local auction, while the furniture was going into storage. He didn't want Carmen to regret selling those pieces that had been hand-carved by her great-grandfather.

Someday they might have children. Then she'd want them to have something from her past.

The mere thought was enough to stir his blood. Or maybe his blood was being stirred by the sight of Carmen, who'd stepped onto the back porch.

She was wearing faded jeans and one of his flannel shirts. Her hair was a tumble of golden curls and there was dirt on her face.

She'd never been more gorgeous.

With steps that were more a jog than a stroll, he moved across the yard and vaulted up the stairs. His heart soared as she walked directly into his arms.

He thought back to the first moment he'd seen her standing on the beach. Her beauty had been luminous. As if she was glowing from inside.

He'd known he was in trouble. He just hadn't known it was a forever-and-ever kind of trouble.

"It's about time," she murmured.

He planted a kiss on top of her tousled curls, breathing deeply of her lemony scent.

"Did you miss me?"

"Maybe a little."

"Just a little?"

She snuggled closer. "Maybe a lot."

"Mmm. I like the sound of that."

He pressed another kiss to the top of her head before urging her back into the house. The icy breeze was starting to pick up. They needed to finish up and get on the road to the airport.

Reaching the living room, he glanced around at the barren floors and walls.

"Do you need me to do anything?" he asked.

She shook her head. "The movers hauled everything to the storage unit you rented. All we need to do is drop the key by the real estate office." She paused, glancing around with a small sigh. "It feels so empty."

He pulled her tight against his side. "Are you sure you're ready to give up this place?" he demanded. "You know there's no hurry to make a decision."

She sucked in a deep breath, squaring her shoulders. "It's time. My grandfather would be sad to see the place falling apart. He would want a family here who are willing to devote their lives to the land." She turned to meet his worried gaze with a small smile. "Besides, I'm ready to put the past behind us and concentrate on the future."

He leaned down to press a lingering kiss against her lips. "Our future."

"Our future," she readily agreed.

Lifting his head, he studied her upturned face. "Ready?"

"Yeah." She reached to grab his hand. "I'm ready."

Holding hands, they walked out the door, facing the world together.

Read on for a thrilling extract from Alexandra's
latest romantic suspense novel

PRETEND YOU'RE SAFE

Available now from Headline Eternal!

Prologue

Frank Johnson had endured his fair share of floods. He'd been born and raised on the small farm that butted against the bank of the Mississippi River. Which meant he'd spent the past sixty years watching the muddy waters rise and fall. Sometimes sweeping away crops, cattle, and during one memorable year, the barn that had been built by his great-grandfather.

The levee that'd been built by the Corps of Engineers over a decade ago had provided a measure of security. Not that he'd been happy when they'd come in and scooped up his fertile land to create the barrier. Frank was a typical midwestern farmer who didn't need the government poking their noses, or bulldozers, into his business. But eventually he'd had to admit it was nice not to have the waters lapping at the back door every time it rained.

But this was no typical rain.

On the first of February the heavens had opened up, and six weeks later the torrential rains continued to pound the small community. The river had become an angry, churning, destructive force as it swept toward the south. Frank watched in concern as the water had inched closer and closer to the top of the levee. He knew it was only a matter of time before it spilled over the ridge and into his back field.

But when he woke that morning, it wasn't to find the levee had been topped. Nope. It had been busted wide open. As if someone had set off an explosion during the night.

With the resignation of a man who'd lived his entire life dependent on the fickleness of nature, he'd pulled on his coveralls and boots before firing up his old tractor and heading down to see the damage.

Dawn had arrived, but the thick clouds and persistent drizzle shrouded the farm in a strange gloom. Frank pulled the collar of his coveralls up to protect his neck from the chilled breeze, starting to feel like Noah. Had he missed the memo from God that he was supposed to build an ark?

The inane thought had barely formed in his mind when he allowed the tractor to roll to a halt. As expected, his fields had become pools of brown, brackish water. In some places the nasty stuff was waist deep. There were also the usual leaves, branches, and pieces of flotsam that'd been caught in the swirling eddies.

What he hadn't expected was the long, dark object that he spotted floating in the middle of his pasture.

His first thought had been that it was a log. Maybe a piece of lumber torn from a building. But a piece of wood wouldn't make his stomach cramp with a sense of dread, would it?

Climbing off his tractor, he'd reached into his pocket for his cell phone. His unconscious mind had already warned him that whatever the floodwaters had washed onto his land was going to be bad.

And it was.

Really, really bad.

Chapter One

First came the floods. And then the bodies . . .

Jaci Patterson was running late.

It all started when she woke at her usual time of four a.m. Yes, she really and truly woke at that indecent hour, five days a week. On the weekends, she allowed herself to sleep in until six. But this morning, when she crawled out of bed, she discovered the electricity was out.

Again.

The lack of power had nothing to do with the sketchy electrical lines that ran to her remote farmhouse in the northeast corner of Missouri. At least not this time. Instead, it could be blamed on the rains that continued to hammer the entire Midwest day after day.

When the lights grudgingly flickered on an hour later, she had to rush through her routine, grateful that she'd baked two dozen peach tarts and several loaves of bread the night before.

As it was, she'd barely managed to finish her blueberry muffins and scones before she had to load them into the back of her Jeep. Then, locking her two black Labs, Riff and Raff, in the barn so they didn't destroy her house while she was gone, she headed toward Heron, the small town just ten miles away.

Predictably, she was barreling down the muddy lane that led to the small farm that'd once belonged to her grandparents, when she discovered the road was blocked before she could reach the intersection. *Crap.* Obviously the levee had broken during the night, releasing the swollen fury of the Mississippi River.

It was no wonder her electricity had gone out.

Grimacing at the knowledge that her bottom fields, along with most of her neighbors', were probably flooded, she put the Jeep in reverse. Then, careful to stay in the center of the muddy road, she reversed her way back to the lane. Once she managed to get turned around, she headed in the opposite direction.

The detour took an extra fifteen minutes, but at least she didn't have to worry about traffic. With fewer than three hundred people, Heron wasn't exactly a hub of activity. In fact, she ran into exactly zero cars as she swung along Main Street.

She splashed through the center of town, which was lined with a small post office, the county courthouse that was built in the eighteen hundreds, with a newer jail that had been added onto the back, a bank, and a beauty parlor. On the opposite side was the Baptist church and next to it a two-story brick building that the local celebrity, Nelson Bradley, had converted into a gallery for his photographs. Farther down the block was a newly constructed tin shed that housed the fire truck and the water department. On the corner was a small diner that had originally been christened the Cozy Kitchen, but had slowly become known as the Bird's Nest by the locals after it'd been taken over by Nancy Bird, or Birdie, as she was affectionately nicknamed.

Pulling into the narrow alley behind the diner, Jaci

hopped out of her vehicle to grab the top container of muffins, which were still warm from the oven. Instantly, she regretted not pulling on her jacket as the drizzling rain molded her short, honey-brown hair to her scalp and dampened her Mizzou sweatshirt and faded jeans to her generously curved body.

With a shiver she hurried through the back door, careful to wipe the mud from her rubber boots before entering the kitchen.

Heat smacked her in the face, the contrast from the chilled wind outside making the cramped space feel smothering.

Grimacing, she walked to set the muffins on a narrow, stainless-steel table that was next to the griddle filled with scrambled eggs, hash browns, sausage, and sizzling bacon.

The large woman with graying hair and a plump face efficiently flipped a row of pancakes before gesturing toward the woman who was standing at the sink washing dishes. Once the helper had hurried to her side, she handed off her spatula and made her way toward Jaci.

Nancy Bird, better known as Birdie, was fifteen years older than Jaci. When the woman was just seventeen she'd married her high school sweetheart and dropped out of school. The sweetheart turned out to be a horse patootie who'd fled town, leaving Birdie with four young girls to raise on her own.

With a determination that Jaci deeply admired, Birdie had bought the old diner and over the past ten years turned it into the best place to eat in the entire county.

At this early hour her clients usually consisted of farmers, hunters, and school bus drivers who were up before dawn.

"Morning, Birdie." Jaci stepped aside as the older woman efficiently began to place the muffins on a large glass tray that would be set on the counter next to the cash register. Many of the diners liked to have a cup of coffee and muffin once they were done with breakfast.

"Thank God you're here."

"I'm sorry I'm late. The electricity didn't come on until almost five."

Finishing, Birdie grabbed the tray and bustled across the kitchen to hand it to her assistant.

"Take this to the counter," Birdie commanded before turning back to Jaci with a roll of her eyes. "The natives have been threatening to revolt without their favorite muffins."

Jaci smiled, pleased by Birdie's words. She'd learned to bake at her grandmother's side, but it wasn't until she'd inherited her grandparents' farm that she'd considered using her skills to help her make ends meet.

Leaning to the side, she glanced through the large, open space where the food was passed through to the waitresses.

The place hadn't changed in the past ten years. The walls were covered with faded paneling that was decorated with old license plates and a mounted fish caught from the nearby river. The floor was linoleum and the drop ceiling was lit with fluorescent lights.

There were a half dozen tables arranged around the square room with one long table at the back where a group of farmers showed up daily to drink coffee and share the local gossip.

At the moment, every seat was filled with patrons wearing buff coveralls, camo jackets, and Cardinal baseball hats.

Jaci released a slow whistle. "Damn, woman. That's quite a crowd," she said, a rueful smile touching her lips. The rains meant that no one was able to get into the fields. "At least someone can benefit from this latest downpour."

"Benefit?" Birdie sucked in a sharp breath, her hands

landing on her generous hips. "I hope you're not suggesting that I'm the sort of person who enjoys benefiting from a tragedy, Jaci Patterson," she chastised. "People want to get together to discuss what's happened and I have the local spot for them to gather."

Jaci blinked, caught off guard by her friend's sharp reprimand. Then, absorbing the older woman's words, she stiffened in concern.

"Tragedy?" she breathed.

Birdie's features softened. "You haven't heard?"

Jaci felt a tremor of unease. She'd already lost her father to a drunk driver before she was even born, and then her grandmother when she was seventeen. Her grandfather had passed just two years ago. She was still raw from their deaths.

"No, I haven't heard anything. Like I said, the electricity went out last night and as soon as it came back on I started baking. Has someone died?"

"I'm afraid so."

"Who?"

"No one knows for sure yet," Birdie told her.

Jaci blinked in confusion. "How could they not know?"

"The levee broke in the middle of the night."

"Yeah, I figured that out when I discovered that the road was closed . . . Oh hell." She tensed as her unease became sharp-edged fear. The levee had broken before and flooded fields, but the neighbor to her south had recently built a new house much closer to the river. "It didn't reach Frank's home, did it?"

Birdie shook her head. "Just the back pasture."

"Then what are you talking about?"

"When Frank went to check on the breach, he saw something floating in the middle of his field."

Jaci cringed. Poor Frank. He must have been shocked out of his mind.

"Oh my God. It was a dead person?"

"Yep. A woman."

"He didn't recognize her?"

Birdie leaned forward and lowered her voice, as if anyone could hear over the noise from the customers, not to mention the usual kitchen clatter.

"He said it was impossible to know if she was familiar or not."

"I don't suppose he wanted to look too close," Jaci said. If she'd spotted a body in her flooded field she would have jumped into her Jeep and driven away like a maniac.

"It wasn't that. He claimed the woman was too . . ." Birdie hesitated, as if she was searching for a more delicate way to express what Frank had said. "Decomposed to make out her features."

"Decomposed?" A strange chill inched down Jaci's spine.

"That's what he's saying."

Jaci absently glanced through the opening into the outer room where she could see Frank surrounded by a group of avid listeners.

When Birdie had said a body, she'd assumed it had been someone who'd been caught in the flood. Maybe she'd fallen in when she was walking along the bank. Or her car might have been swept away when she tried to cross a road with high water.

But she wouldn't be decomposed, would she?

"I've heard that water does strange things to a body," Jaci at last said.

Birdie tugged Jaci toward the back door as her assistant

moved to open the fridge. Clearly there was more to the story.

"The body wasn't all that Frank discovered."

Jaci stilled. "There was more?"

"Yep." Birdie whispered, as if it was a big secret. Which was ridiculous. There were no such things as secrets in a town the size of Heron. "Frank called the sheriff, and while he was waiting for Mike to arrive he swears he caught sight of a human skull stuck in the mud at the edge of the road." Birdie gave a horrified shudder. "Can you imagine? Two dead people virtually in his backyard? Gives me the creeps just thinking about it."

Jaci's mouth went dry. "Did Frank say anything else?"

Birdie shrugged. "Just that the sheriff told him to leave and not to talk about what he found." Birdie snorted. "Like anyone wouldn't feel the need to share the fact they found a dead body and a skull in their field."

A familiar dread curdled in the pit of Jaci's stomach.

She was being an idiot. Of course she was. This had nothing to do with her past. Or the mysterious stalker who had made her life hell.

Still . . .

She couldn't shake the sudden premonition that slithered down her spine.

"Is Mike still out at Frank's?" she abruptly demanded, referring to the sheriff, Mike O'Brien.

"Yeah." Birdie sent her a curious glance. "I think he was waiting for the Corps of Engineers to get out there so they could discuss how long it would take for the field to drain." She wrinkled her nose. "I suppose they need to make sure there aren't any other bodies."

More bodies.

A fierce urgency pounded through her. She might be

overreacting, but she wasn't going to be satisfied until she spoke to Mike.

"I need to go."

"You haven't had your coffee," Birdie protested.

"Not this morning, thanks, Birdie."

"Okay." The older woman stepped back. "I'll get your money and—"

"I'll stop by later to get it." Jaci turned to pull open the back door.

Instantly a chilled blast of air swept around them.

"What's your rush?" Birdie demanded.

"I have some questions that need answers," she said.

"With who?" Birdie demanded, making a sound of impatience as Jaci darted into the alley and jogged toward her waiting Jeep. "Jaci?"

Not bothering to answer, Jaci jumped into the vehicle and put it in gear. Water trickled down her neck from her wet hair, but when she'd gone into the diner she'd left the engine running with the heater blasting at full steam.

Which meant she was a damp mess, but she wasn't completely miserable.

Angling the vent in a futile effort to dry her soggy sweatshirt, Jaci stomped on the accelerator and headed back toward her house. This time, however, she swerved around the barrier that blocked the road, squishing her way through the muddy path that led along the edge of Frank's property.

It was less than ten miles, but by the time she was pulling her vehicle to a halt, her stomach had managed to clench into a tight ball of nerves.

It didn't matter how many times she told herself that this had nothing to do with the past, she couldn't dismiss her rising tide of fear.

Ignoring the avid crowd of onlookers who were

gathered at the edge of the field, Jaci skirted around the wooden barrier, her gaze taking in the sluggish brown water that had surged through the broken levee. Branches and debris swirled through the field. But no body.

Thank God.

"Jaci." A male voice intruded into her distracted thoughts as a skinny man dressed in a dark uniform stepped in front of her.

She forced a smile to her lips. "Morning, Sid."

The young deputy nodded his head toward the flooded field, trying to look suitably somber.

"I guess you heard the news?"

"Yep." Jaci's gaze moved over the deputy's shoulder, landing on the man who was pacing along the edge of the road with a cell phone pressed to his ear.

Sheriff Mike O'Brien.

HEADLINE
ETERNAL

FIND YOUR HEART'S DESIRE...

VISIT OUR WEBSITE: www.headlineeternal.com
FIND US ON FACEBOOK: facebook.com/eternalromance
CONNECT WITH US ON TWITTER: @eternal_books
FOLLOW US ON INSTAGRAM: @headlineeternal
EMAIL US: eternalromance@headline.co.uk